"Oh, bloody wonderful," said Timaeus. "Hiking over hill and dale, up and down mountains and through leech-infested swamps. I'm not exactly the hardened wilderness explorer, you know."

"You think maybe you can save the world by sitting in an armchair and sipping brandy before the fire?" demanded Sidney. "If you aren't willing to face a little hardship, why did you embark on this damned quest?"

"Why *shouldn't* one be able to save the world while sipping brandy before the fire?" asked Timaeus. "What is it about quests that involves dire peril and travail? Who arranges these things, anyhow?"

"Ask Vic when you see him," said Sidney. "He seems to be the expert on quests."

"All very well for you to say," complained Timaeus. "Not that we've got a chance of success without Vic, you know. What are we going to do if we reach Arst-Kara-Morn without him? Knock on the Dark Lord's door and say, 'Please sir, release the spirit of Stantius Human-King so the forces of freedom can beat your nasty orcs and things, and we can all go home?' Vincianus is the only one who has the slightest idea how to—"

"I swear to all the gods," said Sidney, "I can't imagine how I ever got hooked up with such a whiner. We've got to go after Broderick; we don't have any choice. Come or not, see if I give a damn."

Tor Books by Greg Costikyan

MAGIC OF THE PLAINS
By the Sword

CUPS AND SORCERY
Another Day, Another Dungeon
One Quest, Hold the Dragons

GREG COSTIKYAN

ONE QUEST, HOLD THE DRAGONS

Book Two of
Cups and Sorcery

TOR
fantasy ®

A TOM·DOHERTY ASSOCIATES BOOK
NEW YORK

This is a work of fiction. All the characters and events portrayed in this book are fictitious, and any resemblance to real people or events is purely coincidental.

ONE QUEST, HOLD THE DRAGONS

Copyright © 1995 by Greg Costikyan

All rights reserved, including the right to reproduce this book, or portions thereof, in any form.

Cover art by Paul Jaquays

A Tor Book
Published by Tom Doherty Associates, Inc.
175 Fifth Avenue
New York, NY 10010

Tor® is a registered trademark of Tom Doherty Associates, Inc.

ISBN: 0-812-52269-9

First edition: May 1995

Printed in the United States of America

0 9 8 7 6 5 4 3 2 1

FOR VICTORIA

cast of characters

Our Heroes

timaeus d'asperge, *Magister Igniti*
sidney stollitt, of the firm of Stollitt & Pratchitt
nick pratchitt, likewise
kraki kronarsson, descendant of Gostorn Gaptoothéd,
  Mighty Pie-Eater
jasper de mobray, *Magister Mentis*
vincianus polymage, absent more often than not
frer mortise, adept of Deeset

Biddlebourgeois

barthold, Baron Biddleburg
bertram, his heir, *Magister Aeris*
broderick, regent, Barthold's younger brother
captain blentz, of the castle guard
beatrice of the band, rebel and love interest
mr. bates, the butler
mistress mabel, of the International Amalgamated
  Sisterhood of Witches & Allied Trades
master woodsley, a yeoman
marek and gaston, soldiers
master gorham, a stonewright and rebel sympathizer

Hamsterians

lotte, an innkeeper
pablo von kremnitz, Leftenant, Mayoral Foot Guard
hamish siebert, Lord Mayor of the Most Serene Republic
  of Hamsterburg
guismundo stantz, "The Spider," Minister of Internal
  Serenity
renée wolfe, his best agent, *Magistra Umbrae*
gerlad, graf von grentz, patriarch of the *gens* von
  Grentz and a leader of the Accommodationists

julio von krautz, patriarch of the *gens* von Krautz and ineffectual conservative

fenstermann, the reluctant torturer

mauro and kevork, guisardieres

stauer, master of the Pension Scholari

agent g, of the Ministry of Internal Serenity, seventh in a strictly limited series

chad, a troll

millicent, egbert, and rutherford, house guests of the Graf von Grentz

magistra rottwald and serjeant kunz, lackeys of von Grentz

ALSO

beliel, an elf

HOLD THE DRAGONS

Timaeus d'Asperge stood unsteadily before his parlor window, snifter of brandy cradled in one hand and meerschaum in the other. Out there, a cold, late-winter rain gave a glossy patina to the cobblestones and stoops. Wind pattered rain against the window, hard enough to rattle the panes. He shivered, though the coals were heaped high in the grate and the room was warm enough to be uncomfortable to anyone who wasn't a fire mage. He became suddenly aware that he was weaving on his feet, late hours and too much brandy catching up with him—and that the parlor windows extended to within a cubit of the floor. If he were to lose his footing and pitch forward, he'd find himself cracking his skull open on the slate flags of the sidewalk below. He began to contemplate retiring to his bed, another dull day completed.

And they were dull days, he had to admit. He had his master's, he had enough wealth to live comfortably the rest of his days, he had his clubs and his companions—but it didn't seem enough. He almost missed the adventurer's life, the moments of blind terror and adversity; but the purpose of adventure was wealth, after all, and he had that now, in sufficiency. Perhaps his father was right, he reflected; he needed a wife, children, a life. Or perhaps he should return to the university, and pursue a doctorate; heaven knew what he would do with another degree, but the pursuit of one would give him at least the illusion of purpose.

Sighing, he set down his drink—tossing it off would only render him more inebriate, something he really didn't need—and put one hand on the window frame, to brace himself as he took a last look out into the cold, wet dark before going to bed. There was something reassuring about the fury of the weather; something that said that the world of nature continued oblivious to the works of man, that human strife was immaterial; something that said—

"Boodabooodaboodabooda!"

A horrible white apparition sucked up against the glass of the window, face smeared against the pane, body sprawled askew. A creature of the night, an undead, a vile shapechanger—Timaeus leapt back in alarm, pipe flying. He shouted the Words of a spell—

"Heh heh," chuckled the apparition through the window. "Gotcha."

It was, Timaeus realized disgustedly, some decrepit wino, some filthy beggar who had crept up the stoop and flung himself against the adjoining parlor window. Timaeus stormed into the hall and flung open the door, to give the bum a piece of his mind—

Rain crashed into cobbles. Water plastered the old man's white hair to his skull; he smirked toothlessly at Timaeus. "Gotcha, Timmy," he said.

"Vic," said Timaeus resignedly. "What the devil are you doing out on a night like this?"

"Need to talk with you, Timmy," said Vic.

"Don't call me Timmy, by Dion," said Timaeus. "No one's called me Timmy in fifteen years. Come in, come in; you must be chilled unto death."

"Nope," said Vincianus, coming in. "Reshishtance to cold. Eashy enough shpell."

Timaeus held open the door as Vic entered, and got a whiff of the old man. "I say, Vic," he said, "when did you last bathe?"

Vic came in, levered himself arthritically onto the settee, and snatched Timaeus's snifter, the contents of which he gulped greedily down. "Let'sh shee," he said. "The Third Interregnum, wash it? No, I dishtinctly recall a bath during the War of the Liliesh. Or, wait; didn't I shower in—"

"Never mind," said Timaeus, yanking on the bellpull. "More brandy?"

"Never turn that down," said Vic.

By the time Vic was on his third snifter, Reginald appeared at the door to the hall, yawning and tying the belt to his robe. "Yes, sir?" he inquired.

"Sorry to wake you, Reginald," said Timaeus apologetically, "but we have an unexpected guest. Could you draw Vincianus a bath?"

Reginald gave Vic a glare of undisguised loathing. "Certainly, sir," he said distantly. "This way, if you will."

By the time Reginald returned, with a well-scrubbed and faintly rebellious Vic, Timaeus was snoring soundly on the settee.

"By crumb!" roared Kraki. "You have the temerity to ask Kraki, son of Kronar, for a raise? You effete civilized putz, I spit on you!"

"See here, mate," said the clerk defensively, "I'm your best salesman, I am. How many blades have I sold in the last fiscal quarter?"

"Folk buy swords from Kraki because Kraki have best

swords," shouted the barbarian. "Not because puling pantyvaist inveigle them! Out of my shop!"

"You can't fire me, you lout!" shouted the clerk. "I quit! And much luck to you, I don't think!"

"Bah!" shouted Kraki. "Get out! Before I smite you, hip and thigh!"

Kraki glared through the plate glass into the morning sun. The clerk marched down the street, out past the gilt letters that read "Fast Kraki's Flashing Swords" and "Barbarian Blades Are Better!" The swine was his best salesman, no doubt about it, but to ask for a raise! Was this the way of honor? Was this the way of courage? He want a raise, he should demand it like a man, not wheedle like a puling babe! Scum-sucking civilized turds, they were all alike.

The door tinkled as a customer entered. Some fop, in a faggotty hat and hose. As he examined the blades in their brackets against the walls, the stacked daggers and knives, he took snuff from the back of his hand. Kraki curled a lip.

"I say, my good man," said the customer. "Would you have something in an épée."

"Épée, you catamite?" snarled Kraki. "I do not sell such filth. Ve have honest, manly veapons here. Here, look at this claymore. Sixteen pounds of hard-slung steel, fit to smash the pate of the fiercest foe, honed to a razor edge."

"Err, yes," said the fop, "but I am rather in the market for a duelist's weapon. I'm afraid this is just a tad too heavy—"

"Too heavy?" said Kraki. "Too heavy for the likes of you, belike. A hatpin, you vant; or perhaps a letter opener. Here." He handed the fop a cheese knife. "This should do you. I vill not sell good steel to the likes of you. Get out of my store."

"Well!" said the dandy. "I never!" And he left.

Kraki glowered out into the morning sun. It had seemed like a good idea. Who knew weapons better than he?

Would they not flock to buy their blades from Kraki, son of Kronar? Barbarian chic would see to that. But it hadn't worked. You had to write little numbers in books and do something mystical with them; they never came out right. And the damned government wouldn't let you slay the accountants for the lying cheats they were; by crumb, the Financial Accounting Standards Board would see some changes, if he were king!

What would they think of him, back home? They would laugh at him, that's what. Win a fortune by force of arms, and sink it all into some stinking shop. Ach, what an idiot he was. He should build a pile with the skulls of his creditors, that's what he should do, and ride off to slay dragons.

"And on the night of October the seventeenth, on or about the eleventh hour of the clock," droned the prosecutor, "did you or did you not forcibly enter the premises of one Johnson Merriweather the Third?"

"I did not," said Nick Pratchitt.

The prosecutor raised an eyebrow. "And yet," he said, "we have heard the testimony of Officer Sams of the Town Guard, that he found you in the guest bedroom closet in Mr. Merriweather's mansion after being summoned to the house by Mr. Merriweather. Are you calling Officer Sams a liar?"

"No," said Nick. "But I didn't enter the house forcibly. I was invited."

"I see," said the prosecutor, with heavy sarcasm. "You were invited into the house as an honored guest, which is why, when Mr. Merriweather went to investigate a noise that disturbed his repose, you found it necessary to secrete yourself in a closet."

"Nonetheless," Nick insisted, "I was invited."

"And who," said the prosecutor, "invited you? A little birdie?"

"Samantha," said Nick.

The prosecutor's jaw dropped. There were titters from the gallery. "Mrs.—Mrs. Merriweather?" he said.

"Uh huh," said Nick.

The prosecutor shot a look of black hatred at Mr. Merriweather, who had evidently failed to alert him to the possibility that Nick's testimony might follow these lines. "I see" he said in annoyance. "And *why* did Mrs. Merriweather invite you inside at so late an hour?"

Nick gave him a wicked grin. "I prefer not to say," he said.

The prosecutor snorted. "Even if your chances of avoiding conviction depend on your testimony?"

Nick glanced at the jury, and adopted an expression of false nobility. "There are some things," he said, "that a gentleman does not discuss."

There were more titters from the gallery. Merriweather *le mari* looked mortified.

The prosecutor whirled on the judge. "Your Honor," he said in a long-suffering tone, "I ask for a short recess."

The judge, a shrunken little man in black robes several sizes too large for him, roused himself from an apparent reverie, and quavered, "Wherefore?"

"There are matters," said the prosecutor, "I must discuss with the complainant."

"Granted," said the judge. "We shall reconvene in an hour."

One of the women on the jury, a plump but not unattractive matron of at least forty, gave Nick a hard stare. He winked at her, and smiled as she blushed from the neckline up.

From far away came the sound of the monsoon. Somewhat closer, a cough sounded; a panther in the jungle, that was it. A panther coughed, amid the dense foliage of the—

"Excuse me, sir," said the panther. "Your bath is drawn and ready."

Timaeus opened sleep-gummed eyes. Dwarves beat out magic blades inside his skull. Reginald stood there, looking crow-like in black clothes.

"Dammit," croaked Timaeus, "what time is it?"

"Nearly eleven," said Reginald.

Timaeus closed his eyes. "Wake me at two, then, if you will."

"Ahem," said Reginald with determination. "Excuse me, sir."

Timaeus opened one aching eye. "What is it?" he moaned.

"Your guest, sir," said Reginald.

"What guest?" said Timaeus.

"Vincianus Polymage, I believe he is called," said Reginald.

Timaeus recalled something dimly. "Yes," he said. "Let him sleep, too."

"He has been up," said Reginald, "since six."

"All right," said Timaeus, sighing. "Keep him entertained then, please." He closed his eyes.

"Ahem," said Reginald.

"What the devil is it?" snapped Timaeus, opening his eyes again and instantly regretting having done so.

"Mr. Polymage has ensconced himself in the kitchen," said Reginald, "where he has located all Cook's pans, and is in the process of preparing cornmeal flapjacks."

"Yes, good for him," said Timaeus testily. "If he wants to make himself pancakes, by all means let—"

"He has been cooking pancakes since six this morning," said Reginald. "We've been out four times for additional cornmeal."

Timaeus gazed wordlessly on his valet.

"He keeps on talking about 'the Legion,' and muttering something about 'An army travels on its stomach.' 'The boys will be hungry,' he says. I estimate we currently have fifteen linear cubits of stacked flapjacks."

Timaeus groaned and sat up. After a moment, the urge to retch faded. "All right, all right," he moaned. "I'll try to talk sense into him. In the meantime, have the girl take the pancakes down to Father Thwaite's mission. No doubt they can find some use for them."

"Very good, sir."

"Really, Priscilla," said Laura, long nails slicing fivefold paths through the air in a gesture eloquent of disdain, "this notion of yours is quite impossible."

"Look, Mom," said Sidney. "Figures don't lie. Room-nights are down fifteen percent compared to last year's figures, the girls are idle four hours out of every ten, our gross receipts are down by a third—"

"I'm aware of the numbers," said Laura. "But—"

"Aware of the numbers?" protested Sidney. "The hell you are! You never look at the damned numbers! That's why you wound up in hock to the mob the first time round. You—"

"Priscilla, you are *such* a child, sometimes," said Laura. "When one has been in the business as long as I, one develops an instinct for these things. I'm aware that business is slow. With the war on, business is slow everywhere; just one of those things, you know. We must carry on—"

"It doesn't matter *why* business is down," said Sidney in a dangerous tone. "What matters is, what are we going to do about it? How can it hurt to advertise, to—"

"To have pimps standing on every street corner, saying 'Psst! Wanna have a good time?' " said Laura contemptuously. "Madame Laura's is not some disease-ridden neighborhood cathouse, my dear. We run a first-class bordello, and I won't stoop—"

"Ma!" said Sidney. "It's not like that! We're talking about well-dressed gentlemen standing outside the better clubs, handing out discreet pasteboard cards. Cards, by the way, printed with an original etching by de Lauvient—"

"*Avant-garde* dauber," sneered Laura.

"A first-rate artist," said Sidney with determination. "And the legend merely says, 'Madame Laura's,' with the address. Of *course* it's important to retain our reputation for discretion and exclusivity; of *course* we wouldn't want to do anything downmarket, anything . . ."

"Déclassé," supplied Laura.

"Anything déclassé," said Sidney. "But we do need to drum up some business, and—"

"Next you'll have the girls standing out front and hiking up their skirts," said Laura. "My dear, you must leave the business to more experienced heads. Really, Priscilla—"

"Stop *calling* me that!" shouted Sidney.

"Now, then, dear," said Laura. "If you're going to scream at me, I refuse to continue this conversation—"

"*What* conversation?" shouted Sidney. "We don't have conversations! I propose ideas, you sneer at them, then you lecture me! That's your idea of a conversation!"

"Darling, you might give some slight consideration to the notion that perhaps I do have some idea what I'm doing," said Laura. "I *have* been running this business for close to thirty years, you know."

"Running it into the ground, that's what you're doing," shouted Sidney, hurling the card samples onto Laura's desk and storming from the office.

The heavy wooden door slammed behind her. Why, oh *why* had she let herself get dragged back into the business? She stamped down the richly carpeted hall, past the rows of oaken doors with their brass numbers. Six was the only one occupied at present, she noticed; faint moans came from within. One room out of twelve, on this floor. "Slow" wasn't the word for business.

Well, it *had* been necessary to bail her mother out, hadn't it? Couldn't leave her in hock to the elven gangsters. And that left Sidney with half the family business; could she stand aloof and watch as her mother drove it into the ground once more?

She'd run away from home once before. "Running away isn't the answer," Father Thwaite had told her.

Well, then, she thought savagely, what *is*?

"Yes, yes, delicious, thank you, Vic," said Timaeus, not entirely happily.

"Eat up, eat up, boyo," said Vic, slapping him on the back and smiling broadly. "Can't march on an empty shtomach."

"Mmm," said Timaeus through a mouthful of pancake; it wasn't half bad, actually. He reached for a cup of tea to wash it down. "Now, then; what was it you wanted to talk to me about?"

Vic stared at him blankly. "Talk . . .?" he said. "What wash your name, shonny?"

Timaeus sighed. "Timaeus d'Asperge, Vic," he said patiently. "Remember? I found the statue of Stantius?"

Vic blinked. "Found the—wash it losht?" He frowned, and mumbled puzzledly to himself.

Reginald entered, bearing a folded newspaper atop a silver tray. "I thought you might want this, sir," he said, handing it to Timaeus. "Special edition."

And it was. *The Durfalian News-Gazette* was a morning paper; it was unusual for them to print an edition so late.

"ISH FALLS!" screamed the headline. Timaeus didn't think he'd ever seen type quite so large.

Vic peered over his shoulder. "Ish fallsh!" he said excitedly. "Orcsh are gonna be all over the Bibblian plain. Better get your ash in gear, shonny."

"What do you mean?" asked Timaeus

"Get your damned companionsh together and get cracking on this quesht, by cracky!" said Vic. "No more dillyfuddling around, or you're going to wind up in shome troll'sh larder, that'sh what I shay. You and half the human race."

"Off on this quest thing, again, what?" said Timaeus tiredly. "You know what the others say—"

Vic smiled faintly. "Ashked 'em recently?" he said craftily. "Maybe they've changed their mindsh. Like you have, eh, Timmy?"

Timaeus blinked. Had he? Taking Stantius to Arst-Kara-Morn still sounded like suicide, did it not?

He looked at the headline. The gods, duty, and nation, what? A comfortable life didn't look like it was in the cards. If he stayed here another few months, he'd probably wind up drafted.

Yes, actually; perhaps he had changed his mind.

"We do not," said the majordomo freezingly, "permit riffraff in the Millennium."

"Riffraff!" protested Nick. "What do you mean, riffraff?"

"Please," said the majordomo. "I suppose you imagine that, that *thing* you are wearing makes you appear to be a gentleman. The very supposition marks you out as the most vulgar, gutter-dwelling—"

"Ahem," coughed Timaeus. "He's with me."

The majordomo's jaw dropped. "This—are you certain, sir?" he said.

"Yes, I'm afraid so," said Timaeus apologetically. He could see the wheels turn in the man's mind; no doubt within minutes it would be all over the servants' quarters that Timaeus d'Asperge had problems with gambling debts. Certainly Pratchitt looked every inch the racetrack tout.

"I thought these duds were first-class," Nick complained as Timaeus guided him up the wide marble stairs. "Fellow in the shop said they were all the rage."

"Really, Nick," said Timaeus. "Checked hose? And

your hat looks like an admiral's. Next time you want to buy something to impress anyone other than your lowlife companions, do let me know. Or Sidney; she's had enough exposure to—"

"Don't talk to me about Sidney," Nick said. "She's still mad at me for—"

"There you are, Nick," said Sidney. She sat in an armchair by a small teak table, wearing, in deference to the customs of the club, a modest black dress. Jasper hung in the air nearby, while Vic sprawled back in his own armchair, snoring. Reginald had managed to get Vic, at least, into suitable attire. "Glad to see you're still out of jail," Sidney said.

"I ought to be, given my legal bills," said Nick. "You can't believe what lawyers charge—"

"If you'd stop cuckolding rich men," said Sidney, "you wouldn't wind up in court so much."

"Yeah, I suppose," said Nick, "but the problem with cuckolding poor men is they'd rather kill than sue you."

"You don't have to do either," said Sidney. "If you need your ashes hauled, I can get you a very good deal."

"That's not the point," said Nick. "It's the chase that's interesting, not the conclusion."

"Now, now," said Timaeus. "Let's not fight yet, shall we? Where's Garni?"

"If you'd kept in touch," said Sidney freezingly, "you'd know that he left for Dwarfheim months ago. Death in the family, or something."

"Errm, well, yes," said Timaeus, fumbling with his pipe. "I have been rather preoccupied, haven't I?"

"No," said Nick. "You just didn't want to talk to your—lowlife companions, wasn't that the phrase? Rather hob-nob with—"

"Well, I apologize if it seemed that way," said Timaeus. "But—"

"But nothing," said Sidney heatedly. "Nick's right. You—"

A crash sounded from the stairwell. "By all the gods!" came a bellow. "Kraki, son of Kronar, goes vhere he vills!"

"Oop," said Timaeus, rising hastily. "Better go collect Kraki, what?"

There was an awkward silence in his absence. Nick tried to catch the eye of a waiter—Timaeus could probably be induced to pay for the drinks—but they seemed to evade his gaze with consummate ease. "So, Sidney," he said at last, "how's business?"

"Terrible," she said. "And Mom's driving me nuts."

"That was predictable," said Nick.

"You're enjoying yourself, I suppose?" she said resentfully. "Always wanted to be rich. Now you can spend every waking hour chasing—"

"Actually," said Nick, "I'm pretty sick of it. I'm in court all the time, I don't dare pull off a heist because I've got enough troubles, and anyway, I don't need the money; I can only spend so much time at the track before I go nuts—you know, a life of leisure is not all it's cracked up to be."

"Poor boy," said Sidney coldly. "What about you, Jasper?"

"Actually, you know," said the green light, "I've been quite enjoying myself. Joined up with some youngsters in a couple of little forays into the Caverns; felt good to be on an expedition again. And those lads desperately need a wiser head among them, I must say; not making adventurers like they used to. Either that, or I've forgotten how much of an idiot I was when I first started out."

"You've taken up adventuring again?" said Sidney. "Why would you risk your life like that? You don't need the money."

"True enough," said Jasper, "but business is down at the

shop, and—you know, I quite enjoyed our little run-in.
When Timaeus asked me if I wanted to join you in your
venture, I—"

"Venture?" said Sidney. "Oh, no—Vic's quest? Is that
what this is about?"

Timaeus approached with a glowering Kraki. "Ale,
lackey!" Kraki shouted at one of the waiters. "Bring it
quick, by the gods, or you feel the bite of barbarian steel!"

"Simmer down, Kraki," said Timaeus.

"You vant another shop?" Kraki said to Jasper. "I give
to you. Make very good deal."

"Very generous of you, to be sure," said Jasper, "but—"

"I ride for northland tomorrow," said Kraki. "Get out of
stinking city. Had enough."

"I thought you said you'd help Vic on his quest,"
Timaeus said.

Kraki blinked. "Vell, sure," he said. "Good idea, test
mettle against all the forces of evil, for sure. But I thought
all you pansies said no, yah?"

"We're having a bit of a rethink," said Timaeus.

"*You're* having a bit of a rethink," said Nick. "Me, I've
got a court date at two o'clock. Throwing my young life
away on some fool—"

"You haven't seen the papers?" said Timaeus.

"Sure," said Nick. "The orcs have overrun Ishkabibble.
So?"

"Stay here, and you'll be drafted within the year. I guar-
antee it," said Timaeus.

Nick contemplated that. "Probably," he said. "But—"

"Do you know what the casualty rate was on the Ish
front?" said Timaeus.

"Well," said Nick. "Yeah. But I can always cut out for
Far Moothlay, or—"

"Good heavens!" said Jasper in astonishment. "I knew
you were a cautious fellow, young Pratchitt, but I had no

idea you were a craven swine! When the nation calls, will you not answer?"

"No," said Nick, "I won't."

Vic, who had woken up some time ago and had followed this exchange with interest, began to speak Words of power. The others fell silent and watched him until he was done. Vic pointed at Nick and spoke the final Words; a line of viridian energy stretched from his finger toward Nick's crotch. "Better come along, shonny," he cackled.

"Why?" said Nick.

"Or your thing'll fall off," said Vic.

"My—"

"Yup," said Vic. There was silence for a long moment.

"Just promise me one thing," Nick said.

"What'sh that?" Vic asked.

"No dragons," said Nick. "All right? Is that too much to ask? Orcs and trolls and basilisks, fine; goblins and wyverns and the gods know what-all, jake by me. But leave out the dragons, okay?"

"What've you got againsht dragonsh?" demanded Vic. "Fine traditional part of a quesht, dragonsh."

"I don't like dragons," said Nick. "I don't like unicorns, either, but I'm just asking about dragons. All right? No dragons, or I stay."

Vic shrugged. "Do my besht," he said. "Can't promishe shome fool lizard won't shtick hish head where it oughtn't to be. But we aren't heading into dragon country, anyway."

"All right," said Nick. "I'll come, then."

"That just leaves you, Sidney," said Timaeus. They all looked at her; she looked rather uncomfortably back.

"What about Father Thwaite?" she said.

"I've already asked him," said Timaeus. "He's under strict orders, apparently. I talked to the abbot, who seemed to appreciate the direness of our task, but he refused to release Thwaite from his vows. Perhaps correctly; while it is true that he's been on the wagon for some time, we cannot be confident of his sobriety once he departs the monastery."

"And Garni's gone," said Sidney. "Oh, hell, I'll come. If they're going to be drafting every man in sight, business is going to dry up entirely."

"Suicide," moaned Nick.

"Buck up, man," said Jasper in disgust. "Are we not heroes? Does not the right triumph?"

"No," said Nick, "and no. What about the statue? Every wizard in the world will be able to track us as we travel; when we get to the Dark Lands, we'll be snatched up instantly, like hors d'oeuvres on a tray."

"Have a little faith," said Vic. "I put a shpell on it. Short of an invishibility to magic thing. Nobody'sh going to be detecting that shtatue, or my name ishn't Polykarpush Magicush."

"Your name *isn't* Polykarpus Magicus," Timaeus pointed out.

"Jusht hedging my betsh," said Vic.

"How very reassuring," said Timaeus.

"Shpeaking of hors d'oeuvresh—they have lobshter on the menu here, Timmy? Didn't get to be two thoushand by shitting around waiting for lunch, by cracky. Which way'sh the dining room?"

PART I.

OMNIA VINCIT AMOR

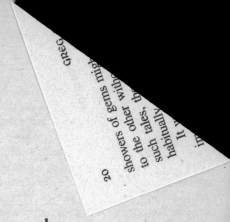

GREG

20

showers of gems might
to the other with
such tales, the
habitually
It
in

1.

Above the mountains shone a brilliant sun, casting its rays across an azure sky. Green-clad slopes lifted upward to snowy peaks; the cool mountain air was freshened with the scent of pine. Across the wilderness stretched a single road; and along that road, upward into the mountains, came a merchant caravan, consisting of a single wagon and outriders.

An observer—a bandit, say, lurking in the woods atop one of the many rises cut through by the road—would have seen nothing amiss in the scene. There is considerable trade up and down the road, for the Iscabalian Way is the most direct route from Urf Durfal to Ishkabibble, and the Biddleburg Pass, toward which it rises, the most convenient traverse across the Dzorzian Range. And the riders, diverse lot though they were, were clad as merchants might be clad. Oh, not the bare-chested barbarian, to be sure, but it was usual for merchants to hire guards of one kind or another, in these unhappy times. Legend has it that, in the days of Imperium, an undefended lass bearing armbands of gold, roped pearls, and

...t have ridden from one end of the land ...ut molestation; alas, whatever the truth of ...e modern world is far less orderly. Merchants ...travel with armed guardians.

...would have taken close inspection to shake the initial ...pression. A keen eye might have seen that one of the riders rode quite adequately without a mount; indeed, without corporeal existence whatsoever, as he consisted solely of a small point of green light, flitting through the air at sufficient speed to remain abreast of the horses of the others. Another of the merchants was a wizard of at least minor power, as he proved by lighting his pipe with a spell—enveloping his head in flames in the process, to no ill effect. And the sight of an ancient codger, snoring toothlessly at the rear of the wagon, might have raised questions also; what purpose would merchants have in hauling a senile old graybeard about?

It is well, therefore, that our observers, whatever their other characteristics, were neither as keen-eyed nor as questioning as they might have been.

Fleecy clouds floated lazily across an azure sky. Mighty firs rose from either side of the road, limbs stretching outward as if to catch the benison of the sun. The air was cool, the breeze a gentle one. It was the sort of day that lifts the soul, that seems to beckon one on to adventure. On such a day, it would take grim determination to feel anything less than contentment.

Sidney Stollitt glowered distrustfully at the trees. Behind every curve she expected an ambuscade. She, who walked the roughest streets of the city without fear, felt utterly out of place in this bucolic wilderness. Her unease was merely sharpened by the lightheartedness of her companions: No one was keeping a proper watch.

Kraki Kronarsson rode behind, chanting the sagas of his barbarian youth to himself. Nick Pratchitt rode aboard the wagon, reins in his hand and idly speculating on the like-lihood that the mountains were inhabited by dragons. Vic, as usual, was sound asleep, snoring into his scraggly white beard. And the mages, Timaeus and Jasper, rode ahead, talking good-naturedly of nothing much.

"Amazing engineering, those Imperial chaps, what?" said Timaeus about the stem of his pipe. Smoke curled into the pine-scented air. "I mean to say, running a road into these mountains at a constant grade. Couldn't be done to-day, I should think."

Jasper floated alongside, matching the speed of Timaeus's mount. "Oh, I don't know," said the green spot of light. "Magical knowledge has increased, if anything, since Imperial times."

"Nonsense," said Timaeus. The doctrine of decline from the Golden Age was the fundament of all historical knowl-edge, or so he had been taught at university; he was sur-prised that as educated a man as Jasper could hold so ill-informed an opinion. "The works of the ancients vastly outshine anything accomplished in the modern age."

Sidney grimaced, studying the road ahead. The grade might be constant, but it was uphill; they were climbing into the mountains, whose white-capped peaks lifted high on the horizon ahead. The horses pulled onward, smoothly but under some strain; they would need to be rested soon. The road curved frequently, no doubt to maintain the grade; there was no telling what might lurk behind the next twist or turn.

Far up the road and high into the mountains, Sidney could just barely see the ramparts of Biddleburg Castle. With luck, they would reach it by nightfall. It was wedged between two mountains, athwart the Iscabalian Way, the seat of Baron Biddleburg, who ruled all the land for, say, half a day's ride from his castle. A petty domain, but not a poor one; the geography conspired to let him impose a stiff tariff on the trade that went up and down this road.

To either side of the Iscabalian Way was dense coniferous forest—pines, firs, and hemlocks. Sidney examined the woods mistrustfully. Bandits, familiar with the land, could appear from the greenwood at any moment—and melt away once they had despoiled the caravan.

"I say," said Timaeus, "here's an example, up ahead. To keep the road level, they had to cut through the hill. To reduce the rock to magma and clear a path—"

"Bosh," said Jasper. "How typical for a fire mage to propose an incendiary solution. Rather than melting your way through the rock, wouldn't it be easier to cause the earth to subside?"

Yes, there was a road cut ahead. Cliffs, perhaps eight cubits in height, rose to either side of the road. Atop the cliffs were trees. A perfect spot for an ambush, Sidney thought unhappily. A foe would have the advantage of them, atop the cliff, protected by the wood. . . . She rode up toward the two magicians.

"Cause the earth to subside?" said Timaeus indignantly. "How the deuce does one cause the earth to subside? You seem to imagine that ordering solid rock from place to place is as easy as squishing pureed vegetables with the flat of a knife!"

"Perhaps it is," insisted Jasper, "if one is an earth mage—"

"Listen," interrupted Sidney, "we're riding along as if we don't have a care in the world. For all we know, these woods are filled with bandits. And that cliff up there is an ideal spot for an ambush. In fact, there are ideal spots for ambushes about every three yards on this damn road—"

"Don't be absurd, my dear," said Timaeus. "This is a civilized area. I'm sure the road is well patroll—"

Sssssh-THUNK. A clothyard shaft protruded from the headboard of the wagon, inches from Nick's ear. He had been cracking pecans, and froze in an attitude of surprise, a handful of nuts halfway to his mouth.

"Stand as I bid ye, fellows, lest subsequent shafts find deadlier mark," rang out a voice—curiously, the voice of a woman. And there on the cliff above crouched a good dozen rùffians, unkempt as one might expect brigands to be, wearing worn and patched clothing in green and brown. Each held a longbow, each with an arrow nocked, each string drawn full back.

Sidney drew a ragged breath. Her sword was of no use; there was no way to close with the highwaymen before they could shoot. "Timaeus!" she whispered urgently, trying not to move her lips. "A fireball . . ."

But he was ahead of her. He was chanting in a low voice, hands waving over his head in a ritual gesture. One hand held his meerschaum pipe, which—

—went spinning off across the road to smash into the scree of shale at the base of the cliff. "I say!" protested Timaeus, peering woundedly toward it.

"No magic," quoth the female voice, "or the next shaft shall pierce thy throat."

"Dash it all!" said Timaeus. "That's my best pipe!"

There was a scurry of motion from Kraki's direction. He was crouching atop his horse, standing on the saddle; arrows shot toward him as he launched himself in a mighty leap toward the cliff top, sword already drawn. Shafts whizzed past him as he grabbed the cliff edge, scrambled over it, raised his sword—

A quarterstaff smashed into the side of his head. He was propelled groggily back over the cliff, bouncing off the shale and smashing into the road below.

A woman in forest green stood atop the cliff edge, quarterstaff in her hands. Close-cropped hair shone brilliantly red in the afternoon sun. "That will be all, I trust?" she inquired in an amused tone.

Sidney looked about. Kraki was sitting up, groaning and holding his head. Timaeus chewed his lower lip unhappily. Sidney herself saw no point in resisting.

Nick was surveying the woman with a definite leer. Sidney gave a silent snarl.

Where, she wondered, was Jasper? The green light had
disappeared.

The woman dropped lightly to the roadbed, quarterstaff
still in hand. The line of bowmen remained atop the cliff,
bows drawn, unmoving. "Good morrow, gentles," the woman
said cheerfully. "We'll take up donations, now, if you will."

"Donations?" inquired Timaeus.

"Quite so, quite so," said she. "The poor groan under
the usurper's oppression. 'Tis our unhappy task to alleviate
their plight by extracting revenues from travelers. Your
purse, now, and yarely, if you please."

"So the money you steal goes to the poor?" asked Nick
skeptically. "A coin or two doesn't stick to your fingers?"

"Certes," said the woman, giving him a smile. "How
would we live elsewise? Come, sir; your purse."

"Can I ask your name, doll?" said Nick.

She tossed her head, as if she were used to having
longer hair. "You are taxed," she said, "by Beatrice of the
Band." With a dagger, she cut Nick's purse loose from his
belt, and pocketed it.

"Taxed?" sputtered Timaeus. "This is nothing but common brigandage!"

"The hypocrisy of the aristocracy," Beatrice said sardon-
ically, as she lifted Timaeus's purse. "It is taxation when
Broderick's men dig up the meager grain a peasant stores
against famine, or burn an entire village when coin is not
forthcoming—but brigandage when we take a little pelf for
better cause. Come, our taxation is lighter, and more just."

"A fancy excuse for stealing," said Sidney. She had
nothing much against theft, herself, but rather balked at
such self-satisfied moralizing.

"Fancy or not," said Beatrice cheerfully, accepting Sidney's purse. "Without divine sanction, temporal power is
mere oppression."

"Who is this Broderick?" asked Timaeus. "I had thought
Baron Biddleburg's name was Barthold."

Beatrice looked at him more closely. "It is," she said. "He is senile. His brother has taken the reins of power, curse him."

"And what of Bertram, the heir?"

"That twit?" said Beatrice with contempt. She had finished collecting funds from the party. "We shall leave you with the contents of your wagon, as the baron's men would be upon us before we could finish searching. And now, *adieu*." With that, she ran to the cliff face, where one of the brigands had lowered a rope. She hurled her quarterstaff upward—another bandit caught it—and clambered up the rope with a monkey's agility.

And as quickly as they had come, the brigands were gone, fading away into the woods.

There was silence for a moment. Timaeus dismounted and went to get his pipe.

"Mighty adventurers we," said Sidney savagely, "unable to repel a passel of backwoods banditti."

Kraki pulled himself up the side of the wagon. "Vhere is vhisky?" he demanded. "My head hurts like devil."

Nick was still staring dreamily up at the cliff, a vague smile on his face. "You," said Sidney, giving him a poke. "If you'd had the guts to back Kraki up . . ."

"Oh, come, Sidney," said Timaeus, packing his pipe. "We're lucky we didn't suffer worse."

A point of green light spiraled down from above their heads. "Bracing, what?" said Jasper. "Nothing like a moment of mortal danger to put a little spring in your step, eh?"

"And where the hell were you?" demanded Sidney.

"Oh, I was about, never fear," said Jasper. "Please be so good as to check your purse, Miss Stollitt."

"My purse? Some hairy peasant is pawing through it at this very—"

Sidney realized that her right hand had touched the purse at her belt. Slowly, she opened the drawstring, emptied the coins into her hand, and counted them. It was all still there. "But I saw her take it," she said.

"Quite, quite," said Jasper in a self-satisfied tone. "She saw it, too. Or thought she did."

The others had realized that they, too, retained their wealth. "I say," said Timaeus admiringly, "how did you do that?"

"Oh, simple enough," said Jasper. "A mental suggestion or two . . . trivial, really. It seemed the easiest way to defuse the situation."

"Good work," said Sidney reluctantly. "But we'd better get organized before they realize they've been taken and come back. I want you flying overhead, Jasper, to warn us if anyone's waiting along the road. I want Nick to ride well behind, to sneak up and help if we're caught again; and I want Kraki—"

The barbarian groaned.

"Never mind," said Sidney.

Evening was nigh, the sun's rays slanting low from the west. Ahead, the pass was blocked by the walls of Biddleburg, which protected both the castle itself and the small town that clustered about it. The road led toward a gatehouse, a grim stone structure with arrow slits, allowing enfilade fire across the road, and a portcullis, now raised but evidently ready to bar the way. The opening itself was large enough to admit two carts abreast. Two soldiers stood with axes, along with their serjeant, who looked quite bored.

"I say," complained Jasper. "Is this charade really necessary?"

"We've been over this before," said Sidney. "Rumors about the statue are running rampant. Traveling incognito, while keeping Stantius hidden, is our best hope of getting unmolested to Ish—"

"Yes, yes, but see here," said Jasper. "If we approach the castle as the noblemen we are—"

"Some of us are," pointed out Nick, whose father had been a riverboat sailor and whose mother had eked out a meager living as a washerwoman.

"Yes, but the point is, they'd gladly greet us as guests. Instead, we shall be forced to flop in another louse-infested publick house—"

"Stop whining," said Sidney. "Don't lice have minds? You're supposed to be a wizard of the mental arts; tell them to leave you alone."

"It's—"

"Enough of this," said Nick. "They'll overhear us. Merchants all, remember, now."

And it was indeed so; they were within hailing distance of the guards. Jasper zipped into the wagon—they wished to avoid explaining the wizard's peculiar appearance—and Nick, who had the reins, brought the wagon to a halt upon the serjeant's signal.

"Name," said the serjeant in a bored tone.

"Nicholas Frauenstein," said Nick. "Of Frauenstein et Frères. Merchants and purveyors."

"Right," said the serjeant. "Commercial business?"

"Yes," said Nick.

"Cargo?"

"Carpets and housewares," said Nick. "Bound for Hamsterburg."

"Righto," said the serjeant. "Bring her in the gates, and we'll have a look. You'll have a bill of lading?"

"Yes, of course," said Nick, a little annoyed. He hadn't anticipated a search, but geed up the horses, and moved them at a slow walk within the gates. The rest of the party followed with their mounts. "Can you give me an estimate of the toll?"

The serjeant looked up from a sheaf of papers, on which he was making a note. "Sixpence a person, extra penny per mount. Ten percent tariff on estimated cargo value."

Nick choked. "Ye gods," he protested, "that's awfully steep!"

The serjeant gave him a nasty smile. "Don't like it, take your wagon over the mountains, me lad."

As soldiers opened the flaps enclosing the wagon's cargo, Nick studied the sheer slopes flanking Biddleburg town. You'd have to be a mountain goat to climb them, he thought; they were bare rock, the slope approaching vertical in places. Scant chance that an irate merchant, incensed by the tariff, would find an alternate path.

"Who's the old duffer?" asked a soldier.

Vic was sitting up in the rear of the wagon, blinking sleepily at the searchers. "What'sh going on?" he demanded querulously. Sidney left her horse in Kraki's care and helped the old man out, guiding him to where the others stood. Soldiers began to haul rugs out and unroll them beside the road, to ease appraisal.

"Look here," said Nick to the serjeant. "Is this really necessary? I mean, this search." Jasper could probably take care of himself, but the gods forbid they should find the compartment where the statue of Stantius was stored.

"Standard procedure," said the serjeant, turning over the corner of a carpet to examine the degree of wear to the backing.

"Ah, perhaps an exception to standards might be in order?" said Nick. "One might be prepared to extend a gratuity . . ."

The serjeant chortled happily. "Attempted bribery," he said. "Another ten shillings to your toll, boyo."

Nick scowled and went to join the others. "I'm beginning to think I prefer bandits," said Sidney.

"Stiff-necked bastards," said Nick.

"Vhy not let me kill them?" said Kraki.

"Good plan," said Sidney sarcastically, giving his skull a sharp rap.

"Stop that!" said Kraki, wincing—but he took her point. He was not in any shape for combat.

Vic was blinking a little sleepily in the daylight. "Kill?" he said. "Kill who?"

"We'll survive," said Timaeus resignedly. "It's only money, after all. And then, down into the valley—"

"Only money!" said Nick. "What do you mean, only—"

"Whatcher say, serjeant?" inquired a soldier, examining a gaily patterned Nokhena. "Think it's worth a hunnerd quid?" He had unrolled the rug to examine it more closely.

"Call it two," said the serjeant, giving Nick a nasty glance and a grin.

"Two hundred pounds!" said Nick. "I bought that wholesale for—"

"Hallo, Serjeant Jenks," said a voice. "What's all this, what, what? Shaking down another greasy merchant?"

It was a young man, dressed in hose and a waistcoat of surprisingly stylish cut—surprising, given how remote Biddleburg was from the centers of civilized life. He seemed fit, cheery, and obviously of the nobility, given his clear anticipation of deference from the soldiers; despite a prominent overbite, he struck Sidney as quite handsome.

"Yes, Sir Bertram," said Jenks.

The young man surveyed the company. "Further contributions to the exchequer are never amiss—hallo." He started a bit, and peered closer. "I say, hallo, d'Asperge. What brings you to these parts?"

Timaeus, who had been doing his best to disappear behind Kraki, straightened up and sighed. "Hallo, Bertie," he said. "Pip of a day, what?"

"The sun doth shine and the birds do play, you mean? Yes, yes, quite. I say, Jenks, pack up all this trash, will you? And send it up to the castle. Why didn't you write to tell me you were coming, Timaeus, old man? We'd have broken out the old fatted calf."

II.

they sat in an enormous room that might have been the great hall of a lesser castle, but was here only one sitting room among many. At one end, a fire roared in a vast fireplace. Banners and tapestries hung from the walls, the floor was carpeted with rugs that compared favorably with the ones that lay in their own wagon, and heavy furniture was scattered in conversational groupings. They had all been assigned rooms down the hall, and this was a convenient place to gather.

"An old school chum?" said Sidney. "Why didn't you *tell* us Baron Biddleburg's heir was an old school chum?"

Timaeus puffed a little embarrassedly on his pipe. "Well, it didn't seem relevant, really," he said. "I mean, here we are; and we'll have to stay at least a couple of days, you know. Only polite. I had hoped we could simply pay the toll and continue on our way."

"Well, at least we'll save some money," said Nick.

"I must say," Jasper said, "you really might have told

us, old man. That is, it should have been our collective decision whether or not to approach young Sir Bertram. For myself, a night or two of rest in decent accommodations is all to the good; surely our quest is not so urgent as all that."

Vincianus was peering querulously about. "Quesht?" he quavered. "Where are we?"

"Biddleburg Castle, Vic," said Nick soothingly.

"Biddleburg, Biddleburg," said Vic. "Ushed to have quite a shellar. When'sh dinner?"

Timaeus had spotted a liveried servant approaching. "Rather soon, I believe."

"Good evening, ladies, gentlemen," said the servant. "Sir Bertram has asked that you join him in the Great Hall for an apéritif."

Three men awaited them at the far end of the Great Hall. There was Bertram, resplendent in gold doublet and hose. To his left, an elderly man sat in an armchair, a brass-knobbed walking stick in one liver-spotted hand. To Bertram's right stood a man of late middle age, wearing a blue velvet doublet and a silver chain, weary blue eyes above a salt-and-pepper beard.

Bertram bent over the old man. "This is Timaeus d'Asperge, Pater," he said. "We were at university together. My father, Barthold, Baron Biddleburg."

"Glad to meet you, sir," said Timaeus.

"Nnnn-nnnn-nnnn," said the old man. "Nnnnn."

"Sorry about that," said Bertram apologetically. "Since Pater's seizure ..." He shrugged. "And my uncle, Sir Broderick."

"How do you do," said Timaeus, shaking Broderick's hand.

Broderick peered at Timaeus rather sharply, as if he had heard the name before, and possibly not in a positive context. "Timaeus d'Asperge, eh?" he said. "And your companions?"

"Ah, Sir Jasper de Mobray," said Timaeus. The green light bobbed in midair. "Kraki Kronarsson, of the north."

"Vhen do ve eat?"

"Patience," said Timaeus. "Sidney Stollitt and Nicholas Pratchitt." They alternately curtsied and bowed, Sidney feeling quite out of place in the gown the servants had laid out for her. "And Vincianus Polymage, of the White Council."

Vic had been peering about confusedly, but looked up at his name. "Eh?" he said. "What'sh that?"

Broderick's eyebrows shot up at Vincianus's name. "Greetings all," he said. "And welcome to Castle Biddleburg. Please accept my apologies, but there is a matter I must attend to immediately." And he bustled away.

"Ah, there's Uncle Broderick for you," said Bertram. "Always bustling about on important business. Whisky, anyone? Or a glass of wine?"

The makings stood by on a sideboard, and two servants had appeared to do the honors.

"You got shome of the Shang du Démon?" asked Vincianus.

Bertram inclined his head respectfully. "Yes, of course. Delbert, the '88, I think."

"Very good, sir," said one of the servants, and whisked off to the cellars.

The others settled for Moothlayan whisky or, in Jasper's case, for the Dzorzian sherry that stood on the sideboard. "Broderick's been a great help," Bertram said. "Really rallied round after Pater's seizure. Don't know what I'd do without him."

"One gets the impression he's running the barony virtually unaided," said Timaeus, slightly censoriously.

"Well, yes, but dash it, Tim, you know I was never any good at sums and such. I'm just not cut out to be the wise and benevolent lord. Broderick enjoys the work, and he can have it, as far as I'm concerned. Personally, I'd be off for Urf Durfal or Hamsterburg in an instant, if he didn't need me here as a figurehead."

"So he's a stand-up guy, as far as you're concerned?" asked Nick.

"Well, yes, rather," said Bertram.

"Doesn't seem to be the general opinion," said Nick. "Ow!" Sidney had kicked him in the shin.

"Shut up," she said, low and urgent.

"I say, what do you mean?" said Bertram.

"Ah, we had a bit of an encounter on the road," admitted Timaeus.

"Mm?" said Bertram, taking a sip of his whisky.

"With a group of bandits," said Jasper. "Most extraordinary group, oddest justification for thievery I've ever heard, and led by a woman. Beatrice, I think she called herself."

Bertram looked up from his whisky. "Beatrice?" he said thoughtfully. "I knew a Beatrice, once." He looked briefly pensive—not his usual mood, it seemed to Sidney. "Lovely gel," he said almost to himself.

The table was a long affair that looked as though it could seat a hundred, as perhaps it did on occasion. They seemed to be the only guests at Biddleburg Castle, for they, the baron's immediate family, and a man of soldierly bearing introduced as Captain Blentz were the only ones at table. They were seated together at one end, while the other extended off, an infinity of linen and candelabra, toward a vast hearth, where some great beast—a whole steer, or perhaps a doe—was roasting on a spit. A small boy wound a crank to keep the spit turning.

Three footmen bustled about, seating the party, holding chairs, and waving out napkins. Two silver wine buckets stood by the table, filled with ice and bottles. Sidney was

impressed; ice was expensive. Although, she realized, here
in the cool mountains it was probably easier to store ice
through the summer than in the hotter lowlands.

There were three forks, three knives, two spoons, three
glasses, and four plates at Sidney's place. Nick surveyed
this collection of silverware and china and looked nervously at Sidney. "Outside in," she whispered at him; that
was the rule her mother had taught her, and while her
mother had just enough etiquette to be considered vulgarly
nouveau, it was at least more than Sidney herself pos-
sessed. Nick nodded with comprehension—start with the
outermost utensils and work your way in, a clear enough
principle—but puzzled over the butter knife, which lay
above the largest plate: Did it come before, after, or in between the two knives to the right of the plates?

Kraki grabbed his water glass, poured its contents into
his gullet in a single motion, gulped the water, and
crunched on the ice. Sleet spattered everywhere. He
seemed disgruntled to realize that his quaff had not been
alcoholic. One of the servants, apparently divining this,
took a bottle from one of the wine buckets and presented
it to Kraki, holding it so that the barbarian might read the
label. "Some wine, sir?" he inquired. "A white Linfalian,
quite dry—"

Kraki said, "Yah, good," grabbed the bottle, and put it
to his lips. Several large swallows later, he put it down
with a slam on the table before him, wiped his mouth with
the back of his hand, and gave a belch. Realizing by the
servant's expression that some breach of etiquette had occurred, he added, "Ah—thank you."

"Not at all," murmured the ashen servant, moving away.

A butler whose ruddy jowls, frozen expression, and vast
expanse of waistcoat indicated servile dignity fossilized
through years of service held out a large silver platter to
Sidney's right. With a flourish, a footman whisked off the
cover to reveal a broiled fish, dotted with slivered al-

monds. "Troot Omondine, marss?" inquired the butler; it took Sidney a moment to translate this as "Trout Almondine, miss?" She had heard the same accent in the speech of the other servants here at the castle, and more faintly in that of Beatrice, and had tagged it as common to this region; but in the butler, the accent approached the impenetrable. "Uh, please," she said.

The footman deftly removed a smallish section of trout, laid it precisely at the center of the smallest plate in the pile of three in front of Sidney, arranged three overlapping slices of lemon to the trout's right, and placed a small dish of brown butter below the lemon.

She waited as the other members of her group were served; apparently, guests came before family. Nick was served; then Timaeus; then Kraki. Sidney closed her eyes, expecting some unforgivable crudity, but Kraki merely waved the fish away with a grimace of distaste.

"I do hope you'll be staying with us for a few days," said Uncle Broderick as Baron Barthold was served. A footman tied a napkin about the old man's neck while another deftly sliced his section of trout into small pieces, carefully removing the bones. The baron was the last to be served, and everyone tucked in. "I'm afraid that young Bertram is somewhat insensible to the many charms of our mountain realm," Broderick continued, "and no doubt would enjoy the companionship of ones lately from more settled lands. Too, the villagers will be holding the Feast of Grimaeus, our most colorful local celebration, the day after tomorrow, and you may find it of some passing amusement." While Broderick spoke, Baron Barthold had been attempting to eat his fish; one palsied hand held a fork, the other a silver pusher. He would painstakingly push a piece of fish onto the fork, then raise it, hand fluttering like a leaf in a gale, an expression of intense concentration on his face, toward his mouth. More often than not, the fish would fly off at an unexpected angle across the room, gen-

erally to land on the slate flags of the chamber floor, but
at least once to hit Nick on the nose. He diplomatically
picked the fish off his face and deposited it in his napkin.

Timaeus swallowed hastily and cleared his throat. "Well,
aherrrm, as it happens, ah, it seems that we're, ah, expected
in Hamsterburg. Quite soon. While it's wonderful to see
you again, Bertram, old son, I'm afraid that the fortunes of
war, pressure of business, you know the sort of thing ..."
He was floundering, and was evidently relieved when Jasper interrupted.

"Very rude of us, to be sure," said Jasper. The green
light bobbed over his chair; occasionally, a glass of wine
would tilt back and the level of liquid drop, or a fork bob
through space bearing a load of fish, which would abruptly
disappear. "And it is very kind of you to take us in on
such short notice. Still, I fear we must take our leave on
the morrow. If there's any way we can repay your hospitality ..."

"No, no, no, no," said Broderick hastily, obviously annoyed. "Hospitality is, er, hospitality, after all; there shall
be no thought of repayment, of course, none, no, no. Might
one inquire as to the nature of this pressing business?"

Momentary looks of panic were exchanged across the
table; their agreed story, that they were merchants, would
obviously not do. Several began to talk at once.

"Ah—carpets and housewares for, uh, the war effort—"
said Nick.

"We carry diplomatic papers from the Foreign Ministry
of—" said Jasper.

"—plan to join in the defense of the Petty States—"
said Timaeus.

They fell still in confusion.

"I see," said Broderick in an amused tone. There was an
embarrassed silence for a moment. Sidney kicked Nick
under the table; carpets and housewares for the war effort,
indeed! He gave her an injured glare. The servants were

clearing away the fish dishes and silverware now; Timaeus hid his embarrassment by turning away to hand his dish over.

"Uncle, Timaeus tells me that his group had a bit of a run-in with our local banditti," said Bertram, breaking the silence.

"Oh?" said Broderick, eyebrows shooting skyward. "Egad, they're getting bolder by the day."

"Fear not, milord," said red-faced Captain Blentz, hitherto silent. By his speech, he was obviously more than half soused. "We'll flush the blighters out."

"Yes, yes," said Broderick thoughtfully. "I hope you didn't suffer at their hands?"

"No," said Timaeus, "we came out of it—"

"Apparently, their leader is a woman by the name of Beatrice," interrupted Bertram.

"Ah?" said Broderick, eyeing Bertram; it seemed to Sidney that this was no news to Broderick.

"You don't suppose that could possibly be the daughter of Sir Benton of Bainbridge?" inquired Bertram.

"That traitor?" snapped Broderick. "It was a fine day indeed when he was broken on the wh—" He interrupted himself with a cough, realizing abruptly that this was not appropriate dinner conversation. "A rebel," he explained. "Rose in arms against my brother the baron. We were forced to give him justice."

Sidney looked at the baron, who looked back with haunted eyes, a sliver of fish adhering to his lower lip. "Nnnn-nnn-nnn," he said.

"Terrible, terrible," murmured Jasper.

"Decadent times," said Timaeus soothingly. The footmen had reappeared with an enormous wooden bowl containing mixed fresh greens, along with a silver ewer containing a dressing, and a cubits-long pepper grinder.

"But his daughter . . ." said Bertram.

"I'd heard she had entered a religious order," said Broderick.

"Wouldn't she inherit . . . ?" asked Bertram. The butler grandly scooped up a substantial helping of the salad and plopped it on Sidney's plate, while a footman prepared to dish out the dressing and another refreshed her wine.

"No, no," said Broderick. "We have a salian law here, you know that. Besides, the man was a traitor; the estate reverts to the barony." He gave a wolfish grin.

"Ah," said Bertram. "Still, it seems an odd coincidence; both called Beatrice, both with red hair—"

"It would reflect poorly on us if you were beset by bandits again," said Broderick to Timaeus, hastily changing the subject. "Under the circumstances, I must insist that you accept an escort until you reach the border of the barony."

"An escort?" said Timaeus, a little surprised. "Well, of course. Why not?"

The salad crew had reached Kraki's place. "Pah," said Kraki, spitting on the floor. "Is for rabbits. Don't you have any food fit for a man?" The butler was obviously a bit unsettled, but merely motioned the servants to the next place around the table.

"Oh, I say, never fear, old man," said Bertram comfortingly. "There's roast greep for entrée."

"Greep," said Kraki with disgust. "Ach, more fish."

"Fish?" said Bertram, goggling. "What do you mean, fish?"

"Oh, heavens," groaned Timaeus. "Not another—"

"Fish?" said Broderick, sitting bolt upright at the head of the table. "Ye gods, barbarian, where did you get the notion that greep are fish? No, no far from it; the greep is the noblest of animals, a full-antlered beast larger even than the moose of which we hear tell. Well do I know that mighty creature, for it abounds in the crags and pinnacles of our mountainous domain . . ."

GREEP ROTI

It is wary prey; some say the mighty greep is smarter even than a man, and who am I to gainsay them? For I have hunted the greep for forty years, man and boy, pursuing that monstrous animal through woods and over mountains, in fair weather, sleet, and snow. And ofttimes, I have returned empty-handed, for the greep is a wily foe, and only the wiliest of hunters may bring it low.

Shall I tell you of the first time I slew the greep? [*Well, actually,*" interjected Jasper, but Broderick was not to be dissuaded from telling his tale.*] It was forty years ago, when I, a stripling of sixteen, set out in dead of winter, the wind near enough to freeze a man to the marrow. "Egad, Broderick," my father said, "you are mad, to venture forth on such a day."

It was not madness, but youth. It was my fancy to pit myself against the worst that nature could offer, the starkest cold of all. I swaddled myself full and deep, draped a cloth about my mouth to shelter my lungs from at least the cold's sharpest bite, and took my longbow from the armory. For though it is a yeoman's weapon, I have trained in it from infancy, at my father's behest.

I went forth on snowshoes, lunging with a will over the crisp white that blanketed the land. After some time, I climbed a rise, reached its peak—and saw, in the streambed below, a monstrous greep, full seven points, the noble head gnawing at the bark of a tree. There is little sustenance for the greep kind, in the dead of winter; they must forage where they may, and mayhap the bark of a tree was all the nourishment it had found, that bitter day.

Instantly, I went to earth—or to snow, if you will. Stealthily, I reached over my back, toward the bow which, strung, I had slung over my shoulder—

But I got no further than that, for with a snort, divining the presence of a foe, the greep looked up, and looked directly to me with curiously sapient eyes. It bounded, and away.

I rose again to my snowshoes, and lunged after.

'Tis said that a man has the stamina to outrun any beast, and mayhap that is so, on a level plain, in fair weather; but we struggled up and down mountain peaks in the deadliest frost of deep winter. I had no faith that I would be victorious over the greep; but I was young enough to wish victory with peculiar fierceness. I could see the hoof-prints of the greep before me, the strange, semicircular indentations of its splayed toes, toes that gave it traction even in deep snow. I followed the prints relentlessly.

I came to a stream, running quickly enough that only a thin layer of ice sheltered its waters from the cold; quickly enough that no snow lay atop the ice. And here, the greep had followed the stream, taking to water in desperation.

Which way had it gone? A frightened beast would flee downstream, the easy path; but upstream of me, a twig was bent, and the ice was broken, and a branch was missing its load of snow. I was not deceived. I turned uphill, and labored on.

And upward, and upward. Soon, the trees were thinned out, becoming scraggly, and I recognized that I was nearing the timberline—

I saw the greep! The flit of a white tail, lean brown legs leaping through snow. Seemingly, it had waited here, to see if I should venture this far—and, spotting me, had dashed away once more.

I cursed; my bow was over my shoulder still, and I had missed perhaps my only chance. I took my bow in my hands—awkward, you see, to walk in snowshoes, the swinging of the arms constrained by a weapon—and strode onward.

It had been cold by my father's stead; here, a thousand

cubits upward, it was colder still. I had accounted bitter wind by my father's house; here, it was the very whip of demons, lashing out across the bare countryside. From the Dzorzian Range eastward, there is no mountain of equivalent height until you come to Oceanus. A thousand miles and more, that wind raged across the continent, until it battered itself against the mountain where I stood; and batter it did, in fury to find itself opposed.

I could feel my mustache freeze, the water of my breath instantly transformed to ice. In sudden fear, I began to check my extremities: Were my fingers white? If I rubbed my ear with snow, did the flesh still sting? This was madness, I realized: to come so high, expose my flesh to this rawness. This was how men died.

I labored on. There was no turning back. I would take my greep, or die.

Whiteness skittered across rock. More often than not, my snowshoes grated on stone instead of snow, for the wind scoured the mountainside free of snow as quickly as snow fell.

And it was falling now; somehow in my single-mindedness I had failed to note when the clouds turned gray and began to disgorge their load of snow. I could see no farther than a half dozen cubits ahead, flakes whipped across my vision in a blur of white.

Where was the greep? It left no tracks, not on this bare rock; and in the snow, I saw it no—

A snort. A glimpse of brown. I drew back an arrow and loosed it—to see the arrow snatched away by the fierce wind.

Onward, onward. At times, I cast forward in despair, feeling that I must have lost the trail; but always, I managed to find some spoor, some trace. And I lunged—

Into space.

My stomach lurched, both physically with my sudden fall, and spiritually with my sudden realization that I had been *outfoxed* by a beast. Do you understand? Man is differentiated from the animal only by his intellect; and this dumb creature had out-thought me. It had led me to a cliff, knowing I could see only inches ahead, and maneuvered me off . . .

I fell for a brief eternity, certain I was falling to my death . . .

There was an impact. It came to me that I was alive; more than alive, uninjured. There was whiteness all about me, a tunnel upward to dim gray sky; I had landed in a drift, and the snow had been thick enough to break the fall.

I trashed about in deep snow, making no progress; it caved in about me. At last I calmed, thought things through, and removed my snowshoes. I reached up, and slammed one into the snow above me, pulling myself upward, then slamming the next in. In this fashion, I climbed, until I found myself, almost hot with exertion, lying atop the drift.

The wind was slight, here, in the lee of the cliff. Dimly, dimly, far above me, I espied a blur of brown. I peered, through drifting snow; it thinned enough that for an instant I saw a brown-furred head, a hint of antler—

It was the greep. It peered downward, trying to discern whether or not I had met my doom.

In an instant, I was on my feet, an arrow nocked and drawn to my ear. I could see the greep only as a blur of brown; but—

I loosed the shaft, and instantly drew another, hoping I would be permitted another shot before the creature fled—

The brown was gone. I had lost—

Something smashed into the drift, scant cubits from where I stood.

It was the greep. I scampered over the snow, and peered down into the crater it had smashed in the drift.

It stared back at me, fear and hatred, hot anger in its gaze. The shaft of my arrow protruded through the jaw, out one cheek: a flesh wound. But that had been enough to startle the beast, cantilevered out over the cliff, peering downward at me. And it had fallen out, as I had . . .

Perhaps, given time, the greep could have clawed its way out of the drift; but I proposed to give it none. My first shaft struck it in the eye; it roared its pain and hatred, flailing desperately at the snow that caved in about it. A second time I shot, and hit its throat, lifeblood squirting crimson on white snow. And the third—but it was dying.

And as that great beast, its antlered head thrashing in pain through whiteness, as it breathed its last, I knew I had found my destiny. So would I defeat all who stood before me; so would I triumph against all adversity.

In that instant, I accounted myself a man.

And I thanked the greep, truly I did; I thanked it for showing me the vital struggle, the fierceness that underlies all creation.

Down the mountainside, I knew, was the village of Bainbridge, though I could not see it in the drifting snow; a few hours' trek, by snowshoe. I cut the greep's head from its body—I could carry no more—and I made my way to the village. There, they met me with celebration: It was accounted a great deed, to take so impressive a stag of the greep, at sixteen, in such a storm.

The greep's body froze in the snow; and, frozen, remained fresh until, some days thereafter, we sent out a party to recover its flesh.

And it roasted there, in yonder fireplace, upon that very spit.

I do not think I have ever tasted meat so fine.

During the telling, the salad had been taken away, broiled eggplant and peppers with herbs had been served, and the diners had been presented with a clear broth, to cleanse the palate before the main course. There had been a new wine with each new dish. It was clear by the time that Broderick ended his tale, however, that the *pièce de résistance* was in the offing. A parade of servants had appeared with a variety of platters. There were cardoons in a butter sauce, celeriac and bitter herbs, game hens perfumed with cinnamon, parsleyed potatoes, and fresh peas with mint. There was a deep, rich brown gravy, fresh bread of several kinds, and herb butter to slather on it. But all this was by way of side dish. The servants had wheeled in a cart bearing a load of wilted greens, had trundled it over to the fireplace, and had carefully removed the whole roast greep from the spit. Three strong men had been needed for that task. Now the butler stood over the carcass, whetting an enormous carving knife.

"And so," Broderick ended at last, "I bid you, sup; eat deeply of the richness of the greep, and imbibe as you do his wisdom. We may only hope that some portion of the greep's nobility, his courage, and his fierce desire for existence will infuse us with his flesh."

"Good story," said Kraki approvingly, pounding his fist on the table hard enough to make the glassware jump. Bertram, on the other hand, looked as if he were going off his head with ennui.

One of the footmen approached Sidney deferentially and asked her what portion of the greep she desired. "I'm not familiar with cuts of greep," she said, realizing there was no polite way to avoid eating it entirely. "Perhaps you can make a recommendation." He suggested a filet of the tenderloin, and she assented. Another servant appeared with the desired cut, while the first went to obtain requirements from the other guests. Kraki requested ribs, by which, it became clear, he meant the beast's entire rib cage.

"Wine, miss?" inquired the sommelier, holding a bottle out to Sidney. She had never seen its like. It was green. The label proclaimed it a *"vin chartreuse d'appellation Royaume Dzorzique."* This struck Sidney as unlikely, since the kingdom of Dzorz hadn't existed in almost two hun-

dred years. Uncertainly, she said, "Please," and watched as
the green liquid flowed three-quarters of the way up a
fluted glass.

"And you, sir?" the steward asked Vincianus, showing
him the bottle.

The oldster left off gumming his greep steak and peered
at it for a long moment. "Pretty young for a vin
chartreushe, ishn't it?" he said dubiously.

"Sir? Perhaps a tad, sir. But the 5530s mature a little
young; a century and three-quarters seems about right."

"A chartreuse?" said Jasper delightedly. "My, my,
Broderick, you do set a good table."

"Out of my usual range, to be sure," said Timaeus, obviously impressed.

Broderick beamed.

"We've always kept a good cellar," said Bertram, a little
proudly. "The Barons of Biddleburg have been high-class
lushes for four hundred years—"

"Nnnnn! Nnnnn!" said Baron Barthold. The old man
was shaking his head violently. By the sommelier stood
another servant, bearing a wine glass and a twist of paper
on a platter.

"Now, Pater," said Bertram concernedly. "You really
must have your philter. Doctor's orders, you know."

"Nnnn!" said Barthold.

"Come, brother," said Broderick. "If anything can make
your medication palatable, surely it is the Dzorzian. Drink
up, now!"

Barthold made a choking noise, and shook his head
again.

"If you're good," wheedled Broderick, "there's puff
pastry and ice cream for dessert."

"Nnnn," said Barthold more mildly. With unhappy eyes,
he watched the sommelier pour a glass of wine, untwist
one end of the paper, and empty a powder into the glass.
White crystals dissolved quickly in the liquid.

"Awfully sorry, Pater," said Bertram apologetically, "but it's for the best, you know. In your condition . . ." He took the wine glass and held it to the old man's lips. Barthold closed his eyes and, misery writ on his face, choked down the wine.

"I do apologize," said Broderick. "Happens every night, I'm afraid. He can be a trial."

"Nnnn," muttered Barthold censoriously, eyes still closed.

As a servant carried away the empty bottle of chartreuse and the twist of paper, Sidney dropped her dessert fork, reached down to pick it up, and quite deliberately tripped the man. The wine bottle smashed on the cold stone flags of the castle floor, the silver tray hit with a noise like a gong, and the man landed awkwardly on one arm.

"Oh!" Sidney said, springing up. "How clumsy of me. I'm so sorry. Please, let me help you."

"Quite all right, ma'am," said the servant. "My fault, I'm sure."

"Aye," said the butler freezingly. "If woon canna' watch where woon poots woon's feet, woon sharr find woonserf stoking the stove an' eating wi' the oopstairs maids. Fetch a broom at oonce and clear this mess awa'."

"Yes, Mr. Bates," said the servant. "Sorry, Mr. Bates. At once, Mr. Bates." And he scurried away.

Sidney reseated herself, the twist of paper tucked into her garter.

III.

the room was a study, of sorts. That is, it had the usual accoutrements of a study: numerous bookshelves, ornate armchairs, a globe, a crystal ball, tables and writing supplies. But the dust on the books was thick, indicating they were rarely consulted; and every available surface was covered with maps and papers. Broderick might be an efficient administrator, but he was not a neat one.

A fire burned in the hearth and an oil lamp gave a little light, but the corners of the room lay in shadow. Captain Blentz sat sleepily in a chair, while Broderick prowled restlessly.

"What?" said Blentz in blank incomprehension. "Why?"

"Why do you need to know?" demanded Broderick irritably. "Just do it."

"But Sir Broderick—"

"Bah! I don't know why I bother with you, Blentz. Still haven't found that Beatrice bint, have you, me boy? Bertie's on to it, you know; if you don't off the bitch, and soon, I'll likely wind up killing my own nephew to avoid a stink. Damned awkward, too; too much unrest in the barony as it is, the idiot is a useful figurehead."

"We'll catch her," said Blentz heavily. "These things take time."

"Time is what we don't have, man! Well, look here. This job is surefire. I don't see how you can miss. Fail me this time, and you'll find yourself out the gate with nothing but your sword and your trousers. With your record, I don't fancy your chances of finding another position."

"Yes, but look here; I mean, one thing to kill a peasant or two, but—"

"It's very simple," said Broderick. "They are carrying an object of great value. I want it. They have agreed to accept an escort to the barony's border; you are to provide it. Halfway between the castle and Bainbridge town, to minimize the chances of anyone either here or in the village learning the truth, you will turn on them and butcher them all. You will have the element of surprise; if you can't kill them before they know what's what, you are a buffoon indeed. Bury them a good distance off the road. Inside their wagon, probably in a hidden compartment, you will find a large statue. Burn the wagon and its contents. Return the statue surreptitiously to me."

"Sir, I don't know that the men will do it. After all—"

"Damnation, Blentz! There's a pound *argentum* in it for each of them."

"Ah," said Blentz. "And for me?"

"Greedy, greedy, Blentz," said Broderick in a warning tone. "Your position here is less than secure, you know."

"It's murder we're talking about," said Blentz doggedly. "I won't—"

"You won't what, Blentz? Cat got your conscience? A moral void at your soul that only the sparkle of gold will assuage? Very well; ten pounds for you, if you succeed."

"Fine," said Blentz resentfully, rising from his chair. "If that's all, I'm to bed."

"Go along, then," said Broderick, waving a hand. "I just hope you remember all this when sober."

"Not likely to forget," grunted Blentz, and wandered unsteadily out.

When Blentz's footsteps had died away, Broderick sighed, then went to examine the crystal ball. He gave it a sharp rap with a knuckle and spoke a Word. The crystal began to emit a faint yellow glow.

"Yes?" said a bass voice in a bored tone.

"Private message," said Broderick. "*Ex*: Sir Broderick de Biddleburg, Biddleburg Castle, Barony of Biddleburg. *Ad*: Gerlad, Graf von Grentz, Drachehaus, the Enclave, Free City of Hamsterburg. *Re*: Yours of the fourteenth. Begin. I may be able to obtain object in question. Please define quote considerable sum end quote. Other parties interested. Respond soonest. Thirty."

"Very good," said the voice. "How will you be paying?"

"I have an account with the Royal Bank of Dwarfheim," said Broderick. "You should have the records."

After a moment, the voice spoke again. "Very well, sir. Will that be all?"

"Yes," said Broderick, turning away as the crystal went dark.

Through slitted eyes, the cat atop the bookshelf watched the crystal's light die. Broderick pinched the oil lamp's wick into darkness, then shuffled out of the room himself, leaving it lit only by the dying embers of the fire.

The cat rose to its paws and arched its back in a stretch. As it did, there was a noise from one of the study's two windows. The cat caught the hint of a shape outside the glass, a moment of movement—and then the shape was gone.

The study was two stories up. Could the exchange be-

tween Broderick and Blentz have had a second observer?
wondered Sidney. And if so, who might that observer have
been?

She jumped to the floor, and fastidiously licked away
the dust of the shelves. When her toilet was complete, she
slunk back through the hallways toward her room.

Without the castle, the morning was brilliant, a jolly sun
casting light across a lucid sky, birds twittering happily,
gentle zephyrs wafting the pines. Jasper's bedroom was
somewhat gloomier: Its windows were small and deeply
set in thick walls, designed for defense rather than illumination. And the thick walls of the tower kept the air uncomfortably cold, colder than the world outside—a
blessing on hot summer days, no doubt, but a bit of a trial,
Jasper thought, at the moment. He had the windows open
to admit a little warmth.

Still, he pottered cheerfully about, preparing his toilet.
The green light moved over the floor, floating alongside a
straight razor. "Tum-tiddle-um-tum-tie," hummed Jasper.
"Tum-tiddle-tiddle-tiddle-um-tum-tum." A strap of leather
hung from a washstand; the free end of the strap rose in
the air until the strap was tight and parallel to the floor.
The razor began to strop itself.

After a while, the razor floated over to plunk itself
down on the stand. "Hey nonny-nonny, tiddle-um-tum-
day," sang Jasper. A brush dipped itself in water and began
to swish about in a mug, developing a lather. The brush
rose and swished itself through the air, depositing a vague
hemisphere of lather on invisible space. If one had looked
carefully, one might have been able to discern the shape of
a chin.

A cat jumped through one of the open windows, landing
in the deep window well.

The razor rose from the washstand and began to scrape
at the lather that hung in midair. Jasper hummed still, but

it was now the hum of a man with a closed mouth: "Mmm-hmmm-hmmm-mmmm-mmm-hmm."

Sidney transformed. "Jasper," she said. "I—"

The razor gave a sudden jerk. *"Yow!"* shouted Jasper. Flecks of blood appeared amid the lather and began to drip onto the floor. "By Dion, Sidney, you startled me. I do hope I have some sticking plaster." The floating lather moved over to Jasper's trunk, from which bits and oddments began to fly.

"I'm sorry, Jasper," said Sidney, not sounding particularly apologetic. "I have some information to impart."

"Hmm? Yes, good, here it is." A jar of sticking plaster unscrewed, and a dollop of the substance moved out to smear itself across empty space. "Say on, then."

Sidney sighed. "The walls have ears," she said.

"Do they?" said Jasper in a surprised tone. The lather turned to face each of the walls in turn. "I don't believe so, Sidney," he said dubiously. "In another room, perhaps?"

"Are you being purposefully dense?" demanded Sidney. "Look here. There are servants everywhere in this damned castle. I don't want to run the risk of being overheard. You're a mentalist, aren't you? Read my mind."

"Ah! Do you mind if I finish shaving?"

"No, no, just hurry up."

Jasper completed his toilet. When he was finished, the green point of light flitted over to hang before Sidney's forehead. "Now, then," said Jasper. "Hmm. Good heavens! Can't say I think much of Sir Broderick's notion of hospitality, hmm? More goes on in this castle than meets the eye."

"That's for sure," said Sidney. "Listen, we can't leave, you see?"

"Ye-e-es," said Jasper slowly. "Well, that is, we could, but it would be a risk. Maybe more of a risk than we ought to take."

"Definitely more of a risk than we ought to take," said Sidney, a little irritated. "I don't fancy a battle with scores of hardened veterans, when there's a chance of getting away without one."

"Fair enough," said Jasper.

"Will you tell the others?" asked Sidney. "Or rather, not-tell them?"

"What? Oh, yes. I see. Certainly, my dear."

A buffet breakfast had been laid out on the sideboard in the great hall: sausages, cold roast greep, pastries, pies, and oat cakes, while a servant stood by to take orders for fresh eggs. Kraki sprawled at one end of the table, with a small keg of beer and an enormous platter of sausages—a silver serving platter, Sidney saw. Apparently, he'd simply taken the whole thing from the sideboard. He was halfway through the mass of sausages and wrapping himself outside the remainder with alarming rapidity. Sidney shuddered, loaded a plate of her own, sat down, and motioned one of the servants over for tea.

Just as the servant began to fill her cup, a tremendous *bang* propelled Sidney out of her chair, jostling his arm and spilling tea all over her tunic. She cursed, grabbed a napkin, and began to swab at the stain; Timaeus walked in, puffing contentedly on his pipe. He came over to sit down next to her.

"I wish you'd figure out a quieter way to light that thing," Sidney complained.

"Hmm? Never fear, Sidney; I have a plan," Timaeus said cheerily, patting her on the shoulder.

Sidney looked at him mistrustfully. "If it's like your usual—" But Timaeus was bouncing up again. Bertram had appeared at the door.

"I say, Bertie, old bean," said Timaeus, bounding over and throwing an arm about Bertram. "Come to see us off?"

"Ye gods, man," groused Bertram, "a little less chipper, please! Consider the hour."

"Mmm?" said Timaeus. "Eight, by the clock, and a fine time to be alive."

"Oh, shut up," said Bertram, moodily picking up a plate and scraping some of the cold greep onto it. "A fine trick, I call it, to give a chap hope for some entertainment, then to disappear virtually before one may finish saying 'Hail fellow and well met.' Here I'd hoped you'd stay at least a fortnight—"

"Well," said Sidney. "Actually—"

Timaeus waved an insistent hand at her. "Sorry, you know, the way of the world; rush, rush, rush, insistent business, dashing about hither and yon . . . But I say, why don't you come with us as far as the border? We can at least chat along the way."

A light dawned as Sidney appreciated Timaeus's idea; if Bertram came along, Captain Blentz wouldn't dare kill the young heir's friends. Unless—he killed Bertram, too. They could always blame it on the bandits—maybe this wasn't such a good idea.

Bertram looked almost cheerful as he considered the proposal, then sighed. "Sorry, Timaeus. I'm afraid I'll have to give you a *nolle prosequi* on that. Uncle would never allow me to go with you."

"Whyever not?" Timaeus demanded.

"He wouldn't trust me to turn back at the border," Bertram said apologetically. "He'd be afraid I'd just keep on going with you. And he might be right; I'd be tempted. But, well, my duty is here, dash it. Must try to keep things together during Pater's illness, you know . . ."

Timaeus was chewing his lip. "Well—but—"

"We go today," said Kraki with finality. "It vill be glorious." He smiled and belched, obviously enjoying the prospect of combat.

Bertram sat down at the table with his plate, looking askance at the barbarian. "Glorious?" he said.

Somebody had to do something, Sidney saw. She said, "Timaeus, dear, why don't we stay on for a few days? I can't imagine our contacts in Hamsterburg will worry about a day or two spent on the road, and we are, if anything, ahead of schedule. And this festival they're having tomorrow does sound grand." She gave Bertram a winning smile, which he returned. Jasper whizzed into the room in time to catch the last of this.

Timaeus merely goggled at Sidney; this was not what he expected to hear from her. Barked orders and curses were more in her line.

"I say, yes," Jasper said. "Nothing like a few nights in a feather bed after camping out on the road for weeks."

"Yes, do stay, Timaeus," said Bertram. "You've no idea how tedious it gets out here in the provinces, far from the city lights."

"You make it sound very attractive," complained Timaeus. "Oh, very well. I suppose it's inevitable."

Kraki snorted, looking faintly disgruntled.

"Hurrah!" said Bertram as Broderick entered. The older man made a beeline for the tea. "Oh, Uncle," said Bertram, "good news! Timaeus and his crew have consented to stay on for a few days."

Broderick's head whipped around. He studied Timaeus with narrowed eyes, then broke into an ersatz grin. "Yes, yes, wonderful news, glad you've seen the light. Well, well, well. We shall have fun. Tea, dammit, milk and two sugars."

Kraki, Nick, and Broderick had ridden off hunting; Jasper had gone with them, at Sidney's insistence. "Hunting accidents," she had said. "Too easy. Keep an eye on them." So the old adventurer had sighed and agreed to go. Timaeus and Bertram were off in another wing of the castle, playing billiards and drinking port. And no one knew where Vincianus was; snoozing away someplace, in all probability. This, as Sidney had hoped, gave her the opportunity to go into town.

She doubted two hundred people lived in Biddleburg. The streets were cobblestone, for the most part, with the houses quite close together. Except for the main road, which ran from the eastern gate to the western, through what passed for a market square, the streets were too narrow for wheeled traffic. Eyes followed Sidney wherever she went; her Durfalian street clothes were evidently startling to the Biddlebourgeois, whose women were clad mainly in multiply layered homespun. And no one had taught them not to gawk. Sidney felt quite out of place.

Still, half an hour of wandering the village's byways had taught her nothing, except that carpenters were building a platform in the market square, presumably for use in tomorrow's festivities. She had failed to find any sign of an alchemist. Sighing, she approached a butcher in the marketplace. He held a squawking chicken by the legs.

"Excuse me," said Sidney. The man looked at her briefly, then laid the chicken's neck on a block of wood. "I'm looking for an alchemist's. Could you tell me—" The butcher raised a cleaver and—*thwack!*—severed the creature's neck. The head hit the floor and blood spurted. "—where I might find one?"

The butcher laid the cleaver aside and scratched his chin with one hand while the other still held the chicken's legs, its wings flapping wildly in its death throes. "Warr, marss," he said. "Eeant un in toon, y'ear. Mebbe ee Owd Warch'rr hep ye." He stuck the chicken's feet in a hook, shifted his grip to its body, and yanked down; the feet were pulled off the legs, leaving tendrils of fat and gristle.

Sidney was beginning to feel faintly nauseated, and hadn't the slightest idea what he had said. "Yes, thank you," she said, turning away, and began to wander off.

"Nar, nar!" said the butcher, tossing the chicken into a pot of boiling water. "Eer, marss; up t'Arpers Ane." He pointed off to the left, across the square to the opening of an alley. Sidney blinked; this was something, at least. "Thank you," she said, with somewhat more feeling. The butcher took the chicken out of the water with a pair of tongs and began to pluck it.

Up the alley only a few feet was a storefront. Across the window was painted the name "Mistress Mabel," and under that, "Knows All • Sees All." Nothing was visible through the grimy glass except for a haphazard display of bottles, red plush hearts, and arrows, obviously intended to imply that love potions were for sale, and a fat gray cat that lay just inside the glass, staring malevolently at Sidney.

On the door was a small coat of arms, with a scroll held in a wyvern's claws. On the scroll were the words "International Amalgamated Sisterhood of Witches & Allied Trades."

It wasn't quite what she had in mind, Sidney thought, but perhaps it would do. She turned the bat-shaped knob and entered.

The gloomy shop was filled with choking smoke. It was lit only by dim sunlight, filtering in through the grimy window, and a low fire in a hearth at the rear. Before the hearth, an old woman sat in a ragged platform rocker, her feet up on an ottoman in the shape of a man on his hands and knees, his back bearing up the cushion, an expression of despair on his face. In her mouth was a corncob pipe, smoke curling out from her lips above her wispy beard. The gray cat leapt from the window, puffed up its fur, and hissed at Sidney.

"Beewzy," shouted the old woman in a high-pitched voice. "Behave, now. Coostomer."

The cat gave the woman an astonished glare and slunk off into the shadows.

Sidney took a glance about the shop. Bundled herbs hung from the ceiling. Against the brick wall were shelves, held up by cast-iron braces nailed directly into the mortar. The shelves held an assortment of bottles and boxes, half of them knocked sideways and most covered with dust. At the center of the room was a rickety table, on which lay an assortment of fortune-tellers' cards. On either side of the hearth, in the brick, were ovens, and over the fire was a kettle, bubbling away. Mistress Mabel pulled herself painfully to her feet, picked up a snake-knobbed cane that had lain between her legs, and hobbled arthritically toward Sidney. "Wha' can owd Mabel dee for ye, larss?" she said. "Loove potion, mayhap? Terr ye foortune? Soomething tee pertect ye from gettin' wi' chird?"

"No, Mistress," said Sidney. "Actually, I was looking for an alchemist, but there doesn't seem to be one in Biddleburg."

"Nar, nar," said Mabel, peering nearsightedly at Sidney in the dimness. "Too smarr a toon, Bidderburg be . . ." She gave a sudden start, backed away a bit, and made a warding gesture. "Worf!" she said. "Ye'rr nar be payin' ye're tricks on me, y'unhoory bint."

Sidney blinked; it took her a moment to untangle this, but when she had, she gained a measure of respect for the old woman's talent. "Not a wolf," she said. "A cat. And the taint of chaos need not mean a desire to do anyone harm. I wish your help, and I'm willing to pay for it."

The old woman stood for a long moment, hunched over with both hands on the knob of her cane, puffing on her corncob pipe. "Arright," she said at last. "If nar harm's to coome to any at Bidderburg, I'rr hep ye."

Sidney produced the twist of paper from her purse. "This paper," she said, "recently held a white powder. I saw someone pour it into a glass of wine, in which it dissolved. I was told it was a medicine. I'd like to know what it is."

The old woman stood unmoving. She puffed smoke for a moment. "Why?" she said at last.

"I fear an old man is being poisoned."

The old woman reached out a hand, the fingers twisted with arthritis. "Gie it here," she said. Sidney handed over the twist. The old woman took it, sniffed the paper, and muttered a few Words, then toked on her pipe and blew smoke onto the paper. The smoke glowed faintly green. "Aye," she said. "Poison, o' oon kind ar anither. If ye want tee knoow what kind, ye sharr have to coome back tommorrer."

Sidney let out a long breath; she hadn't realized until that moment that she had been holding it. "Tomorrow? But I—"

"Sayin' it's poison be easy enow," said the old woman irritably. "Five shirrings for that oon. Assayin' it, that be far more difficurt; take me soome time. If ye want ter know, it'rr cost ye a poond, and ye moost coome back tomorrer."

"All right," said Sidney, and began to count the money out onto Mabel's table.

"Keep yer coin," snapped the old woman. "I'rr take the five shirrings, but the rest coomes when the job be doone."

Sidney nodded, and began to retrieve her change. Mabel set the twist of paper carefully down on the table, levered herself gratefully into a chair, and said, in a low voice, "Froom the castle, I suppoose?"

Sidney studied her before carefully responding, "Yes."

The old woman sighed. "Not soorprised," she said. "See ye tommorrer."

IV.

Dinner that night was cold roast greep, bread, cheese, and ale; by custom, the baron's household provided the food for the Feast of Grimaeus; the castle kitchen was in a frenzy of preparation. The guests were left to dine on leftovers and put themselves to bed, while work continued belowstairs.

The morning dawned gray and curiously warm. The clouds were a solid bank, high above; there was no immediate rain, but many in Biddleburg eyed them uneasily, hoping nothing would spoil the celebration. At eight, a procession left the castle, bearing platters of food, cartloads of bread, enormous casks of beer, roast pigs, pastries, chickens by the score. The *chef de cuisine* accompanied them, fussing about and ensuring that the food was properly set out on boards in the market square; he was exhausted, but would not sleep until the feast had ended.

By ten, virtually the entire town was in the square, gossiping and eating. Farmers, woodsmen, charcoal-burners came from all over the baron's demesne for the celebration.

At eleven, with a fanfare, the baron's party—including Timaeus and the others, as honored guests—left the castle. It was the custom to walk, but Baron Barthold was led down to the village on a palfrey, in respect for his infirmity.

Sidney walked through the narrow streets of the village with Bertram, trailing the rest of the party. "Dreadful town," said the young heir. "Beastly dull."

Gingerbread loomed above cobblestone streets. "I don't know," said Sidney. "I think it's charming. Quaint."

"Quaint," said Bertram, goggling at her. "Yes, that's the word, by Fithold. Quaint indeed. Well, we must put a good face on it; the people will expect a degree of gaiety, today. Anyhow, I am looking forward to the needlepoint competition."

It was Sidney's turn to goggle. "Needlepoint ... ?"

"Yes," said Bertram, puffing up a bit, "took it up at university, very soothing. I have a piece in here, the Lonely Tower at Hamsterburg, all in cross-stitch; I have high hopes for it. At least a third prize, or perhaps a second."

"I see," said Sidney.

"No hope for a first, of course," said Bertram. "Mistress Mabel will have that one sewn up." He giggled, adding, "As it were."

"Mistress Mabel?" said Sidney. "The witch? She does needle—"

"Tch tch tch," said Bertram, mildly censoriously. "We don't say 'witch,' you know. They're very sensitive. 'Wise woman' is the preferred locution."

Sidney snorted, but forbore from comment. After all, Mabel's damned door proclaimed her a witch, so what was the—

"The young heir," said a voice, in a slightly contemptuous tone. They turned; a young man stood at the corner of an alley, in forest green, a bow slung over his shoulder. A hood covered his head, which, along with the dimness of the alleyway, made it impossible to make out the lad's features.

"Good morrow, lad," said Bertram with good humor. "Come for the archery competition?"

"I have," said the boy. "Will your uncle be in it?"

"I believe so," said Bertram. "He sets great store by his skill with the bow."

"Good," said the boy. "Then one of us will be man enough to stand up to him, at least."

"What do you mean?" asked Bertram.

The boy leaned forward, speaking quickly and urgently. "Can you truly be insensible to the plight of the folk?" he said. "Bainbridge looted, villages pillaged, good men broken on the wheel for no more crime than questioning Broderick's fitness to rule—"

"This, this is treason," said Bertram, shocked and uncertain.

"Treason, or love of truth," said the youth, then turned and fled down the alley.

Bertram frowned after him. "There's something familiar . . . ," he muttered, then shook his head. "Insolent pup, what? Come along, Sidney." He strode after the rest of the party, toward the market square.

Sidney hesitated long enough to take a brief look down the alley; it ended in a wall, not ten cubits in, but there was no sign of the youngster. A puzzle; but no doubt he was spry enough to climb a wall. She shrugged and followed Bertram.

They entered the market. Cheers rang out; Captain Blentz and a few of his men went on ahead, to clear the way. The cheers for the baron seemed genuine, while the townsfolk seemed to treat Sir Broderick with fearful deference and Sir Bertram with genial, and slightly contemptuous, good humor. Both Broderick and Bertram spoke easily with the townsfolk as they strolled across the square, telling a joke or asking after someone's health.

The party from the castle took their seats on the wood platform, Sidney next to Timaeus. She peered both left and right; there was no obvious way to sneak off, not without attracting undue attention. She was in plain view of the entire crowd below. How, then, was she to meet with Mistress Mabel?

Sir Broderick rose and made a brief speech, welcoming the folk in the name of his brother, the baron (who waved, somewhat shakily), and thanking them for their loyalty over the year (there were faint jeers at this). Sir Bertram donned ermine robes, which the butler had brought from the castle, and made a brief invocation imploring the goodwill of Grimaeus, who evidently was some regional spirit or deity.

And then the contests began. Mountaineers strove to climb a cliff near the edge of town; it was clearly visible from the market square, and each wore a piece of colored cloth pinned to his back, so that everyone could cheer his favorite. The first to the top was promised a purse of coins. Then there was a contest for lumberjacks; several large tree boles were brought into the square, and men vied to determine who might chop through one quickest. A quilting bee was next; Sidney was asked to act as one of the judges for this contest, her gender apparently being sufficient qualification, but managed to decline the honor. There was an ale-quaffing contest—Kraki won that one— and a display of wolves' pelts, on which the barony apparently paid a bounty, with a bonus going to the hunter who had killed the largest number of the beasts.

The needlepoint display was next; each contestant brought out her (or in one case, his) best work of the previous year. They were mounted on easels put up before the platform, and the judges—all women, by their dress the wives of prosperous townsmen—strolled up and down, examining them. Bertram stood nervously by his own offering, talking occasionally to the crowd, who seemed to think that the heir's choice of hobby was a marvelous joke. Broderick scowled blackly, no doubt believing the whole affair a blot on the family escutcheon, raising unnecessary questions about Bertram's manliness.

Sidney was faintly charmed at blond Bertram's nervousness; as the baron's son, surely he was guaranteed a place at the finish? "He's very handsome, isn't he?" she said, loudly enough that Timaeus heard her.

The wizard, who had been puffing on his pipe, took it out of his mouth. "What?" he said. "I mean, really. Bertram? Handsome? Bertram, handsome? I say . . ."

Sidney gave him a faint smile.

Bertram had been a good judge of his chances; he took second prize. Mistress Mabel appeared, leaning on her snake-knobbed cane. It occurred to Sidney that the old woman looked more tired, in the light of day, than she had in her shop; there were dark circles under her eyes, and she stifled a yawn as she hobbled painfully up to collect her own prize, a small purse. Sidney hoped for some word from Mabel, but she passed Sidney's place without a glance.

The needlepoint competition was followed by a dowsing contest. Then there was a ball game, one new to Sidney. It was evidently a free-for-all, with no teams, in which the player who ended a period of time in the ball's possession was considered the victor. There were several injuries in the course of that one.

When the herald declared that the archery contest was about to begin, Sir Broderick sprang up with a gleeful smile. "At last!" cried he. A servant handed him his bow and a quiver of arrows, and he leapt off the platform to take his place with the other contestants.

Captain Blentz and his men cleared an aisle down the center of the square, along the path of the main road. The road beyond the end of the square was cleared likewise, so that an errant shaft would not injure anyone. A target was placed at the far end of the square, perhaps twenty ells from the archers, painted with concentric circles of different colors.

A dozen contestants waited, each with a bow. Sidney watched as Broderick strung his weapon, slipping one end of the bowshaft behind his leg and pulling down on the other with his full weight; that bow, thought she, must be quite difficult to draw. Another contestant caught her eye, a slim man in green pants and tunic, perhaps a forester. He wore a hood—and Sidney recognized him as the lad who had spoken to Bertram. She wondered at his foolhardiness: A word from Bertram to Captain Blentz, and the boy would be decorating a gibbet. Sidney looked to where Bertram sat and saw that he, too, was studying the lad in green, a quizzical frown on his face—but Bertram apparently did not intend to betray him.

As the only nobleman among the archers, Sir Broderick shot first. "A burr's-eye!" went up the cry, in the accent of the region. "A burr for Sir Brodick!" Sidney saw that it was so; Broderick's arrow was in the target's center. The others shot in turn; every four shots, a boy would run out and remove the arrows, clearing the target for the next archer. Each arrow was carefully returned to its owner. "Uncle fletches his own shafts," Bertram confided, "using eagle feathers and glue from boiled greep hooves." Sidney supposed their arrows were equally precious to the other bowmen.

Eight of the twelve had managed bull's-eyes at this range; the other four were counted out of the competition, and the target was moved back, to a distance of forty ells. Two men carefully paced the distance out, using a rope knotted at intervals. A little breeze had picked up, and Broderick cocked his head at the sky, perhaps gauging the weather, before releasing his second shaft. It shot true and fair, to hit the target square again; "A burr!" went the cry.

The hooded lad was, by chance, the next up, the intervening archers having been removed in the previous round. He stood a moment, string pulled back, before releasing his arrow; it shot forth and ...

There was a long pause while the judges studied the target. Eventually, one shouted out, "Ho, Wordsrey hath sprit yoor shaft in twain, Sir Brodick"—and they brought back Broderick's splintered arrow.

For a moment, Broderick seemed dismayed; but he mastered himself, and said, in friendly fashion, "Well, good Master Woodsley; you have a fine eye."

"Aye," the lad responded, raising his voice likewise, so that the crowd might hear, "an eye that gauges the worth of a man as readily as it spies out a target." Hearing the voice again, Sidney realized that something about it was peculiar. It was a reedy tenor, rather high for a man, but that was not wholly unusual in one so young; it was, she decided, the accent, or rather, the near absence of one, that sounded odd. Master Woodsley was, by his garb, a simple woodsman; yet he spoke like an educated man.

Broderick frowned at the words. "An eye that gauges the worth of a man"—yes, well enough; but did that eye find Broderick meritorious or meretricious? Was it praise or insult? By the tone, perhaps insult.

Broderick laughed, a little harshly. "Well, the next round shall tell."

The other archers took their shots; of the remaining six, only two hit the bull's-eye.

The target was moved back again, to a full fifty ells. Sidney could barely see the bull's-eye now, save as a tiny, distant dot. The light, it suddenly occurred to her, was rather dim; she looked up at the clouds and saw that they had darkened since the morning. She wondered whether rain would soon begin.

Broderick stood quite a long time with his shaft drawn back before loosing it—and when he did, it flew with a definite loft, arching over the street to plunk into the target. The judge's voice shouted out, a little fainter now with distance, "A burr!" And there was almost a sigh through the crowd.

Woodsley stood forth and almost negligently fired. "A burr!" again came the shout, and there were murmurs of approbation. Broderick was blank-faced, but by the redness of his ears, bursting with rage. The other two bowmen took their shots, but one hit only the inner ring, while the other, perhaps rattled at having come so far in the competition, missed the target entirely.

Again the target was moved back, another ten ells. Again Broderick toed up to the line, drew his shaft, held it, released—"Inner ring," came the shout. Broderick's mouth compressed to a thin line; but he might win still, if Woodsley's shot was no better.

Woodsley stood forth. He was less certain this time, holding his hood at an angle to gauge the wind before drawing, holding the arrow by his ear for a long moment before releasing—

"A burr!" came the shout.

There was a murmur of awe through the crowd—and then all eyes went to Broderick, to see how he would react. He wore a tight smile, but put out his hand to Woodsley genially enough, saying, "Well shot, Master Woodsley. You have a keen eye indeed. I would see the face of the man who has bested me."

Woodsley put a hesitant hand to his hood, but said, "Sir—I would not—I—"

Barely containing a snarl, Broderick reached out and flipped back the hood of green.

There was a rumble of thunder; only Sidney seemed to notice.

Beneath the hood was close-cropped red hair—

"Beatrice!" shouted a voice from the crowd. "Beatrice of the Band!" And there was instant confusion.

It was she, Sidney saw, breasts strapped down, clothing baggy enough to hide her form. She was running down that long cobblestone street now, toward the gate at the far end of town, the road already cleared of obstruction for use as a firing range. Broderick watched her flee, but only for an instant before calmly drawing an arrow from the quiver at his back, setting the string of his bow in its notch, pulling back the string, aiming at Beatrice's back—

"Uncle! No!" shouted Bertram, leaping off the platform and running for the archers' station. But before he could reach his uncle, a burly, bearded man in peasant garb darted from the crowd and hurtled shoulder first into Broderick, sending the shot wild and knocking the nobleman to the ground.

The first fat drops of rain spattered on dusty cobbles. Men and women ran to and fro in the crowd, as others of the Band made their presence known and ran off likewise down the street, urging defiance on the crowd. Bertram reached Broderick in time to help his uncle to his feet. "Blentz!" Broderick was screaming. "After them, Blentz!"—and indeed, the captain was running after the Bandsmen, sword in hand, puffing badly. With him ran a half dozen soldiers, looking as if the last thing they wanted to do was catch up with the bandits and be forced to fight them on more or less equal terms. Without horses—all the horses were back at the castle, save only Baron Barthold's palfrey—the guardsmen's chances of catching Beatrice and the Band were slim.

Men, women, and children were scurrying for cover, whether from the danger posed by naked blades or the discomfort of falling rain it was hard to say. The *chef de cuisine* was dancing with rage, berating his *sous-chefs* and maidservants: "The pastry! By damn, save the pastry! The rain will ruin it!" But the castle staff was in an uproar, too, goggling after the bandits, running about in insensible panic.

"Should we do something, do you think?" said Jasper.

"I vant to kill someone," said Kraki, who had his sword out and was looking wildly around, "but who?"

"Precisely," said Timaeus, looking unhappily into the rainy sky. "Why do Broderick any favors? Or those bandits, either."

"Bunch of foolsh, that'sh what I'm hooked up with," said Vincianus. "Don't have the shenshe to come out of the rain." He began a ritual chant.

"Put that thing away," Nick said disgustedly to Kraki. "You'll only get it rusty."

Kraki looked at him a little guiltily, then sheathed his weapon.

"Vic has a point," said Timaeus. "Why don't we go—"

Thunder crashed. Everyone jumped—"Vic's gone," said Sidney.

"Ah," said Timaeus. "Teleported back to the castle, I suppose. Not a bad notion—"

"Don't you dare!" said Sidney. Timaeus's own teleport spell left a fireball at his place of departure; unpleasant for those left behind, albeit useful when leaving someone you didn't particularly like.

Broderick was still running about and giving orders, but Bertram had seemingly disappeared into the crowd.

"Look," said Nick. "I don't see any percentage in staying here. Why don't we head back to the castle?"

"Righto," said Jasper. "Let's." He floated off the platform, followed in more conventional fashion by Nick and Sidney.

"Nnnnn-nnnnn!" said Barthold, still seated in his chair, his gray mustache drooping with wetness.

"Good heavens," said Timaeus. "Mustn't forget the baron. Here, give me a hand. Can you walk, my lord?"

"Nnnn," said Barthold.

"Drat," said Timaeus. "Is the palfrey still about?"

"Ran off," said Nick.

"Never mind," said Kraki, who picked Barthold up, jumped off the platform, and began to stride toward the castle.

It occurred to Sidney that she still had an errand to run.

V.

Timaeus dripped water onto the slate flags of the Great Hall. His red hair was plastered to his skull, his beard dewed with droplets. Garments sucked wetly against his skin. "Damnation," he fulminated miserably, "this castle is normally overrun with servants; where the devil are they when a man needs them?"

"Scurrying about town, I'd guess," said Nick, shucking his soaked jacket and draping it across a chair, "looking for bandits or hiding from them." He was red-faced and exuberant.

"Servants?" said Jasper, whizzing gaily about. If he was affected by the storm, it didn't show. "Timaeus, old man, you are a fire mage, after all; surely you don't need a servant to start a blaze." Logs and kindling were already laid in the fireplace; all that was needed was a spark.

Timaeus muttered something, then waved his hands a bit and said a Word; a bolt of flame shot across the room, blasting into the hearth. Logs went tumbling like skittles, but when they had settled down, the fire was positively raging.

"How is it that you're not soaked?" said Timaeus nastily. "Bloody green pipsqueak." He went to bask before the fire, standing almost to the flames; his hose began to give off steam.

"Umbrella," said Jasper.

Timaeus eyeballed the speck of light, which was settling into an armchair. Umbrella? Timaeus hadn't seen an umbrella. But then, he never saw much of Jasper in any event.

"Vhat's his problem?" asked Kraki, dropping Baron Barthold into another armchair.

"Fire mage," said Jasper in good humor. "Can't stand the wet, any of them. Magical opposites, you know."

"Hallo, hallo, all," said Bertram, breezing into the hall. "Timaeus, old man; did you ever see such a goddess?"

"Mm?" inquired Timaeus, shaking each limb in turn, in an effort to dislodge drops of water.

"I mean to say, what a creature! What an exquisite creature. And what cheek! To beard old Uncle Broderick in his own den, as it were! I say, there's the woman for me."

Timaeus stared at Bertram openmouthed. "Surely you can't be—"

"Oh, I know, I know, chaps; I'm dreadfully sorry. I suppose you're all pining for that xanthous beauty yourselves, that gloriously—"

"I say, Sir Bertram, old bean," said Jasper. "What the devil are you babbling about?"

"What?" said Bertram, thunderstruck. "You mean to say, you weren't as poleaxed as I?"

Kraki wandered over to the sideboard and thoughtfully fetched a full decanter of Moothlayan whisky for Baron Barthold, who held it uncertainly in one shaky hand. Normally, a servant poured two fingers for him when he wanted a drink; but Kraki had different ideas about the proper way to quaff strong drink, ideas he was demonstrating with a magnum of ancient Dzorzian sherry. He chugged it down like water.

Nick sat on the stones before the hearth, back to the blaze, cleaning his fingernails with a dirk and smiling faintly at Bertram. Nick fancied himself an expert in—if not affairs of the heart, at least affairs of the flesh. In his judgment, Bertram had about as much chance with Beatrice as a dachshund with a St. Bernard. Nick was beginning to wonder whether he himself might have an opportunity . . .

"I see not," said Bertram wonderingly. "Hard to imagine. How could you not instantly have fallen for that veritable fount of pulchritude, the beauteous and valiant—"

"All right, all right, for goodness' sake," said Timaeus irritably. "We appreciate the immediacy of your lovestruck state. Now do shut up and let us dry out, there's a good chap."

There was an awkward silence.

"Look here, young Bertram," said Jasper. "It's all very well to have fallen in love, but what do you plan to do about it?"

"Err—well, yes," said Bertram, digging for earwax. "I had given it a modicum of thought. You see, Beatrice is a bandit, after all, in rebellion against the lawful rule of her rightful sovran; and whatever meritorious characteristics Uncle Brod possesses, a willingness to forgive and forget is not among them. I take it, therefore, I must woo and win her, presenting the old relative with a *fait accompli*."

Everyone mulled over this for a moment; light flashed from the windows, followed momentarily by the crash of thunder. It was pouring still, out there.

"I shall—I shall need your help, of course," said Bertram uncertainly. "I'm afraid I am not, ah, altogether, ah, a sophisticate in these matters of the heart."

Timaeus snorted, and fumbled for his pipe.

"Well well well," said Jasper, his voice thick with emotion. "Of course you shall have our help, my lad. Of course we shall do everything in our power to see that a successful conclusion is brought to the love between you and the beauteous Beatrice."

"We will?" said Nick.

"Are you daft?" demanded Timaeus.

"Silence!" Jasper thundered. "Of course we shall! Are we not heroes? What else does our duty demand? *Omnia vincit amor; et nos cedamus amori,* as the poet says."

Kraki contemplated this as Bertram babbled thanks and Timaeus boiled. He didn't understand the fancy talk, but as he understood it, heroism involved slaying your foes, building pyramids with their skulls, and hearing the lamentations of their women, preferably as you had your merry way with said women. He didn't quite see where love came into it; but Jasper usually knew what he was doing, and it certainly sounded more interesting than lolling about the castle and swilling the local liquor, which seemed to be the alternative on offer.

"If you think for one minute," Timaeus declared, his pipe at a determined angle, "that I intend to charge off into the raging storm in the cause of some fatuous infatuation, than you're as feebleminded as Bertram here."

Nick said nothing; the prospect of seeing Beatrice again was increasingly appealing, and whatever Jasper thought, Bertram did not strike him as much of a rival.

"I say," said Bertram, shocked.

"I go," said Kraki.

"Good man," said Jasper. "And Timaeus, I must say, I am shocked; to deny your plain duty—"

"Duty? You old fool," shouted Timaeus, "our duty is to get the damned statue of Stantius to Arst-Kara-Morn, not to run off to help the chinless wonder, here, with his love life—"

"I say!" said Bertram. "That's quite—"

"First," said Jasper freezingly, "I would ask you to keep

your voice down. And if you must shout, you might consider refraining from bellowing our deepest secrets to the winds, especially when you well know that our host is far from friendly."

"What? Nonsense, nonsense, I have only the most amicable—"

"Not you, Sir Bertram. Second, I must say, Timaeus, I am deeply wounded at your cold, hardhearted attitude. It is indicative, I should think to say, of the callous modern outlook; here we have a young man smitten with a beauteous maid, a maid the mortal enemy of his uncle, star-crossed lovers—"

Timaeus snorted. "If I recall correctly, when the subject of Bertram was mentioned, Beatrice's comment was 'That twit.' This hardly sounds like the passionate cooing of the enraptured lover."

"She said what?" said Bertram.

"Listen to me, dammit!" shouted Jasper. He sighed heavily before continuing. "How to put it? A maid the mortal enemy of the young man's uncle. An uncle who— well, forgive me, young Bertram—an uncle who has designs on our own possessions. Not to mention our lives."

Bertram blinked. "How do you—"

"Yes, dreadful man," said Timaeus. "And so?"

"And so. If we are to leave the castle safely, with our possessions, we must either neutralize Uncle Broderick, or hoodwink him in some way, yes? And how better to do so than to enlist the aid of the young heir and his blushing bride-to-be?"

"I have a hard time imagining Beatrice of the Band as a blushing bride-to-be," said Nick, who had spent a considerable amount of time imagining Beatrice in a number of different roles, none of them involving a standing position.

"I have better plan," said Kraki. "Vhy not kill all the soldiers in castle? Then ve leave."

"I like Kraki's plan better," grumbled Timaeus. "*Omnia vincit amor,* eh? You're really going to put your faith in that old saw?"

"Bah, d'Asperge," said Jasper roughly. "Where's your sense of adventure? Of romance?"

"Taking a long and pleasant rest before the fire with a snifter of brandy," said Timaeus.

Jasper snorted. "Let's go, shall we, Bertram? We'll obviously get nothing out of this insensitive clod." He lifted from the armchair and headed toward the door.

"Yes," said Bertram plaintively, "but what's this about Uncle Broderick having designs on—"

"Oh all right, all right, all right," said Timaeus irritably. "Coming, coming. I don't suppose you have such a thing as a mackintosh about the place?"

Rain spattered off cobbles. Sidney was soaked through by the time she got to the door of Mistress Mabel's shop. The bat-shaped knob turned in her hand and the door opened. The cat arched its back and backed away from her, spitting madly.

"Beewzy!" shouted Mabel. The old woman was on her feet before the fire, cane raised as if to strike at the animal. "Where's yer manners?" The animal fled into the dimness of the shop.

"Don't blame her," said Sidney apologetically. "She smells a strange cat ... It's only natural that she defend her home."

Mabel lowered the cane and rested her weight upon it. She did look tired, thought Sidney; it had not merely been the light of day that had made her seem that way. "I see," said Mabel thoughtfully. "Well, enow. Naow, let me see." She hobbled over to one of her shelves and selected an enormous leather-bound tome. With it under one arm, her free hand clutching her cane, she turned and began to hobble for the table at the center of the room—a slow process, burdened as she was by the volume's weight. "Here, let me," said Sidney, taking the book and placing it on the table.

"Thankee," said Mabel, flinging the book open with a crash. With authority, she spoke a Word. Between Mabel and the tome, a patch of air turned fuzzy; Sidney, peering over Mabel's shoulder, saw the letters of the page grow enormously in size, seen through the patch of air. Mabel's finger ran up and down the page, the patch of fuzzy space following. Sidney presumed that the spell was intended to allow the old witch's ailing eyes to read the small and rather crabbed letters of the tome.

Mabel turned several pages, ran a crooked finger down a line of text, then moved aside so that Sidney could read and said, "Here," tapping an entry and stifling a yawn.

" 'Venenum Opinici,' " read Sidney aloud. " 'We have it on ancient authority that the venom of the opinicus is of especial efficacy. The monster's poison sac lieth against the lower portion of the skull, hard by—' "

"Niver mind," said Mabel impatiently. "Gie me that." She took the book back, flipped a few pages, and said, "Read here."

Sidney cleared her throat and read once more. " 'The earthly nature of the venom of the opinicus, which may be refined from the raw venenum through distillation and titration, is itself a poison, acting directly upon the black humors of the body. In small doses (a grain per stone), it induceth confusion, echolalia, thickness of speech, and black moods; at somewhat heavier doses, lassitude and depression, spasms, seizures, and severe speech impediment, sometimes such that the subject may be incapable of communication entirely. Above doses of a dozen grains per stone of body weight, it induces terrible seizures, often leading to death . . .' This is horrible."

"Aye," said Mabel heavily. "So it be."

"You found traces of *venenum* on the twist of paper I brought you?" Sidney asked.

"Aye," said Mabel.

Sidney reread the passage. "Is there anything to be done?" she asked.

Mabel played with the knob of her cane. "Mayhap," she said. "The venoom be quickly metabolized, ye ken. Barthord moost be remedicated every dee, or so."

"You figured out that it was the baron?" asked Sidney.

"'Twere nar great trick," snapped Mabel. "See here, now. A sight increase in doosage, an' the owd man be dead. But, stop piesoning him, an' he'rr recoover in a dee or two. Och, mayhap he'rr niver be quite the man he were, but he'rr be in his oon right mind."

Sidney considered this for a moment. "I'm not sure we have a day or two," she said.

"Och, aye," sighed Mabel wearily. "Wherefore have I spent a seepress night, preparing a pootation." From under the table, she produced a plain stone jug that, by the words baked into the glaze, had once held the ginger beer of Jos. Eisdorfer, Brewer, Tsugash City, Lesser Dzorzia. "A sip or tee, and owd Barthord wirr recoover on the instant, at a cost in strength and pain."

"This is wonderful, Mistress," said Sidney. "It is, however, more than we had bargained for. What do I owe you?"

"Nothing, rass," said Mabel roughly. "I sharr ask the owd man foor recompense."

"The baron?" asked Sidney.

"Aye," said Mabel, hobbling over to the wall, where a heavy shawl hung. She took it from the hook and flung it about her shoulders. "Sharr we be off?"

Sidney blinked. "I suppose there's no reason not to dose the baron now," she said.

"Aye, aye, get a move on," said the old woman impatiently. She had taken a broom, and sat astraddle it now, the straw up toward her face and the shaft behind. She patted the shaft behind her, indicating that Sidney should take a seat.

"Is it wise to fly in such a storm?" asked Sidney; in truth, it was raging outside still, rain slashing down onto the cobblestone street, visible even through the grimy window.

"It'd take me a coon's age tee hobble oop the hill ersewise," said Mabel. "Coome naow, dammit."

So Sidney sat behind. Mabel shouted a Word, and the door flung open, crashing against the outside of the building. Another Word, and the three of them—the two women and the broom—slashed out through the door and up into space, barely missing the overhang of one of the buildings as they leapt into the sky.

Sidney clutched Mabel's ample waist for dear life, wondering how the nearsighted old witch could see in the raging storm.

"How are you going to find her?" asked Nick as they climbed the spiral stair.

"Sir Bertram," said Jasper. "Would you have anything belonging to Beatrice? A piece of clothing, perhaps the arrow she used today? Anything that might have come into contact—"

"I have a lock of her hair," said Bertram, removing a small packet from a pocket near his heart. "Would that do?"

Jasper halted in midair. Everyone else stopped climbing the stairway with him. "Lock of hair?" he said, flitting about the ribbon-tied auburn strands that Bertram displayed. "How did you get that?"

"Oh," said Bertram embarrassedly, tucking the envelope back into his jacket, "we were childhood sweethearts, you know."

"No, I didn't know," said Jasper severely. "When was this?"

"Well, you know, her father, Sir Benton of Bainbridge, was one of the few noblemen around. She and I played as children, and when I was sixteen, I was quite sweet on her."

"And then?"

"Well, and then, I went to university, you know," said Bertram. "And well, with one thing and another, you know ..."

"O thou inconstant heart," said Jasper accusingly. "No wonder she thinks you're a twit."

"Did she really say that?"

Without another word, Jasper had begun flitting up the stairs again, and the others likewise resumed their climb.

"Is that," said Timaeus, "the same Sir Benton your uncle broke on the wheel?"

Bertram cleared his throat. "Afraid so," he said apologetically. "Apparently the old man rebelled against my father, his liege—"

"You weren't here?"

"No, I was at Durfalus University. Father had his stroke, and Uncle Broderick came from his own demesne, in the Lesser Dzorzia, to help out. Apparently—"

"And Benton, outraged at Broderick's usurpation, took arms to defend Baron Barthold, his liege, against the conniving younger brother—"

"You think so?" said Bertram thoughtfully. "That's not how Broderick tells the story."

"Bertram," said Timaeus, almost fondly. "You really are a twit, you know."

"I don't know," said Bertram. "You see, Uncle's been very kind to me. I don't know how I'd manage the barony without—"

"Of course he's been kind," said Timaeus irritably. "You're a useful figurehead."

"Yes, but—"

"Here we are," said Jasper cheerily. "Hand over the old lock, my boy."

"Here" was a watchtower; the windows gave onto what might have been a glorious view, if the wind and rain hadn't restricted visibility. Unlike much of the rest of the castle, it had not been modernized; the windows were unglazed, and the cold stone floor was slick with water swept through the windows by the breeze. Thunder crashed outside as lightning blasted a pine tree, down there on the mountainside, into flinders. Kraki was leaning out a window, into the rain, letting the wind whip his hair and the water spatter against his skin, a fierce smile on his face. Timaeus shuddered and drew the mackintosh he'd been lent close about his body.

Somewhat reluctantly, Bertram handed over the lock of hair to Jasper. "What are you going to do with it?" he said.

"It's no good our blundering about the forest in search of Beatrice," Jasper pointed out. "Your uncle and Captain Blentz are already doing that, I imagine, and Beatrice, woodswise as she no doubt is, won't want to be found. We shall have to use magical means."

"But how—"

"I am a mage of the mental arts, dear boy," said Jasper condescendingly. "There aren't too many human minds out there in the forest; the region is lightly inhabited. Even so, picking out one would be difficult, without some token of its person; but I have a lock of her hair, which, by the principle of similarity, is tantamount to having Beatrice here, by our side. It shall be but the work of a moment to locate her."

And as Jasper spoke Words of power, the green light spiraled up, up over the heads of the others, into the air of the high tower chamber. Thunder crashed, and—

"I sense her," Jasper said. "To the north-northeast.

Come, we shall have to act quickly; I can maintain the spell for a time, but keeping it active requires power."

"Right," said Timaeus, heading for the stairs. "We'll have to get our horses."

"No," said Bertram. "I think not."

Timaeus looked up in alarm. "What do you—"

"After all," said Bertram, "I am *Magister Aeris*." And he began to chant. Thunder flashed and power drew about him.

"A wizard, too?" said Nick. "I hadn't realized—"

"Why do you think he went to university?" said Timaeus irritably. But he looked rather worried.

"What's wrong?" said Nick.

"He's attempting a fly spell."

"Yes," said Nick. "That makes sense. So?"

Timaeus sighed. "Bertram did not exactly cover himself with scholastic glory," he said.

"He didn't take a first?" said Jasper.

"No," said Timaeus. "Far from it. But that's not the worst of it."

"No?" said Nick.

"No," said Timaeus. "Air mages have no power over earthly human flesh, but great power over the zephyrs of the air."

"So?"

"So their idea of a fly spell is a tornado."

"What?" said Nick, alarmed.

But before Timaeus could respond, ears popped as air pressure precipitously dropped. They were sucked forcibly out the tower window.

Timaeus flailed, his mackintosh flapping about him as he and the others began to plummet down, down through driving rain, the ramparts of the castle speeding upward toward them in the gray day, an instant of frozen terror—

Another gust of wind smashed them upward at the last

instant, whipping them up and away, lofting them in a high curve out over the forest, out to the north-northeast.

Was that a witch on a broom, there in the aether? Whatever, it was of no account; they were soon far beyond the crone, whipping out over the wilderness, tumbling willy-nilly through the sky.

The gust failed. Again they plummeted toward the forest green, enormous firs like daggers stabbing upward into the sky as they fell—

Again the wind gusted, whipping them upward and on.

Timaeus moaned, soaked to the skin, his mackintosh no use in this wildness, stomach lurching, bile rising in his throat.

Firs whirled crazily below as they plunged downward, down, limbs snapping, branches scratching faces, until they smashed into the needle-covered forest floor.

There was a moment of silence, broken only by the whistle of the wind through the trees above, the crash of thunder, the steady drip of rain—and moans of pain.

Jasper, who had flown under his own power, circled down. "What ho," he said. "Bracing, what?"

Timaeus sat up, spitting out pine needles, wiping rotted leaves off his face. His cheeks were scratched, bits of twig were stuck in his beard, and he was soaked to the bone. "Bertram!" he roared. "By all the gods, I shall roast you until your eyeballs pop! You silly twit, if you ever do that to me again, I'll—"

There was a moan of agony. Kraki was stooped over Bertram's form. "Clench your fist, man," the barbarian said. "Breathe through the pain."

"What's wrong?" asked Nick.

"S-sorry, chaps," came a ragged voice. "I seem to have busted the old gam."

They all crowded around Bertram. He was white-faced; his right leg lay at an awkward angle. Nick crouched, took

out a dirk, then pulled away Bertram's hose and ran a
razor-sharp edge up the garment, splitting it open. There
was a large bruise on the front of the leg, where the bone
pressed against the skin. "Not a clean break," was Nick's
opinion. "I don't dare try to set it without a healer."

"Dandy," said Timaeus. He hauled out his pipe and
thumbed the bowl disconsolately; the weed was almost
certainly too wet to light. "Well, perhaps I won't kill you,
Bertram, old son; looks like you're having a go at it yourself."

"Someone must go for help," said Kraki.

They considered this. In the wilderness, halfway up
some mountain, with no clear idea of their location, in the
midst of a thunderstorm—the prospect of help seemed
pretty remote.

"Ah," said Jasper. "Not to fear." And with that, the
green spark zipped aloft, into the cover of the branches
above.

"Jasper, dammit!" shouted Timaeus. "What are you going to—"

"Hold, an you value your life," said a voice. There was
a thunk, and an arrow vibrated from the bole of a tree, not
inches from Nick Pratchitt's head.

"Not again," complained Nick.

"Well," said Timaeus, "we *were* looking for trouble."

"I kill them now?" asked Kraki.

"Oh, I suppose not," said Timaeus.

"No more talk!" rang out that voice, and a slim, green-
clad figure stepped out from behind a tree, holding a bow
of yew.

"Hallo, Be," said Bertram weakly.

"Watch out!" shouted Sidney into the rain-swept air.
The window, all glass and lead runners, loomed before
them, flanked by the stone walls of Biddleburg Castle—

With a crash, they hurtled through the glass, tumbling to the stone floor.

"Damn arr moodern contrivances to herr an' goone!" spat Mabel. "Tha's where me tax mooney goes, instarring grass in every window in Bidderburg Castle, by arr the demons!"

Mistress Mabel had a ragged cut in her left hand, but it did not appear to be serious. Sidney herself felt uninjured, though she was soaking wet and chilled to the bone. Glass and strips of lead lay everywhere across the room—a bedroom, apparently untenanted at present. At least there were no trunks, bags, or personal accoutrements, though the bed was made and the room recently cleaned. Sidney had no idea where in the castle they might be.

"First thing is to find the others," said Sidney. "Broderick will be hard-pressed to stop us, with Timaeus and Kraki to lend a hand—"

"Brodick be oot in the woods, searching foor Beatrice," said Mabel. "Nar need to woory aboot him, foor the nonce." She was hobbling for the doorway.

"Pardon me, Mistress," said Sidney apologetically, "but perhaps we'd move faster if I carry you." And she swept the older woman up.

"How oondignified," said Mabel. "Hurry, hurry, hurry. Tha's the trooble with this new generation." But she clasped her arms about Sidney's neck, and suffered herself to be carried.

Mabel was heftier than she appeared; by the time Sidney reached the Great Hall, she was staggering. She let Mabel gratefully down on a bench.

"Timaeus!" she shouted. "Jasper! Kraki! Halloo!"

There was no reply.

"Nick? Vincianus?"

Still no reply.

"Where the blazes can they be?" she demanded.

Mabel sighed. "I terr ye, yer friends are not important, naow. We moost find the baron, and dose him, afore Brodick retairns."

"No one else is here," said Sidney in annoyance. "What makes you think—"

"Nnnn-nnnn-nnn," said a voice from an armchair. It was at the far end of the enormous room, facing away from Sidney and Mabel and toward the fire. Mabel rose, and the two women walked toward it.

"I might ha' know," said Mabel disgustedly. There was the sharp odor of whisky. Kraki had left Baron Barthold with a flask of Moothlayan single-malt, but without a glass; alone and bored, Barthold had removed the stopper and had tried to sip whisky through the flask's narrow neck. Unfortunately, his coordination was not up to the task, and he had splashed nearly as much of the whisky on his neck and clothes as he had managed to get into his mouth. Even so, he gave them a loopy smile; Sidney judged he was well potted.

"My lord," said Sidney, "Mistress Mabel has prepared a potation that, we believe, will cure your illness."

"Nnnn-nnnn!" said Barthold, waving a liver-spotted hand that, unfortunately, held the flask of whisky, sloshing more of the liquid onto his armchair. There was the glint of panic in his eyes.

"Naow, naow," said Mabel. "Settle doon. Not that stooff that Brodick hath been feeding ye; he's been piesoning ye by degrees, ye ken."

Barthold's face lit up, and he nodded his head rapidly. "Nnn-nnn-nnn!" he said emphatically.

"You knew that?" said Sidney. "Why didn't you let Bertram know?"

Barthold rolled his eyes.

"Never mind," said Sidney, chuckling. "Here. Mistress Mabel says it's good for what ails you." She held the jug up to his lips, and the baron greedily swallowed.

When his teeth began to rattle against the jug, Sidney decided he'd had enough. She pulled away. The old man was sitting bolt upright in the armchair, vibrating like a tuning fork, his face as red as a beet, the knuckles of his hand white around the neck of the whisky flask. Sidney tried to take it from him, but his grip was too tight.

He shook this way for a minute or two—Mabel began to look concerned, and took a wrist to measure his pulse.

But at last, he slumped back into the chair.

There was a long moment of silence, while Barthold rested.

Then, a rusty, aged voice sang,

> "John o' Dell hath run away
> and I am full of sorrow.
> my heart left with him on the day
> and shan't come back tomorrow."

Barthold sat upright and opened his eyes. "By Dion," he said, "I can speak."

VI.

Timaeus, Nick, and Kraki sat with bound arms. Timaeus was red with anger at the indignity. Nick looked preoccupied, as indeed he was; he was busy pulling a strip of sharpened metal out of his left sleeve with the fingers of his right hand. He kept it there for just such eventualities, and was reasonably confident of severing his bonds within minutes. Kraki looked unruffled; he, too, was reasonably confident he could free himself in short order, albeit through brute strength rather than any such clever stratagem.

"Firefies cooming oot wi' the end of the rain," said a bandit, shooing Jasper's green light away with the swat of a hand. Jasper dodged quickly enough to avoid contact.

Bertram lay, unbound, at the center of an attentive group of bandits, Beatrice with them. A fat friar felt all over Bertram's leg, his hands glowing faintly blue. "Compound fracture," the friar said cheerily. "Have you right as rain in half a tick." He chanted a bit, and poured some wine onto the ground as an offering, then bent his tonsured head over Bertram's leg again. "Shan't hurt a bit," he said, placing one hand on each side of the break and giving the leg a sudden, vicious twist.

"*Aaaaaaaaaaah!*" screamed Bertram.

Kraki scowled. "Get hold of yourself," he said sternly. "Are you a voman?" Beatrice turned to smile faintly at the barbarian.

"If that's your idea of not hurting—" said Bertram.

"Now, now, chin up," said the friar. "Here, have a swallow of this." And he gave the young noble a wineskin.

Bertram squirted a bit into his mouth, grimaced, and swallowed. "It has medicinal qualities, I suppose?" he said dubiously.

"Oh, aye, aye, medicinal qualities," chuckled the friar. "Drink enough of that, and you'll feel no pain, I'll warrant. Drink too much, and you'll be dancing up the trees, busted gam or no." He took up a chant again, moving his hands up and down Bertram's leg. "Bed rest for a week, me lad," he said. "Keep that leg immobile; I'll rig up a splint for you. And you'll need a cane for a week after that."

"Thank you, Brother," said Bertram.

"Not at all," said the friar.

"What do you in the greenwood, Sir Bertram?" asked Beatrice coolly.

"Looking for you, actually," said Bertram, almost apologetically.

"Indeed?" said Beatrice, slightly surprised.

"Well," said Bertram. "Actually, I came because . . . Well. In springtime, a young man's fancy—No, that's not how to put it. How shall I begin?"

"At the beginning," suggested Beatrice, slightly testily.

"Err—yes," said Bertram. "Um—Look here, Beatrice. You were marvelous at the fair, you know. First-rate marksmanship—"

Oh, stop babbling, you idiot, said a voice in Bertram's skull.

"Who said that?" said Bertram.

"Who said what?" said Beatrice. "Speak up, Sir Bertram, and yarely. Our Band has many tasks to which we must attend, foremost among them the evasion of our pursuers. We have not the time for persiflage. Spit it out."

I said that, said Jasper. *Jasper de Mobray. Telepathically, to belabor the point.*

"Do I have to talk back?" said Bertram.

No, thinking will do, said Jasper.

"Sir Bertram," said Beatrice coolly, "my patience is sore pressed. We must choose between taking you hostage and abandoning you here; I am inclined to keep you as our captive, perhaps to bait a trap for the usurper. But I demand to know your reason for pursuing us. Are you in truth in your uncle's pay, as many claim?"

Ask to speak to her alone, said Jasper.

"Ah—may we speak privately?" said Bertram.

"Wherefore?" demanded Beatrice.

You have a message for her ears alone, said Jasper.

"I have a message for your ears alone," said Bertram. I do? he thought.

"Oh, well enow," said Beatrice, turning to the bandits. "Good my fellows, Sir Bertram and I shall talk *en privé*; I bid you, give us space in which to converse."

"But mistress," protested a bandit. "He may intend ye harm—"

"Am I some silly wench, to require your protection?" demanded Beatrice. "Move off, an I command ye."

"Bertram, what the devil are you up to?" asked Timaeus worriedly.

"Don't worry," said Bertram uncertainly.

"Don't worry?" grumbled Timaeus to Nick as they were led away. "There's no telling what the twit will do."

Now then, said Jasper.

"Now then," said Bertram.

Don't parrot me, damn it, said Jasper. *I was just saying—*

"Now what?" said Beatrice. "See, here are my ears; where is your message for them?"

Look here, said Jasper. *Bring up some fond remembrance. "Remember that beauteous May, when we wove garlands out of the new-blossomed buds," something like that.*

"Beatrice," said Bertram, looking a little desperate. "Remember the time we climbed Mount Arsna, and picked blueberries together?"

"Yes," said Beatrice, leaning against a tree, strung bow in one hand but no arrow nocked. "You put a spider down my dress, as I recall."

You did that? said Jasper.

"Yes, but ... Oh, it's no use. Look here, Beatrice. I'm hopelessly in love with you. I know it's useless, but—"

"You're what?" said Beatrice incredulously, pushing away from the tree.

"Yes, I know, dash it all, not very romantic to put it like that, but there it is, you know. I can't imagine why I didn't see it years ago. I—"

"Well, I like that," said Beatrice. "You disappear off to school, never a letter; your uncle tortures my da to death, systematically loots the barony, and dispossesses widows and orphans while you look benevolently on—"

"Well, ah, I know there's been an increase in taxes," said Bertram apologetically, "but Pater did let the roads get into terrible repair, and—"

"Have you seen anyone fixing the roads?" demanded Beatrice, face reddening, her freckles becoming even more prominent. "And be quiet until I'm done! 'Struth, you haven't the brains of a newt, Sir Bertram de Biddleburg. If anyone had a duty to interest himself in the barony and see that justice was done after your father fell ill, it was you;

and yet there you sit in that damned castle, lapping up Broderick's lies and taking your ease, while—"

"Well—"

"Be silent!" shouted Beatrice, chest heaving with emotion. "You love me, you say? Pah! I'd sooner have a greep for a lover!" And she turned sharply away and strode for the bandits, who looked quite interested, having caught at least the end of this exchange.

Bertram groaned. "That's it then," he said miserably. "Could you lend me a dagger or something, Jasper? So I can kill myself now and save everybody the trouble?"

A chuckle came from the "firefly." "Buck up, old son," said Jasper. "You did rather well, I thought. At least you got it out."

"But she despises me," moaned Bertram.

"Opposites live side by side in the human heart," said Jasper.

"What is that supposed to mean?" said Bertram.

"And how are you, my dear lady?" asked the Right Honorable, the Lord Barthold, Baron Biddleburg, as he tottered unsteadily from his chair.

"Sit ye doon, ye owd foor," said Mabel. "Ye'rr be weak yet."

"And thank you too, Miss—?" said Barthold, sinking back into the armchair.

"Stollitt," said Sidney. "Sidney Stollitt."

"Where is that weasel Broderick?" asked Barthold weakly.

"Oot wi' his men, hoonting poor Beatrice doon, I warrant," said Mabel, peering into Barthold's eyes and thumping his chest.

"He won't have taken the whole guard," said Barthold. "I must rouse them against him, bar the castle gate, send word to the folk in the town below—"

"Werr, ye're fit enow," said Mabel. "Ye ought tee be in bed, me boy."

"I'm not yout boy, madam," said Barthold, reaching out and giving Mabel a resounding slap on the flank. "Though there was a time when I wouldn't have minded being."

"Nar a' that," said Mabel, grabbing his wrist but sounding more pleased than scandalized.

"Do I have your gracious permission to hobble to the armory?" asked Barthold.

"Nar, ye dee not," said Mabel. "Ye're tee weak stirr."

Sidney sighed; her arms still ached from carrying Mabel. "I'll have to carry him," she said resignedly.

Mabel chuckled. "Gee on apace, then," she said. "I sharr coome a'ter."

Luckily, thought Sidney, Barthold was not too great a burden; the stress of the poison had reduced him to skin and bones, and he had not been a large man to begin with. Still, Sidney walked as quickly as she was able, more because she wished to rid herself of the weight than because she felt a need for speed. With Barthold to direct her, it did not take long to find the armory.

Within, a half dozen soldiers lounged about, some snoozing, a few dicing. Weapons were scattered here and there, but none of the lot wore armor.

Sidney set Barthold down in the doorway, letting his feet drop before standing him up. The baron peered about at the men.

"Hallo," said one of the soldiers, spying the two in the doorway. "Who's that?"

"It's the old man," said another. "And that wench with Bertie's friends."

The first elbowed the second in the ribs. "Where's your manners, Gaston?" he demanded. "With *Sir Bertram's* friends. How do you do, miss? May we help you?"

"Now, you louts," said Barthold, his thin voice giving

hint of former power, "on your feet! I want the portcullis down and the watchtower manned. And I—"

"He's talking!" said one of the soldiers.

" 'Sblood, Marek," said Gaston. "You do have a talent for stating the obvious."

"That's bad," said Marek, worriedly. "Sir Broderick won't like it."

"By all the gods, I gave you an order!" shouted Barthold. "I'm the head of this household, and I demand that you prepare to defend this castle against my damnable brother!"

The soldiers looked worriedly at one another. "Meaning no offense, my lord," said one at last, "but Sir Broderick's the one who issues our pay."

"I—I never . . . ," sputtered Barthold.

"In fact, we'd better hold him until Sir Broderick returns," said Gaston worriedly.

"Are you sure?" said Marek. "I mean, he is the baron; if we do the wrong thing, we could wind up—"

While the soldiers debated, Barthold turned and began to march away. Sidney backed away from the door with him.

Several soldiers grabbed weapons and headed for the door. Cursing, Sidney snatched at the knife in her thigh sheath. She had not thought it necessary to wear weapons to the Feast of Grimaeus, and had not been back to her room since the morning; only a reluctance to go wholly unarmed had made her wear this unobtrusive blade.

"Now, ma'am," said Gaston, "that's really not necessary. We're just going to hold you until Sir Broderick returns. There's no need for violence."

Looking at six swords, Sidney sighed. "I'm sorry, Lord Barthold," she said. "I think we'd better do as they say."

Barthold's mouth was a thin line above his weak chin. "I agree, my dear," he said.

Down the corridor, Mabel slipped around the corner;

Sidney saw her out the side of her eye. With relief, Sidney realized that the witch knew of their predicament.

Bertram lay in a makeshift stretcher, the poles trimmed saplings, a torn blanket slung between them. The bandits were evidently ready to move.

Beatrice surveyed Timaeus, Kraki, and Nick. "What shall we do with you?" she said.

"Och, Beatrice," said one of the bandits. "We hae nar choice but tee kirr them. We canna leave hostires behind oor back."

Kraki looked up at this and smiled. "Good," he said. He bounded to his feet, wrenched his hands free of his bonds with a grunt, and charged into the bandits, knocking them asprawl. There were shouts of anger, and soon Kraki was in a tangle of men, arms and fists flying, quarterstaves thumping uselessly at such close quarters. Beatrice danced about, shouting orders.

There was a sudden bang and a flash of light. Beatrice turned toward it—Timaeus stood there, freed of his bonds, urbanely tamping his pipe, while Nick, likewise free, had grabbed a quarterstaff and was swinging it experimentally. He was familiar with urban stick fighting, but such a large stick was beyond his experience.

"Really, Lady Beatrice, there is no need for this," said Timaeus.

"It was not in my mind to order you slain," she said irritably. "The barbarian acted in hasty wise—"

"Yes, yes," said Timaeus. There was another explosion—Beatrice ducked as flames enveloped Timaeus's head, but soon realized this was not an attack. The wizard puffed contentedly on his pipe, smoke curling out into pine-scented air. "He's having a ball, I have no doubt. Call them off, and we shall discuss the matter."

"Gervais!" shouted Beatrice, turning toward the struggling knot of men. "Egbert! William! Enough! Break off, I charge ye!"

Gradually, the fighters untangled themselves, leaving a panting, grinning, black-eyed Kraki standing at the center, on the balls of his feet and ready for a renewed struggle. The bandits looked considerably more battered than he. "Vhat is problem?" said Kraki. "I have not yet even broken any bones!"

"You see, my lady," said Timaeus, "you make a mistake in believing that we are your enemies."

"Even so?" said Beatrice skeptically. "We have robbed you; you sup at the usurper's table; you accompany this fool." She gestured toward Bertram, who winced at being so described. "What should I take you for but foes?"

"My good lady," said Timaeus, "on the contrary, we have come to join your band."

"I beg your pardon?" she said, arching a skeptical eyebrow.

"I can't imagine why you should think elsewise," said Timaeus, pausing for another puff. "Our good friend, Sir Bertram, has broken with his uncle, recognizing at last the evil he has wrought within the barony. In companionship, we join with him, as he comes to plead his love for the beauteous Beatrice."

There were jeers and hoots from her men at this.

"You've broken with Broderick?" Beatrice demanded of Bertram.

"Well, ah, that is—" said Bertram. The light that was Jasper darted down from the trees and gave Bertram's leg a sharp jostle. "Ouch! Yes, I've broken with Uncle Brod."

"Well, why didn't you say so, Bertie," said Beatrice, shaking her head, "instead of going on about the need to fix up the roads? I mean, really."

"Well, ah; the decision was a rather sudden one . . . ," said Bertram plaintively.

"If you have in truth come to join your fortunes with

our own, Bertie," said Beatrice, "we shall find good use for you. But you, friend wizard; how can I know to trust you?"

"Well . . . you know," said Timaeus, "glad to help out a fellow Old Durfalian. I mean, old school ties are the ties that bind, and . . . and so forth." He saw that this logic was not having the intended effect on Beatrice. He gave a cough and tried again. "As it happens, we have a rather valuable cargo, which good Sir Broderick has been plotting to seize, killing us in the bargain."

"Verily, that sounds like the man," said Beatrice, "but how did you learn of this scheme?"

"We have our means," said Timaeus. "Don't we, Jasper?"

"Quite so," said Jasper, inches away from Beatrice's left ear. She started and whirled—to see nothing but a point of green light.

"Your servant," said Jasper, bobbing.

"I—see," said Beatrice.

"Indeed," said Timaeus, "it would be in our interest to remove Sir Broderick from power."

Beatrice arched an eyebrow. "My aims are not so grandiose," she said. "My men are doughty, but 'gainst hardened warriors . . ." She shrugged.

Timaeus puffed smoke thoughtfully. "Even with magical support?" he suggested. "And the legitimate heir at the van?"

"At the van . . . ?" said Bertram, looking faintly ashen.

"We shall have to hold council," said Beatrice, smiling and serious.

Sir Broderick stamped into the guardroom, scattering water from his waxen coat, a floppy felt hat on his head. "Damnation, Blentz!" he thundered. "I've had it up to— what's Barthold doing down here?"

The baron, who had been napping in an armchair, woke

up with a start. "Good day, brother," he said dangerously. "How d'ye do, you despicable swine."

Broderick was obviously startled, but quickly rallied. "Good heavens, an unexpected—and remarkably rapid—recovery. Well, this is good news. Glad to see you back on your—"

"I shall expect an immediate accounting of your expenditures since your arrival here," said the baron, "and access to your files. To start with, you may order these men to release me; they seem to be under the misapprehension—"

"See, here, Barthold," said Broderick. "You don't seem to understand—"

"I understand quite well!" said Barthold, standing unsteadily up in rage. "I am giving you a chance to make amends! Cooperate, and I shall do my best to see that your reputation emerges from this mess unbesmirched—"

"Oh, shut up," snapped Broderick. "You always were a moralistic jackass, do you know that, Barthold? Marek, Gaston—take him to the dungeon."

Blentz, puffing and red-faced, sparse hair plastered to his skull with the wet, had come into the room in time to hear the end of this exchange. "Sir Broderick," he said. "Is that wise? If word gets out—"

"Be quiet, Blentz," said Broderick, sinking down in the armchair that Barthold had vacated. He seemed unhappy, surprisingly calm, almost moody. "I see no alternative," he muttered to himself.

Blentz looked as if he had something to say, but held his tongue.

Abruptly, Broderick became aware that Sidney was still present, sitting on the floor with her back to the wall.

"Damnation," he said. "And a witness, too. Better lock her up as well. Separate cells, mind."

* * *

They moved through the dripping woods. From ahead and to the flank, birdcalls came: not the natural song of the wild, but reports from Beatrice's scouts. At present, Beatrice wished to avoid contact with Broderick's men, something she could best achieve with advance warning of their presence—hence the need for scouts. Timaeus was impressed with this show of military expertise on the part of a pack of peasants and woodsmen.

He, Nick, and Kraki walked with Beatrice. Bertram and his bearers brought up the rear. Though this was climax forest, with little ground cover, the bearers were forced to step over fallen logs or dodge tree limbs from time to time. The stretcher was rarely level, and often jostled. Bertram was still suffering considerable pain, and the unevenness of the path did nothing to relieve it. He had been quite happy, therefore, when Jasper had resumed their *sub rosa* conversation; at least it kept his mind off his leg.

Well, all right, Jasper, said Bertram, *if you fellows really think it's wise, I'll go along. But, I mean, good heavens, we're talking about war. Brother against brother, sword and flames, blood in the streets sort of thing.*

Fiddlesticks, said Jasper, flitting above the stretcher. *Do you want Beatrice or not?*

Well, yes, rather, said Bertram.

Well, then, it's obvious enough, isn't it? Misled by your evil uncle, you aided him in his usurpation of your father's demesne, but now love has burgeoned in your breast. The beautiful Beatrice has shown you the error of your ways, the scales have fallen from your eyes, epiphany has struck bolt-like from the heavens, and so forth and so on. Therefore, as the valiant young heir of the House of Biddleburg, you will ride forth, rally the folk of the realm, and lead them, together with the doughty woodsmen of the Band of Beatrice, 'gainst Biddleburg Castle. Having gained the ramparts, you will free your father from durance vile, wed the noble Beatrice, and unite the people of your realm, former rebel and loyal townsman alike, in glorious harmony. Wedding bells ring, the heroic couple walk off into the sunset, hallelujah and hooray, omnia vincit amor.

Yes, well, said Bertram, *it sounds very neat. But, you know, I'm really not the blood-and-thunder type. You want someone like, like your friend Kraki—*

Kraki? Nonsense, not his style at all. He'd just kill everyone in sight, and sell everyone else into slavery. No, for this kind of job, you want the young but stalwart heir—

Oh, come on, Jasper, whined Bertram, *there's no point, really. She despises me, I'm completely useless as a man of war, I'm—*

Snap out of it, said Jasper, practically shouting in Bertram's brain. *Do you want her or not?*

Well, rather.

Then play the role. Besides, chin up. She did call you Bertie, after all.

She did, didn't she? said Bertram. *Do you think that's a good sign?*

My dear chap, said Jasper, *I think the thing is practically in the bag.*

Mr. Bates rang the gong in the Great Hall; it was dinnertime at Biddleburg Castle. He stood stiffly by the main entrance, ready to guide the guests to their appointed places. An antipasto was on the table, and back in the kitchen the *chef de cuisine* had already prepared a cold vichyssoise, a *mélange* of fresh vegetables, and the dessert, a *tarte aux framboises,* and was busy with the finishing touches for the rack of lamb with rosemary. Mr. Bates, who was no mean trencherman himself, rather hoped that Sir Broderick would eschew another of his interminable hunting stories tonight, as the butler hoped to retire to the Steward's Room as quickly as possible, in search of his own sustenance. Rack of lamb was one of Bates's particular favorites.

Broderick arrived, looking a little flustered; he had barely had enough time to change out of his wet things and into appropriate garb for dinner. "A bit of the Moothlayan, Bates, if you please," he said, and gravely accepted three fingers of whisky.

Broderick paced a bit about the hall, sipping his drink, while Bates stood as impassively as ever. After several minutes, Blentz opened the door and walked rather awkwardly into the room. He'd been asaddle all day, and his thighs were feeling the strain.

"Where's Bertram," snapped Broderick, "and his damnfool friends?"

"Haven't seem them," said Blentz shortly, sagging into an armchair.

"What about it, Bates?" demanded Broderick.

"If ye please, sor," said the butler, "I've nar seen them since the morning. Sharr I inquire amoong the staff?"

"Please," said Broderick, and so the butler departed.

Blentz stared moodily into the fire, and Broderick poured himself another drink. After several minutes, Bates returned.

"I'm soorry, sor," he said, "but the staff has seen nar hide nar hair oof Sir Bertram, nar oof his friends, since the incident doon in the toon."

Broderick was rather alarmed at this news. "Neither hide nor hair?" he said incredulously. "I thought I saw them leaving the square toward the castle as we set out in pursuit of the rebels."

"Mayhap, sor," said Bates apologetically. "The staff was in toon, ye ken, foor the festivities, and did not return tirr later. They may hae coome, and departed."

"Departed for where?" asked Blentz tiredly.

"Begging your pardon, sor," said Bates, "boot I canna say."

Blentz groaned. "I suppose you'll want me out searching the woods again," he said to Broderick—but the man was gone, running out the door.

Blentz sat up and peered at the antipasto. He was famished, but it would not do to start in on the food, not before everyone else arrived. He and Bates exchanged glances, both feeling rather put-upon.

"Shall I bring in a cheese tray, sir?" inquired Bates.

Blentz smiled in relief. "Just the thing, Mr. Bates," he said. "Thank you very much."

"Noot at arr, sir."

Broderick and Bates returned almost simultaneously, Broderick, in a reversal of roles, holding open the door so that Bates, bearing an enormous silver platter set with crackers and a large wheel of brie, could enter the room. "They left the wagon," Broderick said with satisfaction.

Blentz blinked a minute; he had forgotten about the wagon. "And the statue—"

"Still there," said Broderick.

"May I take it, sor," asked Bates, "that we wirr be ony three at dinner?"

"Three?" said Broderick.

"You, sor," said Bates, "the good captain; and the baron, of coorse."

Broderick blinked. "Ah, I see," he said. "No, Mr. Bates, my brother won't be coming down to dinner tonight; he's somewhat indisposed, I'm afraid."

"Sharr I have a tray taken oop, sor?"

Broderick cleared his throat. "Ah—no, thank you, Mr. Bates; why don't you bring the tray here, and I shall take it up myself, after supper."

Bates's impassive faced betrayed nothing, but internally he felt a quiver of alarm. Why would Sir Broderick want to prevent him from seeing Sir Barthold? "Just as ye say, sor," he murmured. "If ye wirr take your paces, then, gentermen, I sharr ca' the wine steward."

* * *

The fire crackled; they burned hemlock, a wood notorious for sparking. It was down to the embers now. About the camp, snores resounded. Nick found himself wakeful.

In such a mood, he knew, it was pointless to lie abed, mind whirring uselessly. He got up and went to relieve himself and drink at the purling stream.

Returning, he caught sight of a figure: Someone stood atop the rise that flanked their campsite. Nick's breath caught; the profile was indubitably that of a woman. He climbed upward.

Up here, there was little sound; merely the soft breeze, soughing through the pines. The stars spread gem-like across the velvet sky. Beatrice stood gazing at them, one booted foot atop a boulder, leaning on the shaft of her bow.

"Beautiful, isn't it?" Nick said.

"Aye," said she, half turning toward him. " 'Tis nearly enough, the glory of creation, to justify the vileness of mankind."

"Are all men vile, then?" asked Nick, standing closer to her. He drank in her scent; to another, the smell would not have been attractive. There was rarely time or opportunity to bathe, in the greenwood, as Beatrice's odor gave evidence, but to Nick, at that moment, it seemed the veriest perfume of paradise.

"Vile enow," said she.

"I'd show you different," Nick murmured.

She permitted him to kiss her, then drew away. "I think not," she said.

He smiled quizzically at her. "Life is short," he said, "and pleasure fleeting; we must take it where we may. How better to spend an hour, in this soft air, under the distant stars?"

"Fool," said Beatrice softly. "How do you imagine a woman may lead this band of bandits? Either I must have all men, or none."

"Who's to know?" said Nick, reaching an arm around her waist.

"Actions have consequences," said she, lifting his hand away.

"And youth and love must have its way," said Nick.

Beatrice laughed. "Sirrah," she said, "to hear *you* speak of love is even less credible than to hear it from Sir Bertram."

Nick gave an unwilling smile. "Well," he said, "if you won't, you won't."

"And I won't," she softly said.

Nick nodded and trudged down the slope, back to his bedroll, where he spent a sleepless, lust-tortured night.

Beatrice got little more sleep than he. Broderick, she saw, watching the wheeling stars, had robbed her of her youth, as well as her inheritance. The latter she might regain, but the former was forever gone.

VII.

At dawn, Master Gorham, the stonewright, stood at the center of Bain Bridge, for which the barony's second town was named, staring critically down at the bridge's stone supports. The River Bain was swollen with yesterday's rain, white water crashing down its channel. Master Gorham had lived with that noise all his days, the constant susurrus of the stream against which Bainbridge lay, a comforting burbling that lulled the citizens of the town to sleep each night. He hardly noticed the sound most days, but this morning had been woken by a change in its tenor. The stream had been full before the rains, still running with snow melt from the high mountain peaks above Biddleburg; but rain had swollen it almost to its banks.

It was not flooding that concerned Gorham; the Bain's channel was deep. Rather, he was concerned for the bridge.

It was impossible to tell from this vantage, but he feared that the waters were undermining the piers, the stone pil-

lars on which Bain Bridge stood. In earlier days, the mere
suspicion would have been enough to charm a fat contract
for repair from Baron Biddleburg; alas, Sir Broderick was
a more tightfisted man. Worse than that, thought Master
Gorham; he was a tyrant, or so the citizens of Bainbridge
accounted him, for he had hanged a half dozen of the
townsfolk's men, in punishment for their support of Sir
Benton's rebellion. Broderick would be letting no contracts
to Bainbridge's stonemason, Master Gorham told himself,
no matter the state of the bridge's repair.

Because he was up so early, and on the bridge that led
into town, Gorham was the first to spy the approach of
Beatrice and her men. He looked at them wide-eyed for a
moment, then turned and hurtled toward the village.

By the time Beatrice and the others arrived, half the village was already in the courtyard before the Greep Cou-
chant, the inn at the center of town. In better times, the
whole community would have turned out for such an
event; but half the village, apparently, thought discretion
the better part of valor, and had no desire to risk meeting
rebels, in revolt against a lord who had proven his vindic-
tiveness, especially well-armed rebels who might prove as
dangerous as the enemy they fought. Sir Broderick had
few friends in Bainbridge town; but that did not mean that
the Band had many.

"Madam Helsing, Master Gorham, Mistress Entright,"
said Beatrice, nodding to folk she had known from childhood, "I bid ye well."

"Get ye gone froom here!" shouted Madam Helsing.
"We hae suffered enow in your famiry's cause. Why dee
ye endanger us again?"

"Be quiet, woman!" shouted Mistress Entright. "E'er
has the house of Bainbridge served the toon well! Wourd
ye kiss the whip tha' scourges ye?"

"Marss Beatrice," said Master Gorham worriedly, "too

many toonsfolk hae suffered for us to greet you joyfurry. Can we ask why you—"

"What, you too, Master Gorham?" said Beatrice.

Gorham looked blank for a moment.

"I am not 'Miss Beatrice,'" she said, projecting her voice like one accustomed to addressing crowds, speaking in a conversational tone but with sufficient volume to reach everyone present. "Nor Mademoiselle Beatrice, nor yet Madam Beatrice. Sir Benton, my father, is dead; he hath no male issue. Wherefore, I inherit his title and demesne; I hight Lady Beatrice, a peeress of right, though Baron Barthold has not yet received my oath of fealty. Before he may do so, he must be freed from his brother, who usurps—"

"So said yer father, and see what good it did him!" said Madam Helsing.

"Though Sir Brodick's rure be oonerous and his taxes bear heavy, it wourd seem to be lawfur," said Master Gorham apologetically. "He says he acts foor the baron while Barthord is sick, and he has the suppoort of Sir Bertram, the heir. You say he is a usurper, but lacking proof—"

"I say she's right!" said a voice from behind Beatrice, from amid her Band.

"Who speaks?" said Master Gorham.

"Stand me up, lads," said Bertram. They set down his stretcher and helped him to a standing position, a shoulder under each arm to bear him aloft despite his broken leg. "I do, good sir," said Bertram.

"You say your ooncle acts wi'oot the baron's consent?" asked Gorham skeptically.

"Well, you know, the old pater doesn't seem to be in much shape to consent to anything. That is, the old *tête* is more than a little *au fouillis*. Ding dong, nobody home, if you follow my drift."

"Then," said Gorham slowly, "the right tee rule descends on the shouders oof the heir. So it is oop tee ye tee determine whether Sir Brodick acts legarry oor nar."

"Well, Uncle Brod does seem rather to have taken advantage of the situation, what? All these taxes and such; heaven only knows where the money is going. And to kill Sir Benton—I mean, going a bit far, I thought. The old relative has overstayed his welcome, if you ask me. A bit. He needs a firm talking to, I believe."

"Do ye suppoort Lady Be in her reberrion against Sir Brodick, then, Bertram, our baron-to-be?" shouted Mistress Entright.

"Err, well, perhaps," said Bertram. Timaeus gave him a poke. "That is to say, I suppose so." Beatrice turned toward him, fire in her eyes. "Yes, definitely," Bertram added hurriedly. "Unquestionably. We must rise and march on Biddleburg Castle! All hail the revolution! One for all and all for one! Down with the usurper! Bainbridge, arise! Fight, Durfalus, fight! And, er . . . so forth."

"Hurrah!" shouted Mistress Entright. "Hurrah foor Beatrice and Sir Bertram!"

Suddenly, there were caps in the air; everyone was leaping about like mad and shouting and hugging each other. Madam Helsing and a few of the others seemed unconvinced still, but Master Gorham, at least, was soberly nodding. Though he was not as exuberant in his support as many others, it was clear that the crowd was on Beatrice's side. The townsfolk were in and among Beatrice's men, now, slapping them on the back, the hostility between town and forester forgotten. *"Donec ero felix,"* someone shouted, the motto of the House of Biddleburg, and soon the crowd took it up as a chant. Beatrice was flushed with righteous fire, while Bertram looked surprised and rather pleased with the dramatic effects of his words. *"Donec ero felix,"* they shouted, the words resounding across the valley, echoing from the mountains.

"Yes," said Timaeus to Jasper, "only let us hope we are."

As dungeons went, reflected Sidney, the one below Biddleburg Castle was far from the worst. Not that Sidney was a great connoisseur of dungeons; the only one she had ever visited, before now, was the one in Urf Durfal, where she had briefly been interred on a petty larceny charge, and while that had been dank and gloomy, it had been no worse accommodation than the cheaper sort of rented flat in the dingier slums of the city. Her cellmates had complained of the rats, but the rodents had merely served as between-meals snacks for Sidney—and not for long, as the bars of the cell had been wide enough for a cat to squeeze between them. She had left before the charge against her had been brought before a grand jury; she imagined it was still outstanding.

Still, even if Sidney's personal experience with dungeons was limited, she had heard the usual tales, of rat-infested filth, dark tortures by the light of fires in which red-hot irons lay, and so forth. This sort of thing was a staple of popular fiction, though the role of the dungeon in such works varied, depending on whether the story was intended to be edifying, entertaining, or prurient. Neither the dungeon of Urf Durfal nor this one lived up to the standards of fiction: no despairing graffiti, no distant screams, no aged lunatics capering in nearby cells, no hooded torturers considering their tools.

The dungeon of Biddleburg Castle, unlike that of Urf Durfal, was not dank. There were a mere four cells—no doubt crime was not a particular problem in so small a realm—and while they evidently hadn't been dusted in some time, neither could they quite be described as filthy. Their guard, far from being a sadistic, hunchbacked maniac, was a fat little man named Lem, who sat in a room down the corridor, playing endless games of solitaire and munching on apples. The closest Biddleburg Castle came to torture, apparently, was the impossibility of avoiding the noises Lem made in the course of these activities: "Shuffle, shuffle, shuffle. *Crunch*, munch, munch. Flip, flip, flip, flip, flip. *Crunch*, munch, munch, munch." Sidney could have done without it, although, to be sure, it was greatly preferable to a red-hot poker in the eye.

Indeed, not only was the dungeon less than horrific, some attention had actually been paid to the comfort of its occupants; Sidney's cell held both a chamber pot and an upholstered, if rather lumpy, sofa, which had served quite well as her bed for the night. Sidney wondered at the intelligence of whatever servant had placed the sofa here; it was old and worn, and no doubt the thought had been that use in the dungeon was preferable to throwing it out, yet ... She could feel springs through the bottom of the couch. Its presence reassured her that Biddleburg had scant acquaintance with hardened malefactors.

Well, thought Sidney, if they're so unworldly as to put the thing here, I'd be remiss if I didn't take advantage of it.

There were two cells across the way, but both were vacant. "My Lord Barthold," Sidney said. "Can you hear me?"

"Yes, my dear," came a voice from the cell next door. Lem wandered into the corridor, blinking at its dimness; his candlelit room was rather brighter. "Sorry, milord," he said apologetically, "but Sir Broderick has ordered that there be no conversation between you."

"He has, has he, the insolent pup!" shouted Barthold. "And how d'ye propose to stop us, tell me that, me lad!"

Lem's jaw worked weakly, perhaps on a bit of apple lodged in his teeth. "Uh—I don't ... I'll have to—"

"Look," said Sidney. "Let's not make trouble. We won't talk, if that's the rule."

"The devil you say!" said Barthold. "I'm damned if I—"

"My lord," Sidney interrupted. "If you hope to get out of here, the last thing you want is Broderick to storm down here."

"And why is that?" demanded Barthold.

Because any fool could escape from this setup in six seconds flat, Sidney thought to herself. "Please take my word for it," said Sidney a little sharply. "Give me a little credit, please; if it weren't for me, your vocabulary would still be limited to the letter N."

Barthold muttered something under his breath, and then reluctantly said, "Very well, I shan't utter a peep. Go back to your damned apples, you cretin."

"Thank you, miss," said Lem in relief. "If there's anything I can get to make you more comfortable, you let me know, you hear?"

"The keys to this cell, my sword, and a dozen cubits of rope would be nice," said Sidney.

Lem chuckled. "Sorry, miss," he said. "But really, you let me know if you'd like something special from Cook, or a book, or something."

"Thank you, Lem," said Sidney. "But nothing for now."

Lem touched his brow, and went back to his cards and his apples.

And now, thought Sidney, for the sofa. She lay on the floor on her back and slid under the couch. She ripped open the ancient, fragile cloth at its underside, pulled away handfuls of cotton ticking, and yanked at a spring. On the third try, it parted with a sproing, and came out the bottom of the sofa.

She considered it for a moment, then took it over to the wall, where a single tiny window admitted a little light. The end of the spring was quite dull. The wall was uneven, chisel-cut rock, but someone had taken the bother to saw-cut the granite slab that served as the windowsill, meaning it was smooth enough to use as a whetstone. Sidney began to scrape at it with the spring.

Scritch, scritch, scritch. She worried about the noise, but Lem apparently heard nothing over the sounds of his own mastications. It took Sidney ten minutes before she was satisfied with the sharpness of her spring.

She laid it by the door to her cell, took on cat form, and stepped daintily through the bars. Outside the cell, she transformed again, reached into the cell for the spring, and considered it for a moment.

There was movement from the cell next to hers; Barthold peered out at her, with interest. Sidney was, of course, naked; therianthropy was no gentleman's magic, designed to include such niceties as the need to clothe one's nakedness, but a disease, a condition, a curse. Her clothes were back in her cell. She put a finger to her lips to enjoin the baron to silence, then placed the spring just outside the vacant cell directly across the hall from her own.

"Oh, Lem," she said. "Could you come here for a moment? I've thought of something."

Lem's chair scraped in the other room. Sidney became a cat, and went to sit inside the vacant cell.

Lem came blinking down the corridor and looked into Sidney's now-unoccupied cell. "Yes, miss?" he said. His eyes had not yet adjusted, and it took him a moment to realize that no one was there.

By then, the cat had stepped back out of the vacant cell. Sidney resumed her human form, bent swiftly down for the spring, and leapt for Lem's back, wrapping her left arm around his waist and holding the sharp end of the spring to his jugular. "Move or talk, and you're a dead man," she said urgently.

Lem froze. With her left hand, Sidney drew his sword. She stepped back, tossed the spring into Barthold's cell—just in case—and switched the sword to her right hand.

Then she rested the point of the sword against Lem's kidney and took the ring of keys from his belt.

"Take off your shirt," she said.

"Please, miss," Lem whined. "I got a wife and—"

"I'm not going to kill you," she snapped. "Not if you keep your voice down, and take off your damned shirt."

"What do I do with this?" Barthold asked with interest, holding up the spring. Lem began to shuck his shirt.

"I don't care," said Sidney. "Better than no weapon."

When Lem had his shirt off, she handed the keys around to his front and said, "Open the baron's door." He swallowed, but did so. Baron Barthold came out to join her.

"Now unlock mine," Sidney ordered.

"Well done, my dear," said Barthold. "Kill this fellow, and let's be on, shall we?"

"No no, please, I don't—" babbled Lem. He almost turned around, but the pressure of the sword at his back dissuaded him.

"I promised I wouldn't," said Sidney with irritation. "Open the door to my cell!" Fearfully, Lem fumbled at the keys. He finally found the right one, and unlocked Sidney's cell.

"Very noble," said Barthold, "but if we leave him here, he'll be screaming bloody murder in nothing flat."

"True," said Sidney. "Pick up the shirt."

"What?" said the baron, studying the garment in question, now lying on the floor, with some distaste.

"Pick it up!" said Sidney. Grimacing, the baron did so. "Now rip off the sleeves."

The baron gave them an experimental tug. "You know," he said, "I'm not precisely the fine figure of a man I was in my salad days. And my skills as a seamstress are noticeably nonexistent. I don't believe I—"

"Here, take this," Sidney snarled, giving Barthold the sword. "Kill him if he so much as peeps."

"Gladly," said Barthold. Sidney reached for the shirt,

nipped at the cloth with her canines, and ripped off the sleeves. Turning about, she noticed that Barthold was swinging the sword experimentally, clearly contemplating a thrust through Lem's back.

"Don't do that if you want my help," she said.

"Oh, very well," said Barthold.

Sidney took back the sword and pushed Lem into the cell. "Turn around," she said. He did. His eyes grew large as he realized her state of dishabille. "Stand behind the door, and put your arms through the bars," she said. He did so with alacrity. She tied his wrists securely with one sleeve.

While she had been doing this, Barthold had wandered into the guardroom and had returned with an apple, which he was about to bite into. "Give me that," said Sidney.

"What?" said the baron.

"The apple," said Sidney. Barthold passed it over. She inserted it into Lem's mouth, pushing it in till his jaws creaked. And then she tied it into place with the second sleeve, knotting it behind his head.

"Walk forward," she told Lem. He did, until the cell door clanged shut. She locked him into what had been Barthold's cell.

And then she entered her own cell, and put her clothes back on.

"Very neat," said Barthold, surveying her work. "I believe I'll get another apple. Would you like óne?"

VIII.

"When I get my hands on young Bertram's scrawny neck," said Broderick, "I'll ... Blentz! Wake up, man!"

Captain Blentz awoke with a start and peered, bleary-eyed, around at the study. "Just as you say," he said thickly, having no idea what Broderick had been yammering about. Why had he ever taken this damnable job? It was full morning now, sun shining horribly bright through those glassed windows; his eyes ached abominably. Broderick had kept him awake all night, fulminating and scheming and getting precisely nowhere. Blentz yearned for a less hyperactive employer.

Marek came running into the study. "My lord," he gasped. "There's an army coming up the Hamsterburg road!"

"An army?" scoffed Broderick. "Idiot! There's no army—Duke Schofeld is a dotard, he's not going to invade, and the orcs have got to get through Hamsterburg before they get anywhere near these mountains. There can't possibly be an army out there."

"B-b-but my lord," sputtered Marek. "I've seen it with my own eyes. Hordes of them! Thousands! Serried ranks of soldiery, great siege machines, magical wards and flying demons—"

"We must flee!" gasped Blentz.

"Oh, do calm down, you two," said Broderick. "Let's go have a look."

So they climbed up to the watchtower. Broderick leaned out a window and peered down the road, shading his eyes. He pulled back in and studied an inscription on the wall. Broderick was no great collegiate mage, but he was not wholly unacquainted with the practice of magic. This castle had been built with a number of useful enchantments, not least of which was the scrying magic of the watchtower. The runes, carved into the stone walls, declared the necessary spell for those who had forgotten it; " 'Epekt glamor tsuganish,' " read Broderick slowly.

The view out the window changed; suddenly, from Broderick's standpoint, it displayed a cardinal, sitting on the branch of a chestnut, at remarkably close quarters. Broderick cursed and moved his head; the view swept across space at amazing speed, small changes in viewing angle and distance causing different portions of the world outside the tower to come into focus. It was several moments before Broderick was able to find precisely the right spot from which to see the approaching "army."

"Serried ranks of soldiery," he said. "Great siege machines. You imbecile! It's a rabble, is what it is. The townsfolk of Bainbridge, waving pitchforks and kitchen knives. Come to complain about the taxes again, I imagine. I wonder at their temerity; a quick cavalry charge should scatter . . . Good heavens."

"What is it?" asked Blentz.

"Timaeus is with them," said Broderick. "And—yes, there's the barbarian."

"I don't fancy a cavalry charge against fireballs," said Blentz worriedly.

Suddenly, Broderick started. "And that bitch Beatrice too!" he said, turning wide-eyed to Blentz. "By all the gods, they're conspiring against me! The townsfolk, the rebels, Timaeus and that lot—Oh, gods; Miss Stollitt is one of them; they must know we've got Barthold in the dungeon."

Blentz was looking more and more alarmed. "We must flee!" he said.

Broderick turned red. "Is that your invariable response, Blentz? Flight? Turn tail at the slightest opposition? No wonder you're a blithering blunderer as a soldier, you flibbertigibbet. Here we sit in the finest natural fortress this side of Miller's Seat, and you want to flee at the approach of a batch of housewives and lumberjacks? Raise the drawbridge, lower the portcullis, man the damned ramparts, and heat up the boiling oil. We'll teach the fools what it is to tangle with Broderick de Biddleburg!"

"What—what about Bertram?" said Blentz worriedly. "If he's with them, the town below will rise, and—"

Broderick checked, the idea occurring to him only now. Could the young idiot be quite such a fool? Well, yes, as it happened, he could.

"Go prepare the men, Blentz," said Broderick. "I must think."

Damnation, but it was all falling apart. Barthold *compos mentis*, Beatrice in league with d'Asperge and the Bainbridgers, Bertram gods knew where ... Biddleburg Castle could withstand a siege from that ill-armed rabble for an eternity, if need be, but spending the next seven years holed up in this damned drafty pile of stones was not what he'd had in mind when he'd launched this fool scheme.

"Screw your courage to the sticking place," he told himself. He would do the necessary, whatever it might be.

Now, thought Broderick, suppose Baron Barthold were to appear on the ramparts of Biddleburg Castle, in full control of his faculties, and tell the crowd to disperse, that his brother Broderick had his every confidence . . . That would do the trick, wouldn't it?

Barthold would never do it, of course. He'd spit defiance even with a blade at his back. Torture wouldn't sway him, nor threat of death—

Wait a minute. Threat of death might very well do it. Not Barthold's, of course, but suppose Broderick made clear his intention of slaughtering as many of the townsfolk as possible. Boiling oil had its uses, of course.

It wouldn't play for long, would it? But it should be sufficient to disperse the crowd; and something might always turn up.

If he could sell the statue, he'd have enough money to raise an army. And through the crystal, he could contact mercenary captains. A sufficiently large force could crush all opposition; after enough folk decorated gibbets, resistance should cease. Barthold and Bertram could disappear in all the uproar, leaving him legitimate heir. All it took, Broderick thought, was fortitude and sufficient ruthlessness.

He'd win this one still, he decided. After all, he'd never lost yet.

He hurtled, two at a time, down the tower's circular stairs, yanking himself around the curve by the railing.

The army, if it may be dignified by such a term, of Sir Bertram and Lady Beatrice encountered no opposition as it approached the walls of Biddleburg town. Broderick had recalled the guard from the town wall, concentrating on the defense of the castle itself. They made their way to the central square, makeshift banners flying, people singing songs and shouting *"Donec ero felix."* There two sturdy foresters hoisted Bertram to the wooden platform, erected for the Feast of Grimaeus and not yet disassembled. He was flushed with exhilaration, his previous self-doubts erased by the evident enthusiasm of the crowd. As curious townsfolk began to stream into the square, he confidently addressed them.

"Biddlebourgeois!" shouted Bertram. "How d'ye do? Um—you all know me, I suppose. Ah—up there, in the castle, lies Uncle Broderick, the, er, usurper, I suppose you might say. Since he showed up hereabouts, we've had all sorts of unpleasantness. Bloodshed and, um, bloodshed." Someone in the crowd shouted something. "Oh?" said Bertram. "And taxes of course. Beastly things, taxes. I say, it's about time to take a firm line with the old relative. What? I mean, enough is quite enough; there is a limit to hospitality, and Uncle Brod does seem rather to have trod over the edge. So, um, as the heir to the throne, I call upon all good folk to join me in rising against Uncle's tyranny. What ho?"

"See here, yoong Bertram," said a skeptical graybeard, "it's arr very werr tee talk aboot turfing oot Sor Brodick; boot he hath the castle and a hoondred men. How can ye hoope to o'erthrow him?" All eyes went to Bertram as the folk took the oldster's question to heart.

"Well," said Bertram, "I mean, here we've got the people of Bainbridge, the Band of Beatrice, an old school chum with fantastic magical powers, and, er, so forth. And our cause is just, our—how does it go?—our strength is as the strength of ten because our cause is pure, and all that rot; I mean, we can hardly fail, what? Screw your courage to the sticking plaster, as Pater used to say. No, that doesn't sound quite right. Nail your courage to the sticking plaster? Something like that."

"Och, werr, that's as may be," said the graybeard.

"However, I dinna care tee risk me life foor tha." There were murmurs of agreement from the crowd.

"What?" said Bertram, sounding shocked. "After the murders, the taxes, all that sort of thing, you're willing just to let things go on? What about freedom?"

"I canna eat freedom," said the old man. "How wirr things be different when ye rule?"

"What? Why, um, the Band will return to peaceful pursuits, Lady Beatrice will be restored her lands, brothers will be reconciled, the huntsman will return to his courses and the farmer to his lands, charity and goodwill will rule among men, and the heavens will reflect the harmony of the temporal realm. Yes?"

The graybeard rolled his eyes. "And what's tha' tee me?" In the crowd, people were shaking their heads and beginning to drift away.

Beatrice leaned over and whispered in Bertram's ear. "Oh!" said Bertram. "Yes, of course. We'll have to do something about all those nasty tax increases. Yes, very good; we'll cut two pee off the sales tax, and abolish the inheritance levy." The crowd looked slightly more interested, but still undecided. "No? How about three pee off the sales tax, eliminating the capitation and the gabelle, and halving the *ad valorem* duty on spirituous liquors?" There were smiles and murmurs from the crowd, but still no obvious enthusiasm. "Oh, bugger all," said Bertram. "Let's just go whole hog and eliminate the lot. A tax holiday, that's the ticket! No taxes for a full year, forgiveness of all debts outstanding, and a free pint of bitter for every man!"

"Hurrah!" shouted the crowd. "Hurrah for Sir Bertram!" Hats flew into the air, folk gamboled about like madmen, and many went to get ancient, rusting swords, or billhooks or axes, so they might say they had joined in the final assault on the Tyrant Broderick.

"Tough crowd," muttered Bertram to Beatrice, as she helped him descend the platform.

"You spoke well," she said, smiling.

Only the most prestigious of servants ate in the Steward's Room: Bates, of course; the groom of the chambers; the lady's maids; and the personal gentlemen of the castle's guests. There was silence, save for the sounds of ingestion, as the assembled set to their breakfasts. The eggs were almost cold, alas, for Bates had been late in arriving; something had detained him in the Great Hall, where he served breakfast to the lords and ladies and their guests before the servants ate their own repast.

There came a knocking at the main door to the Steward's Room; an unusual occurrence. Few of the lesser servants would dare to intrude without strong reason. Still, it was always possible that Sir Broderick had called specifically for Bates or one of the others.

Bates wiped his jowls and said, "Coom in." The door opened a few inches, displaying the face of one of the scullery maids, looking rather intimidated. "I'm sorry tee interrupt, Mr. Bates," she said. "Boot Sir Brodick's spats ha' gone missing in the wash."

Lambston, Broderick's valet, looked up from his hash. "Damnation," he said. "I shall have to go."

"Of coorse, Mr. Lambston," said Bates, nodding sagely. Seeing to Broderick's equipage was Lambston's personal responsibility, and it would go hard with him if Broderick's clothing was not prepared and properly laid out when the man was ready to dress.

Lambston pushed back and bustled out the door, closing it behind him. "What the devil do you mean they've gone missing?" he demanded, voice fading as he and the scullery maid made their way down the corridor.

Bates cocked his head to one side; when he judged

Lambston was sufficiently distant, he called, "Ye may enter now, Susan."

The rear door opened, and one of the upstairs maids entered. She peered about the Steward's Room with interest, for she had never seen it before; the lesser servants snatched their meals when they could, in the kitchen. "Och, Mr. Bates," she said, impressed by the table's bounty, "ye do serve quite a spread." In truth, the food was quite the equal of that served in the Great Hall; the *chef de cuisine* ate in the Steward's Room too, and made sure that his companions dined well. Saucily, she snagged a muffin.

The other servants regarded her askance; for a lowly maid to dine in the Steward's Room was unheard of. Indeed, if it had not been clear that she was here at Bates's behest, they would have set at her in the manner of the wolfpack dealing with a rogue that had forgotten its place in the pecking order. "Susan," said Bates soberly, "have ye seen the baron?" Among Susan's responsibilities was making Barthold's bed.

"It's terriber odd," she said through a mouthful of muffin. "His bed hasn't been slept in, nar the sheets turned doon."

"Nar did he break his fast," said Mr. Bates, lips pursed over ruddy countenance. "I canna think where he may be."

"Is that what this is about?" asked the groom of the chambers.

"Yes," said Bates. "The missing spats are a mere red herring; I had Lambston sent off on a wird goose chase, so that we might speak freely." Lambston, being Broderick's man, could be expected to report to his master.

"Sir Bertram and his friends have disappeared as well," pointed out the groom of the chambers.

"Aye," said Bates, "but they can take care of themserves; the baron, however . . ." He sighed. "Moreover, Sir Brodick maintains the baron is aboot the castle, though I ha' seen neither hide nar hair of him." He told

them how Broderick had insisted on carrying up the baron's tray the previous night. "And it was returned
untooched to the kitchen," he said gloomily.

"Do you fear foul play?" asked the groom of the chambers.

"I dee not know what I fear," said Bates, "but we must
search foor him."

"If he is dead," said Sir Bertram's valet, "what sharr we
do?"

"Then, we sharr ask the young master," said Bates with
finality. The others groaned, misdoubting Bertram's judgment, but Bates only looked the sterner. There came a
knocking at the main chamber door.

"Lambston," whispered the groom of the chambers; it
was a logical surmise, as Lambston had been gone long
enough to locate the "missing" spats.

"Joost a second, Mr. Lambston," said Bates loudly.
More quietly, he said, "Can soomeone scout oot the dungeon? If he's—"

"I say," said the door. "Open up in there, Bates."

Surprise was not an expression that came easily to
Bate's face. Indeed, *expression* was not something that
came easily to Bates; under normal circumstances, his face
was frozen in a sort of supercilious obsequence, a dignified mien that altered not a jot no matter how it might be
tested. But at this instant, an observer might have noted
that Bates gave a definite start, that his eyes revealed an
instant of surprise, perhaps even a moment of fondness.
"Open the door, Susan, if you will," he said calmly,
gravitas already restored.

Susan, wide-eyed, did so, for she too had identified the
voice. There in the hall stood Barthold, half supported by
Sidney; behind him was Mabel, leaning on her cane.
"Coome in, my lord," said Bates. They did; one of the lady's
maids hastily evacuated her chair so that Barthold might sit.

"You must hide us, Bates," said Barthold.

Bates drew himself up indignantly. "My lord!" he protested. "This be yer seat. Ye moost not skurk aboot like a dormouse—"

"Have you seen Timaeus?" asked Sidney. "And the others of my party?"

"Nar, marss," said Bates. "They've been oot since yesterday."

"Damn," she said.

"Better free than captive," Barthold told her. "Bates, I fear my brother will try to kill me if he finds me; and he has the allegiance of the guard. I am putting you all in great jeopardy by asking this, I know, but I have nowhere else to turn."

Bates practically quivered with pride and indignation. " 'Tis a sorry pass, my lord," he said. "A sorry pass. We sharr hide ye, of course; we sharr not fail ye now."

"Ye can coont on us, me lord," said the groom of the chambers. There were "ayes" and murmurs of agreement from the others.

A sharp knock came from the door. "There must be some mistake about these spats," said a voice. "Open up, Mr. Bates."

"Take them oot the back passage, Susan," whispered Bates to the upstairs maid. Wide-eyed, she nodded and, cramming the greater part of a muffin into her mouth, led them down a narrow hall.

Bertram, Beatrice, and the others retired to the White Crag, Biddleburg's tavern, to hold a council of war. "Well, I mean, frontal assault, what?" said Bertram. "The right will triumph, eh?"

"Yes," said Kraki. "Ve vill dye the ramparts red vith our blood."

"No, thou silly boy," said Beatrice to Bertram. "That were an approach of desperation, to assault a fortified position with a force of militia and foresters."

"Is that right?" said Bertram doubtfully. "I'm afraid I

avoided military science like the plague at university. What else is there to do? I mean, there's the castle—I imagine Uncle Brod has it sewn up tight by now."

"Now," said Beatrice meaningfully, "is when our magicians must do their all."

"What?" said Timaeus, a little startled.

"Quite right," said Jasper. "We'll have to take a section of the wall. I fly, you teleport; between fireballs and a mind control or two, we ought to be able to neutralize the immediate defenders. We can find some ladders, I suppose? The Band can scale the walls behind us, then—"

"Not all of us are invisible," complained Timaeus. "You don't run any great risk, but all it takes is one spear in my gut—"

"There, there, old man," said Bertram, "screw your courage to the—is it 'spirit gum' I'm looking for?"

"Oh, shut up," said Timaeus testily. "How I ever got involved in this—"

"Look," said Nick. "Why don't we try a parley first? If I were Broderick, I'd be tempted to cut and run."

"You speak wisely," said Beatrice.

A brisk spring breeze blew across the ramparts of Biddleburg Castle, fleecy clouds scudding across the sky. The air was warm and redolent with the smell of growing things. Down below, the town was a scene of feverish activity, hammers banging, saws sawing away, the townsfolk preparing ladders and siege machines. Every once in a while, members of the Band would loft an arrow toward the castle walls; their aim was poor, at this distance, in this wind, but the defenders stood nervously behind crenellations, exposing themselves as little as possible.

"What do you *mean* they've escaped?" shouted Broderick.

"I'm sorry, my lord," said Marek, "but I found the cells empty, save for Lem here—"

"You pathetic pismire," said Broderick, turning on Lem and almost screaming.

"I'm s-s-sorry, my lord," said Lem, shaking in the face of such wrath. "They overpowered me, and—"

"Overpowered you? Overpowered you? A woman in a party dress and a man old enough to be your great-grandfather? Gods, we can't spare the men to comb the castle now."

"My lord," said Captain Blentz soothingly. "If we loot the treasury, take the wagon—a cavalry charge can clear the road—we can be in Hamsterburg, rich men, in days. There comes a time when discretion—"

"You puling wretch," said Broderick, striking Blentz in the face hard enough to leave a crimson mark beneath the captain's stubble. "The next man that talks of flight shall hang. We shall slaughter them, slaughter them all if need be; there is no going back now, no course for us but blood-shed and victory. Rivers of blood may yet flow, and years of desolation pass over—"

"Yes, my lord," said Blentz, backing away. "As you say, my lord."

"A party approaches, sir," said Marek.

And it was true. Coming up toward the castle gate was a group of seven, under flag of truce. Broderick strode along the wall, down toward the gate tower, Blentz scurrying after.

A pot of oil was bubbling there, its fire tended by Gaston. Broderick stood, leaning out from the wall, the tower stair behind him, fearlessly exposing himself to the fire of the archers below—but no arrows came, for the Band was under strict orders to avoid combat till the parley had reached its conclusion.

Bertram was there, in a stretcher born by two foresters. With him were Beatrice and Timaeus; also Master Gorham, of Bainbridge, and Banker Billings, of Biddleburg town.

"Hallo, Uncle," said Bertram.

"Hallo, there, Bertie," said Broderick. "You have made rather a hash of things, you know."

"Well, um, here we are," said Bertram awkwardly. "I say, old man; why don't you open the gate, what? Clemency all round, gaiety and celebration, you can go home to the Lesser Dzorzia no worse for the wear."

"Idiot!" said Broderick. "You and I could have squeezed this barony till the pips squeaked, sucked it dry, lived like kings. You could have gone back to live the high life in Urf Durfal; now, there is nothing but the grave before you. Shall I surrender this fortress to a rabble? Shall I surrender a fortune to my feebleminded nephew? Am I a fool? Begone."

There was a clatter on the tower stairs; Broderick did not look about, perhaps taking the noise for reinforcements. Cannily, he eyed the distance between Bertram's party and the gate, their position relative to the pot of boiling oil; and he reached out one hand to grab the handle of the pot, preparing to tip it over and french-fry his foes—

Suddenly, a cane whacked Broderick in the temple, sending him sprawling against a merlon.

"That'rr be enow o' that, ye caitiff!" said a quavering, elderly voice. Agape, Broderick looked up to see Mistress Mabel, her wispy beard quivering with righteous rage, atop her broom, one hand waving her snake-knobbed cane, circling back through the air for another whack.

From the tower stair burst the servants, Mr. Bates in the lead with an enormous carving knife. Behind him, a footman carried Baron Barthold, the elderly nobleman still too weak to manage the stairs himself. And behind him came Sidney, with her own sword and mail. The other servants, armed with an assortment of cutlery and decorative weapons, pried from their places on the walls of the Great Hall, fanned out across the ramparts.

"Marek!" bellowed Broderick, drawing his own sword. "Gaston! To me! Treachery!"

Soldiers backed uncertainly toward Broderick, weapons out.

"Shall a valet or a scullery maid master you?" shouted Broderick to his men. "Screw your courage to the sticking place!"

"Sticking place! That's it, by Fithold," came Bertram's voice faintly from below.

"Look here, Blentz," Barthold said. "How d'you think the townsfolk will react when you slaughter their baron atop the castle wall, before their very eyes?"

Blentz was ashen, eyes casting about desperately for some means of escape.

By now some score of men had come up to surround Barthold. "Overlapping shields," he ordered. "Slow advance; we'll cut them to ribbons."

"And then what?" demanded Blentz. "We'll be stuck here for—"

"Shut up, you puling wretch!" shouted Barthold. "One more whine from you and—"

"And what?" shouted Blentz back. "Who commands these—"

"Captain Blentz," said Baron Barthold, "surrender, and I give you my word that you and your men may depart this place, unharmed and unhindered."

Blentz looked to Barthold, face a blotchy red, mouth in an angry line. The color of Blentz's face heightened until he looked as if he were about to burst, like a kettle under pressure. "Done," he said at last, practically spitting the word.

Broderick turned on Blentz, thunderstruck. The guardsman looked hesitantly first toward the nobleman, then to their own captain, who sheathed his blade with finality and nodded toward them to do likewise. Gradually, they stepped away from Broderick, lowering their shields and putting their weapons away.

The tableau hung for a long moment, Broderick staring

in shock at Blentz, holding a fighting stance still, his sword wavering in the air.

"Put that silly pig-sticker down, Broderick," said Baron Barthold at last. "It's over."

Broderick pivoted toward his brother, his sword still aloft. His expression turned from shock to grim decision. He tossed his weapon into the air, tumbling it end over end, grabbed it by the blade—cutting a gash in his hand—and rested the pommel on the stone flags of the wall. He held the point to his stomach, and made to throw himself onto his own sword—

Sidney darted forward and tumbled into Broderick shoulder first, knocking him away. Two beefy footmen dived for the man, holding him down and binding his hands.

"What'd you do that for?" demanded Barthold querulously.

"What?" said Sidney, a little surprised. "He was going to kill himself—"

"Yes, yes," said Barthold testily. "Would have been the neatest thing. I shan't slay him, of course; he's family, after all. Have to keep him in a cell for the rest of his life, beastly nuisance. Take him down to the dungeon, thank you, lads."

"I say," said a confused voice from below. "Is that you, Pater? What's going on up there?"

Barthold peered over the wall. "There you are, you miserable sod," he said severely. "How these loins ever produced such a sorry skink as you is beyond my powers of comprehension. I can't imagine—"

"Hold thy tongue," said Beatrice, looking up severely at her lord. "Your son has been the very font of courage and ambition; when at last he realized his duty, he did it with all his main."

"I did?" said Bertram wonderingly.

"You did," said Beatrice, taking his hand.

"Well, well," said Barthold, sounding rather pleased. "Open the gate, someone, won't you?"

IX.

the hall boy cranked away, raising the portcullis. Bates spoke to the master of the hounds, who turned to fly down the tower stair to unbar the gate. As the castle's massive door creaked open, a cheer resounded from the town, echoing from the very battlements; virtually as one, the populace of the barony—Biddlebourgeois, Bainbridger, and forester alike—shouted triumph. Beatrice turned and gaily waved them forward; soon folk poured into the castle courtyard. Barthold stood bemusedly in the window of the tower, staring down at the tumult and waving to acknowledge the cheers. He turned to Bates and said, "Ale all around, Mr. Bates; I trust we have casks enough in the cellar?"

"I sharr attend tee it, my lord," said Bates with satisfaction, and made his way sedately down the stairs.

When the ale arrived, the assemblage quickly turned into an impromptu celebration; the folk raised stoups of ale, and steins, and mugs. Bates was hard-pressed to find containers enough, for soon a fair portion of the barony's population stood in the courtyard, the crowd overflowing through the gates to the field before the walls.

Barthold gave a short speech, thanking everyone for their loyalty, and telling them of his poisoning; there were hisses, and the folk called out for Broderick's death, but Barthold did not acknowledge the cry. Beatrice, too, spoke, announcing that this was a time for reconciliation and asking that her men forget and forgive whatever offense others of the barony might have given them in the course of the struggle. And lastly, Bertram spoke. His speech was short and rather lackadaisical, but it was cheered to the echo. "Hurrah for Sir Bertram!" the folk cheered. "Hurrah for the tax holiday."

"The what?" asked Baron Barthold sharply.

"Tax holiday," said Timaeus, nose in a stein of ale.

"Tax *what*?" said Barthold.

"Better ask Bertram," said Timaeus, slightly amused.

Barthold cast about for his son, but caught no glimpse of him. Bertram was off at one side of the courtyard, back against the wall, staring yearningly at Beatrice, who stood amid a knot of Bandsmen, laughing and talking gaily.

Jasper had laid out the scenario so neatly; what was it he'd said? "Having gained the ramparts, you will free your father from durance vile, wed the noble Beatrice, and unite the people of your realm in glorious harmony." Wasn't quite how it had worked out, was it? He hadn't won the castle in heroic battle; the castle had more or less liberated itself, albeit Blentz probably wouldn't have surrendered if there hadn't been an army outside the walls. True, Beatrice was being slightly kinder to him than before, but only slightly; if Jasper had counted on Bertram's heroism and selfless devotion to win her over, he'd had scant opportunity to display those qualities.

It had been a pipe dream from the start, he realized miserably. He had always known he was not among the brightest men; his ambitions had been limited to membership in a decent club, a good box at the races, an adequate cellar, and an income large enough to live in reasonable comfort. He had not asked to be made heir to this backwoods demesne, nor to lead men in battle, nor to act the hero.

He considered searching out Jasper and asking the wizard's advice, but decided against it. He had a fair idea what that advice would be; something along the lines of taking her in his strong arms and passionately declaring his love. Jasper was an incurable romantic, and Bertram had no desire to expose himself to inevitable rejection. Especially not in public. And besides which, thought Bertram, pinching his biceps, he had the arms of an upper-class wastrel, not a hero of yore.

About him, folk laughed and sang and drank themselves insensible; it had the feeling of a day that would live in their memory always, the day the barony was liberated from the Tyrant Broderick. Their joy only increased his misery. The whole barony, it seemed, was happy this day, every man and woman, save only he.

Well, maybe not the whole barony, Bertram thought. I imagine Broderick isn't too chuffed right about now, either.

"Good morning, Sir Bertram," said Bertram's valet, yanking the draperies firmly back.

Bertram groaned, shading his eyes against the bright sunlight. "You are a tyrant, Smythe; you know that, don't you?" he moaned.

"Terribly sorry, sir," said Smythe, lifting the teapot from the tray he had placed by Bertram's bedside table and pouring a cup for his master. "It is nine of the clock, and the household has already assembled in the Great Hall; your father was asking for you particularly."

"Ye gods," complained Bertram, "after carousing all

night, they're up at this hour? My head feels as if a dozen blacksmiths have been using it as an anvil all night long."

"I had anticipated this, sir," said Smythe, proffering a mug containing a viscous yellow liquid. "Your usual pick-me-up."

Bertram shuddered, but accepted it. "Ah," he said, "the first terror of the day." He quaffed it in a single gulp, lunging for his teacup to wash it down. He gasped, gave a single hoarse cough, and said, "Effective, if brutal."

"I've laid out a set of clothes for you, if you don't mind, sir—"

"Yes, all right, Smythe," said Bertram, maneuvering his limbs over the side of the bed, "but I shall need some assistance with this leg of mine."

"I had anticipated as much," said the valet.

Bertram was dressed in surprisingly short order; almost as soon as he was, someone tapped at the door. While Bertram leaned on his crutch and fiddled with his cravat, Smythe opened the door.

It was Beatrice. Bertram's heart took a leap to see her; she wore a black velvet dress, flounced fashionably below the waist but tight above it, a dress épée belted at her middle. Freckles were dusted across her face, her arms, her upper torso; with difficulty, Bertram stopped himself from imagining where else they ran. "Good morning, Bertie," she said cheerily. "Coming down?"

"I suppose," said Bertram, levering himself toward the door.

"Here, let me," said Beatrice, and took his free arm in her own, providing some support. Bertram's mouth went dry at the touch; he wasn't quite certain whether he was in misery or ecstasy. They made their way out the door and down the hall.

"The baron's mood is sunny," Beatrice said. "He rose at six, and has been cheery since. He was perturbed by your promise of a tax holiday, I fear."

Bertram groaned. "I'd forgotten about that," he said. "Oh gods, he'll kill me."

She patted his arm. "I spoke with him about it," she said.

"And?" said Bertram as they neared the grand stairs.

"He accepts that it was a necessary gesture. At any pass, there's always the revenues of the toll road."

"I suppose," said Bertram gloomily, nonetheless dreading his arrival in the Great Hall. He swung his crutch out and placed it on the first stair below, stepping down with part of his weight on Beatrice's shoulder. They stopped talking for a moment, progress down the stairs requiring a degree of concentration. It was difficult work for Bertram, made the more difficult because his heart beat like a rabbit's at Beatrice's touch. He was in agony, for he knew that whatever there had once been between them was lost; he had been inconstant, had failed to correspond while at school, had foolishly believed the lies of his uncle. Had she not made clear how she felt? True, she had mellowed toward him since that disastrous conversation in the woods, but love, once lost, cannot be renewed. He longed for the hour she would leave to return to Bainbridge, for her presence was painful; simultaneously, he dreaded that moment, for the parting would no doubt be a final one.

He would join the fight against the orcs, that's what he would do; perhaps he could get himself killed in some futile, bloody charge. Yes, that was the ticket; a meaningless, anonymous death in the meat-grinder that was war, the perfect anodyne for spurned love—

"So," said Beatrice softly, "when shall we wed, my love?"

Bertram was in the process of levering his crutch down the next slick marble step. He gave a sudden lurch. The crutch went flying. Beatrice made a grab for him, but too late; his legs crumpled, he fell down the stairs head first, pulling his limbs into a fetal position, cartwheeling down the high marble steps. At last, he thumped into the carpet at the bottom of the stairs, rolled across the floor, and hurtled into a priceless Dzorzique tabouret, smashing it, the smoked-glass lamp atop it, and several guineas worth of bric-a-brac to flinders.

Hands at her mouth, Beatrice peered down the stairs. "Bertram?" she said. "Are you all right?"

"What, me?" said a happy voice from a pile of rubble. "Never better, my love. Absolutely peachy. Blissful, in fact. Do summon a cleric, though, if you will; I fear I've broken the other leg."

Beaming for all he was worth, Baron Barthold held high his fluted glass of *vin chartreuse*. "To the girl next door," he said. "To hearts entwined. I want you to know, my dear, you've made more than one man very happy today; I only hope you can make something of this sorry excuse of a son."

"Hear, hear," said the assembled, sipping wine. They all sat down at table, while servants circulated with an enormous platter holding hotcakes and pastries. It was unusual to quaff wine at breakfast, but the baron was in a celebratory mood.

A footman entered and marched smartly up toward Barthold, leaning down to whisper in the baron's ear.

"All's well that ends well, what?" said Jasper with satisfaction, green wine disappearing into a spot of green.

"Bosh, Jasper," said Timaeus, "you do have a gift for cliché—"

"Have either of you seen Vic?" interrupted Sidney. "I haven't seen him since he teleported away after the archery competition."

"No," said Timaeus, turning toward her in concern. "I truly haven't—"

"I'm sorry," said Barthold, rising somberly. "I'm afraid I have bad news." All eyes were on him at once.

"What now?" said Timaeus.

"It appears that my brother has escaped. Apparently, he picked the lock with a length of spring metal—"

Sidney smacked her forehead. "Damn!" she said. "I should have told the servants to get rid of that couch."

"That's not all, I'm afraid," said Barthold. "Messieurs, mademoiselle; it appears that your wagon and its cargo are gone."

Nick shot to his feet. "What?"

Barthold looked quite apologetic. "Our best horses, and your wagon, are missing from the stable."

"Out of the frying pan into the fire," said Jasper.

"You are really becoming quite tiresome, do you know that?" said Timaeus.

"Ve vill track him down and kill him," said Kraki.

Sidney pushed back her chair with a sigh. "Well," she said, "no rest for the weary."

"Not you too," complained Timaeus.

part II.

another week, another wilderness

1.

Black and silver was the night, the black velvet of the sky, the silver of stars and moon; black conifers looming upward, the stones of the road silver in reflected starlight. In the stillness of the night came black fury; the beat of hooves on stone, the rumble of wheels, the crack of a whip. Broderick half-stood atop the cart, knees absorbing jolts, lashing the horses onward.

He spared no thought for mishap; despite what he had claimed, the road was in excellent repair, the curves gentle and the grade slight between Biddleburg and Bainbridge. He thought rather of pursuit: He had hours at most before his absence was discovered. And when it was, there would be pursuit, no doubt of that; perhaps his kin would be content to see him gone, but Bertram's friends would surely pursue their property.

In the cart was Stantius, ensconced below the floorboards. The cart had no other load; Broderick had tossed the rugs to lighten it, had not cared to risk discovery by spending time to locate and load supplies. He'd get hungry, he knew, but speed was of the essence. That statue alone was his fortune, wealth enough to buy an army, a kingdom. Pah, let his brother have this petty little land in these impoverished mountains, surviving off its meager tolls; if he could make good his escape, untold riches awaited him. And riches were power.

The cart had no load save for Stantius—and an old man, wrapped in a blanket, toothlessly cursing Broderick's unrelenting and uncomfortable haste. Somehow, Broderick had failed to see the old man; perhaps some slight glamor of magic was to blame.

Hooves beat on stone, wheels rumbled. The wagon creaked as they tore around a curve.

Ahead on the road were dim shapes, silver moonlight glinting off silver mail. A chill ran down Broderick's spine; should he charge on regardless, hoping they would go down under the horses' hooves? But no, he saw pikes, spearheads glowing with magic in the darkness: enchanted weapons. The horses would simply run themselves onto the pikes, and that would be that. "Hyaw!" he shouted, hauling back on the reins. The horses slowed, slowed, came to a halt bare cubits from the waiting—children?

No, not children, Broderick saw; their stature was slight, but they were not humans of any age. Large black eyes stared out from beneath silver helms, ears pointing upward: elves.

Half a dozen blocked the road, kneeling, pikes set to intercept his horses had he charged on; another half dozen stood in the trees, holding elven longbows with arrows nocked.

From the woods stepped another elf, hands empty, sword at belt, tasseled cap above merry expression. "Hiya," he said cheerily.

Bright morning sun poured in through watchtower windows. Jasper flitted impatiently about. "Speed is of the essence, my lord," he told Barthold. "My companions ready their horses even now. We must—"

"Hold on, hold on," said the baron irritably, still out of breath from the climb. "He's only had a few hours, we may still be able to see something—"

"Yes, yes, but do get on with it," said Jasper.

The baron read the runes incised in the wall about the window, refreshing his memory of the scrying spell. Like his brother, he was no collegiate adept, but any nobleman was expected to have a certain capacity for magic. He had always keenly felt the lack of deeper knowledge, in fact, which was why he had insisted that his son attend university. Panting between syllables, Barthold read the spell.

He walked carefully about until the road toward Urf Durfal came into view. Then he slowly moved his head to bring sections of it into focus, mile by mile, down the mountain and toward the barony's border.

"Well?" said Jasper, the point of green light hanging expectantly above Barthold's shoulder.

"Settle down, damn it," said the baron. There was nothing down the Durfalian way. He moved to the opposite window and began to survey the eastern road, down toward Hamsterburg. Several moments passed.

"Hold on," he said.

"What is it?" demanded Jasper.

"How very odd," said the baron.

Jasper made a noise indicative of exasperated inquiry.

Barthold said, "Come here." The light flew directly toward him. "Take careful note of where I stand," said the baron. "I shall move aside; take up my position, and read the spell you see on the window above you."

The baron moved; Jasper read the spell. After a moment, he said, "Well?"

"Don't you see it?"

"I have an excellent view of a small pond and a beaver.

I hadn't known they had orange teeth; why is that, do you think?"

The baron studied Jasper's position. "Move about a bit, until the road comes into focus."

Experimentally, Jasper flew in slight circles, until he said, "Oh. I see what you mean."

Down there on the road, perhaps a half dozen miles from the castle, was the wagon, apparently abandoned. The horses that had drawn it were out of the traces, tied to nearby trees, cropping quietly at the brush on the roadside verge.

"Where could he have gone?" wondered Jasper.

"An excellent question," said Barthold.

"I don't suppose the statue is still there," said Jasper.

"You'd better go have a look," said Barthold.

Jasper flew out the window toward his companions, who waited expectantly in the courtyard below, already mounted.

Nick poked his head out of the wagon. "It's gone," he reported.

Sidney sighed; she had expected as much. Jasper flitted about, apparently mumbling some kind of spell, perhaps hoping to pick up the traces of Broderick's presence. Baron Barthold sat his horse patiently, looking rather tired. Timaeus disconsolately thumbed weed into his pipe, while Kraki merely looked bored.

Beatrice, who had been kneeling in the vegetation along the verge, rose to her feet. "Look here," she said, sweeping a hand to indicate the brush around her.

"Ah, yes," said Timaeus. "Weeds. Goldenrod, isn't it? And are those lupines? Is there anything in particular we're supposed to be seeing?"

"Look at the color," said Beatrice.

They were silent for a moment. "It's a lighter green,"

said Nick. It was true; a swath of the vegetation was lighter in color than the weeds around it.

"Quite so," said Beatrice, nodding. "It is the light green of early spring, of new shoots putting forth. Why this should be, I cannot say."

"Hmm," said Timaeus thoughtfully, tamping his pipe. "Suppose one were to haul a heavy object through the wood—"

"How?" demanded Jasper.

"How should I know? Suppose they had some great draft horse—"

"A damned great draft horse," said Jasper. "Stantius must weigh a ton."

"Do shut up until I'm finished, there's a good man," said Timaeus irritably. "Suppose they were to drag it through the woods; it would leave an unmistakable trail, would it not?"

"Assuredly," said Beatrice.

"Suppose then that a nature mage was among them, who might order the vegetation to grow behind, to cover the evidence of their passage. Would not such vegetation be lighter in color, as are new-grown plants in the early spring?"

"Interesting," said Jasper. "But if Broderick had such a wizard as an ally, why did he not summon the mage to help him defend Biddleburg Castle against us?"

"Maybe the wizard wasn't an ally," said Nick. "Maybe Broderick was ambushed."

"By whom?" asked Sidney.

"Who can say?" said Timaeus.

"Well," said Jasper after a brief silence. "Look here, My Lord Barthold; I presume that Sir Broderick's personal effects remain at Biddleburg Castle?"

"I assume so," said Barthold. "If I were Broddy, and I'd just escaped from the dungeon, I wouldn't go skulking

about in search of the odd pair of socks before running
away."

"Good," said Jasper briskly. "Then let's find those
socks, and I shall use the same spell to trace the baleful
Broderick that I used to locate the beauteous Beatrice.
Shall we return to the castle?"

Sidney sighed. "Might as well," she said. "It looks like
this is going to be a long pursuit; we'd better get some
supplies together."

"Damn," said Nick as they saddled up. "I wish we knew
where Vic was."

"True," said Timaeus, wheeling his horse. "His absence
is disturbing. Given the fact that his wits are only intermit-
tently keen, it may be he's forgotten our whole enterprise."

"It's not that," said Nick, clucking his mare into motion.
"It's—I always figured Vic would save our bacon, if push
came to shove."

"Beg pardon?" said Timaeus.

"I figured, if we got into deep trouble, he'd always bail
us out," Nick explained. "After all, he's got the power of
a dozen mages. Even if he isn't altogether there, in mortal
danger he'd probably snap to."

"Our own private *deus ex machina*," said Timaeus. "A
nice thought."

"Doesn't matter anyway," said Sidney shortly. "He isn't
here."

They rode onward.

The socks were brown, worn, and quite odoriferous.
They hung below the point of green light; despite Jasper's
near invisibility, one got the impression he was keeping
them as distant from his invisible nose as he was able.

"I hadn't meant socks in the literal sense," complained
Jasper. "I meant it in a metaphorical way. Anything associated sufficiently intimately with the man himself will
do."

Timaeus chortled. "You'd be hard put to find anything more intimately associated with Broderick," he pointed out. "They are imbued with his very, ah, essence."

"Yes, well, essence, in the sense that a perfume is an essence," said Jasper. "Not essence in the sense of unique character—"

"I'd say they capture Uncle's unique character quite well, actually," said Bertram from his sedan chair, to which his broken legs confined him. "His morals stink; so do his socks. His welcome has worn thin; so have the heels."

"Can't ask for better similarity between spell object and target than that," said Timaeus complacently.

"All right, all right," grumbled Jasper. "Here goes." He chanted his spell.

"Anything?" asked Sidney when he was done.

"Yes, actually," said Jasper. "He's—this way." The green light flew in a straight line toward one end of the chamber.

Beatrice watched it, then glanced out the tower window. "East by southeast, I make it," she said. They bent over the map on the table.

"Are you sure?" said Sidney incredulously, looking up at Jasper.

"This direction, all right," said Jasper. "No mistake. Unless someone else has been wearing these things."

"Scant chance of that," said Bertram. "I found them balled up in his boots."

"You can't have gotten the spell wrong?" Sidney said.

"I have not," Jasper replied.

Timaeus peered over Sidney's shoulder at the map. "But you have him striking straight across trackless wilderness," he said.

"The wildwood," agreed Beatrice.

"Leagues and leagues of it," said Sidney, a finger tracing the route.

"Very well," said Jasper. "Let us gather provisions, and go."

"But how could he possibly carry the statue through—" said Nick.

"How should I know?" said Jasper. "We'll ask him when we find him."

"You'd best leave your horses," said Beatrice. "That's mountainous terrain; the vegetation is quite dense, and there's little forage. They'd just slow you down."

"Oh, bloody wonderful," said Timaeus. "Hiking over hill and dale, up and down mountains and through leech-infested swamps. I'm not exactly the hardened wilderness explorer, you know."

"You think maybe you can save the world by sitting in an armchair and sipping brandy before the fire?" demanded Sidney. "If you aren't willing to face a little hardship, why did you embark on this damned quest?"

"Why *shouldn't* one be able to save the world while sipping brandy before the fire?" asked Timaeus. "What is it about quests that involves dire peril and travail? Who arranges these things, anyhow?"

"Ask Vic when you see him," said Sidney. "He seems to be the expert on quests."

"All very well for you to say," complained Timaeus. "Not that we've got a chance of success without Vic, you know. What are we going to do if we reach Arst-Kara-Morn without him? Knock on the Dark Lord's door and say, 'Please sir, release the spirit of Stantius Human-King so the forces of freedom can beat your nasty orcs and things, and we can all go home?' Vincianus is the only one who has the slightest idea how to—"

"I swear to all the gods," said Sidney, "I can't imagine how I ever got hooked up with such a whiner. We've got to go after Broderick; we don't have any choice. Come or not, see if I give a damn."

"Oh, I'm coming, I'm coming," said Timaeus unhap-

pily. "But I don't have to like it. I don't suppose you'd
come, Lady Beatrice? We could use a woodswise companion."

"See here, Timaeus," said Bertram, slightly alarmed.
"You won't be taking my betrothed away, will you?"

"I'm sorry," said Beatrice. "I'm needed here. The
barony—"

"Yes, yes," said Jasper. "But it would be useful to have
someone who knows the woods. Could a member of the
Band perhaps be persuaded to join us?"

Beatrice thought for a moment. "Frer Mortise, I think,"
she said.

They stood in the castle courtyard in the new day's
light, the sky still rosy, the air a little chill. Timaeus picked
up his pack uneasily. "This must weigh five stone," he
said.

"Two, two and a half," said Sidney, bustling about and
making sure the last of the supplies were packed away.
"Kraki, help him get it on, will you?"

"Sure," said Kraki genially, slinging his own pack easily
over one shoulder. "Turn around. Put arms back. Here ve
go."

Timaeus did as requested, extending his arms awkwardly behind him.

"Oopsy-daisy," said Kraki, looping the straps over
Timaeus's shoulders and letting the pack go. Timaeus staggered under the weight. "Good heavens," he grumbled.

"Chin up," said Jasper, zipping about.

"I don't see you with a pack," said Timaeus.

"Couldn't fly," said Jasper. "Limit to the weight I can
carry."

"Very convenient," said Timaeus.

Beatrice approached with a lanky, long-haired man.
"This is Frer Mortise," she said cheerfully. He was pallid,
painfully thin, and wore circular spectacles with lenses that

were almost black. His garb was forest green and at his belt was a large silver sickle. He bore a gnarled wooden staff, and a pack at his back, like the others. He nodded in greeting.

"What's your cult, Brother?" asked Timaeus.

"Deeset," said Mortise, in a reedy, high-pitched voice. The moon goddess; nature-aligned, but with some fairly unpleasant traits. Her worshipers were mostly elves, women, and therianthropes. Sidney smiled.

"Vhere is Nicky?" inquired Kraki.

"Yes," said Timaeus, "where is he, Sidney?"

"What am I, his keeper?" she said. "How the hell—"

"Here he is," said Jasper.

Nick approached, looking faintly uncomfortable. Behind him, one of the scullery maids trudged slowly, eyes red with recent tears. As Nick took up his pack, she burst into sobs again, turned, and ran back toward the kitchen door.

"What are we waiting for?" Nick said. Beatrice was looking at him rather coldly; to his surprise, he blushed.

"Ve go," said Kraki.

And they departed.

They climbed a rise, feet sinking into the leaf mold; oaks and chestnuts stood about them. Timaeus lagged behind, already puffing. Mortise strolled with him, quite at ease.

"Wonderful day," said the cleric. Timaeus grunted.

"Look," said Mortise, pointing to a large, shelf-like fungus growing from the bole of an elderly oak.

Timaeus looked. "Edible?" he asked.

"No," said Mortise. He reached up into a hollow in the tree and pulled out a squirrel. The little red creature chattered in rage and tried to bite the cleric's hand, but he held it too expertly.

Mortise pulled his sickle from his belt, whacked off the creature's head, and sucked blood from the stump of its neck. "Want some?" he asked, holding out the limp little body.

"I'll pass, thanks," said Timaeus faintly.

Sidney sprang for the brook's far bank. Her foot slipped on mud, and she went sprawling full-length into the water. Kraki, who had bounded over the brook with consummate ease, gave her a hand up. "Good thing varm day," said Kraki. "You dry out qvickly."

"Yeah, I suppose," said Sidney, shaking her limbs. A little sandbar along the bank of the stream held a footprint of some kind—not the print of a human sole. Her attention captured, she examined it more closely. It was a hoofprint, rather horse-like but quite large.

Mortise leapt lightly across the stream. He studied the print Sidney had found. "Unicorn," he said.

"Unicorn?" said Sidney unbelievingly. They were rare and notoriously skittish.

"Sure," said Mortise, and headed off into the woods.

Timaeus came up, panting heavily. He splashed heedlessly through the water and nearly ran into Sidney. He stopped and teetered for a moment under the weight of his pack.

"Unicorn," said Sidney, nodding toward the hoofprint.

He stared at her uncomprehendingly for a moment; gradually, a glimmer of understanding penetrated fatigue-dulled eyes. He glanced at the hoofprint. "Pshaw," he scoffed.

"Mortise says it's a unicorn," she said.

They camped in a pine grove on a gentle slope above a stream. Mortise had shown them how to pitch the tents, and had collected enough wood to start a blaze, something they all appreciated; the day had been warm, but the night sky was clear and their elevation was high. The temperature was rapidly dropping.

Nick scanned the skies above them. He was acutely

aware that dragons inhabited the Dzorzian Range.
Vincianus had promised there wouldn't be any, not on this
quest; but Vincianus wasn't around, and had probably forgotten his promise anyway. It would be just their luck if
some dragon took it into its head to have them for dinner.

They wouldn't have a prayer of defeating a dragon, not by
force of arms; and, Nick realized uncomfortably, one of their
two wizards would be useless against a wyrm. Fireballs
wouldn't faze a monster that belched fire after every meal.

Timaeus sat on the needled ground by the fire, leaning
back against his pack, eyes half closed with fatigue, luxu-
riating in the warmth. A copper pot bubbled above the
blaze, filled with skinned squirrel, mushrooms, and wild
onions—Mortise's gleanings of the day.

They heard the crash of a large beast in the woods.
"Dragon!" shouted Nick, looking for someplace to hide.
Everyone else leapt for weapons—except for Timaeus, who
barely roused himself enough to look.

It wasn't a dragon. An ogre walked into the circle of
light cast by the fire. He stood a good ten feet tall. His hair
was matted and filthy; he was clad in uncured deer hide,
and a knife as long as Kraki's sword hung at his belt. In
one hand was an enormous wooden bucket.

"Die, foul vight!" shouted Kraki, hurtling toward the
monster. His sword bit into the ogre's leggings, through
deer hide and into the straw the monster had packed within
them for warmth. It was doubtful the blade penetrated as
far as the ogre's flesh.

"Hey!" boomed the ogre. "Don't do dat." He kicked
Kraki across the clearing. The barbarian tumbled, plowing
through pine needles to smash into the trunk of a tree.
Somehow, he managed to keep his grip on his sword.

The monster upended his bucket over the fire, extin-
guishing the blaze and splashing Timaeus, who sprang to
his feet, fatigue forgotten. "What is the meaning of this?"
Timaeus shouted.

"Very bad fing, fire in woods," scolded the ogre, waving a sausage-like finger. "Nasty bad humans. Make forest fire. Scare all liddle animals." And with that, he turned and strode away, tree limbs cracking in his wake.

There was silence for a moment. Kraki stood up, shaking each of his limbs in turn, making sure nothing was broken. Timaeus poked disconsolately at the sodden remnants of their once-cheery blaze. "Damn it all," he said. "I'm freezing." In truth, it was rather cold.

"I don't think it's a good idea to start another fire," said Nick, greatly relieved it hadn't been a dragon after all. "He might come back."

"Then ve kill," said Kraki.

"Sure, pal," said Nick. "You did such a good job the first time."

"He got me by surprise," protested the barbarian. "Am I not Kraki, son of Kronar, son of—"

"Shut up," said Sidney. "There's no point in fighting that thing if we don't have to. The last thing we need is for someone to get badly wounded out here, miles from nowhere."

Timaeus sneezed, visibly shivering. "Fine," he said. "See if I care. I *like* pneumonia."

"Get out of those wet clothes," Mortise advised.

Timaeus grunted and went to search through his pack. Mortise retrieved the stew pot, which, miraculously, had not been upset. He pulled out a squirrel leg and bit into it. "Well," he said, "it's *partly* cooked."

Disconsolately, they sat in chilly darkness, eating half-raw rodent and onions still fresh enough to bring tears to the eyes.

"Rise and shine!" sang Nick. He and Mortise were already puttering about, striking tents and packing up. Timaeus woke, bleary-eyed and fatigued. He habitually rose early, but this was absurd; there was the merest glimmer of rose on the horizon. He had slept like the dead, exhausted from the previous day's trek, but his back was killing him. He peered under his bedroll and saw a root that must have been pressing against his spine for hours. "Tea," he moaned.

"No fire," said Sidney, handing him a stick of something brown. "Here."

Timaeus held it gingerly, at arm's length. "And what, pray, is this?" he asked.

"Beef jerky," she said, masticating a stick to prove the point. "Breakfast."

"Ah," said Timaeus. "Excellent." He essayed a bite and nearly lost a molar.

"Makes you feel like a new man," said Jasper, whizzing over to help Nick pack. "Nothing like the great outdoors—"

"Ye gods," muttered Timaeus. He went over and took a tin of tea leaves from his pack, then grabbed Mortise's pot and headed down to the stream.

Sidney hustled over and grabbed his arm. "I said no fire. We don't—"

"Unhand me, madam," said Timaeus. "I shall start no blaze." Reluctantly, Sidney let go, but followed him down to the stream to make sure. Timaeus washed out the pot, filled it with water, dumped a quantity of leaves into it, then chanted a brief spell and thrust his fist into the water. After a few moments, it began to boil around his hand, the water turning brown as the tea infused it. "There, you see?" said Timaeus. "Nary so much as a whiff of smoke." He withdrew his hand and headed back up the hill, steam rising from the pot. Sidney snuck a glance at his hand, half expecting it to be scalded red, but it seemed unaffected by its immersion in boiling water.

Everyone accepted a cup of tea, with thanks. Timaeus sat down on his pack to enjoy his morning pipe and cuppa, but before he had even poured his second cup, Sidney was ordering him to his feet. "We've got leagues ahead of us," she scolded, "and no time to waste."

Timaeus groaned, lurched to his feet, and consented, grumbling, to have Kraki hoist up his pack once more.

When they reached a grove of oaks, Mortise called a break for lunch. Everyone removed packs and began to prepare for the meal. Everyone, that is, except for Timaeus, who did not appear until minutes later. He staggered into the grove, drenched in sweat, panting raggedly, and stumbled blindly onward. He might have staggered back off into the woods, oblivious to the others, if Sidney hadn't taken his arm and brought him to a halt. He stared at her dumbly for a while, then crumpled to the ground.

It was a good ten minutes before he roused himself even enough to light his pipe. Sidney, worried, brought him a flask of water, which he gulped greedily down. "It'll get better," she told him.

Timaeus considered that for a moment. It was a difficult concept to grasp. Better? In what sense? Were there superior and inferior versions of torture? And which was the better? The most painful, or the least? "Define your terms," he said tiredly.

The others were already preparing for departure. "We've got to go on," Sidney said. "Jasper claims Broderick's lead is widening. We don't dare stop—"

"Mm hm," said Timaeus, not considering further conversation worth the effort. He got to his hands and knees, then used a nearby tree to pull himself erect. Pipe clenched in his teeth, he extended his hands behind his back and waited until Kraki got the hint, lifted Timaeus's pack, and dropped it onto his shoulders.

Under the impact, Timaeus pitched face forward into leaf mold. Coals spilled from his pipe into the leaves, which started to smolder. Nick stamped them out.

Haltingly, Timaeus got to his hands and knees, crawled to his pipe, and pocketed it.

"I take his pack," said Kraki, already wearing his own.

"Are you sure?" said Sidney. "Two packs are a good fifty pounds."

"Good," said Kraki. "Then maybe I break a little sveat." Muscles like steel cables bunched in his arms.

Timaeus was scrabbling at a tree, trying to get to his feet once more. Kraki removed the wizard's pack; Timaeus hardly seemed to notice, except that he was now able to stand erect.

They climbed onward, up a ridge, Sidney trailing with Timaeus to make sure he did not fall too far behind.

The little glade was pleasant after the cool dimness of the forest, a roughly circular space where only grasses and wildflowers grew. Leaf-dappled light played across the ground. Perhaps a fire had cleared the trees here, and they had not yet grown back; perhaps some local peculiarity of the soil prevented the growth of timber. At the glade's center stood a boulder, perhaps glacial in origin. Not far away, a charming stream purled. All in all, the place seemed most inviting to travel-wearied wanderers. Sidney called a rest.

Timaeus came out of the forest, hobbling as if shackled. Nick guided him to the central boulder; the wizard lay with his back against it.

Kraki dropped his packs and shook his head like a dog; droplets of sweat flung everywhere. "Ho!" he said. "Feels good to vork for a change. Ve go on or camp here?"

"If we can make a few hours before sundown, we should," said Sidney, feeling a little tired herself. "I say we—"

She was interrupted by a snore. Timaeus lay openmouthed, drooling a bit into his beard.

"Oh, hell," said Sidney.

Jasper, who had muttered the Words of a spell, said, "He's a little farther away now than last evening."

"Broderick, you mean?" said Nick.

"Yes," said Jasper.

"How does he do it?" demanded Sidney. "He's laden with that statue, he's got to be in his fifties—"

"And he's apparently traveling with a unicorn," said Jasper. "No knowing what he's up to."

"How much farther away?" asked Sidney.

"I'm sorry; I'm afraid I can't tell. It's really a directional spell; he's off in that direction," Jasper said, pointing roughly to the east-southeast. "I can get a vague sense of distance from the strength of the feeling, but not much more than that."

Sidney looked at sleeping Timaeus. "I suppose we'd better camp here," she said regretfully. "We're not going to catch up soon, anyway, so there's no point in driving ourselves beyond endurance."

"*Our*selves?" said Nick pointedly.

"We're in this together," said Sidney.

"I don't think this is a good place," said Mortise apologetically, looking about the glade and frowning slightly.

"Why not?" asked Sidney.

"It doesn't feel right," said Mortise.

"Vhat?" said Kraki. "Don't be silly. Vater that vay." He pointed to a stream, not far off in the woods. "Good drainage. Soft grass to lie on. Make fire by boulder, shelter from breeze. Sleep under open stars. Fine campsite."

Mortise looked uncertainly about. "Yes," he said uncertainly. "But—"

Kraki was already unrolling his blanket.

Mortise sighed and opened his leather pouch. He'd killed three woodlarks and a number of finches during the day. There wasn't much meat on songbirds, but woodlarks were actually quite delicious. And he had the eggs from one of their nests. Still, it wasn't really enough for dinner.

Jasper was watching him. "Not to worry," he said, and the green light zipped away into the woods.

A half hour later, Nick was contemplating the necessity of making a meal of cornmeal mush. "Is this all we've got?" he complained.

"There's raisins, pemmican, jerky, and hardtack," said Sidney. "Enough to live on for several days, but something fresh would be better."

"Fresh?" said Nick. "You call cornmeal mush fresh?"

"Come off it, Nick," she said. "It's better than—"

A doe came walking into the campsite. She walked over to Kraki and stood there, silent and trembling. Everyone stared in astonishment.

"Well, hurry up," said Jasper irritably, flitting through the air behind her. "Kill her, by all means. I can't control her forever, you know."

Kraki drew his sword.

"Better if you age the meat," said Kraki sleepily and gave an enormous belch. The remains of a haunch lay before him.

"Didn't like it, I can tell," said Nick with satisfaction; he had prepared and roasted the deer.

Mortise gathered up the scraps and went to throw them into the latrine. He regretted that; better to throw them into the woods and let animals eat the remains—but they wouldn't want to be bothered by predators and animal noises tonight.

By the time he got back, everyone else was asleep. He hesitated; he still felt a sense of wrongness about the place.

He sighed, then took his bedroll and walked several paces into the wood before laying it down. Perhaps the others were right; what was there in the woods to harm them?

Moving out of the glade might be a pointless precaution, but he felt the better for it.

II.

It started as a single note; a single haunting note, like the sound of a flute in the hands of a master: low, rich, evocative of loss. Sleepily, Sidney raised her head from her bedroll and looked about the campsite. The fire had gone out, only a few embers remaining. Above, a sliver of moon glinted silver. In the cool night air, fireflies played, green lights winking out and reappearing. If she hadn't been a city girl, it might have occurred to Sidney that it was late, near midnight: too late for fireflies. And early in the year, yet, for them to appear in such numbers.

A birdcall, she thought, and turned over to go back to sleep.

At the edge of her consciousness, a song began to play. It did not occur to her to wonder at that; half asleep, she took it for a dream. It was slow, sad, ancient music: a single flute. No, it had not the metallic sparkle of a flute; it was more like a recorder, rich wooden tones.

And then the music changed. Joining the flute was another, and a string instrument as well. Sidney was no musician, but she thought it might be a lute. Still the music mourned; what, precisely, she could not say, but she could feel the sense of loss. She lifted her head again.

The little meadow was bright now; not the bright of day, but full-moon bright—peculiar, for the moon was a crescent still. Atop the boulder by which they'd built the fire was a creature; a little goat-legged creature, with the goateed face of a man. At his lips were pipes; not a flute at all, nor yet a recorder, but panpipes. His legs were crossed, one hoofed foot moving to the music's beat. He never seemed to breathe, playing the music continually. About him, fireflies glowed.

Smiling, Sidney sat up and listened. Somehow this struck her as completely natural, that there should be music here. It never occurred to her to wonder whether this was dream or reality, whether the creature meant them well or ill. There were no questions, only the music, and wonderment only at its beauty.

Those fireflies were not insects; not fireflies at all, but fays, glowing winged creatures, shaped like tiny men and women. Sidney had heard of them before, but never seen them; they were kin, somehow, to the elves. They hovered in the air like hummingbirds, listening attentively to the tune.

Where were the other musicians? Sidney looked about. One sat at the foot of the rock, lute in hand. It was a raccoon, for all that it was dressed like a man, furred face bending seriously over the lute, clever clawed fingers plucking the strings. And the other piper—was nowhere to be seen. Pipes floated in the air by the foot of the rock, as if the piper sat there; but whoever played them, if indeed they did not play themselves, was invisible. None of this struck Sidney as unusual.

Her companions were awake now, too, sitting up and listening to the music. Their faces betrayed nothing but peace, gentle concentration, perhaps a touch of the music's own melancholy.

And the music changed.

It was sprightly, laughing, exuberant now; the pipes seemed practically to chuckle, but with a rueful tinge. It was music that might be played in a city under siege, the enemy outside the gates, the end a matter of days, the carousers determined to seize a moment of joy before the horror to come. The goat-legged creature was practically bouncing atop his rock now, arms and head swinging with the music. The fays began to dance in the air, dashing wildly about the glade, pairing off and flying around in intricate arcs, a gay pavane. Sidney was smiling now, her heart in her throat, completely captivated; she found her own feet tapping, her fingers moving.

Jasper was flying too, trying somehow to dance with the fays, his light a deeper green than theirs, but not dissimilar. He was slower, clumsier than they, but they took his participation good-naturedly, clustering about him and guiding him into the pattern of the dance.

And the music changed again. It was desperately exuberant, desperately fast. It spoke of life and death, the wild hunt, Dionysian frenzy. Enthralled by the sound, Sidney found herself on her feet, dancing too. Her motions were hesitant at first, but rapidly grew surer. The others were dancing also, joy and exuberance on their faces, dancing across the glade. They would pair for a moment, dance off again. Others were present, too; young deer leaping about, owls flitting through the air amid flying squirrels. Even the very grasses seemed to move, as if they, too, felt the music's enchantment.

The dance went on and on; one song seemed to begin where the last one left off. At times, the music slowed, the dance became a somber minuet; at times it rose again to a frenzy, Sidney bounding about, practically flying through the air, in surefooted motions like none she had ever performed before. At times only one instrument spoke, or one of the players would sing, in a peculiar language she did not know. When the music became fastest and most frenzied, invariably all three musicians played.

Sidney began to tire. And still she danced. She could feel the fatigue of her limbs, but it didn't seem to matter. She danced on and on, until her legs seemed something alien, outside her body, whirling away there below her. When the music slowed, and the dance with it, they would tremble a bit; but as the pace quickened, they would quicken too, dancing unrelentingly.

When she would chance to dance a few steps with one of her companions, his face would hold the same bright fierceness, the same exuberance she felt; but as time passed, she began to recognize the symptoms of fatigue. Their eyes seemed to sink into their sockets, black circles growing outward from them. Their faces became gaunt and shrunken, but still they danced on . . . and on . . . and on . . .

Frer Mortise didn't hear the music. But he was attuned to the magic of the woods, and as the spell began to take hold, he turned in his sleep, bothered by the flow of energy, until he, too, awoke.

Silver light shone from the glade.

He leapt to his feet and ran toward it, halting just outside the ring. For that was what it was, he now saw: a faerie ring, a place of power. Most such were marked out by standing stones, or toadstools; he would have recognized it before, if it had been so indicated. He heard no music, but he saw the dance, the flitting fays, the mindless, ecstatic faces of his friends.

He saw the players, there within the ring; the goat-legged man he recognized as an aspect of the god Fithold. The others he could not identify.

"Sidney!" he shouted. "Timaeus!" And he called the others, too, but none of them so much as glanced his way.

Should he enter the ring, and bodily draw them forth? No, he thought; he would simply be enraptured by the spell, as they had been. He mumbled prayers—then, struck with inspiration, fetched his sickle and felled a sapling. Holding one end, he extended the other into the ring, in the hope that the dancers would stumble against it, come to their senses, that the spell would be broken . . .

He stood there for long moments, waving the stick about. The dancers seemed oblivious to its presence, taking no conscious note of it but evading it with amazing agility. It seemed to bother them not in the least.

What the devil could he do? He stomped around the ring in frustration, shouting himself hoarse. Beatrice had charged him to guide and protect his companions; and here, mere days into the woods, were they ensorceled and in peril.

He looked up at the sky; the moon had set. He prayed to Deeset regardless, drew on his link to the goddess to power a spell—but it failed. That was a god, or an avatar of one, there within the ring; and the faerie ring itself was no feeble power. He could not overcome it.

Not, certainly, with the moon as slim as it was now. It was recently out of the new, a thin crescent when in the sky. His power waxed and waned with its extent. When it reached the full, perhaps he might fight this spell, perhaps he could break his companions free . . .

But that was eleven days from now, he realized with despair. Could they survive for eleven days, without food or drink, caught in the faerie dance? Well, yes, they might; time passed oddly for those ensorceled by the fays. What seemed a night might be a century, and eleven days outside the ring might be mere moments for those inside.

The sky was tinged with rose, now, the sun beginning to rise. And as the air lightened, the scene within the faerie ring faded away, fays and musicians and humans evaporating like the morning dew.

They would return, Mortise knew, with the setting sun, to dance away another night. And another, and another, and more to come; they would dance, if he could not save them, until their deaths.

The glade was quiet, now, serene; birds twittered in the trees. The bedrolls and packs of his companions were scattered across the grass; those, at least, had remained.

With a groan of despair, Mortise sat on the boulder at the glade's center, his head in his hands.

For long hours, he debated what to do. He considered digging trenches across the glade, or building barricades of logs, or damming the nearby stream and flooding the land; but he feared none of this would work. Indeed, it might simply cause his companions to trip, fall, injure themselves, and continue their ecstatic dance without regard for injuries. He might merely advance their deaths.

He saw only two possibilities: He could wait eleven days, until the night of the moon's fullest extent; or he could leave the glade in hope of finding aid.

He might as well spend eleven days traveling as sitting here in despair, he supposed.

If he were to leave, should he return to Biddleburg, or continue the pursuit of Broderick?

He could think of no one at Biddleburg with the power to aid him; but then, he knew no one in the Hamster-Dzorzia, whither Broderick was seemingly bound.

He shrugged, and searched the packs until he found Broderick's socks. He closed his eyes and concentrated; some faint remnant of Jasper's spell remained. East-southeast, that was where Broderick headed.

Before he left, he took a last glance around the glade; the packs of the others were strewn across the grass. Animals might rip them open in search of food, he realized;

and so he picked them up, and hung them from the branches of trees.

He shouldered his own pack, took up his walking stick, and hiked resolutely east-southeast. Without the others to slow him down, he made good speed.

Some days later, Frer Mortise smelled a campfire, the smoke on the wind. It was night, a few hours after sunset. He pulled forth the socks again and closed his eyes, but felt nothing; if any power remained in Jasper's spell, he was not sensitive enough to feel it any longer. The people camped ahead might include Broderick, but again might not.

He eyed the sky through a gap in the trees; Deeset was waxing, but still slim. There was less than an hour before she set.

Mortise hesitated, then decided to take the risk. He should have enough time. He took on owl form.

His gear and garb fell away, onto the needled forest floor. The owl flew up through the trees and circled once, fixing the place in memory. It would not do to lose his equipment, Mortise thought.

He flitted above the trees. The moon shone slantwise through thin wisps of cloud; the firs looked dark below. Bats shared the air with him, as did another owl or two; Mortise heard an annoyed hoot, as the owl whose territory this was took exception to his presence. Below, he spotted a flying squirrel, leaping from one tree to another; almost without thinking, Mortise folded his wings, dived, and snatched it from the air. He bit the creature's head off, then landed in a tree to rip at its flesh.

He hadn't had anything to eat for hours; the squirrel was delicious. But this was unwise, he realized; time was short.

He darted through the forest, dodging the boles of trees. The campfire was just ahead now. He came to a perch on the branch of a white pine, just outside the perimeter of the camp.

There was a babble of speech; high voices, silver tones: elves.

Mortise advanced crabwise down the branch to get a better look. A dozen or more. They had the statue of Stantius, sure enough; they'd set it up by the fire, and someone had put a peaked elven cap on Stantius's up-turned face—a joke, perhaps.

Some sort of stew bubbled over the fire. Several elves were singing, while another group played cards.

Mortise gave a start; one of the card-players was human, an old and toothless man. The old man looked up from his cards, stared directly at Mortise—and winked.

Mortise was terrified; would the old man betray him? But the human, whom Mortise did not recognize, merely returned his attention to his cards.

Mortise heard a noise from beneath his tree, the scuffle of a boot on leaves. He looked down; another human, gray-haired but not as old as the other, was sneaking out of camp. Mortise identified this one easily enough: Broderick.

One of the elves turned at the very same noise—but at that instant, Vincianus threw down his cards and yelled, "Grand spatzle!"

Hoots and groans came from the card-players; the singers broke off, their song interrupted. Vincianus jumped up and did a little dance of victory, waving his hands—and suddenly, the air was full of explosions and colored lights, exuberant magic to express the old man's pleasure at winning.

Broderick ran flat out away from the encampment.

The old man was providing a distraction, Mortise saw, to allow Broderick to escape. Should he follow Broderick, Mortise wondered, or stay with the statue?

Before he could decide he realized with a start that the moon was already sinking behind the—

Oh, fudge, he thought. The moon had set. He was trapped in this form until it rose again—late tomorrow afternoon.

Mortise sighed internally, and flitted silently after Broderick.

Broderick paused at the forest edge to survey the land beyond. Nearby, Mortise came to a landing on a tree, grateful for the rest.

Parallel ridges ran out from the Dzorzian Range, cutting the countryside below into valleys. The slopes were terraced, planted with grapevines and olive trees; the valley floors were patchworks of wheat, corn, and fields left fallow. Here and there stood farmsteads, isolated clusters of buildings, and peasants' huts. Down the left slope was a village, a cluster of buildings along a road; no lamps burned now, in the hours before the dawn.

Broderick came to a decision and made his way downward, toward the town. At each terrace edge, he crouched and let himself over the lip.

Mortise took to the air behind him and circled high into the night sky. Sharp owlish eyes easily picked out the figure of Broderick, struggling down the ridge; indeed, saw mice scutting amid the still young corn, rabbits in a farmstead's vegetable patch. Mortise contemplated a snack, but feared losing track of Broderick.

Dawn neared; with each of Broderick's steps, they left Mortise's gear farther behind, a heap somewhere off in the forest. At dawn, Mortise would need to depart; he had no wish to brave the day's harsh glare, not with sensitive owlish eyes. He hoped Broderick would soon find a place to rest.

At last Broderick came to the road along the valley floor, and made quicker progress along it toward the village. There he hesitantly surveyed each building in turn, until, with apparent satisfaction, just as the eastern horizon began to lighten, he came to the village's only inn.

He began to hammer on the door, shouting. Mortise glided down to a landing atop the stable's peaked roof to watch. Mortise was thankful; doubtless Broderick would take shelter here. Mortise could flit back to the forest, find his gear, and return soon after.

After some moments, a candle appeared at an upper window; and shortly afterward the door was unbarred and opened. A haggard, middle-aged woman in nightclothes stood there, holding a candlestick.

"Hola, woman, your best mount, and on th'instant," Broderick said sharply.

Bugger, thought Mortise. Doesn't the man ever tire? Broderick clearly intended to ride onward, and Mortise could not pursue.

"Well enough, good sir," said the woman sleepily, "but a deposit will be needed, and we must agree on the rental—"

Broderick drew a blade. "Your life will be deposit enough, methinks," he said, "and as for rental, you may request it of your lord."

The woman made to slam the door, but Broderick pushed inward. The door slammed behind them both.

Unhappily, Mortise watched the door, swiveling his head from time to time to survey the eastern sky; but no one returned, not for several moments, though there were crashes and muffled oaths from within the inn.

At last, Mortise took flight again, and headed back toward the woods.

Frer Mortise slept, head under wing, until the late afternoon, when the moon finally rose. At last able to return to human form, he donned his clothes and collected his things.

It was not until the evening that, trailworn and weary, he returned to the fields where he had left Broderick. Familiar now with the lay of the land, he managed to come to the forest edge not atop the ridge, but down in the valley. This at least spared him the difficult descent down the terraces.

He took comfort from the waxing moon; if danger was near, so at least was his goddess. In the few days yet to go, though he had scant hope now of finding help for his friends, he hoped at least to learn of Broderick's fate, and perhaps the statue's, too. The faerie ring was two days' travel, if he went swiftly; he still had time to gather provisions and return.

Across the fields came the lowing of cattle, returning to their pens. From huts and houses, tendrils of smoke reached skyward, fires cooking the evening repast. Down the road, Mortise could see the inn where Broderick had been; he noticed its sign, as he had not before: a broken column, surmounted by an olive branch. Other men, and some older women, were heading there likewise, no doubt to quaff a pint of ale or stoup of wine after the day's hard labor.

The door stood open; within, there was comfort and cheer, the hearthfire casting warmth and light across the taproom. When Mortise appeared, conversation trailed away, as the locals took in his habit and sickle; a wandering priest, clearly, his cult not readily apparent. He seemed harmless enough, so the lull in conversation was momentary.

Two young children ran about, bearing cups and sometimes platters of food; the clientele knew them, it seemed, and would pop them onto their knees, or tell them a joke before asking for another ale. A third, a babe, crawled on the bar itself, plashing its hands in a puddle of wine.

A group of people clustered about the woman at the bar. Mortise recognized her as the innkeeper from whom

Broderick had demanded a horse. She had a shiner about
her left eye. She came around the bar and approached him.

"Good evening, Father," the innkeeper said. "May I be
of help?"

"Not 'Father,' " said Mortise. "Merely 'Frer,' if you
will. I could use a bite to eat, and a place to spend the
night."

She hesitated. "May I ask your cult, Brother?"

"I follow Deeset," he said.

"Oh—very well," she said. "We can spare some pottage
and the local wine; and if you don't mind the hayloft,
there's room in the stable."

Mortise blinked; the offer of charity was unexpected. He
could pay, of course—but perhaps he'd take her up, in the
interest of appearing a harmless itinerant, and secretly
leave her a stack of coins on the morrow. "Thank you," he
said. "May I sit by the fire?"

"Of course," she said, snagging one of the children.
"Get the friar a bowl of pottage, Albrecht," she said.

"Righto, Ma," said the boy, and ran off toward the
kitchen. The innkeeper rejoined her circle.

"It just goes to show," said a red-faced and portly man,
taking up the conversation where it had paused, "you need
a man about the place, Lotte."

"And you'd like to be my man, is that it, Johnny?" the
innkeeper said, pouring a mug of wine and motioning
Mortise to take it.

There was general laughter, as Johnny turned even more
red-faced. "That's not what I had in mind," he protested,
"though I'm not saying I wouldn't, either. But all sorts
come down the road. And with the war on, there'll be
more. One man with a sword stole your best horse, Lotte,
you have to think about that. Think of the children, if not
your own safety. We should take turns, sleeping here—"

"I think," said a woman with the lined face and large

hands of a lifetime of labor, "people who open the door in the middle of the night get what they deserve."

"Thank you kindly, Tanya," the innkeeper said in an annoyed tone, "but I can't afford to turn away custom."

Mortise sat on the bricks of the hearth and sipped his wine, listening. Albrecht appeared with a bowl of brownish, lumpy stew, and dropped it unceremoniously in Mortise's lap. Mortise wolfed it down, scooping it up with pieces of bread. It was the usual thing; an inn generally had a pot bubbling away above the kitchen fire at all times. Into it went leftover scraps of meat, vegetables, occasional bones, and water to keep it all from burning. It served as the basis for stocks and gravies, but was edible alone in a pinch. Years of continuous simmering gave it a rich, meaty consistency. Mortise thought it quite satisfactory.

He hoped they would mention where Broderick had gone; but the topic did not arise, and Mortise had no desire to raise suspicion by asking.

Besides, he was looking forward to a good night's sleep. He could always ask Lotte tomorrow.

Mortise awoke in late morning, nose filled with the warm scent of hay. At the far end of the loft, golden sunshine poured from an open window. A beam protruded out over the road there; Mortise supposed they used it to hoist up bales of hay.

It took Mortise a moment to realize what had awoken him; more than sunlight poured through that window. He heard the voices of a good many men in conversation, the tinkle of harness, the clopping sound of horses on the move. Mortise climbed over bales of hay to peer into the road.

An army marched through the town. Not a large army; perhaps twenty horse and forty foot. The latter bore polearms of some kind, oddly shaped blades waving in the air.

The van had already passed, but Mortise peered up the road; at the head rode two men abreast, a woman between them. One of the men, even from behind, Mortise identified as Broderick; that salt-and-pepper hair, that arrogant stance were pretty well imprinted in the memory of any Biddlebourgeois who had lived through the time of tyranny. The other was evidently a nobleman; behind him rode a footman bearing his arms—a dragon displayed, gules on argent. His armor was curiously stark for a nobleman; the modern fashion was for increasingly elaborately decorated arms, but his mail was plain as plain. Functional, Mortise supposed.

The woman wore a mage's robes; and by the color, she was evidently of the College of Fire.

"Think we'll have time for an ale, after?" said one of the soldiers passing below Mortise's perch.

"If you don't watch where you put your bloody guisard," snarled another, "you won't have an after, Mauro, you turd."

"All right, you lot," said another commandingly, "save it for the elves."

Elves? thought Mortise.

Of course! Broderick had made some kind of deal; they were off to take the statue from the elves.

Mortise lunged toward his clothes.

By the time he'd gotten his clothes on and made it out of the stable, the party had left the village and was winding its way along a cattle path, up the southern ridge.

Mortise watched them a moment, wondering how much use cavalry would be amid these terraces; a charge down these slopes would mean risking your mount's legs with every drop.

He ran down the road and skirted someone's wheat. To follow the cattle path himself would be to court disaster; they would wonder why he followed, and might detain him. Instead, he'd have to struggle up the ridge some distance away, hoping to avoid notice. It was hard work, pulling up the terraces; and the grapevines around him gave no shelter from the hot sun—and not much more from observation.

By the time he reached the ridgeline, he was panting. He had made good time up the hill—better time, in fact, than the soldiers, who were still some paces from the ridge's peak, perhaps fifty rods distant. Mortise, feeling uncomfortably exposed, began to descend the ridge's far side. Perhaps he could find a hiding place before the soldiers reached the ridgeline themselves.

Indeed, a perfect place presented itself: a copse of trees, standing alone on the valley floor. He must first descend the ridge, then walk several minutes to get there, but once there, could observe Broderick and the army without fear of being seen.

He made haste, running down the slope and leaping from one terrace to the next. Mortise reached the valley floor and peered back up the ridge. Could he make it to the copse before the soldiers reached the ridgeline?

Alas, no; the cavalry was just beginning to cross the ridge, the men leading their horses slantwise down the slope—more or less in his direction. Mortise cursed—then noticed that the intervening plain was planted in wheat and maize. If he crawled, the plants would shelter him.

And so, on hands and knees, he skirted the periphery of the wheatfield—to plunge into it would mean swaying stalks of wheat, which the soldiers might observe. The next field was maize; he wove his way between the stalks, green leaves a canopy over his head. It was cool, down here by the earth, the leaves filtering out the harshest rays of the sun.

After some minutes, he stuck his head up high enough to essay a glimpse of his surroundings. The soldiers were closer now, he saw; indeed, they had taken up position in the very wheatfield he had left moments ago. The cavalry had remounted and had formed up in ranks at center, flanked on either side by the foot. The latter were in tight formation, guisards held parallel and forward. They were clearly expecting trouble. And they were facing him.

Mortise yanked his head down and hugged the cool earth. He was directly between the soldiers and the copse of trees.

Could the elves be amid those trees?

In sudden terror, Mortise realized: It was more than likely. Elves are creatures of the woods; if forced, for some reason, to travel across a cultivated plain, they would make camp, if at all possible, amid some stand of trees, some little wood.

"Deeset aid me," Mortise whispered into the dirt—but he was facing the wrong way, not toward the heavens; and anyway, the moon had not yet risen.

Stalks of corn cracked. A single footman rode past Mortise, close enough that the friar could see the froth about the horse's bit. He bore a white flag.

This relieved Mortise somewhat; they were going to try to parley. He wasn't going to be trampled to death by charging cavalry for a little bit longer, in any event.

The footman dismounted not far away and planted his flag.

Long moments passed. Mortise wondered whether he should try to crawl off—but with the footman so close feared even to breathe, lest that give him away. He dithered, until he heard a voice speak.

"Hiya," it said. It was a cheerful voice, rather high-pitched. "What's shaking?"

An elf, Mortise thought.

The footman cleared his throat. "The Graf von Grentz would speak with you under flag of truce," he said.

"Jake by me," said the elf.

The footman blew a horn—Mortise nearly leapt out of

his skin—and, a moment or two later, another two horses passed within yards of Mortise. One bore Broderick; the other, the nobleman Mortise had seen before—the Graf von Grentz, he presumed. Though von Grentz retained his armor, Mortise saw, both noblemen had left their swords behind.

"I hight Gerlad, Graf von Grentz," said a deep, curiously calm voice.

"Howdy," said the elf. "You can call me Beliel. Hiya, Broddy, old buddy."

"Greetings, Beliel," said von Grentz. "Are you aware that you are in Hamsterian territory?"

"Gosh, is that so?" said the elf, slightly sarcastically. "Golly. Well, you know how it is, if it's Tuesday, this must be Ishkabibble. Got my passport here somewhere, just a sec . . ."

"To be specific," said von Grentz, "you are in County Weintroockle, a fief of the House von Grentz. My demesne, in other words. Which you have entered, bearing arms, leading several dozen elves at arms. An armed invasion, in point of fact. Can you offer any reason why I should not order the lot of you killed out of hand?"

"Well jeez," said Beliel in an aggrieved tone. "If we'd known you'd be such a prig about it. I mean, we haven't actually done anything; no villages pillaged, no cities put to the sword or nothing. Just merry old elves, singing our merry song as we voyage merrily across the land. Maybe it's technically armed invasion, but gosh, let's keep this in perspective."

There was silence for a long moment.

"Then," the elf said, rather more nervously, "there is interspecies comity to consider. I mean, with the war with the orcs and all, you wouldn't want an international incident opening a breach among the Free Peoples, would you?"

There was another pause.

"Would you?" said the elf again.

"Mr. Beliel," said von Grentz, "you will order your folk to leave the thicket of trees ahead of us, one by one, and lay down their arms. You will permit my men to make a thorough search of your equipment."

"And then?" said Beliel.

"You will be escorted over the border," said von Grentz.

"And our things?"

"Your what?"

"Our possessions?"

"Your weapons will be returned to you upon your departure. Items of contraband will be confiscated. Your legal possessions you may retain."

"Gotcha," said Beliel. "There's this statue, see. We don't plan on giving it up."

"Indeed," said von Grentz. "Sir Broderick and I have discussed it at considerable length. I believe you stole it from him, and I fully expect you to return it."

Beliel snorted. "No," he said.

"No?" von Grentz inquired.

"No," said Beliel. "Negative. Nugatory. Nope. Uh uh. Nosirreebob. The opposite of yes. No—"

There was sudden violent motion from where the speakers stood, and the elf's voice broke off. Then Broderick bellowed, "Surrender, or your leader dies!"

Mortise dared a peek. Broderick had grabbed the elf and held a knife to his throat. Even to possess a knife was a violation of the rules of parley; to hold a negotiator hostage was a criminal act in every human, dwarven, and elven realm. This was loathsome, Mortise thought, even for Broderick.

Even von Grentz looked rather disgusted, but not enough, apparently, to force Broderick to put the elf down.

The elves' response was a shower of arrows. One of the horses went down, neighing in terror. Beliel wriggled out of Broderick's grasp and shoved Broderick's own blade, still in Broderick's hand, into Broderick's stomach.

That was all Mortise saw before he hit the dirt once more. An arrow plunged into the earth scant inches from his head.

A horse screamed in pain; an arrow must have found its mark. Moments later, another horse thundered close by Mortise, at a gallop—von Grentz, crouching low over his mount's neck, was off to rejoin his army.

Mortise went to hands and knees and began to scuttle away, keeping his head down but hustling to get out from between the army and the elves. Things were going to get pretty hairy pretty damn soon—

Things got hairy even sooner. Mortise started, rising inches into the air almost before he heard the report of thunder; a fireball had exploded a few rods distant. A full-throated, many-voiced roar rose from behind, and the beat of hooves on earth; the air above him was filled with flitting arrows.

Moaning in terror, Mortise gave up hope of escape and simply clutched the earth for dear life. Another fireball exploded, and another; the air was filled with smoke now. Fortunately, it had been a wet spring; Mortise didn't think the maizefield would burn, not yet, anyway.

The cavalry thundered past; one horse missed stepping on him by inches. And then there were screams and confusion amid the smoke, the thunderous charge becoming hesitant, breaking up under fire; and then horses galloped back, not far distant, several with empty saddles.

Things were quieter momentarily; the quietness only made the screams of the wounded more piercing.

A silver shadow drifted to a halt before Mortise; the cleric looked up and saw a beast that stood at least twenty hands, silver pelt marred by soot from the fires, eyes reddened with anger and fear, horn a deeper red with the blood of men. The unicorn sniffed Mortise for a moment, but forbore to kill him. It drifted on, as silent as the wind.

Mortise gasped thanks to Deeset; his connection to the goddess—a deity beloved of elves as well as men—was the only reason he could conceive for the unicorn to spare him.

There were several more explosions; the smoke became denser. Crashing noises could be heard through the stalks of maize. A pair of boots passed by him.

The foot was advancing, he realized, under cover of the smoke. They had broken their tight formation and moved forward individually, to make them less vulnerable to archers. No doubt they'd regroup at the forest edge.

In moments, he heard the clangs of steel. Then Mortise felt magic energy discharge—and the very stalks of maize that had sheltered him until now bent down and began to rip at his flesh.

Screams from the wood told him that the soldiers were similarly beset. Quietly and grimly, Mortise used his sickle to cut himself free from the maize.

As quickly as it had come, the spell passed. The sounds of battle continued now, amid the roar of the fire; orange flames licked the sky. They were burning the trees, he realized; a fire mage was with von Grentz, and they were destroying the elves' only haven.

Wet spring or no, the whole valley would soon be in flames.

He dared a peek. The trees were a mass of struggling men, horses, and elves. Von Grentz himself, wielding an enormous sword, strove against the unicorn.

Mortise turned; the ridge behind was empty. The army had passed.

He leapt to his feet and hurtled away.

Feet whirled. Music played. Sidney danced.

Time passed, unreckoned time. So must time be to a

beast, which has no way of measuring it, which has no appointments and no intentions beyond the next meal. Time passed; and it didn't seem to matter how long a time.

It didn't seem to matter. Only the music, the dance, the beautiful creatures, both natural and magical, about her; only these things mattered.

Sidney collided with Frer Mortise. She had never stumbled or collided with anyone before, in all that long time. Mortise was standing stock-still, not far from the rock at the center of the glade, staring straight upward, upward at the moon.

It was a full moon.

Some remote corner of Sidney's mind noted the fact, but failed to recollect that the moon had been a crescent when they had gone to sleep. It didn't seem to matter. Hesitantly, she resumed the dance, mad music swirling about her.

"Lady Deeset!" shouted a high and reedy voice. "Hear me!" And stock-still within the circle, a motionless point within exuberant motion, Frer Mortise began a prayer, his eyes upward to his goddess.

His words cut through the music like a knife. The dancers turned toward him, steps slowing, until they stood unsteadily still.

One by one, the players stopped playing, music dying, turning sour, like a bagpipe blatting as its bag empties.

The moon seemed somehow to have grown until it covered half the sky. Though each of the humans stood at a different point within the glade, each of them saw the same thing: the figure of Mortise, silhouetted against an enormous lunar orb. The priest looked angry and stern, shouting the words of his prayer.

A raccoon scurried away into the forest. The goat-legged man gave a wordless snarl, leapt off the rock—and never hit ground, disappearing in midleap. As the humans came groggily to, they looked about the glade—but the fays were gone.

The moon was back in its accustomed place, its accustomed size, but a full moon still. Mortise was kneeling now, chanting another prayer, this one in thanks to his goddess.

Sidney fell to the earth, overcome by fatigue, legs trembling uncontrollably. So did the others, sprawling across the glade.

"Good heavens," said Timaeus, chest heaving with exhaustion. "What was that?"

"You slept in a faerie ring," said Mortise, moving from form to form to make sure they were alive. To each he handed a flagon of water.

Sidney looked about the glade; it was nearly circular, in truth, but there were no toadstools, no standing stones to mark it as such.

What there was gave her a start: On easels about the glade stood parchments, stretched across triangular and hexagonal frames. On each parchment were painted mystic symbols. At four points around the circle—the compass directions, she realized—stood braziers, from which wafted scented smoke.

"What are those?" she asked, pointing.

Mortise looked. "It was no small enchantment," he said apologetically. "It took effort and preparation to break it."

"We should have listened to you," said Jasper. "You did feel uneasy about this place, didn't you?"

"Yes," said Mortise. He handed each of them a stick of jerky. As he handed one to her, Sidney realized the intensity of her hunger.

" 'I could have danced all night' takes on a new meaning," said Nick tiredly.

"Ow law i ee," Sidney said, then swallowed, the jerky only half masticated, and tried again. "How long did we dance?"

"Eleven days," said Mortise.

There were muttered oaths and exclamations, then silence as they chewed.

"Thank you, Brother," said Jasper at last. "We owe you a great deal."

Mortise coughed. "You'll need rest," he said. "I know you're all tired, but I'll have to ask you to move out of the ring. Crawl, if you have to."

And they did.

The morning was as pretty a day as one could hope for; clear skies, bright sun, gentle breezes. Sidney itched to go, but Mortise insisted they spend a day resting. "You've got eleven days' eating to catch up on," he said, flipping a cornmeal flapjack in a skillet over the fire. When it was done, he gave it to Sidney, hot out of the pan. She managed to choke it down with stream water. They had neither syrup nor sugar among their supplies.

"What I don't understand," said Jasper thoughtfully, "is why."

"Vhy vhat?" asked Kraki.

"Why did this happen?" asked Jasper. "I've heard the stories about faerie circles, of course; but in the stories, the fays always have some good reason to hate their victims. But what have we done to the fays? Or the elvenkind? Or the denizens of the woods? Apart from killing a few squirrels, I mean."

Mortise nodded. "They normally avoid humans," he said. "They wanted to kill or delay us. I couldn't say why."

A shiver ran down Sidney's spine. Certainly some creatures wanted them dead, or delayed; Arst-Kara-Morn might well know of their quest. But the fays were allies of the elvenkind, and therefore of humanity, in the war against the east; there was no sense in it. They should have wished the humans well, if anything.

"Eleven days," she said. "Broderick could be anywhere!

We have no idea what happened to the statue. It could be—"

"Well," said Mortise deferentially, "not *no* idea."

"What?" said Sidney.

So he told them.

"Elves?" said Jasper.

"Yes," said Mortise.

"Why elves?" asked Jasper.

"Who knows?" said Timaeus shortly. "What does it matter, anyway? It sounds like this von Grentz fellow has it, anyway."

"That old man with the elves must have been Vic," said Nick.

"But vhy did he—are the elves good guys?" said Kraki. "Vhat is Vic—"

"Who knows?" said Timaeus. "The ways of senility are unaccountable."

"We've *got* to get going," said Sidney.

"Tomorrow," said Mortise firmly.

Toward the evening, Jasper essayed a spell. Sidney watched as he spoke Words of power, spiraled upward into the air in a complex dance—those dirty socks waving in the air below him—and hung there, over the camp, moving slightly this way and that. "Damn," he said at last.

"What is it?" asked Sidney; Jasper zipped down to her level. Timaeus listened in, filling his pipe, while the others busied themselves, packing away belongings and washing the dirty dishes at the stream.

"I'm not sure I can say," said Jasper uncertainly. "Broderick . . . Something has changed."

"Yes," said Sidney. "He's escaped from the elves and gone off with von Grentz and the statue. Is he off in the same direction as before? East-southeast?"

"Yes," said Jasper, "the same direction Frer Mortise traveled. But that's not what bothers me."

"What does?" asked Timaeus.

Jasper sighed. "Something has changed. Something has happened to Broderick. I sense him still, but the character of the sensation has changed."

"Changed how?" asked Sidney.

"I'm not sure," said Jasper. "But it feels like something has happened."

"Like what?" demanded Sidney.

"My dear, if I knew, would I not say?" said Jasper irritably. "Maybe he's found religion. Maybe he's been magically transformed into a newt. Maybe he's—how should I know? The sensation is different, that is all. We'll just have to go and see."

Sidney went to sleep fretting over the morrow—but, surprisingly, slept like a log. Exhaustion will do that to you, she muzzily supposed as she dropped off.

III.

Pablo von Kremnitz crept down the dusty passage, the glowing opal on his finger his only light. One side of the narrow corridor was brick, the other lath and plaster, the footing uncertain on unboarded joists. The Maiorkest was riddled with such passages, with secret doors and accessways, with spy-holes and traps. His épée was out, probing uncertainly at the dimness before him.

Not far away, a thin line of light shone across the corridor, visible by the motes of dust that passed through the beam. It came from a spy-hole, drilled through the wall, a hole permitting surveillance of one of the Maiorkest's many chambers. Von Kremnitz had passed many such holes; he went to this one, as he had to others, and pressed an eye to it. Here, between the walls, it was difficult to get one's bearings; he hoped the sight of the room beyond the hole might tell him where he was. He should be near the Dandolo Room, if the gods were with him and he had not made a wrong turning, but—

Yes, excellent! Through the hole, he caught a glimpse of an armchair and, beyond it, a stained-glass window, bright with afternoon light. Only three rooms in the Maiorkest had stained-glass windows, and the Dandolo Room, where the Lord Mayor made his office, was one of them.

His hand ran over the wall, searching for the control of a secret door. If this was indeed the Dandolo Room, there should be one nearby. He felt rough wood, bulbous protrusions where wet plaster had oozed through the laths before solidifying, layers of dust—

There was a clatter. Von Kremnitz froze. The plaster was old, and decayed; he had knocked some of it loose, sending it rattling down the wall and into the space between the joists. Cursing under his breath, von Kremnitz peered through the peephole again, hoping he had not alerted anyone within the room.

A voice, heavy with drink, came muffled to his ears. "Cockroaches in the walls," it said; the speaker must be talking fairly loudly. "They told me there were cockroaches in the walls, in the Maiorkest; an intelligent man might reason that where there are cockroaches, there may be assassins. Come forth, blackguard. These old fingers may not be as dextrous with a blade as once they were, but I shall endeavor to give a good account of myself."

At last, von Kremnitz's fingers found the brass fitting that controlled the secret door, but he hesitated to work it now. Coming to a decision, he sheathed his épée before pulling the lever and pushing back the section of wall on its hinges.

Von Kremnitz took two steps within the Dandolo Room and knelt on the rich Nokhena carpet within. Head down, he said, "My lord, I come not to slay but to rescue you."

"What have we here?" that thick voice said, no longer muffled by the thickness of the walls. "I believe I detect

the odor of the provincial. I have no need of rescue, lad;
at least, there is nothing from which I *can* be rescued."

Von Kremnitz dared a look upward; the Lord Mayor
stood before him, a snifter of brandy in one hand and a rapier in the other. The rapier drooped, no longer at guard,
but not sheathed either. Hamish Siebert was much as von
Kremnitz had imagined him, from glimpses afar, from en-
gravings: a jowly man, with something of the air of a basset hound and an expression of, somehow, mixed jollity
and combativeness. Von Kremnitz had not expected to find
him half sloshed; the redness in his cheeks was surely neither embarrassment, nor an excess of sun, nor the consequence of vigorous exercise.

"My lord," he said, "I am a leftenant of your Foot
Guard. While on private business, I learned of a conspir-
acy against your life, against the, the Hamsterian state. Believing my own superiors compromised, I—"

"Let's see," said Siebert. "The Guelphards? The
Smalkaldians? Fenian's little group? The Mattmark sepa-
ratists? The Accommodationists? Or the Hauliers' Guild?"

"The—the *gens* von Krautz, my lord."

"Oh, yes, Julio von Krautz, bit of an ass, that man. I
shouldn't worry too much about him, if I were you, lad.
Old Julio has all the political *nous* of a particularly unin-
telligent rabbit. I count eleven known conspiracies against
my life, as of this morning, and I don't think we even
bothered to include old Krautz, since he's got about as
much chance of bringing something off as Stantius the
Third has of returning from the grave."

Blushing, von Kremnitz rose to his feet. "It seems I
have been a fool," he said. "Forgive my temerity, my lord;
I shall depart immediately."

"No, no, by no means," said Siebert. "Take a seat, my
boy." He waved his snifter toward one of the armchairs
and, with the motion, apparently realized anew the existence of its contents. He tilted it back, drained it, and made

toward the sideboard. "Join me, won't you? Brandy? Sherry? Or we have an excellent Moothlayan single-malt."

"My lord," said von Kremnitz. "I feel quite the idiot. Please permit me to retire shamefaced to my—"

"Oh, shut up," said Siebert. "Since you won't choose, you shall have the brandy. Here you go." He handed von Kremnitz a snifter practically brimful of the powerful liquor. Von Kremnitz took a gulp of the burning stuff, unsure what else to do.

"Are you any good with that blade of yours?" asked Siebert.

Von Kremnitz cleared his throat. "Yes," he said uncertainly.

" 'Yes'?" said Siebert. "That's it? 'Yes'? No boasting of your prowess, the many fine swordsmen you have bested? No falsely modest declarations of 'some slight expertise'? Merely 'Yes'?"

"What would you have, my lord?" asked von Kremnitz miserably. "I have been in the city mere weeks; I am accounted the finest swordsman in Meersteinmetz, but the finest swordsman in Meersteinmetz may be a mere fumbling provincial, by the standards of the city."

Siebert snorted. "How many weeks have you been here?"

"Three, my lord."

"And in that time, how many duels have you fought?"

"Sixteen, my lord."

Siebert, in the process of sipping his brandy, snorted, then coughed for long moments, trying to clear his nose of the liquor. "Sixteen? Ye gods, you must wear your honor on your sleeve."

"I shall not see the name of my lord, my city, nor my regiment insulted," von Kremnitz said stiffly.

Siebert laughed long and loud. "I see," he said at last, wiping eyes with a lace handkerchief. "Sixteen duels are explained. I imagine it's difficult to walk down the street without hearing someone condemning that wild-eyed radical, the Lord Mayor. If you wish to avoid further contests at arms, I advise you to remain in your barracks. Or frequent the dives of the proletariat; I may be well liked there. Tell me; of the sixteen, what was the disposition?"

"I slew two men; six were sufficiently wounded as to require medical attention. The remaining eight were satisfied with first blood."

"*They* were satisfied with first blood? I see no healing wounds upon you."

"I beg your pardon, my lord. *I* was satisfied with first blood, when they withdrew their vile slanders."

"I see," said Siebert thoughtfully. "I believe I may have use for a young man of your abilities and, um, steadfast loyalty."

Von Kremnitz sat up straighter in his chair. "My lord," he said. "I shall do what I may."

"Excellent," said Siebert. "There are few men of whom I can rely; another is always welcome."

"My lord!" protested von Kremnitz. "Surely the men of your regiment, the ministers of state—"

"Surely," said Siebert mockingly. "Let us have less modesty about the abilities of swordsmen from the provinces, and rather more about their appreciation of political realities. Hamsterburg is a sewer; I am appointed to muck it out; and the rats do not appreciate the attention."

"My lord—"

"Be quiet. You claim to be concerned at plots to my life; rest at ease. Why worry about the inevitable? I estimate my life span at eight months, at the outside. Oh, I try to keep on top of the various conspiracies—the Ministry of Internal Serenity has been suspiciously supportive, but I can't trust Minister Stantz even as far as I can throw him, which is probably a distance measurable only with calipers, as you'll appreciate if you ever meet the man. But there are just too many, you know. I'm seventy-two if I'm a day, I have periodic gout, I have no political following to speak of, and the Hundred *Gentes* elected me only as a placeholder, because they were too quarrelsome to settle on someone with any more political clout. I know I'm a dead man, and my only ambition is to gore as many oxen as I may before some lunatic settles my hash. To mix a metaphor. Drink your damned brandy, my boy."

"Yes, my lord," said von Kremnitz, who, round-eyed, had been neglecting his drink. He choked on another hasty mouthful.

"What is your name, by the way?" asked Siebert.

"Pablo von Kremnitz, my lord."

"Noble, eh?"

"Third son of a knight, my lord."

"Pity," said Siebert. "See here, you know the Graf von Grentz?"

"Socially? No, I—"

"Socially?" snorted Siebert. "My good man, I don't imagine you travel in such circles. You've *heard* of him, yes?"

"Of course, my lord; an Accommodationist, is he not?"

"Yes, quite. Actually, Gerlad von Grentz virtually rules the Accommodationist party. I don't imagine he really thinks we can bargain with Arst-Kara-Morn, somehow keep the orcs from our gates with diplomacy; but neither the military nobilization nor the taxes it requires is particularly popular, and questioning the need for them is good political theater. Very bad policy, to be sure, but good politics, if you follow the distinction.

"He's up to some damn thing—well, that goes without saying, doesn't it? Everybody's up to something, in this lunatic city. Thankfully, Minister Stantz keeps pretty good tabs on what most people are up to, but neither he nor I have much of a take on von Grentz. You see, he's off in the provinces."

"My lord?"

"Doesn't seem so odd to a provincial? Hamsterburg is astorm, lad, half the town trying to kill me, the other half maneuvering to gain power after my death, some portion of them hoping to thwart, or benefit by, or modify the reforms I am imposing. Gerlad von Grentz is not a man to vacate the city at a vital political juncture; no, he should be here, pulling strings with as much abandon as any of them. Instead, he retires to his ancestral castle near some dusty little village called Weintroockle. Make a plonk of some kind out there, I understand."

"What has this to do with me, my lord?" asked von Kremnitz.

"Patience, lad. Word has reached my ear—by way of Stantz, incidentally, meaning I can't trust the information—that a pitched battle was fought near Weintroockle in the last fortnight, between von Grentz's household troops and—nobody seems to know. Von Grentz is up to something, you see; something is going on out there in Weintroockle, and I need to know what. You are a naïf; nobody knows who you are; you're a provincial, so nobody will take you seriously; and you seem quite capable with that blade of yours. Go to Weintroockle, poke around, come back. I'll give you a safe passage, for what it's worth—the gods only know how many Hamsterian citizens are likely to respect *this* Lord Mayor's *laissez-passe*—but use it only as a last resort. Will you do it?"

"My lord has only to command," said von Kremnitz, springing to his feet and to attention.

"Oh, don't be an idiot," said Siebert. "You're probably walking into a deathtrap—although, come to think of it, judging by the frequency with which you duel, walking into a deathtrap may improve your life expectancy. I shan't order you to do anything: It's quite one thing for me to throw my life away on whimsical quixotry, it's quite another for me to ask a young man, with years of sexual potency and any number of flagons of wine ahead of him, to do likewise. I'm asking you to go, but I positively refuse to order it; some scant salve for a much-decaying conscience."

"I shall depart on the instant," said von Kremnitz.

"Righto," said Siebert. He moved to his desk, picked up a quill, and scratched something onto a piece of parchment. "Off you go then."

"I shall not fail you, my lord," said von Kremnitz, kneeling to kiss Siebert's ring.

"Oh, bloody hell, enough of that," said Siebert. "*Au revoir, bon voyage*, the hopes of the city ride with you, and so forth and so on." He folded the parchment, tucked it in von Kremnitz's belt, and pointed the young man toward the secret door. As von Kremnitz crawled into the passage, he felt a resounding slap on his buttock.

Hamish Siebert, Lord Mayor of Hamsterburg, sat at the head of the table, leaning well back, his elbows on the arms of his chair, fingers steepled before him. He waited patiently, a slight smile on his jowly face, as his ministers drifted in.

As always, the cabinet met in the Octagon Chamber, deep within the Maiorkest. Stone walls rose to high windows. Though it was spring, a fire roared in the great hearth; this pile of stones retained the chill of winter well into the hottest days of summer, and for now, it was still rather cold.

Siebert studied the portraits that ran around the perimeter of the room. They depicted mayors past, unsmiling men and women leaning outward from the walls, the frames angled down for better viewing, imposing a sense that these grim potentates regarded the doings of their successors with stern and censorious eyes.

He looked about the table. Yes, they were all here, all but one, studying each other discreetly, no warmth among them. In happier times, they might have passed the time with pleasantries; but in these strained circumstances, with half the city maneuvering for power, conversation was impossible.

Siebert envied the rulers of other states, who might choose their own advisors; his cabinet had been foisted on him by the Hundred *Gentes*, the great families that ruled Hamsterburg, that had elected him mayor in the mistaken belief that he would be a comfortable nonentity. The foreign minister was an Accommodationist, the minister of public works a Smalkaldian, the minister of the Arsenal of the Bleinmetz *gens*. Even that fool Julio von Krautz had his own little piece of the pie, the Department of Drains and Water Supply. In fact, the fat little turd was seated just to Siebert's left, looking as if he were sucking on lemons.

Every faction had its own little piece of the action, its own access to the public purse. That was precisely what Siebert hoped to end.

They were all here but Stantz. Siebert pursed his lips. Stantz's lateness might be a calculated insult, or perhaps merely a way of demonstrating his importance; they could not start without him. Rather, Siebert *would* not start without him; Stantz was virtually his only ally, however untrustworthy an ally he might be. It was hard to trust a man whose files contained evidence of innumerable indiscretions, whose spies were everywhere, who was known to the general public, in hushed whispers, as "The Spider." It was not a reference to his physiognomy.

Siebert frowned irritably and opened his mouth; there was a limit to the length of time he would willingly wait. At that very moment, however, the great doors creaked open at last.

"His Excellency, Guismundo Stantz, Minister of Internal Serenity," announced the footman.

Stantz stood between the two splayed doors, a cane in each hand. He needed two, to support his bulk. Attendants had helped him this far, but now they stood respectfully back.

Painfully, advancing both canes before levering his body behind them, he progressed into the room. He moved with elephantine slowness. "Elephantine" was an apt word; he was three hundred, possibly four hundred pounds.

"I beg your pardon for my tardiness, my lord," said Stantz, in a curiously sweet voice for such a man. "I was delayed *en route.*"

"Confound it, Minister," said Siebert. "We've important matters to discuss."

"Yes, my lord," said Stantz, in his melodic voice. He was halfway to his seat now.

Siebert sighed. "My Lord Privy Purse," he said, "commence, if you will."

Lord Mannheim went to the sideboard. A jeroboam of single-malt stood there: the Isle of Alban, the preferred tipple, so it was said, of Mayor Albertus, the Republic's founder. It was served from the same decanter at the inception of every cabinet meeting.

Mannheim went to each place in turn, pouring a careful two fingers into each tumbler. They would all drink from the same bottle. Just as every Hamsterian citizen drank from the wellspring of the city's life, just as each thrived or suffered with the state, so every minister drank from the same potation. If it was poisoned, they all would die. It had happened more than once in the history of the Republic.

Mistrustful glances were exchanged across the table. Several sniffed their tumblers.

To Siebert's mind, the serving of the Alban stood as a salutary reminder that the cabinet's business was not individual ambition but the Serene Republic's health. There were all too few such reminders.

No one drank, just yet.

Stantz came finally to his chair and managed, somehow, to squeeze his bulk between the arms. He put his canes to-

gether, leaned them against the table, and took his tumbler.
All eyes were on him as he tossed the whisky back.

One could almost hear a sigh pass around the table. Other
ministers reached out for their own glasses and sipped or
gulped the whisky, whatever was their normal practice.

Stantz had the best spies in Hamsterburg. If he thought
the malt was unpoisoned, the odds were that he was right.

The Lord Mayor reached for his own glass and saw that
Julio von Krautz had taken it—the two glasses had been
close to each other on the table. Siebert gave von Krautz
a stare, and reached over to take the minister's glass.

The Lord Mayor took a sip or two of the whisky intended for von Krautz. "Now then," he began roughly. "I
have here a proposal to open bidding on public contracts."

A ripple of astonishment went around the table.

"The proposal applies to all public works, but will affect
most immediately the collection of trash. Hauliers and private citizens may bid on the contract to collect refuse from
individual parishes of the city; bids will be open to public
review, and—"

"My lord!" shouted von Krautz, leaping to his feet.
"This, this is insane!"

"How so?" demanded Siebert coolly, leaning back in his
chair.

"For centuries, the guiding *gens* of each parish has controlled the collection of trash in its own demesne; the ancient firms that perform the work have intimate ties to—"

"Precisely," said Siebert. "It has become a sinecure, a
source of patronage for the *gentes*, to the detriment of public hygiene and at great public expense. By casting collection open to public—"

"Again you attack the very roots of the state!" shouted
von Krautz. "Will you not cease, before you destroy all the
traditions of our city, reduce us to servility before—
before—" He was red-faced now, apparently too enraged
to speak further.

"I am gratified to know," said Siebert dryly, "that the very roots of the state lie in garbage. My lord—my lord, are you all right?"

Von Krautz was pressing his midriff, as if he had gas pains. Or a painful ulcer, perhaps. "It is nothing," he said hoarsely, stiffening his spine. "One by one, you deprive the *gentes* of our privileges; one by one, you attack our ancient traditions; one by one you—hunnnh."

Von Krautz stood now with both hands flat on the table, staring downward at a pad of paper, a quill, an inkpot, all on polished wood.

He made a curious sound.

He vomited blood. Not a little splashed into Siebert's lap.

Julio von Krautz collapsed onto the table.

Siebert looked at the glass in his hand: He held von Krautz's tumbler. He looked at the glass, now stained with blood, that stood just by von Krautz's left temple: That glass had been meant for him.

Siebert's eyes went instantly to those of Guismundo Stantz. Stantz's piggish eyes were staring back.

There were shocked faces, hooded eyes all about the table.

Someone had meant to kill him, Siebert knew. Someone had meant to kill him. Who?

Eleven conspiracies, by this morning's count. And yet—

"This meeting is at an end," Siebert announced, his voice a little shaken. "We shall take up this matter another time. Minister Stantz, I shall expect an immediate investigation."

"Of course, my lord," said Stantz, levering himself painfully to his feet.

They had all drunk from the Alban, every one of them. Yet only von Krautz had died, one man out of all of them. How was that possible? Who could have managed it?

Siebert's eyes followed Stantz, those canes moving slowly forward, those heavy limbs behind.

Who else but Stantz, the Spider, assassin?

IV.

Guismundo Stantz wheezed painfully, collapsed in the chair behind his great, semicircular desk. Sweat rolled off him in rivulets, lungs labored in desperation. It was long moments before he regained control.

He had rushed back from the Maiorkest, back here to the Albertine Lodge, the headquarters of Internal Serenity. He had ordered his coachman to whip the horses on, bracing himself against the inevitable jostling, and had practically trotted through the halls. Now he was paying the price. He wiped his face with a lace-trimmed handkerchief until it was sodden.

He loathed those meetings in the Maiorkest; given the option, he'd never leave this room. Here, in his office, he had everything.

He had light. There were no windows, to be sure; windows admitted light, but also, on occasion, spies and assassins. Instead, light shone from a shaft above his desk, delivered to the enclosed room from the building's roof by a complex series of mirrors and lenses. A contraption hung from the ceiling; from a lens at one end, intense light shone out, illuminating the papers on Stantz's desk— sunlight, directed by levers and pulleys wherever Stantz needed illumination.

He had information. He had speaking tubes to reach subordinates, a newscrystal to keep up to date, scrying globes for magical contact; here he was the Spider indeed, sitting amid his web, spies and sources extending off across the lands of Hamsterburg and beyond. He was alert to every twinge of the web, every jerk that meant a development in the politics of the Republic or the relationship of the powers, alert and ready to scurry, to the advantage of the city.

And he had food and drink. An enormous wheel of Stralitzer sat on the end table, along with a cheese knife and an array of crackers; by it stood an ewer of water and a bottle of syrup of greep—Stantz was partial to greep sodas. And if he desired anything more, the ministry boasted an excellent kitchen, staffed every hour of the day or night, its chef accessible by one of the hinged brass speaking tubes that hung above Stantz's desk.

Lord mayors and grand dukes came and went, but the state went on. And Stantz was a loyal servant of the state. His goal was simple: the aggrandizement of his native city, for which he felt a fierce emotion, one of the few emotions remaining to him. For Hamsterburg, he was prepared to do any deed. Assassination included, to be sure.

Not, however, this time. Siebert was a fool; but war was coming, and Siebert was taking the necessary steps to prepare for war. Stantz had no desire to see him dead, especially since there would be internecine struggle over the succession, struggle that might well break out into civil war.

In fact, Stantz considered, the method of von Krautz's assassination was carefully calculated to cast suspicion on—on Guismundo Stantz. The pouring of the Alban was part of Hamsterian legend; the whole cabinet dies, or none. To engineer the death of a single member was audacious, clever; and Stantz had a reputation for audacity and cleverness. No doubt the whole cabinet believed he had killed von Krautz, had meant to kill Siebert.

As, no doubt, did Siebert. It would be difficult to repair relations, Stantz reflected.

Who might want Stantz discredited, almost more than he wanted Siebert dead?

"Anyone who seeks absolute power," Stantz whispered to himself. Absolute power would necessitate the removal of Stantz; the Lord Mayor might be the power of the state *de jure*, but Stantz had long since become the most powerful man of the *urbs de facto*.

Stantz sat for a long time, eyes moving to the newscrystal, the sound currently low, where the image of a tiny demon sat, reading stories in a bored monotone.

Stantz had not killed von Krautz.

It didn't bother him that von Krautz had died; assassination was a commonplace in the politics of Hamsterburg.

What bothered Stantz was this: He didn't know who *had* killed von Krautz.

That was a shocking failure. He should have known. It was his business to know. In the building above him, Records had files on every nobleman, every merchant, and every thief in the Republic. An army of paid informants blanketed Hamsterburg; he knew every faction, every *gens*, every cabal, knew their names and their ambitions. He knew what three dozen different groups were plotting, knew of eleven plots against Siebert's life—and knew that none was within weeks of fruition.

Something was up. Stantz wanted to know what.

Stantz *needed* to know. Knowledge was his existence. It was almost a physical need.

He pulled down a speaking tube and bellowed, "Bleichroder! Get me Wolfe."

And then he picked up the cheese knife and set to work on the Stralitzer.

"What," said the shadow. It was more of a statement than a question.

Stantz started, the flesh of his upper arm jiggling. He swallowed a mouthful of cheese.

Wolfe occupied the armchair across the desk. Stantz hadn't seen her come in, nor the door open. He barely saw her now, her dark gray clothes blending into the shadows of the chair's depths.

"I wish you wouldn't do that, Ren," he said mildly. Not for the first time, it occurred to him that she was the greatest hole in his security; suborned or alienated, she could kill him far more easily than anyone else. The thought bothered him, but he put it aside. She was loyal, she was well paid, she was indispensable.

Wolfe merely shrugged.

"Julio von Krautz has been killed," Stantz said. "Accidentally; the Lord Mayor was the target."

"All over town," said Wolfe. "Word is, you did it."

"Not I," said Stantz.

"Didn't think so," said Wolfe. "I'd've known."

Stantz nodded. "I need to know who did."

Wolfe looked interested at that, leaning forward so that her scarred face was visible in the light from the ceiling. "You don't know?"

"No," said Stantz, frowning. "That bothers me."

"Me too," said Wolfe, leaning back. "Know how it was done?"

"Yes," said Stantz. "Trivial."

Wolfe leaned forward again; she was actually smiling this time. "Word is," she said, "whisky was poisoned, whole cabinet drank whisky, but only von Krautz died. Word is, impossible hit. Word is, assassin was a genius. Word is, must have been you."

"Impossible hit my ass," said Stantz.

"Large ass," observed Wolfe.

"Thank you kindly," said Stantz, slightly annoyed. "There are at least three ways von Krautz could have been poisoned. The most likely is the simplest: There was a water- or alcohol-soluble poison in the bottom of his glass. Easy enough to accomplish, with a bribe or two to the Maiorkest kitchen staff. Only one glass was poisoned; only one man died."

Wolfe nodded. "I'll work on it."

"Do, Ren," said Stantz seriously. "When you find something, I want to hear—instantly. Any hour of the day or night."

"Fine," said Wolfe faintly.

Stantz blinked; the armchair was empty. He hadn't seen Wolfe go.

"Wow," said the boy enthusiastically. "You have your wild sex orgies down here?" He bounded down the dank steps with enthusiasm. Maybe "boy" was a little unfair, thought Wolfe; he probably considered himself a man. Still, whatever his age, his apparent level of intellectual and emotional maturity made it absurd to think of him as an adult.

"Sure," said Wolfe. "This way."

The stairs ended in a large chamber, lit by flickering torches. Moss covered the stones of the walls; water trickled down the center of the room. Against one wall was an open furnace; around it were tables, fitted with manacles, chains, and blood runnels. More chains and manacles hung from the walls.

"Gosh," said the boy, picking up a bullwhip and examining it. "This is, like, maybe a little too kinky for me. So where are the girls, huh?"

Wolfe grabbed his wrist and locked a manacle about it. "Sorry," she said. "Aren't any."

"Hey!" said the boy. "Let me out, okay? I mean, a joke is a joke, but—"

"Fenstermann!" shouted Wolfe. "Where the hell are you?"

"Coming, coming," said a tired bass voice from down the hall at the far end of the room. Footfalls sounded, and flickering torchlight moved up the corridor as Fenstermann neared the chamber.

"Who's Fenstermann?" asked the boy.

"The torturer," said Wolfe.

"Oh, mama," said the boy. "Look, I was looking for some action, sure, but this kind of thing—"

"It was a ruse, you moron," snapped Wolfe. "There are no girls, no wild sex, none of that crap. I could have coshed you and carried you here, but it was easier to feed you a line of guff."

Fenstermann entered the chamber, bearing a torch. He was bare to the waist, wearing a domino mask and tight pants. His arms looked like the Platonic ideal of the notion of "mighty thews." He looked like he could rip the fangs out of a tyger's mouth with bare hands.

"Oh, gods," he complained, "not another one, Wolfe."

"Sorry, Fenstermann," said Wolfe. "This guy's on the Maiorkest kitchen staff. He may know something about the von Krautz assassination."

"All right, all right," said Fenstermann morosely. He took some pincers, some large knives, and some odd contraptions with big spikes and serrated edges, and stuck them into the furnace. "Look, suppose we accept as a given that ends can justify means. The question arises: Which ends and what means? Torture—"

"Shut up, Fenstermann," said Wolfe impatiently. "Just do the job."

"Look, I'll talk, okay?" said the boy. "Peter piper picked a peck of pickled peppers. Once I met a lass, a bonny bonny lass—I'm talking, see? I'll say anything you want, only please don't—"

Fenstermann turned toward him, holding a long piece of metal with something on the end that glowed red in the dimness of the dungeon. The boy moaned, staring at it like a terrified bird.

"Fine. You set the table in the Octagon Chamber before the cabinet meeting?" asked Wolfe.

"Yeah, that's right," said the boy.

"Von Krautz's glass was poisoned. You do it?"

"Me? Uh, no, no, I didn't—couldn't possibly—I mean—"

"Brand 'im, Fenstermann."

"Your karma, Wolfe," said Fenstermann, waving the branding iron, which was glowing now a duller red. "You really want to spend your next reincarnation as a dung beetle?"

"Just do the job, dammit, Fenstermann," said Wolfe. "Everybody's a goddamn philosopher. I don't ask you to *enjoy* sticking red-hot needles into people's eyeballs, I just ask you to do it. Now stop whining, for gods' sake."

Fenstermann shrugged. "Sorry," he said to the boy, and probed gingerly toward a leg with the iron.

"Yeah, I poisoned the glass! I did it! I admit it! Okay? Stop it! Only I didn't know it was poison. And it was supposed to be for the Lord Mayor, not for Baron von Krautz."

Wolfe raised an eyebrow. "Tell me about it," she suggested.

"This guy, Siggy Hoffmann, he paid me to do it. Gave me a vial of this transparent crystal stuff, told me to put like a quarter teaspoon in the bottom of the mayor's glass. Said he'd kill me if I ever told." The boy's burst of speech ended on a depressed tone.

"How much he pay you?" asked Wolfe.

"Ten shillings," said the boy, subdued.

"Ten shillings?" said Wolfe, astonished. "You agreed to assassinate the ruler of the most powerful state in the human lands for less than a quid?"

"Hey, I didn't know it was poison. And anyway, it didn't kill *him*, it got von—"

"Somebody tells you to put a mysterious substance in the Lord Mayor's drink, and it doesn't occur to you that maybe, just maybe, the stuff isn't going to be good for his health?"

"Well, geez, it occurred to me, but, well, I needed the pelf, see, cause this girl—"

"Spare me," said Wolfe.

They were silent for a while. Fenstermann was smiling, pleased that he wouldn't have to torture the lad after all.

"Well," said Wolfe at last, "we won't give Siggy Hoffmann the chance to kill you."

"Oh, thank you, thank you," said the boy. "I'll do anything—"

Wolfe turned to Fenstermann. "See what the Szanbu cultists'll pay for him," she said. "One of their holy days is coming up soon; they'll need sacrificial victims."

Fenstermann lost his smile. "Yes, ma'am," he said reluctantly.

The boy began to wail.

A whale lay sprawled on the enormous circular bed, its bulk covered only by a blanket. It blew, with a noise like a fireball's explosion. Stantz's snore could wake the dead, Wolfe thought, studying her sleeping employer.

It took some doing to study him; it was pitch black here—no windows, no illumination other than a thin, meager glow through the bottom of the locked and bolted door. She was probably one of the few folk alive who could see in such dimness.

"Guismundo," she said.

Stantz was instantly alert. He thrashed with the blanket, rolled off the bed to smash into the floor with a wet smack, and scrabbled desperately with something.

"Sir," she said, "I've come to—"

Stantz had something in his hand. There was a burp of

blue light, and something spun across space between Stantz and Wolfe, striking her in the stomach. She was propelled by the impact into the paneled wall. A hand went automatically to her stomach, and felt something warm, wet, and sticky: blood.

Flashes of blue light were blasting across the room in a flurry, smashing into the walls and furniture. By the light they emitted, Wolfe saw that Stantz was on one elbow, sitting up, a wand of some kind in his hand. He was also quite naked—something that hadn't been evident when Stantz had been below the blanket but that was now quite obvious and, to Wolfe's eyes, more than a little revolting. She didn't think she'd ever seen anyone with quite so many rolls of fat.

"Stop that, you idiot!" Wolfe shouted. "It's me!"

Stantz stopped firing the wand. "Ren?" he said, then was silent for a moment. "Dammit, I thought I was well protected. How did you get through the wards?"

The room was protected by magic, as well as guards and physical traps. It had taken more than a little work to get within, but Wolfe had been happy to expend the effort, in the service of her own reputation for infallibility. "I have my methods," she said in an irritated tone. "You did tell me to report at any hour of the day or night."

There were loud clicks and bangs; someone was working on the door's locks. "What's that?" demanded Wolfe.

Stantz had got to his hands and knees and was pulling on the bed, trying to stand erect. "The guards," he said, grunting. "I triggered the alarm—"

"Call them off," said Wolfe.

"Can't," said Stantz, finally standing up. "They're to assume I'm being held hostage if—"

The door smashed open. Men darted into the room, fanning out; in instants, three swords were at Wolfe's throat, crossbows bristling with bolts behind the swordsmen.

"Kill him?" grunted one of the guards. Wolfe was slightly annoyed at that, but only slightly; she was aware she cut a rather androgynous figure, and certainly her loose-fitting gray clothes did nothing to emphasize her femininity.

"No," said Stantz, rather embarrassedly, wrapping a blanket around his midriff. "Get us some tea. And a healer for Wolfe."

Fenstermann pushed up the manhole cover and peered down the moonlit alley. He didn't see anyone, so he climbed back down the ladder. "Give me the ten shillings," he told the boy.

"B-b-but . . . What am I—"

"Look, kid," said Fenstermann, "I have to show Wolfe some money to prove I sold you to the Szanbuists. She'll think ten shillings is poetic justice. Give me the money, and I'll let you go."

The boy looked hopeful for the first time in hours. He'd been terrible company, pissing and moaning away in his cell. Only by telling himself that anger was a mortal sin had Fenstermann avoided screaming at the lad.

"You will?" said the boy.

"Sure," said Fenstermann. "I suggest you leave Hamsterburg at once. If Wolfe finds you alive, you won't stay that way long. If people find out you killed von Krautz, your life isn't worth a shaven ha'penny. And if Siggy Whatsisname finds out you ratted on him . . ."

The boy's chin began to quiver again. "But where can I go?"

"Not my problem," said Fenstermann gently, unlocking the manacles. "Just be glad I'm letting you go."

The boy handed him a small purse and scrambled up the ladder.

"Hey," Fenstermann called after him, "slide the cover back over the hole . . ."

Running footfalls sounded, getting fainter with distance.

For a moment, Fenstermann stood staring up at the manhole and the starry sky beyond; then he climbed the ladder

himself, grabbed the manhole cover and dragged it into
place, scowling all the while at the ingratitude of the world.

Stantz was barefoot and bare-chested, if you could call
the folds of flesh sloping from shoulders to midriff a chest.
While the cleric finished his spell and taped the gauze over
Wolfe's wound, Stantz poured a noxious brown syrup into
a glass, covered it with water, stirred, then spoke a brief
cantrip. The water started to foam. Stantz took a sip.

"What's that?" asked Wolfe, as the cleric packed up his
asperger and candle. Oil lamps provided a dim illumination, and a guard stood watch by the door, ostensibly to
take a message if one was necessary, but in reality, Wolfe
knew, to keep an eye on her.

"Greep spritzer," said Stantz, sitting on the bed. It
creaked under the weight. "Want one?"

"I'll pass," said Wolfe.

"Good stuff," said Stantz. "So what have you got?"

"Sigismundo Hoffmann paid a boy on the Maiorkest
kitchen staff to poison the Lord Mayor's glass."

"Are you sure?" asked Stantz, looking surprised. Wolfe
couldn't remember seeing Stantz look surprised before.

"Yes," she said with an edge in her voice. "I'm sure."

"Sorry, Ren," said Stantz, putting his drink down and
rearranging his blanket. "Hoffmann works for Gerlad von
Grentz. Von Grentz is a cautious man. He wouldn't try to
kill Siebert unless he thought he was going to come out on
top in the struggle to follow . . . But why would he . . . ?"

Stantz lifted a fold of flesh to scratch beneath it while
he thought. Wolfe stood gingerly up—there was a twinge,
but not a bad one; the cleric had done his work well—and
went to the sideboard to pour herself a brandy. It was good
stuff; Stantz did not stint himself.

"Are we sure Hoffmann was working for von Grentz?"
asked Stantz. "Someone might have turned him, or he
might moonlight, if someone paid him enough."

"You'd know better than I," said Wolfe.

"Of course," said Stantz. "I'll check the file in the morning."

"You want me to bring Hoffmann in?"

"No, no," said Stantz, shaking his head. Wolfe was interested to see how much of Stantz's body jiggled with the motion. "No need to tip our hand; besides, von Grentz wouldn't have told Hoffmann anything. 'Get someone on the kitchen staff to put some of this in the Lord Mayor's glass,' with a big sum for doing the job. Hoffmann would know it was poison, but not why von Grentz wanted Siebert dead, or much of anything else."

Wolfe nodded. "What do you want me to do?"

Stantz was staring at a framed portrait on the wall: a scowling woman in dress that was several decades out of style. Wolfe guessed it might be his mother. "Von Grentz knows something we don't," he said. "His faction is strong, but not strong enough to force through its own candidate for the mayoralty."

"The *gens* von Grentz?" asked Wolfe.

"Eh? No, no. The Graf von Grentz is an Accommodationist."

Wolfe nodded.

"Von Grentz must think he has something that would clinch his election as Lord Mayor, if Siebert were out of the way," said Stantz, standing, lurching to his feet. "We need to know what it is."

Wolfe sighed. She didn't care, particularly, whether von Grentz was the next mayor or not. Stantz probably didn't, either; he just couldn't stand the notion that someone was keeping him in ignorance.

"You'll have to get into the Drachehaus," Stantz said.

Wolfe had heard the name, but couldn't place it. "Which is?"

"The von Grentz city residence," said Stantz.

"Wonderful," said Wolfe. "I'll bet their security is tighter than a constipate's anus."

Stantz snorted. "Then you, Madame Wolfe, must prove an effective laxative."

Wolfe blinked. "I prefer to think of myself in other terms," she said.

"No doubt," said Stantz. "And now, if you don't mind, I do intend to get a few hours' sleep."

"Fine," said Wolfe. Stantz was between her and a lamp, his shadow long on the floor before her. She stepped forward and—

Stantz blinked; one moment she was there, the next not.

He nodded and went to close and bolt the door.

How had she gotten in? he wondered as he lowered himself onto the bed. He kept the room pitch dark to eliminate even the faintest shadow. That was obviously not enough.

It was sometimes worrisome, having so effective a leftenant.

Someone knocked on the door.

"Dammit," Stantz called into the darkness, "I'm not to be disturbed."

"I'm sorry, sir," came a worried voice from outside; Bleichroder, his personal secretary. "It's the elvish ambassador, and she says it's urgent."

Stantz groaned, sat up, and reached for the blanket. It didn't look like he'd get any more sleep tonight.

He'd need to get dressed for this one; one could hardly meet the authorized representative of a great power with a blanket draped about one's midriff. "Get my valet," he said, and prepared to lurch to his feet, no easy task for a man of his bulk.

The elvish ambassador? What the devil does she want? Stantz wondered.

V.

It took them two days to travel from the faerie ring to the blasted remnants of the trees where the elves had made their stand. They were a haggard, unkempt crew when at last they arrived.

Charred tree trunks poked morosely up from the blackened earth. Before them ran a line of hastily dug graves. Timaeus wandered among them, sniffing at thé air, while the others stood before the graves.

"I have no intention of digging him up, Jasper," said Sidney. "If you say he's in that grave, I'll take your word for it."

"Look," said Nick. "You said yourself that your spell registered some change in Broderick. Death is change, isn't it?"

Jasper said, "Yes, but how can we be sure—"

"Have you ever seen a body that's been in the grave for a week?" asked Nick.

"Well, no. Have you?" said Jasper.

"Uh, no," said Nick. "I don't want to, either. The point is, what makes you think you'll be able to identify him if you do dig him up? Ever bought a steak, and kept it around for a week?"

"Well—" said Jasper.

"I did see him wounded," Frer Mortise pointed out. "The wound might have been severe enough for him to die."

"And it would be awfully convenient, for this von Grentz guy, Broderick dying," Nick said. "I think we've got evidence enough."

"If you want those bodies dug up," said Sidney irritably, "do it yourself."

"I say, look here," said Jasper. "Wouldn't it be best to be sure?"

"Me, I'm sure," said Nick. "I'm also tired and thirsty. We're maybe half a mile from that hamlet we saw earlier. I bet there's an inn there—and I bet every peasant for miles around knows what happened here, and whether Broddy bought it or not. I bet some of them are eating lunch at that inn right now, and I bet they'd be happy to spill their guts for a round of drinks."

"I wouldn't mind seeing Lotte again," said Frer Mortise.

"Good," said Sidney. "Let's go." She turned and led the way toward the town.

"Yes, but—I say," said Jasper. "Look here, we . . . Oh, dash it all." He flitted after the others.

They walked through the hamlet, down the dirt road—it was little more than a cow path, really. Nothing moved in the afternoon heat, save for far-off peasants, toiling desultorily in their distant fields.

They stepped gratefully into the inn's cool dimness.

Lotte stood behind the bar, hammering a tap into a keg. She looked up as they entered, pausing with hammer aloft; an expression of unease passed across her face.

"Hoy there, madam," said Timaeus, pulling out a chair at the first table by the door. "Ales all around, if you will."

Sidney took the trouble to survey the customers before sitting; it went against the grain to sit in the middle of the room, as Timaeus had so unthinkingly done. Better to have a solid wall behind your back. The inn's clientele did nothing to reassure her; rather than the expected mixture of peasants and local lushes, there were only two parties. One was a man sitting alone against one wall, by his mien and bearing a well-to-do mercenary or adventurer, an épée at his belt, clad in frock coat and frilled shirt. The other consisted of a dozen men and women, occupying two booths at the opposite end of the room. Near them, a cluster of pole-arms leaned against the wall; several wore sabers at belt. They were unarmored, but the utilitarian appearance of their garb and a certain coarseness of manner led Sidney to classify them instantly as soldiers.

Sidney was glad they wore no armor; that meant they were probably not expecting trouble. She amended that judgment; by the number of empty bottles on their two tables, they were certainly not expecting trouble. Lotte, finishing the tap's insertion with a few bangs of her hammer, began to fill glasses with ale.

"Travelers, quotha," said one of the soldiers, the words slightly slurred.

"So they be," said another. "Mauro, did I not charge you to watch the road?"

"Aye, sir," said the third, "but I was to be relieved on the second hour, which is long past time."

"Who was Mauro's relief?"

There was silence for a moment.

"You ordered none," said a voice with a hiccup.

"Well," said the one who had questioned Mauro. A hat with a plume sat before him, and Sidney took him for their captain. "No harm done, as they have had the good sense to break their journey at this excellent establishment." The captain got to his feet, stepped over his soldiers' legs with mumbled apologies on both sides, and lurched from the booth toward the table Timaeus had taken.

"Well met, sir," said Timaeus mildly.

"That remains to be seen," said the captain, the words coming with slight difficulty; Sidney judged he, like his subordinates, had been drinking for hours. "May I ask where you are going and what business you have in these parts?"

Timaeus's pipe, between his teeth, rose to a slightly defiant angle before he removed it the better to speak. "Why," he said, "we go where our noses take us, and our business is no man's but our own."

The captain grew red; there was a stir from the booths as soldiers began to realize they might have to rouse themselves soon. "You're going to get us killed," Sidney warned.

"I am not accustomed to being accosted in such rude fashion by drunken riffraff," said Timaeus.

Lotte darted in with a platter and plunked down their ales with dispatch. As she set down Mortise's, she whispered in his ear, "They're bad ones; best leave yarely."

"Bless you," Mortise said loudly, "and thanks for your hospitality." He looked at that moment less like a peaceful cleric than a warrior with the battlelight in his eye.

"Are you aware that you are in the territory of the Serene Hamsterian Republic?" demanded the captain, one hand on the pommel of his sword.

"Are we?" said Timaeus. "Oh, good."

"You may expect, therefore," said the captain, "to be required by the authorities of the Republic to state your business and to display your papers."

"Pish," said Timaeus, taking a slug of his ale. "You do not wear the badge of Hamsterburg."

And it was true; the clasp at the captain's shoulder bore a dragon segreant, gules over argent. Hamsterburg's arms, famed across the human lands, were the hamster statant regardant.

"True," said the captain. "We are of the Graf von Grentz's Guisardieres; this village of Weintroockle lies within the von Grentz demesne." He took a look over his shoulder at the booths, where his company had managed to form into a loose and slightly drunken semblance of military order, took a deep breath, and said, "Wherefore, I order you to produce your papers instantly."

"Oh, very well," said Timaeus mildly, reaching for his pouch. "Madam, another round if you will." While the innkeeper collected the steins, crouching as if expecting open warfare to begin at any moment, he pawed through the pouch's contents until he found his Durfalian *passeport*. The others found and proffered their own documents.

The captain gravely fumbled through their papers while Lotte brought refilled steins. He studied one document carefully, frowning at it, looking over the top of the sheaf of papers at Kraki. Kraki stared back, nose in a stein, one hairy leg on the table.

"Kraki Kronarsson?" the captain said.

"Is me," said the barbarian.

"These papers say you are of the dwarven race," said the captain.

"Is right," said Kraki, nodding, then gave an enormous belch.

"That's absurd," said the captain. Kronarsson stood more than six feet tall.

"If papers say I am dwarf, I am dwarf," said Kraki shrugging. "Is hokay by me."

The captain studied the papers a moment longer, then laid them on the table, stepped back, murmured, "Arms forward," to his soldiers—there were a rustle and clank as they turned into an orderly hedgehog of pole-arms—and announced, "Timaeus d'Asperge, I have orders to take you and your companions into custody."

Lotte cursed faintly and dived behind the bar.

Kraki put down his stein and began to harry the spaces between his teeth with a thumbnail. Neither he nor the others rose. There was silence for a moment. Sidney put her hands on the table, the palms slightly cupped, ready to snatch the throwing knives from her sleeves.

Timaeus said, "That's *Magister* d'Asperge to you," and brought his forefinger to his pipe. There was a loud bang, and flames briefly enveloped his head. When they dissipated, the pipe was lit, Timaeus puffing contentedly.

"Will you come peaceably?" the captain demanded.

"My dear fellow," said Timaeus, "I shan't come, peaceably or elsewise. If we are to have peace, you must desist from this futile insistence."

There came a voice from across the room. "By Dion, I like your spirit." The man in the frock coat was standing, a hand on the hilt of his épée.

The captain eyed the man unhappily. "Are you a Hamsterian citizen, sir?"

"I am," responded the man.

"Then by order of the Graf von Grentz, do not interfere in our business."

"By order of von Grentz, eh? The most despicable of a despised *gens*, an Accommodationist, and a lover of catamites to boot. By the love I bear for Hamsterburg, any enemy of Gerlad von Grentz is a friend of mine."

The captain barked, "Hold," over his shoulders at his men, marched smartly around the table where Sidney and the others sat, and drew his saber, holding it vertically before his nose. "You will withdraw your vile assertion," he stated. Sidney noted that the slur in his speech had disappeared.

"Which assertion?" said the frock-coated man. "That the *gens* von Grentz is despised? That Gerlad prefers his boys below the age of consent? Or—"

The captain shouted, "Draw your blade, or so help me, I shall cut you down where you are."

The frock-coated man smiled and said, "If you insist, good sir." He began to remove his coat, displaying long, white, and somewhat soiled sleeves with lace cuffs.

"Captain," said one of the soldiers uneasily, "we've unfinished business—"

"So vile a slander must not be tolerated," spat the captain. "I charge you, hold."

The soldiers bore unhappy faces, but maintained their formation. Sidney wondered what they must be thinking; a massed formation of guisardieres was effective on the battlefield, and should be sufficient to deal with five or six adventurers—but not if one of them was a fire mage. A single fireball could wipe them out. And they had seen Timaeus light his pipe; they knew what they faced.

The swordsman had finished removing his frock coat. He took his épée from his belt and held it likewise before his face. "My name is Pablo von Kremnitz," he said. "I would be honored to learn yours before I kill you."

"There is no need," said the captain, and gave a sudden vicious cut toward the other's head. The épée twitched, and the captain's saber was deflected upward, missing its target. The captain recovered quickly; they stood facing each other for a moment, both in fighting stance—sword extended, one foot forward, the rear foot pointing away from the body. With a sudden clash of steel, they were in motion again. The captain lunged forward, von Kremnitz dodging aside, the épée's blade angled to deflect a sudden cut. The captain followed his weapon around and brought it back to defensive position.

"Vhy doesn't he have soldiers kill that man?" asked Kraki, studying the passage at arms with interest.

"That would be dishonorable," said Nick. There was a sardonic tone in his voice; he had the thief's amused contempt for aristocratic notions of honor.

Kraki blinked, obviously puzzled. "Someone insult you, you and friends kill him," he said. "Not dishonorable to gang up; good joke on him, ho ho, stupid to make insult vithout pals around for back up. You vant rest of ale, Nickie?"

Tensely, Nick shook his head, scanning the room, like Sidney ready to act instantly if the situation got out of hand. Kraki grabbed Nick's stein and drained it.

Von Kremnitz lunged, the captain twisting out of the épée's way. Von Kremnitz was compelled onward by the momentum of his own thrust, leaping atop the table where Sidney and the others sat, upsetting several steins. Nick, Sidney, and Mortise jumped away, chairs toppling backward; Timaeus sat stolidly where he was, puffing his pipe and leaning back, while Kraki merely removed his leg from the table so that it wouldn't be trod upon and snatched one of the toppling steins, to drain whatever remnants it contained. Swords clashed inches from his face; he studied the swordplay with interest. Sidney itched to plant a dagger in the captain's brisket, but decided against it; there was no telling how his soldiers would react.

The captain had backed off, apparently misliking the advantage the height of the table gave his opponent. Von Kremnitz leaped down, charged the other, ducked under the defensively held saber while sweeping upward with his own blade, struck the captain in the stomach with his left fist, whirled past, and, the captain not quite recovered, cut toward the captain's face with his épée, drawing a line of blood up the right cheek.

Von Kremnitz stamped back and held his épée vertical before his face again. "First blood," he said.

The captain looked shaken, but still angered. "Insufficient," he grated and danced forward, saber sweeping up in a block, then sideways in a cut, a maneuver that might have injured the swordsman's thigh if he had been where

the captain had expected—but he had moved inward, inside the captain's stroke.

For a long moment, they appeared to embrace, the apparent tenderness belied by the thin line of von Kremnitz's
steel protruding from the captain's back.

The captain gave a gurgle and fell, sliding off the blade.

Von Kremnitz assumed a fighting stance, against the
possibility that the soldiers would attempt to avenge the
death of their leader.

"He killed the captain, Mauro," said one.

"I have eyes, Kevork," said Mauro.

"Let us slay the murderer," said Kevork.

"I think not," said Timaeus, standing up. "Your captain
challenged this gentleman; the forms were obeyed. There
was no murder."

"You are under arrest," said Mauro. "Stand aside."

"Kraki, please stand between me and the soldiers," said
Timaeus.

"Hokay," said the barbarian, lumbering to his feet and
pulling his sword from its sheath at his back. The cubits-
long length of steel made both saber and épée look like
toys.

"I believe that my friend can delay you sufficiently long
to allow me to cast a spell," said Timaeus. "I see no wards
among you. If you persist in attempting to capture us, or
offer injury to the gentleman, I will not be responsible for
the consequences. Indeed, under the circumstances, I suggest that it is advisable for you to depart this establishment."

"What do we do, Mauro?" asked one of the soldiers.

While Mauro dithered, Sidney and Nick went to stand
by Timaeus; Sidney produced her throwing daggers, since
intimidation seemed more useful at present than surprise,
and Nick, seeing this, did likewise. To her surprise, Frer
Mortise joined them, displaying his hatchet, which he
tossed and caught repeatedly with his right hand, the

weapon twirling with each toss, but caught always by the shaft. Von Kremnitz joined Kraki facing off against the soldiers, though what use he expected his épée to be against pole-arms Sidney could not say. That left only Jasper. And where was he?

A mumbling was coming from underneath the table, Sidney realized; she didn't quite catch the Words, but suspected it might be a spell.

Several of the soldiers were wavering slightly, as if nearly too inebriated to stand. Their formation was tight enough to keep all erect, though guisards dipped and swung unsteadily. Could they be that drunk?

"I bet they won' riss—riss a fireball in here, Maur'. Room's too small. An' . . . an' . . ."

One of the soldiers fell to his knees and emptied his stomach on the worn, knotty boards of the floor. Another simply collapsed and began to snore. Mauro sat unsteadily down in one of the booths, as if unable to stand any longer.

Soldier by soldier, the formation disintegrated. More than one lost his lunch; several passed out, others managed to sit, looking rather sick, clutching the table as if they needed support.

Jasper was flitting in the air above them now, green light swooping in circles. "Can't keep it up for long," he said quickly. "Tie them up, won't you?" And then he resumed chanting.

"N-no," said Mauro. "Is—is—no. Can' allow . . ." He struggled to his feet, lurched forward, slipped in vomit, and crashed to the floor.

"I vant vhat they've been drinking," Kraki said to Lotte.

"It's not the wine," said Timaeus, "it's Jasper's spell. They were drunk already; I imagine he merely magnified the effect. Sidney, have we enough rope?"

She was already searching through her pack. "I don't think we brought any," she said worriedly. "Didn't need it in the woods, and weight was at a premium."

"Oh, dear," said Frer Mortise. "I'd really rather we didn't kill them."

"Wait a minute," said Nick. He turned to the innkeeper and asked, "You've got a cellar?"

"Aye," Lotte said hesitantly.

"Is there a lock on the door?"

"Oh, aye," she said.

Nick went over to one of the sleeping soldiers, lifted her legs by the bootheels, and pulled her toward the taproom door. "Show me where it is," he said.

"But sir—these are soldiers of the graf, they'll have me hung if I—"

Nick snorted. "We forced you," he said soothingly. "Threatened to kill you, to burn the inn. You were terrified out of your wits."

"Aye," she said in a tiny, tearful voice.

"Besides," said Nick reluctantly, as he hauled the soldier out the door, head bumping on the lintel, "there's money in it for you."

"Oh, aye," said Lotte, sounding much better. She followed him out of the room. "A dozen pounds should do it."

"A dozen what?" came Nick's horrified voice from down the corridor.

Sidney was already stripping the soldiers of their weapons—and their purses. She pocketed the latter, hiding this action from the eyes of the others, more from sheer habit than from any real desire for the small sums these poor wretches were carrying. "Come on, damn it," she said. "Give me a hand. We've got to get them all in the cellar before Jasper gives out."

The green light was circling a little more slowly now, and the Words of Jasper's spell did sound a little more tired.

"Easier yust to cut throats," complained Kraki, but he tucked a soldier under each arm and dragged the two of them toward the door, their boots trailing on the planks behind.

VI.

Jasper's light hung motionless over a bar stool. "Thank goodness," he said. "I'll have some of the local wine, if you will, my dear."

"Righto," said Lotte cheerfully, reaching for a bottle. "Thanks for not trashing the place. I tell you, I practically had a heart attack when—"

"Not at all, not at all," Jasper murmured. "You wouldn't serve a cold luncheon, by any chance?"

"I can rustle up something," she said. "Give me a mo'." She bustled out toward the kitchen.

"I do trust you'll let us stand you a drink or two," Timaeus said to von Kremnitz.

"Of course," said the swordsman, throwing a leg over a stool himself, shifting his belt so that his épée wouldn't stick into the person at the next stool, who chanced to be Sidney. "If you will permit an inquiry . . . ?"

"Mm?" said Timaeus, knocking ash from his pipe.

"The graf's soldiery seem to be well acquainted with

you, good sir. I'm afraid I, however, am ignorant of the House d'Asperge. By your accent, I perceive you to be Athelstani; may I inquire how you came to these parts?"

"Certainly," said Timaeus, extracting pipe cleaners, a cloth, and a scouring tool from his pouch. "We—"

"Wait," said Sidney. "How do you know we can trust this guy?"

Von Kremnitz gave her a wounded look. "My dear," he said, "I *am* a gentleman."

Nick snorted. "Is that supposed to reassure us?"

"I'm not your dear," snapped Sidney. "And I agree, you helped us with those soldiers. But obviously for your own reasons. I—"

"See here, Sidney," said Timaeus, bristling. "We need hardly assume that everyone we meet is a potential betrayer. After all, our intentions are good, our goal—"

"Right, and you're such a good judge of character," said Sidney. "Know how trustworthy someone is right off the bat, every time. Sure. Remember Lenny the Lizard?"

"Yes, but this is diff—"

"And I thought we'd agreed to keep up our cover until we reached Hamsterburg."

"Cover?" said Timaeus. "What, our cover as itinerant rug merchants? Damned thin, even when we had a wagon full of rugs, which, as I may point out, we no longer do. It's—"

"Ach, always argue, argue, argue," said Kraki. He vaulted over the bar, found a five-gallon jug, held it to the tap, and began to fill it with ale.

Sidney and Timaeus glared at each other past a bemused von Kremnitz.

Jasper sighed. "It may perhaps be impolite of us to say so, but we *have* just met. Our reception hereabouts has not, so far, predisposed us to place our trust in chance acquaintances. Perhaps you could tell us a little about yourself."

"Of course," said von Kremnitz, getting off his stool, putting his heels together, pulling a handkerchief from his sleeve, and making a formal bow, waving the handkerchief gracefully. "Pablo von Kremnitz, Leftenant, Mayoral Foot Guards."

The others introduced themselves. Timaeus picked up a pipe cleaner and began to draw it through the stem of his disassembled meerschaum.

"You are, therefore," said Jasper, "an agent of the Hamsterian state?"

"In a manner of speaking," said von Kremnitz, retaking his seat.

"I think it wise, then, for us to maintain a degree of discretion," Jasper said. His glass of wine rose and tilted back. Timaeus snorted and probed at the bowl of his pipe with a tool.

Von Kremnitz stiffened. "You propose to injure the interests of Hamsterburg?"

"Not at all," said Jasper soothingly. "We are, in fact, more or less indifferent to the interests of Hamsterburg. We are more interested in the fate of humanity as a whole. Indeed, of the Free Peoples in their great contest with the Slave States of the—"

"Oh, come on," said von Kremnitz, chortling. "I mean, what do you take me for?"

"Here you are," said the innkeeper cheerily, sweeping into the room with an enormous platter piled high with cold mutton, olives, caponato, bread, sliced tomatoes, and various alimentary pastes.

"My word," said Timaeus, "that does look good." For a long time, the only sounds were those of mastication— joined by thumps and shouts from below.

"Sounds like our friends are recovering," said Nick.

"Are they secure down there?" asked Sidney.

"Only one way out. We pulled up the ladder and barred the door," said Nick.

"Moreover," said Jasper, "I imagine they will be more concerned with the state of their heads than escape for quite a while."

"Hung over, you think?" asked von Kremnitz.

"Massively," said Jasper complacently.

When the repast had been cleared away, Timaeus turned to Lotte. "Now, then, madam," he said. "Within the past fortnight, a small battle has been fought in these parts, has it not?"

"Aye, sir," she said.

"A fellow by the name of Broderick de Biddleburg rode with the Graf von Grentz. A grave with a marker bearing his name lies by the battle site. Would you know if, in truth, his body lies within it?"

"I'm sorry," she said, "I don't know that name."

"The man who stole your horse," Frer Mortise said.

Lotte grimaced. "Yes," she said. "I heard he died. And serve him right."

"The elves had a statue," said Nick. "Did von Grentz take it?"

"Oh," said Lotte, "yes. Most of the town watched from the ridge, you know. Yes, there was a big brown statue with the elves, and the graf put it into a wagon—took the wagon from Johnny Muller without so much as a by-your-leave."

"And where did they take it?" asked Jasper.

Lotte shrugged. "Back to the castle, I imagine," she said.

Sidney cleared her throat. "So much for discretion," she said, nodding meaningfully toward von Kremnitz, who had followed this exchange with interest.

"Broderick de Biddleburg?" demanded von Kremnitz.

"That's right," said Nick.

"Turfed out in a revolution recently, wasn't he?"

"Quite so," said Timaeus.

"And we're discussing the statue of Stantius? Found by adventurers in Urf Durfal?"

"Yes, yes, obviously," said Timaeus irritably.

Von Kremnitz was silent for a moment. "What I don't understand is why you want it," he said.

"Don't," said Sidney.

"It *is* ours," said Timaeus. "We found it, after all."

"You're those adventurers?" von Kremnitz asked.

"Yes," said Jasper.

"That's how the graf's men knew your name, then," said von Kremnitz. "When I heard the story, your name wasn't mentioned, but I suppose it's recorded somewhere."

"Possibly," said Timaeus. "We have tried to be discreet, but everyone and his brother seems to be interested in the damned thing."

"Why don't you sell it, then?" asked von Kremnitz.

"Well," said Sidney, "we have to take it to Arst-Kara-Morn."

Von Kremnitz looked horrified. "Whatever for?"

"Er—I'm not entirely clear on that," said Sidney apologetically. "Vic seems very set on it, though. Cosmic significance, and so on."

"Vic?"

"You haven't met him," said Timaeus.

"Where is he?"

"Beats us," said Nick morosely.

Von Kremnitz looked at them each in turn. "No wonder you lost the bloody thing," he said at last.

"Now see here," said Timaeus sharply. "There's no call for—"

"You probably don't even realize the significance," said von Kremnitz.

"Certainly we do, old man," said Jasper. "The spirit of Stantius, last Human King, is bound therein. Until it be freed, humanity is fated to conflict and dissension, sundered into many states, easy prey for the advancing armies of the east. We must—"

"Bosh," said von Kremnitz, waving a hand. "Fairy tales. The real rub is this: Von Grentz will use it to depose my master, to make himself ruler of all Hamsterburg. And associated provinces. I must return to the city at once. You must come with me; I can promise you the Lord Mayor's assistance in recovering your stolen property."

"Excellent!" said Timaeus, beaming. "You see, Sidney; occasionally, it pays to place your trust in a gentleman."

"It does?" said Sidney skeptically.

"You can promise the Lord Mayor's help, huh?" said Nick.

"Indubitably," said von Kremnitz. "Come, we must be off."

"Right," said Nick. "A lowly leftenant of the Mayor's Guard can bind the ruler of a great human state."

"You have my word," said von Kremnitz stiffly.

But Nick only snorted.

"The old gray mare, she ain't what she used to be," Nick observed.

"We are scraping the bottom of the barrel, rather," said Jasper dubiously, circling Timaeus and his mount for a closer look. Timaeus's horse was indeed a gray mare and, as Nick had intimated, had clearly seen better days. She was swaybacked, her long teeth protruded, and she sighed tiredly as she gazed dumbly at the dusty ground. Timaeus sat atop her, yawning. He was the first to mount up; the reins of the other horses were tied still to a long bar. They looked little more prepossessing than Timaeus's.

"Get a move on, get a move on," said von Kremnitz, bustling around and tightening the cinch on the saddle of his own horse, a spirited white gelding. "Time is of the essence."

Kraki gave an enormous belch. "Ve make sure ve have lots of supplies," he said.

"Yes, confound it," said von Kremnitz. "You've got three times the food you need; it's a two-day journey to Hamsterburg if we push it. What the devil do you—"

The innkeeper approached with a wheelbarrow, in which a cask of ale lay. "Here you are, sir," she said to Kraki.

"Thank you," said the barbarian. He tucked the cask under one arm, untied one of the horses, and vaulted astride her, reins in one hand, cask in the other.

"You can't be serious," said von Kremnitz.

Kraki gave him a wide, snaggle-toothed smile.

"I really don't understand what all the rush is for," said Timaeus, a little sleepily; the ale and the heat of the afternoon were making him drowsy.

"We must get to the Maiorkest as soon as we are able," said von Kremnitz, vaulting to his own mount's back. "That thing in Gerlad von Grentz's hands for more than a week ... I don't care to contemplate ... Well come on, come on, mount up, by all the gods; what the devil are you lolling about for?"

"See here, Pablo," said Sidney nastily. "We barely know you. What gives you the right to—"

"Leftenant von Kremnitz is understandably agitated," said Jasper soothingly. "And he has offered to assist us, Sidney. Do take a horse, my dear; if he is right, we shall find the statue in Hamsterburg."

Sidney muttered something, but consented to mount. Together they set off down the road. Von Kremnitz adopted a trot, and the others were forced to do likewise to stay abreast.

Sidney scowled. "Slow down, dammit," she said. "The horses won't take this for more than—"

"We must get well away from the inn, and quickly," said von Grentz.

"Weeks sleeping on rocks and subsisting on half-raw

squirrel and mushrooms of doubtful provenance," said Timaeus, jouncing up and down uncomfortably, "a fortnight dancing attendance to a bunch of fool fays; the first opportunity to have a good night's sleep in a comfortable feather bed, and we go gallivanting off on a mare with a trot like an overgrown March hare on the dustiest godsforsaken road I've yet to see in the full glare of a blazingly hot sun. What's wrong with a nice, slow walk?"

"How long do you think it will be before our erstwhile hostess lets von Grentz's soldiers out of their hole?" asked von Kremnitz.

"They're probably out by now," said Nick. "If she's going to make the claim that we forced her stick, she'd better let them out as fast as she can."

"Quite right," said von Kremnitz. "And though we took all the horses, they'll pursue. Best we get some distance ahead."

"Yes, all right," said Timaeus. "But tell me, sir; why do you believe our statue will have such an impact on Hamsterian politics? Why such urgency?"

"You don't understand," said von Kremnitz in a frustrated tone. "The political balance in Hamsterburg is exceedingly fine."

"Why should a statue make a difference?"

Von Kremnitz sighed. "The Lord Mayor of Hamsterburg claims regency over all humanity in the Human King's absence."

"Yes," said Jasper, "a claim no one else acknowledges."

"True," said von Kremnitz, "but we take it seriously. The symbols of Empire are used to bolster our Lord Mayor's rule; the Scepter of Stantius, kept in the highest tower of the Maiorkest for centuries, has long been a symbol of the state. When it began to glow, that was taken as a sign of divine confidence in our new lord, Hamish Siebert, my master; and he has need of every confidence, for he has the support of no faction but his own, and it is small."

"How was he elected, then?" asked Jasper.

"No single faction could force its candidate through, and so they agreed on a man they thought a nonentity," said von Kremnitz.

"And is he?" asked Nick.

"Nay," said von Kremnitz. "He is a man of action, a man of his word; already, he has reformed the civil service, instituted a draft, expanded the military, thrown public works to open bidding, put our foreign relations on new and—"

"Yes, yes, all right," said Timaeus. "He is a veritable doyen of virtue. Your opinion is entirely disinterested, I suppose."

"Well," said von Kremnitz, slightly apologetically, "he *is* my lord. But you see, the possession of the statue by someone else would indicate to the superstitious that the mandate of heaven had passed to another. And von Grentz is a big man in the Accommodationist party. I greatly fear we will find open warfare in the streets of Hamsterburg when we arrive."

"Dandy," said Timaeus. "I always like to time my visits to a new city to coincide with riots, rebellion, and plague. I accept that the Lord Mayor will want to recover the statue from von Grentz, but can we trust him to return it to us?"

"Of a certainty," said von Kremnitz heartily. "We have a common objective: to pry the thing from the clutches of the despised von Grentz. And I have no doubt that My Lord Hamish will be touched to the quick, as I have been, by your inspiring quest, the need to free the spirit of Stantius, and the ancient sorcery it involves."

"Good," said Sidney. Privately, she thought otherwise; if the statue was such big medicine in Hamsterburg's rococo politics, wouldn't the Lord Mayor want to keep it for himself? And thinking back, von Kremnitz hadn't been so much touched to the quick by their inspiring quest as convulsed with laughter at its idiocy and futility.

He bore watching, that one.

part III.

intrigue in old hamsterburg

1.

Some love the sun. They delight in blue skies, warm sunlight, the crisp clarity of a perfect spring day. They are morose in the dimness of midwinter, become joyful as the days lengthen, curse the heavens when it rains. They spring happily from bed at the break of dawn, and return yawning thereto as the sun slips behind the world's far edge.

Renée Wolfe was not among them.

Sunlight made her eyes hurt. She liked the peacefulness of gloomy days, the quiet coolness of dripping clouds, the noiselessness of fog. She looked forward to winter, which in Hamsterburg rarely brought snow, instead producing rain, chill winds, and blessedly long nights. But most of all, she loved times such as these, the yawning midnight hours, the moon sailing ship-like through a sea of scattered clouds, stars wheeling serenely in the heavens, the sleepy world at peace. The streets of Hamsterburg were devoid of hubbub, save for an occasional burst of gaiety as a tavern door opened to expel another homebound drunk. There were few abroad, other than she; a night watchman, a late-night carouser, a burglar searching quietly for a place to rob in peace.

She slipped through the night, unseen and unaccounted, until she came where she was bound: the Drachehaus, the mansion of von Grentz.

It was not what she had expected. Oh, the grounds were typical: carefully manicured, the trees now bursting with flowers—cherry blossoms and dogwood. And the high cast-iron fence about it was not unusual, for a mansion in Hamsterburg. But the architecture was uncommon: neither mock-Imperial nor rococo Durfalian, but severely plain. It reminded her of the temples of the Sons of the Morning, who eschewed all ornament and frivolity; it consisted of plain stone blocks, windows placed regularly, towers and crenellations giving a hint of the fortress it could undoubtedly become in time of need. The only real ornamentation stood above the lintel of the great door, a door above high marble steps: It was a dragon segreant, elaborately displayed. Wolfe admired the artistry that had gone into the carving, as well as the cold ruthlessness the figure seemed to convey.

The fence posed no great obstacle, nor yet the walls; it was a warm night, and several windows were open. Still, she hesitated; surely there would be wards, and it would be best to divine their nature first.

She walked slowly along the fence. There were no visible magical effects, which merely meant the inhabitants did not desire that there be such. She did not touch the iron bars, lest even that trigger some magical reaction. At the corner, where the fence turned a right angle, she examined the post carefully.

It was large, round, and evidently hollow. Craning, she saw that, inside the fence, there was a locked metal door in the side of the post. She nodded; spells require a source of power, and many are effected through the manipulation of physical similarity elements. No doubt objects used to create and maintain a magical effect along the fence were stored within the post.

Unfortunately, this told her little of the nature of the magic. Still, she could be sure of several things. There would be a ward to detect physical entry: It might sense the body heat of someone crossing the fence, or the passage of a soul, or the presence of life force, or possibly of mentation. There would undoubtedly be a detection spell to sense the use of magic, and possibly an active spell to suppress the use of the more common methods of magical flight. And there might be spells to inflict physical harm on those who dared to attempt entry, triggered by any of the methods of detection.

She had entered Stantz's bedroom by the means that offered her ingress almost everywhere; she was a mage of the shadows. She had merged with her own shadow, her body, mind, and soul simply becoming part of the trace of light on matter. As a shadow, she could go anywhere where there was at least a little light, at least a little dark; anywhere that was not wholly sealed against entry. She was not completely invisible, so disguised: An alert observer might note a shadow moving without a body to cast it. Still, she was the closest thing to invisible.

That might not suffice here. As a shadow, she had no thickness and could easily slip under the fence; as a shadow, she had no body, and cast no body heat. Still, she would cross the fence; and depending on what wards were in force, that might trigger a response. She needed magic to merge with her own shadow; a ward might register the passage of that magic. She retained her mind and soul in shadow form, and either of those things might be sensed.

An oak tree stood on the other side of the fence, perhaps a dozen feet away. Wolfe looked up; branches extended from the trunk toward the fence, but had been trimmed

where they would have passed above it. She smiled; von
Grentz, or whoever handled his security, had realized that
branches, crossing the line of the wards, might provide a
method of entry.

Had they considered that the tree's mere shadow might
do the same?

The moon was nearly full, full enough that the tree's
shadow was visible on gray grass. Alas, it was but an hour
after midnight, and the moon high above the horizon. The
shadow of the oak was small, and contained wholly within
the Drachehaus grounds. That would change with the passage of time, the motion of the moon across the sky.

Wolfe sighed, then walked across the street. A long wall
stretched there, protecting another mansion, and in its shelter she would be less obvious. She settled down to wait.

Long hours passed. Stars wheeled overhead. The moon
sank toward the horizon. Slowly, the oak tree's shadow
crept toward the fence.

At last, Wolfe rose, stretched, and strolled back across the
road. The shadow extended out across the sidewalk now.

Wolfe whispered a spell. She hardly needed to; she had
trained herself to say the Words of magic silently, a necessary skill for one who, as a shadow, had no voice. Still, it
was a little easier to say the Words out loud.

Suddenly, no Wolfe stood there. Even her shadow was
gone.

Crossing the fence might trigger defensive wards; Wolfe
did not cross the fence. Instead, she merged with the oak
tree's shadow, a shadow both within and without the fence.
She never crossed the fence; she was within and without it,
the mere shadow of a tree.

Silently, a silent shadow cast a spell; and a dark-clad
woman stepped from the shadow of the tree and into the
garden.

No alarms went off; no spells were triggered.

Wolfe smiled.

* * *

The small room's floor was covered with rushes. Each wall was pierced by a single window, an unusually proportioned window, tall and thin: the window of a fortification, from which a soldier might study besiegers while exposing himself as little as possible. There were no besiegers here; outside were gardens, mansions, pleasure lakes and gazebos—the Enclave, Hamsterburg's wealthiest parish. Perhaps the builder had admired the severe lines of fortifications elsewhere; perhaps he had feared the need to fortify his mansion in harsher times to come.

Through the east window, pink rays shone, casting a pink rectangle of light against the rush-covered floor. The other three windows admitted only dim gray illumination; it was barely dawn.

Against the north wall was a niche, and in it a shrine. Against the south was a door: a heavy oaken door, bound in cast iron. A metal bar stood by it, not in use.

Enter von Grentz. The door swung open on well-oiled hinges. He was simply clad, a few yards of untailored cloth draped over a shoulder and around the waist, belted by a velvet rope, clasped by a plain bronze pin. On his feet were sandals. Around the periphery of his scalp ran a thin line of hair, black in parts but mostly gray, close-cropped in defiance of ultimate baldness. In his hand, he carried a single camellia blossom, fresh-plucked from his garden, the petals still bedewed.

He went to the shrine, rushes rustling beneath his feet, and knelt. A bowl of water stood at the center of the niche; a shallow bowl, gently sloping, glazed, fired the tan color of the original clay, unaltered save for a few broad blue lines applied by a brush before firing. Gently, von Grentz placed the blossom at the bowl's center.

Above the bowl, at the back of the niche, plain iron brackets held a naked saber. The blade was highly polished, the hilt wrapped with unadorned hide. Using both hands, von Grentz lifted it from its brackets and held it atop one bent knee, palms upward. He lowered his head to kiss the blade, then returned it to its place.

A shadow moved noiselessly across the rushes and merged with the shadow of the wall beneath the eastern window.

Von Grentz was still, kneeling before the bowl, gazing unseeing into the stone wall of the niche, the rectangle of pink on the floor behind him moving slowly toward its window, the pink transforming gradually to saffron, then to white. He was lost in meditation.

Enter a lich. The door swung open; the creature glided into the room, black robe veiling most of its form, long finger bones protruding from the sleeves. Empty eye sockets turned away from the young morning light, as if uncomfortable at such brilliance. It moved with curious stillness, no sound of rushes crunching beneath its feet, no click of toe bones on floor.

A shadow perhaps shrank closer to the wall; lichs were famously powerful mages. If it thought to cast a detection spell, it might sense that there was more in the shadows of the room than the mere interplay of light and matter.

"You have examined the statue?" inquired von Grentz, without turning around.

"I have," whispered the lich.

Von Grentz stood gracefully and faced it. "And?" he said.

"It is under several spells," whispered the lich, moving into the room's deepest shadow in search of sanctuary from the light; did that shadow flinch somehow away? "The most recent is intended to prevent others from detecting its magical emanations. The others are more complex, more powerful; a binding."

"Yes," said von Grentz, "but is the rumor true? Does it contain the spirit of the Human King?"

"Yes," whispered the lich. "Yes, indeed."

"Excellent," said von Grentz. A smile danced momentarily across those thin lips. "You support our objectives still?"

The lich was silent for a long moment. "Support your objectives?" it said at last. "I have aided you because I have found it useful—and profitable—to do so. But to reach accommodation with Arst-Kara-Morn? That's a fool's game. There is no accommodation, not short of the grave. Nor even then, I fear. You don't have the slightest idea what you're dealing with."

"With what am I dealing?" said von Grentz, raising a skeptical eyebrow.

"Would you have riches beyond your imagining?" whispered the lich. "Power beyond that any man has wielded in millennia? Houris at your beck and call? Whatever your desire, it may be yours."

"I know what I wish," said von Grentz. "I intend to have it. Who are you, that you believe you can grant it?"

"Not I," said the lich. "Arst-Kara-Morn."

"And was it not you who just argued the impossibility of dealing with them?"

"You do not know what you have," whispered the lich. "If you do not give it to them, for whatever price, they will hunt it, and you, for as long as it takes."

"You serve them?" asked von Grentz bluntly.

The lich shuddered. "I do not," it said. It did not add: I have. I shall probably have to again.

"I have another notion in mind," said von Grentz. "But I don't know if you can be trusted."

The lich emitted a curious whirring noise. The sound went on for several moments. It took von Grentz some time to place the noise: The lich was chuckling.

Eventually, the whirring died away. "Do you trust your cat?" asked the lich.

"I don't have a cat," said von Grentz, with considerable irritation. He was a dog person, actually.

"Whom *do* you trust?"

"Granted," von Grentz said, apparently coming to a decision. "Thank you for assisting me this far. I consider myself in your debt. I have ordered a carriage readied to your specifications, with thick curtains drawn over the windows; it will take you to your—"

"Hold," whispered the lich, raising one bony hand.

Von Grentz was silent, regarding the creature. After a pause, it spoke. "You called me here to verify the statue's authenticity, but an historian or any number of wizards could have done so. You wish me to perform some other task, but have decided I am not sufficiently trustworthy.

"Mere possession of the statue bolsters your political position, since the credulous will take ownership to indicate divine favor. I conclude that this other task involves necromancy, and the statue."

Von Grentz made no reply. The two stared at each other for a long moment, blue eyes into empty sockets.

"If I assume you know more about necromancy than the usual layman," whispered the lich, "I come to an unsettling conclusion."

"Would Arst-Kara-Morn still be interested if the spirit of Stantius no longer occupied the statue?" asked von Grentz softly.

"I am not sure you understand the complexities," whispered the lich.

Von Grentz raised an eyebrow. "It seems straightforward enough," he said. "Simply transfer the spirit from the statue into my body."

The lich shook its skull. "No," it said. "The spirit is bound into the statue, by ancient and powerful magic; unbinding will require great power. Moreover, if I were to do as you ask, you would become schizophrenic."

Von Grentz frowned. "But mind and spirit are separable; why should Stantius's mind be reborn in my body?"

"It wouldn't," whispered the lich. "The claim that mind

and spirit are separable is simplistic; mind is the epiphenomenon of spirit in body. Adding a second spirit to your frame would add a second mind to yours—a new one birthed on the instant, most likely without Stantius's memories."

"This is not appealing," said von Grentz. "The idea is impossible, then?"

"No," said the lich. "The trick is to free the spirit of Stantius while transferring its divine aspect to you. That is, not to transfer the actual spirit into your body, but to transfer its association with the divine, to render you king. This will require enormous power."

Von Grentz frowned. "Do you have sufficient power?" he asked.

The lich said, "No, no, you do not understand. I have the skill; the power I draw from death."

"The task will require many deaths?" said von Grentz.

"Precisely," said the lich.

Von Grentz frowned. "Human sacrifice—"

"Is not necessary," said the lich. "A revolution, say, put down as bloodily as possible; a battle, a massacre—"

"Ah," said von Grentz with relief. "Something along those lines can be arranged. What do you want for your participation?"

The lich considered. What did it want? Surcease, it supposed; an end. It gave a soundless sigh. Von Grentz's scheme was mad, of course; the ritual that bound Stantius's spirit was so powerful that a dozen wizards could not unbind it. The lich's only options were to flee, for the Dark Lord's servants would appear as soon as they knew the statue was here, or to stay close to it, hoping to get it away from von Grentz and then use it to ingratiate itself with Arst-Kara-Morn. The latter course seemed the more promising. "I shall think of something," it whispered. "If the carriage is ready, I shall depart now." It turned and glided for the door.

"When will you report?" asked von Grentz.

The lich stiffened. "I shall inform you of my progress," it whispered with disdain, "when I find it useful or advisable to do so."

Von Grentz scowled after the lich. After a time, he turned back to his shrine, knelt, and considered the blossom; then rose, and let himself out by the door.

Wolfe waited several minutes before she allowed herself to slip from the shadow of the wall. And when she did, she became suddenly aware of another presence in the room.

An exceptionally old man lay, back against the wall of the room, atop the rushes that carpeted the floor. A gray, scraggly beard ran around a toothless mouth; his clothes looked as if they had not been washed in weeks. One hand clutched a bottle of wine.

Wolfe felt a frisson of shock; the door had opened only the four times, for the entrances and exits of von Grentz and the skeleton. How and when had the old man entered? And how could she have failed to sense him—she, von Grentz, and the lich as well? He had not been a shadow, she would swear to that; another shadow she would have sensed.

"Won't work," mumbled the old man, peering vaguely at Wolfe's shadow. "Binding'sh too powerful."

And with that, he pushed off the wall, curled up on the rushes, and fell asleep.

II.

"Fetch that dog Stauer," von Kremnitz told the woman behind the oaken desk. She looked up with the gaze of a startled bird, and scurried off down a darkened hall.

Timaeus, Sidney, Nick, Kraki, and Mortise stood blinking in the foyer, Jasper shining faintly near them. The light inside was dim after the glaring sun of the streets. To the left, a door opened on a taproom, where a few souls sat drinking and a middle-aged man mopped the floor with glacial slowness. To the right, a carpeted corridor led past a series of doors, the first apparently that of an office, into which the woman disappeared. Behind the desk she had vacated, a wide set of stairs with curled banisters led upward to a landing.

The office door was reopened; the woman reappeared, along with a grinning, pince-nezed man in frock coat and conservative hose—presumably Stauer. "Leftenant von Kremnitz," he said, bobbing delightedly. "How good to see you again."

"The pleasure is yours," declared von Kremnitz coldly. "I will allow you to repair your late insult by providing these worthies with service of great alacrity and attentiveness, including, it need hardly be said, the finest rooms in your establishment."

Stauer bobbed to each of the others in turn. He mumbled *"Messieurs, madame,"* then threw open his arms and expansively declared, "Welcome to the Pension Scholari. If you will permit, Madame Steuben will show you to your rooms. I will join you shortly to discover your needs—if Leftenant von Kremnitz will come with me to the office?"

Von Kremnitz assented. Sidney scowled, suspicions aroused; what would von Kremnitz and the innkeeper have to talk about? About spying on von Kremnitz's supposed friends? Madame Steuben inclined her head toward the stairs, then led the way upward. Von Kremnitz entered the innkeeper's office; Stauer closed the door, and at once a mumble of voices arose, Stauer's heated, von Kremnitz's cold. Sidney caught only a snatch of the conversation, but that was enough to set her mind at ease. It was Stauer, enraged: ". . . amounting to two dozen pounds, ten shillings and tuppence ha'penny!"

Timaeus sighed with pleasure when he saw the sitting room. He collapsed into an armchair and complacently declared, "Civilization at last."

Sidney surveyed the room; it did make a change from recent accommodations. Since leaving Biddleburg Castle, they had slept in the rough, once in a rather unpleasant publick house where guests were accommodated four to the bed. Four people, that is; the fleas had been uncountable. The Pension Scholari boasted actual bedrooms, each quite clean, the bedding fresh, with empty chamber pots and an ewer of water and a basin for ablutions in each room.

The sitting room itself held deep, upholstered couches, a

chaise longue, armchairs, a bookcase stuffed with novels, and a sideboard bearing a basket of fruit and an array of bottles. French windows gave out on a balcony, where wisteria twined up trellises to form a canopy over the balcony itself. It almost seemed, Sidney thought, giving the room a professional once-over, as if it had been laid out with an amour in mind: The trellis was sturdy enough for a man to climb, one wall bore a balalaika in case one was seized with an urge to serenade, the wisteria scented the air, and one might progress, with a minimum of movement, from couch to chaise longue to the bedrooms, where soft feather mattresses and piles of pillows lay.

Kraki had already found one of the beds; he lay on it, still in his travel-stained clothes, dusty sandals leaving marks on the comforter, snoring face down into a pillow. Nick was nervously checking locks on the windows, peering under the furniture and knocking on the walls; he looked faintly uneasy, mainly, Sidney knew, because with the pension's many windows and unlockable doors, there was no obvious way to secure their quarters. Frer Mortise was standing before the balcony and looking acutely uncomfortable.

"What is the matter, Brother?" Sidney asked.

"The Lady Beatrice bade me accompany you," he said, "but I fear the city is no place for the likes of me."

"We have no hold on you," said Sidney. "You are free to depart when you wish."

"It was Broderick of our land who stole the statue from you," said Mortise. "I will stay until you recover it."

Sidney sighed. "If ever," she said.

A sharp knock came at the door. "It is I, your host," came a voice. "May I enter?"

"Yes, of course," said Jasper, the point of green light zipping toward the door. The handle turned, as if by an invisible hand, and Stauer bustled in, ignoring Jasper and approaching Timaeus. Sidney wondered why people always seemed to assume that Timaeus was the leader of their group. Was it his aristocratic air, or did they sense his profligacy with money and head for the easiest mark?

"Good afternoon," said Stauer. "I do hope everything is to your satisfaction?"

"Everything is most satisfactory," said Timaeus, perhaps a little sleepily in the afternoon warmth. "Would you have any pipeweed?"

"Of course, *monsieur*," said Stauer. "Several varieties of Alcalan blackleaf, and an interesting Moothlayan offering; I shall send a boy up with a selection. I'm afraid I must raise two matters of, ahem, some minor importance."

"Yes?" said Timaeus, sitting up.

Stauer gave a little cough. "As pleased as I am to meet companions of the noble and valiant Leftenant von Kremnitz," he said, "the good gentleman has, in the past, been known to tend toward a lamentable degree of—how may one put it—impecunity? At the risk of indelicacy, I must tell you that this establishment caters to a select clientele, a clientele capable of meeting its, ahem, appropriate charges. The leftenant assures me that you have means of your own, and that—"

"I see, I see," said Timaeus, waving a hand. "You need have no worries on this score. We shall, of course, pay the house's customary charges; if there are details that need settling, I urge you to raise them with my man, Nicholas Pratchitt, who has my complete confidence in financial matters."

Nick, who had been following this exchange with rising alarm, relaxed somewhat, though it was obvious he was nettled at being described as Timaeus's man.

"Excellent," said Stauer with equal relief, turning to Nick. "There is one slight matter which we ought, perhaps, to settle at present."

"Yes?" said Nick.

"It concerns your mounts," said Stauer.

Nick looked curious. "The horses?" he said.

"Yes," said Stauer, somewhat apologetically. "No doubt beasts of such, ah, wisdom and experience, such loyal retainers, have great emotional value for all concerned; yet one wonders at the, um, economic efficiency of boarding them at our establishment."

Nick blinked. "I don't follow you," he said.

Stauer sighed, took off his pince-nez, and polished them with his ruffled neckpiece. "Our stables charge a shilling *per diem*," he said.

Nick choked, unable to respond.

Stauer looked slightly offended at this. "And worth every penny," he said. "We curry them daily, ride them about to provide exercise when their owners do not, attend to their medical needs as necessary, and provide the finest-quality provender, including fresh fruits and vegetables for a change in diet."

Nick snorted.

"Many noblemen, warriors in particular, appreciate this attentiveness to the needs of their mounts, among their prized possessions; on the open market, a trained warhorse of good breeding can fetch as much as—"

"Yeah, yeah, I see," said Nick. "If your horse cost you a hundred quid, a shilling a day to keep it in shape is no big deal. But our horses are a bunch of broken-down nags."

Stauer sighed in relief, and replaced his glasses. "Precisely," he said. "I can suggest more modest accommodations, if you like."

"Maybe you can recommend a good knacker's yard," said Nick. "Glue is about all they're good for."

"If you wish," said Stauer.

"By the way, Mr. Stauer," said Timaeus, "where has Leftenant von Kremnitz got to?"

Stauer bobbed as if delighted to answer the question. "It is, of course, the gentleman's duty to report to the

Maiorkest upon entering the city," he said. "Now, if there's anything—"

"The Maiorkest?"

"Ah? The mayoral palace; our seat of government. The Mayoral Foot Guard is stationed there."

Sidney scowled again in renewed suspicion.

What at first glance had appeared to be a taproom proved to be a bit more than that. A sign above the door bore the legend "Bistrot Scholari." There was an ornate mahogany bar, but the rest of the bistrot was decorated in what might be called dusty nook-and-cranny, lit more by the chandeliers overhead than the few shuttered windows. Innumerable walls divided the space into wood-paneled booths. On shelves sat dusty bottles of wine, dusty books, still-life displays of dusty plaster fruit in dusty baskets, and dusty oil paintings meant to suggest bounty—suckling pigs, cornucopiae, peasants reaping grain. "Six for luncheon, if you please," said Jasper to the *maîtresse d'*, who seemed only faintly startled to be addressed by a mobile point of light. She solemnly curtsied and guided them to a booth. She gestured to indicate where they should sit, then summoned a waiter with a showy snap of the fingers and an impatient stamp of the foot. Before she left, she reached up and took hold of a rod dangling from one of the chandeliers. She pulled on it and the chandelier moved, running on an iron rail bolted to the ceiling, closer toward the booth—presumably so that the diners might more easily study the bill of fare.

The booth was a bit crowded for them all, so Kraki went to take a chair from one of the tables in the middle of the room. The chair was bolted to the floor. Kraki looked puzzled when it did not move at first, then ripped it up with a crash and carried it over, fragments of oak flooring sticking out from the ends of the chair legs.

The waiter watched this with serene unconcern, as if it

were an everyday happening, and said, "I'll just add the repairs to your bill, shall I, *messieurs et madame*?"

"Yes, yes," said Timaeus, waving a hand. "Do you have a wine list?"

"I shall send over the sommelier," said the waiter. "In the meantime, perhaps you would care to study the *carte d'hôtel*." He handed over the menus. Kraki, perched on his chair, took one and held it upside down. Sidney leaned over, took it from his hands, turned it right side up, and handed it back. The waiter bustled away.

Suddenly, from across the room, a woman shouted, "Felicia, thou strumpet! The lad hath plighted me his troth! Wherefore dost thou bestow such lascivious caresses upon his person, thou jade, thou jezebel?" The speaker posed menacingly in front of a booth across the bistrot, clad in a flounced yellow dress, a rapier at her side, long brown hair in a ponytail down her back. A low murmur came from within the booth, where Felicia, a pale woman in peach velvet and a pillbox hat, sat with several companions. Felicia stood slowly and left the booth to stand before the woman in the yellow dress. Whatever Felicia said did not mollify the other, who drew forth her blade and lunged. The reason for bolting the chairs to the floor became instantly apparent; Felicia dodged aside and grabbed a chair, no doubt intending to use it as a weapon.

People exploded from three nearby booths. Felicia, thrown off-balance by the chair's failure to lift from the floor, might well have been skewered by her foe's next thrust, but two men grabbed the woman in yellow, holding her arms. "This is dishonorable," one shouted to her. "She has no weapon to defend herself." At that, the woman in yellow ceased struggling, looking mortally annoyed.

The claim was not wholly true; Felicia had produced a long hatpin, but she too was now surrounded by friends, who both shielded and argued with her. The tableau held for a long moment, the woman in yellow relaxing from rage. Then, Felicia said in a loud and biting voice, "Quite right. The baseborn lad is not worth the bother," and, adjusting her hat, restored the hatpin to its place.

The woman in yellow, peaceably turning toward another booth, twitched at this, but did not turn back. The object of their quarrel, a young man with his hair in ringlets, went with her, looking rather shamefaced. Quiet was soon restored.

While Timaeus and the others watched this exchange with interest, Sidney, seated on the inside of the booth, heard a faint buzzing; at first she took it for an insect and waved a hand, but the rhythm of the noise, it came to her, was the rhythm of conversation. Curiously, she looked about, and noted a hole in the bench on which she sat, where it met the wall—a hole that pierced the back of her bench and, apparently, the bench in the next booth over. It was circular, about an inch in diameter, and appeared as if it had been drilled through the wood at some point in the considerable past, as the wood of the hole was stained with age. She was, she realized, overhearing the conversation taking place in the next booth and, curious, leant back to listen.

". . . Stantz," said a voice.

"It is true, then? The Spider intended to kill the Lord Mayor?" said a second.

"Isn't it obvious? Who else would dare?"

"But do you have proof?"

"Not such proof as could be displayed in court."

"You've had seven days to find proof."

"Look at this," said the first voice. There was a shuffling of paper.

"The bastard," said the other voice. "Stantz has gone too far this time."

"Are you with us, then?"

"Well, I—"

"Are you ready to order?" said the waiter. He stood expectantly behind Kraki, pad at the ready. Sidney missed something of the conversation through the hole, and moved her ear toward it. "Listen to me! The Scepter of Stantius is glowing!" said the hole.

"What would you recommend?" asked Timaeus.

"The *rollatine de veau avec une sauce greepoise* is very nice."

Irritably, Sidney turned away from the waiter, trying to concentrate only on eavesdropping, but the discussion about her made it impossible. She caught mere snatches—including, once, the word "statue," which alarmed her.

"*Une sauce greepoise*, eh? let me guess," said Jasper, slightly sarcastically. "Greeps are a kind of, oh, insect, are they not?"

"Sir? Why, certainly not! Would the Bistrot Scholari serve bugs to its customers? No, no, greeps are a form of—"

"Stop!" shouted Timaeus. "I forbid you to tell us what greeps are."

The waiter was taken aback. "Sir?" he said.

"We are ascetics, every one of us," declared Timaeus, "wholly uninterested in cuisine. We have not the slightest interest in greeps of any form. I will have your plainest loaf of bread, and a glass of water."

"Ah," said the waiter, "but our greeps are like to tempt even a palate such as yours, my good sir. Dug fresh from the—"

"Stop!" shouted Timaeus. "If you say another word, we shall instantly leave."

The waiter put on a sour expression. "Very well, sir," he said. "Will you be having arsenic or strychnine with your water?"

Timaeus goggled. "I beg your pardon?"

"Ah," said the waiter. "Foreigners, I see. It is the custom in our fair city to take poison with one's repast—a sublethal dose, to be sure."

"You're kidding," said Nick.

"No, sir," said the waiter. "I am in earnest. To build up an immunity, you see. Especially among the upper classes, a certain resistance to poison is useful in extending one's life span—"

"Is assassination so common?" asked Sidney, interested despite herself.

"Alas, no longer so common," said the waiter nostalgically. "These are decadent times. Why, in my grandfather's day—"

"No poison, please," said Timaeus, interrupting hastily. "I assume that can be arranged?"

The waiter looked sour again. "Yes, of course, sir," he said. "I'm afraid there will be an additional charge."

"For omission of the poison?" said Timaeus incredulously.

"Unpoisoned food requires special handling," said the waiter disdainfully. "Will anyone else be dining this evening?"

Sidney ordered the bangers and mash. Jasper ordered the veal cutlet. Farther Mortise ordered the steak and fries. "And you, sir?" sneered the waiter to Kraki.

"I take vone of each," said Kraki.

"Sir?" said the waiter.

Kraki's finger stabbed blindly at each line on the menu. "Vone of that," he said. "And vone of that. And vone of that. And vone of—"

"I follow you, sir," said the waiter. "This is a considerable quantity of food, you realize."

"Good," said Kraki, pulling up his tunic to scratch his hairy belly. "I hungry."

"Quite," said the waiter. "No poison all around, I take it?"

They assented. The sommelier had arrived while they

were ordering, but had stood aside while the waiter took the last orders. As the waiter left, he said, "Good evening. I assume you'll be wanting a red wine with—"

"Bin twenty-one," said Timaeus offhandedly.

The sommelier blinked. "Sir?" he said. "But that's a maderized—"

"Bin twenty-one," said Timaeus testily.

The sommelier shrugged, and disappeared.

"You don't even know what wine's in bin twenty-one," said Jasper. "How do you—"

"I'm tired of being patronized," said Timaeus.

"You're in a foul mood, I must—" said Jasper, but Sidney shushed him loudly. She had her ear pressed to the hole again.

"What've you got?" asked Nick.

She shushed again. The others shut up and watched her listen.

"What do you mean?" said one of the voices from the hole.

"You are mistaken," said the other voice.

"How do you mean mistaken?"

"I do not have the files."

"But if you don't, then Freitag was lying!"

"Correct."

"And that means—"

"That means the end."

"The end? *Finis?* Is that all I've ever meant to the *gens?*"

"You were a useful tool. Now you are broken."

There was a choking sound. "You—you bastard," said the second vice hoarsely. "The wine—"

"Was poisoned."

And there was a thud.

A moment later, a man left the booth and strode across the room. He was the very image of a chevalier: spurred boots, épée with ornate hilt, ruffled sleeves, a ragged scar up one cheek. At the bistrot's door he paused, took a snuffbox from his sleeve, opened it, and inserted a pinch in his left nostril while scanning the room. He noted Sidney's eyes—and those of the others—upon him, sneezed delicately into a lace handkerchief, and left.

"Should I follow him?" asked Jasper.

"I don't—no, I suppose not," said Sidney.

"What is it, Sidney?" asked Timaeus.

She showed them the hole and described the conversation. As she did, a waiter peered into the adjacent booth, then hurriedly departed.

"So an attempt has been made on the Lord Mayor's life," said Jasper.

"Von Kremnitz didn't know," said Nick.

"Or didn't bother to tell us," said Sidney.

"Could it have been von Grentz?" asked Jasper.

"They seemed to think it was someone they called Stantz, or the Spider," said Sidney.

"Ah," said Timaeus. "The Hamsterian Minister of Internal Serenity."

Sidney stared at him. "How do you—?"

"I do follow the international news, my dear," said Timaeus, somewhat patronizingly. "What did they say about the statue?"

"I didn't catch that part," said Sidney testily. "You were too busy harassing our waiter."

The waiter who had peered into the booth returned with the *maîtresse d'* and a busboy. Under the woman's direction, they entered the booth, reappearing a moment later carrying a body, that of a heavyset man in checked hose and crimson doublet. They carried him across the floor and out of the bistrot. Several customers watched them go, then returned unconcernedly to their dinners.

"If it were my restaurant," said Nick, "I'd worry that the customers might think the food was to blame."

"Perhaps it was," said Jasper. "Perhaps the chef had too heavy a hand with the arsenic shaker."

Timaeus chuckled. "Everyone does seem remarkably blasé," he said.

Three waiters approached with platters of food. *"Bon appétit,"* said Timaeus, glumly examining his loaf of bread and his glass of water. Moments later, the sommelier appeared with a bottle of wine with a label in Dwarven. He presented it to Timaeus, who blinked; he had known that there were dwarven wines, but had never tasted one. He suspected this was a bad omen; the dwarves ran more to stouts and porters. With a flourish, the sommelier cut off the lead with a small knife, then drew the cork. He poured a finger of wine into a glass and proffered it to Timaeus, who took a taste, rolled it about in his mouth, and looked pleasantly surprised. "Very nice," he said—and it was. It seemed to be some relative of sherry. Upon Timaeus's approval, the sommelier poured each of the other diners a glass. Kraki drained his instantly and said, "More ale."

"I shall send over your waiter," said the sommelier contemptuously, disappearing into the dim recesses of the bistrot.

Nick elbowed Kraki in the ribs. "Read us the label," he said.

"Vhat?" said Kraki through a mouthful of pork cutlet.

"Thought you were a dwarf," said Nick.

"Ho ho," grunted Kraki sourly, and began plowing through the sauerbraten. For a time, the only sounds were those of clattering silverware, mastication and, in the case of Kraki, several extended bass belches.

"I'm not entirely sure I trust von Kremnitz," said Sidney, who had barely touched her sausages. "Maybe we ought to try to find the statue on our own."

"He did offer us the Lord Mayor's aid," said Jasper.

"You think we can trust the Lord Mayor any better than Pablo?" asked Nick.

"A point," said Jasper. "On the other hand, the politics of this city seem more than a little labyrinthine. Without a local patron, we might all too easily find ourselves in the municipal hoosegow."

As Jasper spoke, there was a clatter, a thump, and a swishing noise. Sidney peered out into the restaurant dimness; the noise was that of a chandelier, moving on its runners. And indeed, a chandelier hurtled toward them from across the room, candle flames fluttering with the motion, a booted man in flared trousers, an épée at the ready, hanging from its rod.

The chandelier slammed to a halt at the end of its rail, lit candles toppling onto the floor. The man let go at the last instant, landing dramatically atop their table, one boot in Sidney's mashed potatoes and the other toppling a stein of ale into Kraki's lap. The point of the épée rested against Timaeus's throat.

"I have you now, Greiblitz!" the swordsman shouted. "There'll be no more of your li—I say. You're not Greiblitz."

With a roar, Kraki erupted from his seat, grabbed one of the swordsman's legs, and yanked him from the table. The épée went flying across the room. The two wrestled briefly; when the flurry of motion ceased, the swordsman's feet were kicking in midair, his face turning purple as Kraki gradually crushed his esophagus. "You spill my ale!" shouted Kraki.

"Just what we need at this point," said Sidney, "to murder one of the locals."

"What's the problem?" said Nick. "Nobody's likely to mind. I mean, if people get poisoned every day—not to mention killed in duels—"

"Still," said Timaeus, "put him down, Kraki, there's a good chap."

"My ale," said Kraki dangerously.

"I imagine he'll stand you another," said Timaeus. Kraki grunted, and reluctantly set the swordsman down.

The swordsman panted for a moment, rubbing his neck, then said hoarsely, "Awfully sorry. Glad to replace your ale. And your dinner, miss, if I may. Don't suppose you've seen Greiblitz about? Well-dressed chappie, scar on one cheek, sports an épée, partial to snuff?"

"Yes, yes," said Timaeus. "Poisoned a fellow the next booth over, and left, oh, ten minutes ago. Now do run along, there's a good chap."

"Poisoned a fellow?" said the swordsman in alarm. "Merciful heavens, I'm too late to save poor Grünwald. Marlene will never forgive me." And he ran off toward the bistrot's door, scooping up his sword along the way.

"Well," said Jasper. "Welcome to Hamsterburg."

"My ale!" shouted Kraki after the departing swordsman. Frowning mightily, he sat down and pulled over a plate of schnitzel. "Should have let me kill him," he complained.

"But what about von Kremnitz?" demanded Sidney. "We still haven't decided—"

"Speak of the devil," said Jasper, putting down his dwarven wine. Indeed, von Kremnitz was walking across the bistrot toward them, one hand on the hilt of his épée, peering rather fiercely into each booth in turn, as if he expected to come under attack at any moment. "I say, Leftenant," said Jasper loudly, the green light zipping back and forth in an attempt to attract attention.

"Ah," said von Kremnitz, "here you are, my friends. I have good news. My master, Hamish Siebert, Lord Mayor of this Most Serene Republic, will grant you an audience as soon as you can come to the Maiorkest."

Guismundo Stantz, Minister of Internal Serenity, the Spider, whose web spanned the world, who drew the unwary inward to their final destruction, master of a hundred plots, the ears behind a thousand walls; Guismundo Stantz, secret master of Hamsterburg, was resting. "Just resting my eyes," he would have said, if anyone had asked him what he was doing. That might, to an impartial observer, have seemed an inadequate description. He was slumped far back in his chair, his head dangling at an angle that would inflict a crick in his neck upon awakening, a line of drool suspended from a slack mouth, vast flesh vibrating with his snores. "Snores," too, might be thought inadequate; he roared, a sleepy lion.

About him clustered a dozen brass speaking tubes, curving away through the walls to distant subordinates. Ten or twelve times a minute, the men and women at the tubes' nether ends flinched as their ears were assaulted with a noise like that of the sea, crashing with gale force against the rocks of the shore. None of them dared move too far from their tubes, lest Stantz awaken suddenly and issue them an order.

Half the ministry knew that Stantz was, ah, resting, but none dared awaken him. Men had died for less.

Stantz had spent two bad nights. On the first, there had been Wolfe, and then the damned elven ambassador; on the second, a series of critical reports had kept him glued to his desk. The Accommodationists were apparently plotting a *coup d'état*, and he still didn't know why. Two nights of inadequate sleep had finally caught up with him.

A shadow moved silently up and into the armchair that stood across the desk from Stantz. Suddenly, Wolfe sat in the chair, wincing at the noise. "Stantz," she shouted over the ocean's roar. "Wake up, man."

With the suddenness of a surfacing whale, Stantz jerked into consciousness. He blinked sleepy eyes at the room, then said, "Morning, Ren. Just resting my eyes."

"Resting them since morning, apparently," said Wolfe. "It's late afternoon."

Stantz blinked. "Ah," he said, and reached up to shutter

the speaking tubes; no need to have the rest of the ministry listen in on this. "And how—"

"I've been to the Drachehaus," said Wolfe tiredly. "Took me hours to get in, and hours to get out; von Grentz's security is very tight."

"Well I know," muttered Stantz. "I've been trying to penetrate it from this end."

"Any luck?" said Wolfe.

"Not much," said Stantz. "Broderick de Biddleburg, the deposed regent of a little barony in the mountains, showed up at von Grentz's castle out toward the Dzorz, in a snit about something. This was two weeks ago. He demanded to speak with von Grentz; the next morning, the two of them and a company of soldiers headed out, and came back with a mysterious somethingorother wrapped up in a tarpaulin."

"And then?"

"And then," said Stantz irritably, "our informant's vital functions ceased."

Wolfe snorted. "Fenstermann must be unhappy."

Stantz looked quizzical. "Who?"

"The torturer," said Wolfe. "Friend of mine."

"Why should he be unhappy?"

"He's a humanitarian," Wolfe explained. "Opposed to torture on principle. Says a tortured subject will admit to anything just to—"

"Damn it, Wolfe, are you telling me we employ a torturer with moral scruples? What can Personnel be thinking of? How effective can he possibly—"

"He's very effective, Guismundo," said Wolfe. "I'm sorry I brought it up. He's very skilled. His dad was a torturer, and his granddad before him; it's a family tradition."

Stantz goggled, but sighed after a moment. "The Dungeon Division operates fairly well," he said, rubbing his third chin. "A bad idea to second-guess subordinates, anyway. So tell me about Drachehaus."

"Hmm? Oh, very severe lines, wouldn't be surprised if the architect were a Son of the Morning. Only real ornamentation is a dragon, nicely carved, above the main door. The grounds—"

"Ren," said Stantz, "you may think it cute to be purposefully obtuse, but I am a busy man—"

"Busy sleeping," said Wolfe.

"Be that as it may," said Stantz. "I'm not interested in the Drachehaus itself; I want to know what you learned *inside* the Drachehaus."

"You remember that rumor about the statue of Stantius? Some adventurers in Athelstan supposedly found it, at about the time that the Scepter of Stantius started glowing?"

"Yes, yes."

"Von Grentz has it."

"What . . . the statue?"

"Yes," said Wolfe.

"Ah, the mysterious object under the tarp."

Wolfe shrugged. "Could be. But there's more."

"There generally is."

"Von Grentz wants to use it to make himself king."

Stantz blinked. "Not just mayor, but king? Of all humanity?"

"Righto," said Wolfe cheerfully. "He had a wizzo in to talk about it, a lich—"

"A lich?"

"Yes."

"Unusual," said Stantz. "There are few free lichs; most are tied to their graves, some few enslaved to Arst-Kara-Morn. Blazes, if *they've* got their tentacles in this—but why would they want von Grentz king? Von Grentz actually thought that was possible?"

"He seemed quite hot on the notion. The lich was a little less convinced, but seemed willing to give it a shot."

"Hmm," said Stantz. "Let's see if this makes sense. Von

Grentz gets hold of the statue. This changes the delicate balance of power among the Hundred, so he attempts to assassinate Siebert, hoping to get elected mayor himself. This doesn't work, so he starts to line up the rest of the Accommodationists to put over a *coup d'état*—"

"What?"

"I have indications along those lines, yes. Von Grentz himself has a small army, you know—traditional regiment, out Dzorz way. Guisardieres. Some of the other noble Accommodationists do, too. The only military force in the capital is the Mayor Foot Guard—"

"Unless you count the watch," said Wolfe.

Stantz snorted. "Please," he said. "So while von Grentz is hardheadedly maneuvering to seize power, he's simultaneously playing with mystical folderol, to acquire divine sanction as Human King ... Hmm, you know, even if it proves impossible, the symbolism is important. If he can *claim* to be Human King with any authority, the mob—"

"Yes," said Wolfe, "I see."

Stantz was silent for a long moment. "There's worse," he said grimly.

Wolfe raised an eyebrow.

"I'm the villain of the piece," he said.

"You generally are," said Wolfe.

Stantz smiled. "Well, terror has its uses," he said. "But I'm serious. We're picking up a whispering campaign; von Grentz has the statue of Stantius, the Scepter of same is glowing, there shall be a new human king. By his possession of the statue, von Grentz is marked out to become that man. The foul Spider, Guismundo Stantz, attempted to assassinate the Lord Mayor Hamish, darling of the mob, and plots against him still; von Grentz shall avenge Siebert's death, reach an understanding with the East, abolish the draft, reduce taxation—"

"Is this hypothetical?"

"No, it's all over the taverns," said Stantz. "Sets things

up nicely; they kill Siebert, pin it on me; by the time the *coup d'état* occurs, mobs turn out in the streets to support it. Half the nobility already supports the Accommodationists; with Accommodationist troops in control of the town, the other half can be purged—"

"Soldiers going door to door with naked blades," said Wolfe. "Blood running in the streets. We haven't had anything like that in three hundred years—"

"Correct," said Stantz, nodding sagely. "Our tradition of assassination serves as a safety valve for political violence, obviating the need for more extreme measures. Obviously, von Grentz must be stopped."

"But how?"

"We have to get the statue away from him," said Stantz. "Is it in the Drachehaus?"

"Yes," said Wolfe. "But the place is a fortress."

Stantz shrugged. "You have *carte blanche*," he said. "Spend whatever it takes. Assemble a team and get it. I shall expect it by Friday."

"I've been up all night," she groused. "Can't it wait?"

"Yes," said Stantz. "It can wait till tomorrow—Friday. At which time, I shall expect to see Stantius safely in the Albertine Lodge."

"Explain to me again why this is so vital," said Wolfe tiredly.

"The coup is scheduled for Sunday."

"So, in a pinch, the raid could be on Saturday."

Stantz grimaced. "Yes, yes," he said, "but it's foolish to schedule something for the last possible moment."

"All right," said Wolfe. "Go back to sleep. Meanwhile, I, sleepless, will labor onward."

Stantz snorted. "Haven't you heard?" he said. "The Spider is everywhere. He never sleeps."

"No," said Wolfe. "He just rests his eyes."

It didn't occur to Wolfe until much later that she hadn't

told Stantz about the strange old man who had also, to all appearances, been spying on von Grentz.

"Is this really necessary?" demanded Timaeus in a harsh whisper, his handkerchief to his nose in a largely futile attempt to keep out the dust. He peered down toward his feet, trying to make out the next joist in the feeble light; he had tripped once already, landing painfully across several joists, and had no desire to repeat the experience. He put one hand to the dusty lath to steady himself, and flinched as he dislodged bits of plaster, which rattled down the wall.

"Spies are everywhere," responded von Kremnitz, also whispering, épée out and opal ring glowing. "Be careful."

"Yes, well, this isn't quite how one expects to be received by a head of state," said Jasper, flitting on ahead and pausing at an intersection, uncertain which way to proceed. "When you said 'grant us an audience,' we did have something rather grander in mind."

"I sure as hell wouldn't have put on this damned dress if I'd known I'd be creeping around in the walls like a rat," snarled Sidney. Despite the short notice, she had managed to find suitable garb at a couturière not far from the pension; the seamstress had rapidly altered it to fit. It was black velvet with silver trim, not her preferred manner of dress, but when you met lord mayors and such . . . It was smeared now with dust and cobwebs. Its only saving grace, as far as Sidney was concerned, was that the Hamsterians expected both men and women to bear weapons; the dress had a sling for a sword, and the sleeves were voluminous enough to permit her to carry throwing knives. If she was condemned to wear this frippery, at least she could still go armed.

"We're nearly there," whispered von Kremnitz soothingly. "In fact—" He pressed his eyes to a peephole, and made a satisfied sound. "I must merely find the control for the secret door—here."

There was a clicking sound. Nothing happened. There was a clicking sound again, then, somewhat frantically, the same sound three times in quick succession. "It's not working," whispered von Kremnitz.

"Is hokay," said Kraki. "I fix." He pushed his way past Timaeus and von Kremnitz to the door.

A loud voice reached their ears through the wall. "Von Kremnitz," it said, "is that you?"

"Yes, my lord," said von Kremnitz, equally loudly. "We're having some difficulty—"

"Not to worry," said the voice. "I installed a lock. Just a moment—"

There was a crash. Laths and plaster flew; they squinted as light flooded the secret passage. Kraki hurled through the ragged hole he had smashed in the wall, into the Dandolo Room beyond, plaster dust and rubble flying everywhere.

"I am Kraki, son of Kronar," he roared, holding the point of his mighty sword to Siebert's stomach. "Name yourself, or die."

The Lord Mayor held a tall glass of something bubbly in one hand, his other hand halfway to the hilt of his rapier. Wisely, he refrained from moving his hand any closer to the blade. "I am Hamish Siebert," he said, seemingly unalarmed, "a simple man, but ruler of this city."

"Is hokay," Kraki allowed, sheathing his weapon in the scabbard slung across his back and making toward the bar.

Siebert let loose a long breath, waving his free hand across his face to waft away the plaster dust that hung in the air. "A rather unorthodox entrance," he said. "You might have forewarned me, Leftenant."

"I am sorry, my lord," said von Kremnitz, on his knees before the Lord Mayor. "May I present—" And he introduced each of the others, in turn.

Siebert seemed most interested in Sidney, whose hand he pressed to his lips. "Charmed," he murmured, holding on to her hand far longer than was necessary. Rather self-consciously, Sidney brushed some of the cobwebs off her dress.

"Well, well, said Siebert, waving a hand toward the sideboard. "Help yourself to a drink, if you like; no servants right now, in the interest of discretion, albeit heaven knows how much discretion we can maintain. I've got the usual wards against scrying, you know, but who knows if I can trust the wizards who cast them? Adventurers in the grand style, what? Hauling things off to Arst-Kara-Morn, bearding the Dark Lord in his lair sort of thing. Ah, youth."

"Leftenant von Kremnitz has told you of our quest, then?" asked Timaeus, bringing a finger toward his pipe.

"Yes, of course—must you light that beastly—" There was a bang. "Ah, well, never mind. You're all quite mad, you know."

"How so?" asked Jasper, settling down toward a couch.

"The good leftenant tells me you plan to free the spirit of Stantius, hmm? Whereupon the gods will select a new Human King, or some damn thing, who'll lead us on a glorious crusade to crush the nasty orcs. All very nice, gaiety and celebration, up the side, and so forth. What happens if the Dark Lord takes it from you?"

"The statue?" said Timaeus.

"Mmm," Siebert agreed, nose in his drink.

"Then," said Timaeus, "he'll use it to enslave humanity, presumably the reason for capturing and binding Stantius's spirit in the first place. We'll join the orcs, crush the elves and dwarves, and live as serfs and peons in a vast evil empire for all time to come."

"Something like that, I imagine," said Siebert. "Cheers." He took another long quaff, ice tinkling against the side of the glass. "Is taking the statue to Arst-Kara-Morn therefore the best idea in the world?"

"Well, you know," said Jasper. "Legends foretell, fated to do such and so, the traditions of the quest. Stiff upper lip, must do as duty demands."

"And so forth," said Timaeus. "I'll have one of those; what is it?"

"Genever and greep soda," said the Lord Mayor. "Very pleasant, really."

"Urg," said Timaeus. "Never mind, then. Kraki, some of the single-malt, won't you?"

The barbarian, who had been sampling the bottles at the sideboard one by one, peered at the selection until he found something that looked like a whisky. He picked it up, made certain it was well stoppered, and hurled it at Timaeus. The wizard only just brought his hands up in time to prevent it from bashing him in the head. He unstoppered it, looked about for a glass, sighed, and took a swig from the open neck.

"So you can't be dissuaded?" said Siebert.

"Afraid not," said Timaeus.

"Oh, well," said Siebert cheerfully. "Sheer lunacy, to be sure, but I don't imagine I'll be around to see the outcome in either event. The important thing is to get the statue away from von Grentz before he can turn the Republic into a charnel house."

"Right," said Nick. "And the first step is to find out where he's got it."

"Ah, that I can tell you," said Siebert. "It's in the Drachehaus, his mansion in the city. The leftenant can take you there, I imagine."

"How do you know it's there?" asked Sidney.

"The Minister of Internal Serenity has so informed me," he said.

"The Spider?" protested von Kremnitz. "But he tried to kill you! How can you trust—"

"As to that, the good minister has been sending me these little love notes," said Siebert. "He claims that poor von Krautz was actually assassinated by the Graf von Grentz, who set Minister Stantz up to take the blame. He claims, moreover, that von Grentz is plotting a coup, and a further attempt at assassination. I'd been rather skeptical, but your own news about von Grentz and the statue is independent corroboration, as are the reports that several Accommodationist nobles are assembling their household troops not far from the city. I believe I'm beginning to place some credence in Stantz's little theory."

"If you know where the statue is, can't you just order your army to go and take it?" asked Nick.

Siebert raised an amused eyebrow. "Ah, the rashness of youth," he said. "It isn't quite so easy, you see. 'My army' would mean the Mayoral Foot Guard; the rest is under the command of the Ministry of War, or the Arsenal, or individual noble houses. Von Grentz has his mansion well defended; there would be a pitched battle. I would immediately be accused by the Hundred *Gentes* of seeking to overthrow the ancient and honorable rights of all free citizens by forcibly entering a gentleman's quarters and seizing his property without due process of law; a motion of censure would be introduced, and possibly one of impeachment. That last would require legal maneuvering; no one has actually introduced a motion of impeachment in the Republic's history, although tradition permits it, since it's generally been considered easier just to assassinate the individual in question. Actually, immediate assassination, possibly by the very officers I order to carry out the attack, is the likeliest outcome of any such attempt."

"Then you won't help us?" demanded Sidney.

"My dear!" Siebert protested. "You wound me to the quick! Why, all of the resources at my command are at your disposal."

"What resources do you command?" asked Nick.

"There's the rub," said Siebert, smiling.

There was silence for a moment.

"See here" said Siebert. "Go to the Drachehaus, scout it out. If possible, obtain clear evidence of von Grentz's treason. With hard evidence, I can do much. Even without, perhaps I can help you obtain the wherewithal to invade von Grentz's mansion and steal the statue from it—the aid of a wizard or two, documents, perhaps a few loyal soldiers. Once you know what you need, perhaps Guismundo Stantz can be persuaded to assist us; but while I am happy to assist you as I can, without unduly destabilizing my own precarious position, I have no magic wand, no helpful genie. You must solve your own problems."

"Thanks a lot," said Nick.

Siebert shrugged. "Life is hard. Leftenant von Kremnitz, stay with these people, and assist them however you may; you know how to contact me, if further assistance is needed."

"Yes, my lord," said von Kremnitz.

"May we leave by the front door, please?" said Timaeus. "I've had enough of scuttling through the walls like a roach."

"I see no harm in it," said Siebert. "And now, *adieu*, farewell, stay not upon the hour of thy going." He turned to Sidney. "Do come back and visit an old man sometime, my dear," he said, pressing her hand to his breast. To Timaeus's vast surprise, she actually smiled back.

III.

Wolfe chanted a spell.

A near full moon shone down on the horses, the hansom cab, and its top-hatted driver, casting sharp shadows against the cobblestones of the street. Across the street, behind its iron fence, the Drachehaus stood amid carefully tended gardens. Dark windows declared that nothing disturbed the slumber of those within.

"None of tha' magic, now, miss," said the hansom's driver sleepily, waving his whip at Wolfe and her three companions. "My fare'll be two shillings, and I've an amulet 'gainst illusion. Ye'll—"

With a gesture, Wolfe completed her spell: The carriage and its driver flattened out, as if they had turned from rounded matter instantly to flat portrait; the color leached from them, leaving shades of black and gray; the image distorted, as if it were twisting down toward the shadow cast on the stones; and then they were gone.

Their shadow, etched against the cobbles, remained; a

shadow, now, with nothing to cast it. The whole had happened in a space of seconds.

Wolfe removed a pouch from her belt; it glowed silver in the moonlight, an intricate pattern in black and white rippling across its surface. She chanted again, a brief cantrip this time, and laid the pouch down on the cobblestones. Like water streaming into a drain, the shadow was sucked into the pouch's confines. Wolfe pulled the drawstring and knotted it with satisfaction, then left the pouch on the cobblestones and turned to her three companions.

"Whhhhhhheeeeeeeerrrrrrre," said the brown-robed earth mage, scanning the street in confusion. Agent G nudged the pouch with the toe of her boot. The troll waited patiently for Wolfe to tell him what to do.

"Aaaaaaammmmmmmm," the earth mage said.

A warm breeze rustled leaves. Scattered clouds scudded across the moon. It was late, past midnight. G gave the pouch a harder nudge, surprised that she had been completely unable to budge it. Wolfe smiled faintly at that; the pouch contained two horses, a hansom cab, and a rather beefy man. Wolfe could transform them into a shadow, but that didn't diminish their weight. She had no qualms about leaving the pouch here while they invaded the mansion; thieves might try to steal it in their absence, but she doubted they'd have much luck.

"Iiiiiii?" said the earth mage.

"Quick on the uptake, isn't he?" said Agent G. She was a corpulent, stringy-haired woman, clad for tonight's work in loose-fitting black clothes and an amazing variety of weapons. At her belt were throwing stars, knives, and two swords. Slung on her back was a small crossbow, a case of quarrels, and a rope with a noose. And those were only the visible arms; others were secreted about her person. Wolfe had been glad to get her: The agents of Internal Serenity came in three states—individually lettered, individually numbered, and general release—and of these, the lettered agents were by far the most highly prized. Wolfe had expected to be forced to settle for one of the more numerous numbered agents, but G had been at loose ends and Wolfe had been able to commandeer her.

"Actually, he's a veritable speed demon," said Wolfe as she held up a placard for the man to read. "Earth mages deal with phenomena that change over geologic epochs. As they get older, their metabolism tends to slow down to suit. There are some who move so slowly they can't even interact with the rest of human society anymore." The earth mage had by now brought up his right hand and taken the placard from Wolfe.

"I'll take your word for it," said G. "I thought this was supposed to be fast in and fast out. How's that going to work with a guy who sprints at a slow walk?"

The earth mage was slowly mouthing the words written on the placard: "Please begin your spell."

"He's not going in with us," said Wolfe. "He's just going to get us in."

"Past the wards?" asked G.

"That's the idea," said Wolfe.

The earth mage dropped the placard. He said the first syllable of a Word, still looking a little confused.

"He starting the spell?" asked G.

"Yes," said Wolfe.

"Take him long?" asked G.

"We timed it," explained Wolfe. "It should take him fifteen minutes, give or take a bit. We need to get prepared."

The earth mage finished the first syllable of his Word and started in on syllable two.

"Yeah, okay," said G. "What about the troll?"

"Ook," said the troll. He wore a peculiarly heavy leather harness, and carried no weapon other than a coil of thick rope.

"Chad's coming with us," said Wolfe. "The statue is

supposed to be heavy; we need muscle to haul it out, and they don't come much stronger than trolls."

G sighed. "Trolls," she said.

"Ook!" said Chad. "Trust Chad. Chad good troll."

"He'll be fine," Wolfe said irritably.

G snorted but made no reply. She was watching the earth mage, who drew a deep breath; he had actually completed the first Word of his spell. He began to drone the first syllable of the next.

Wolfe glanced at the moon. "Maybe another ten minutes," she said.

"Dragons," said Nick forebodingly.

"Vhere?" said Kraki, drawing his enormous blade with a scritch of steel and adopting a ready stance.

Nick pointed to the carving above the Drachehaus's main door: a dragon segreant.

Kraki peered at it mistrustfully, perhaps expecting it to come to life.

"Von Grentz's arms, I expect," said Timaeus. "You may recall that his guisardieres bore a similar badge."

"I don't like it," Nick said. "There weren't supposed to be any dragons."

"There aren't," said Sidney. "It's just a carving."

"I still don't like it," complained Nick. "If the dragon is his symbol, he might have one around here somewhere."

"In the midst of a human city?" said Jasper. "Don't be absurd. It would have half the town in flames."

"Sure," said Nick. "Don't pay any attention to me. What do I know? I'm just saying—"

"Oh, bosh," said Timaeus, knocking his pipe against a section of cast-iron fence. Charred pipeweed fell from the bowl and onto the slate of the street. "Do calm down, there's a lad."

"Don't do that," said Nick. "Any mansion that big has got magical wards. Touching the fence might do anything—set off alarms, trigger a magical assault, wake up the dragon . . ."

"There's no dragon, Pratchitt," said Timaeus somewhat irritably, thumbing more weed into his meerschaum. "Anyway, would you make your wards so sensitive as to register the thump of a pipe, or someone brushing up against the fence while strolling down the street? You'd run your guards ragged, charging out to investigate every stray sparrow or inattentive pedestrian."

"Still," said Jasper thoughtfully, hovering just shy of the fence, "the lad has a point. We durst not cross the fence without preparation. If the graf in truth has our statue within his mansion, it will be well protected; our only hope of snatching it is to get in quickly, without triggering alarms, and get out equally fast."

"Pole-vault over fence," suggested Kraki. "Run like damn."

"Hell," said Nick.

"Vhat?" said Kraki.

"Run like hell."

"Yah," said Kraki. "That's vhat I said."

"No, you said—"

"Pole-vaulting won't do it," said Sidney. "Ward effects usually extend upward, as well as along a fence or wall. You'd probably trigger something even if you never actually touched the fence."

"How high upward?" asked Frer Mortise.

"Why?" said Sidney.

Mortise coughed. "I am able, in the light of the moon, to transform myself into an owl. I might fly over the fence."

"A thought, Brother," said Sidney deferentially, "but skulking about a mansion in search of valuables is more in my line than yours. More than once, I've gotten into a warded building in the guise of a cat. You don't want your wards to register animals, after all, or your guards would go charging out after the local mousers seven or eight times a night."

"Perhaps so," said Jasper, "but the wards might be set to detect the passage of a sapient mind, or a concentration of magic—and your therianthropy is a form of magic, after all—in which case you'd set them off, even as a cat."

"You're a were?" demanded von Kremnitz of Sidney, his face bearing a faint expression of disgust. Therianthropy was magically associated with chaos, and in the minds of the ignorant, especially, this meant with evil; von Kremnitz had a trace of the common prejudice against shapechangers.

"Yeah," Sidney said belligerently. "Want to make something of it?"

Von Kremnitz cleared his throat, and hastily turned to Jasper. "Why don't you just read the minds of those within the mansion?" he asked.

"I've already tried, but as I expected, the mansion is warded against just such a thing," said Jasper. "Most noblemen, especially those with political ambitions, protect themselves against the more common methods of scrying."

"Really," said Timaeus, pipe full but unwilling to light it with the concomitant explosion and the attention it might draw, "we ought to retreat and plan this assault in more detail. Nice to know the place is here, would be nicer to be certain that the statue's in it, but an impromptu attack on a well-defended site with no preparation strikes me as—"

"Why don't I just run a recce?" said Jasper, spiraling upward. "I'll try to fly over the wards myself—"

"No," Sidney said, raising her voice to reach him as he rose. "Magical flight is common enough, you're bound to trigger—"

The earth mage completed his last slow gesture, spake his last slow Word. The bricks of the street buckled upward, then fountained aside in a shower of dirt. Where they had been stood a lumpen, earth-colored, vaguely humanoid shape, hulking and massive: an earth elemental, a gnome.

The earth mage began keening—a long, low, sustained note. After a few seconds, he changed pitch.

"What's he doing?" asked G.

"Chanting," said Wolfe. "He needs to tell the elemental what to do."

"Public Works isn't going to like that," said G, nodding toward the gaping hole in the road.

Wolfe snorted. "Come on, G," she said, "you going to tell them who did it?"

"Ook?" said the troll.

"Yes, Chad?" said Wolfe.

"When do we go?" asked the troll.

"Soon," said Wolfe. Under the mage's direction, the gnome had turned to face the fence. Now it was sinking back into the earth, as if gradually merging with it, the magician keening still.

At last the gnome had disappeared within the hole its appearance had caused. Bricks adjacent to the hole buckled upward; dirt began to fly out of the hole in an arc away from the fence, pattering into a growing pile on the sidewalk across the street. More bricks buckled upward, as a low berm began to extend from the hole toward the fence surrounding the Drachehaus. The berm intersected the sidewalk; slate flags tilted at sharp angles. Then the berm passed underneath the cast-iron fence and into the garden beyond.

"Big mole," said the troll. He was right, Wolfe thought; the berm looked like nothing so much as a gigantic molehill.

Inside the fence, the berm extended into the roots of an enormous rhododendron, which tilted up and sideways, coming down on its side with a rustle of leaves and the faint cracks of twigs. A few moments later, there was a shower of dirt within the garden, and the gnome's lumpen shape appeared, shedding soil like water.

"Come on," said Wolfe, and stepped into the tunnel the gnome had dug.

"Fear not," said Jasper faintly from above. "I'll be back in a jiffy. Ta-ta." The green light darted inward, across the fence.

Almost instantly, from within the mansion there came a faint brass sound: the unmistakable noise of a gong. Jasper flitted onward, apparently oblivious to the alarm. Again the gong sounded.

Sidney Stollitt cursed, her words ending in an annoyed cat's hiss. She twined through the bars and scampered across the lawn.

"Hokay," said Kraki. "Might as vell be hanged for a sheep as a frying pan." He swarmed up and over the fence.

Nick seized the bars of the fence. "Idiot," he shouted after Kraki. "You've got about as much *sense* as a sheep. You'll—oh, hell." He clambered up the fence himself, dropped to the nether side, and sprinted after Kraki.

Timaeus, concluding that since the alarm had been given there was no longer any reason not to light his pipe, brought his finger toward the bowl.

There was an explosion; Mortise, startled, transformed into an owl and flitted after the others. The flames about Timaeus's head dissipated after a moment, the fire mage puffing happily.

Pablo von Kremnitz was running up and down the fence, épée in hand, rather wild-eyed. "What ... ?" he sputtered. "They've ... We've got to—"

"We've *got* to do nothing," said Timaeus. "If they want to act like fools, it's not our responsibility to bail them out."

"Ye gods, I thought you people had at least an iota of

sense," protested von Kremnitz. "No coordination, no plan, no—it's disastrous!"

"Didn't we pass an alehouse a block or two back?" asked Timaeus. "Whisky sounds attractive about now."

"Surely we had better do something," von Kremnitz said.

"Well, you know," said Timaeus apologetically, "sneaking about is not exactly my *métier*. Blowing things up is rather more in my line."

The gong had been sounding continuously. From somewhere on the mansion's grounds, there came a curious noise, like a deep barking or a low roar.

"Sneaking about?" said von Kremnitz incredulously. "I'd say any element of sneakiness has long since been lost. And subtlety is not exactly your man Kraki's strong suit."

"Point taken. No reason not to take more drastic measures, then?" said Timaeus.

"I should say not," said von Kremnitz.

"Oh, well then," said Timaeus. He chanted briefly and pointed a finger at the cast-iron bars. He swept the finger back and forth in long strokes, melting a line across the fence. Severed sections of iron fell out, some hitting the earth, others striking the sidewalk with clangs. "After you," said Timeaus, gesturing courteously toward the opening.

"After you," said von Kremnitz, responding in kind.

"No, no," said Timaeus, "after *you*, my dear chap."

Wolfe examined the gnome's tunnel. It was low; she'd need to crawl through on hands and knees. And that meant she'd get covered with dirt. She grimaced fastidiously, but crouched down—and at that moment, a gong sounded from within the Drachehaus.

Wolfe checked. What had set off the alarm? The gnome's passage shouldn't have done it. And indeed, she realized, it had not; the gnome had appeared within the garden well before the alarm had sounded. "Something's gone wrong," she said.

"Uhhhhhhh," said the earth mage.

"I thought you said you'd checked the wards thoroughly," said G.

"I did!" Wolfe protested. "The ward effect doesn't extend underground. The gnome shouldn't have—"

"We're screwed, Wolfe," said G.

"Ohhhhhhh," said the earth mage.

"We don't have a choice," said Wolfe, dropping to hands and knees. Soft earth compressed beneath her palms; the tunnel smelled of rich loam. Wolfe contemplated the likely presence of small, wiggly things.

"This is lunacy," said G. "We're discovered. We daren't—"

"Nnnnnnnooooooooowwwwwww," said the earth mage.

"Shut up and follow me," said Wolfe. "Stantz wants the statue by tomorrow morning. It's my ass if he doesn't have it."

"Tough for you," said G.

"Tough for *you*," said Wolfe, "if you want to keep on working for the Ministry."

G's lips twisted into a snarl. She'd been involved in too many sensitive affairs; if the Ministry ever felt she was no longer to be trusted, she wouldn't live long. Wolfe was not merely threatening her livelihood, but her life.

"Whhhhhhhaaaaaaat," said the earth mage.

Briefly, G contemplated the possibility of killing Wolfe; killed in action, yes, with only G escaping to tell the doleful tale. But it was too chancy, to kill an ally while penetrating enemy territory.

"Dooooooo," said the earth mage.

Wolfe had disappeared into the tunnel. G stepped down into the hole and got onto her knees. The fact that she'd get dirty bothered her not at all; to the contrary, dirt smeared on face and hands would merely make her harder for the enemy to see in this dim light.

"Ook," said Chad worriedly, clambering into the tunnel.

"Iiiiiiii," said the earth mage. Slowly, he blinked. They were gone. "Dooooooooo," he said, finishing the sentence. What *should* he do now?

That was the problem in dealing with hasty folk. They had such short attention spans. Always running off and leaving you standing around at the site of a felony.

He sighed for several minutes. Well, something would no doubt happen within the next few (apparent) seconds; either Wolfe would be back, or someone would arrest him, or perhaps someone would try to kill him.

Experimentally, the earth mage said, "I surrender," as quickly as he was able. It was most unsatisfactory; why were though so damned many syllables in "surrender"? Dreadful word for the purpose; you'd think there'd be something simpler. "Uncle," he said. Would that do?

The moment Jasper crossed the line of the fence, he heard a distant gong. "Bother," he muttered; apparently he hadn't been sufficiently high. Or possibly the wards extended up and over the mansion, a hemispheric effect; he'd heard of such things before.

Well, he was still invisible, mostly, and still capable of flying rather quickly; and he had his magic powers. Reconnaissance was still feasible. He could get into the house and find someone in charge, read a mind or two, and find out where the statue was.

Sidney shouted something at him. Surely they wouldn't be so foolish as to follow him? Well, with any luck he'd only be a minute. If they were such idiots as to cross the fence after him, they'd provide a useful diversion. He'd be back momentarily, and they could all scoot back to the pension for a late meal. A split or two of champagne would go very well, Jasper thought.

He zipped through the still night air. It was late enough that the crickets had ceased their racket. There was no noise, other than that infernal gong and the hoot of an owl behind him. Confound it, not Mortise, I hope, he thought. There was an open window at the bottom floor, a drape blowing gently out into the night as the house exhaled warm air into cooling darkness. Jasper flitted for the window—

There was a sudden impact. Jasper's head and knees smarted something fierce. His vision dimmed for a moment, and when it gradually returned, little things danced in the edges of his sight. He was lying headlong on the grass.

He brought up a hand to look at it, but was relieved to see he was still invisible. Or rather, only his flame remained, the green light at the center of his being; it marked, so he had been told, his soul. He rose back into the air and moved toward the window once more, poking gingerly toward it with a hand.

To all appearances, the window was wide open. And the drape waved through it without obstruction. He sensed a magic there, a diffuse one: another damned ward, this one not along the fence, but protecting the mansion itself.

A ward against magical flight, he thought? Or invisible things? Or—or what?

Jasper de Mobray felt his rings. Rings on his fingers and bells on his toes; well, no bells, actually, but he had rings aplenty. Ten fingers, ten rings. Given a decade or two as an adventurer, one tended to accumulate all sorts of magic items. This one stored magic power; this one commanded Damon; that gave him flight; this invisibility. . . . Very useful, Jasper's rings.

And he'd worn them so long their effect was redoubled. Magic is effected through similarity; his rings had been so long on his fingers, were so intimately associated with him that they were similar, in some sense, to his very soul. And so their effect was intensified, when he used their powers.

But similarity was a double-edged sword. They were so damned similar it was hard to take them off.

Physically hard, too, Jasper thought, feeling his knuckles. He was no longer as young, or as svelte, as he once had been.

Jasper de Mobray sat on the grass before the Drachehaus, left hand twisting the ring on the middle finger of his right, grunting with strain as he tried to pull it off. The damn thing would not come. It would not come. He must get it off; it was the ring that gave him flight. With it off, perhaps he could get through the window. Or it if wasn't that one that barred him, perhaps the left index finger was the one, the ring of invisibility. He hadn't had it off in, oh, a decade at least, but, well, there it was. Damnation, thought Jasper, yanking with all his might, have the damned things grown roots?

In the distance, there was the baying of hounds.

Kraki clambered up an elm, out on a limb, and into a second-story window.

"Oh, my goodness," gasped a woman's voice. "It's my husband!"

Kraki watched with interest, one foot over the windowsill. A naked young man exploded out of the four-poster bed, covers flying. He snatched at his clothes and ran toward the window, colliding with Kraki. For a moment he looked as if he were about to faint, but then steadied. "I don't believe so," he said, "not unless your husband has somehow magically transformed into a half-naked savage with an enormous sword. Anyhow, there's two of them."

"Vhat?" said Kraki, and looked around. Nick was pulling his way through the window after him. "Hallo, Nickie," he said.

A blond-curled head stuck out from between the curtains of the bed and surveyed the scene at the window. "Oh," she said. "I heard the gong; are they barbarian reivers, you think? Traveling by longboat far upriver to plunder the riches of Hamsterburg?"

"Sure, doll," said Nick, eyeing her with interest. "That's us."

Kraki drew his sword and faced the young woman's lover. "Scream and I kill you," he said genially.

"I say," said the young man, "that's rather extreme, don't you think?"

"Egbert," said the woman in a scared voice, "they're going to ravish me! You must protect me!"

The young man started a bit at this and looked about, as if hoping to spy someone else on whom he might fob off the job. "Um, yes," he said. "I suppose. Look here, my good man, there'll be no ravishment here today. Pillaging, yes, all right, we can put up with a bit of pillage here and there; burning, well, if you must, although we'd really rather you didn't, you know. But rapine is right out. I'm going to be very firm on that."

Ignoring him, Nick sat down on the woman's bed and took her hand. "Now, now," he said soothingly. "That's not our way at all, you know. We barbarian reivers really aren't such bad sorts, you know; we just get bad press."

"I must ask you to leave," Egbert said firmly.

"Piss off, shorty," said Nick.

Dismissing Egbert and the blonde as threats, Kraki ran lightly across the room to its only door. He opened it a crack and peered down the hall. There seemed to be only one person in the hallway, an elderly man in nightgown and slippers, holding a lamp in one hand and a stick of some kind—Kraki guessed it to be a wand—in the other. "Be qviet," Kraki said. "Vhere is statue?"

"Statue?" said the young man, still naked, holding his balled-up clothes in one hand. "I don't know of any—unless you mean the bronze fawn by the koi pond."

"Oh, that thing Gerlad has been pottering about with," said the woman dismissively, gong continuing in the distance. "I haven't the faintest idea where it is. He's been very conspiratorial about it, heaven knows why. It's probably in the vault. Or possibly the potting shed."

The old man in the hall had reached the door, and now spoke. "Millicent?" he said, pushing on the door. "Are you all right? Devil knows what's going on with this racket."

"Oik," squeaked the young man, and threw himself out the window. There was a loud thud and a groan as he hit the ground, apparently having missed the limb of the elm tree.

Kraki had unthinkingly resisted the old man's shove against the door, and the oldster, now alarmed that an ajar door should not open easily, hurled himself into it, shoulder first.

Kraki stood away. When the old man's shoulder hit the door, it resisted not at all. The door smashed open, the old man tripping over the rug just inside and stumbling headlong across the room. He dropped the lamp, which smashed on the floor, spilling oil, and, arms flailing, flung his wand upward.

Unable to halt himself before staggering the full length of the room, the old man stumbled into the knee-height windowsill and hurtled out the window.

Kraki had thought that the wand was made of wood, but it must have been of porcelain or some similar substance. It dropped in a long arc onto the bricks of the hearth, where, as Kraki watched, it smashed to flinders.

The magic energy contained in the wand was instantly discharged in a brilliant, noiseless flash. Kraki had the misfortune to be looking directly toward the actinic glare.

From outside, there was another thump and a loud "Ouch!" as the old man hit the ground. "I say," said the old man after a moment, "very decent of you to break my fall, Egbert."

"Ah—glad to oblige," said the young man.

"Although," said the old man, voice tinged with sudden suspicion, "how is it that I find you here, half-clad, beneath my wife's window?"

"Vhere are lights?" said Kraki, whipping his head from side to side. He couldn't see anything except for a large, blue orb, hanging in the darkness before his eyes.

"You're blinded," said Nick. "The flash. Me too, I'm afraid."

"That makes three of us," said Millicent. "Are you going to ravish me now?"

Nick considered this. It was an attractive proposition in a way; on the other hand, mere physical release had never interested him particularly. It was the pursuit, and its successful conclusion that aroused him; the proof that he was found desirable, the guilty pleasure in cuckolding other men. Actually, he found the notion of rape rather distasteful. No, he regretfully concluded, he wasn't going to ravish the fair Millicent. Just not his style. Besides, he really ought to stick with Kraki . . .

The hand he had been holding wriggled out of his own and began to caress his leg.

Hmm. Then again . . . Nick grinned into darkness. "Ha ha," he said. "I have you now, my lovely."

"You devil," said Millicent breathlessly, sitting up and pressing her bosom against his chest. "I beg you, be gentle."

The gnome froze. After a moment, its nose fell off. Little clods of dirt pattered to the lawn. G poked it with a finger; it was, she saw, no longer animate, nothing but a vaguely humanoid pile of earth.

"This way," said Wolfe, briskly pushing through some hydrangeas. G and the troll followed. Lights had appeared in the mansion ahead; people were shouting, and somewhere dogs barked excitedly. G scowled, reluctant to press on as it became increasingly obvious that their target was alerted.

Wolfe halted suddenly, wiping at her dirt-smeared face with an equally filthy sleeve. G stumbled into her from behind. "What is it?" said G, peering over Wolfe's shoulder.

A door at the rear of the house had opened. From it, dogs ran.

Not mere dogs, G saw; they were the size of ponies, their foreheads low, their eyes aflame. From their massive fangs, blue fire dripped toward the ground, the incandescent slaver burning points of black into the lushness of the lawn: hellhounds. The animals ran toward them.

G was prepared to face almost anything, but fearsome demonic monsters rather larger than she were low on the list. She hesitated almost a full second before reaching for her weapons. Even that, she suspected, was a futile gesture; the beasts would be on them in instants, would tear them to shreds, would—

Would turn and tear around the corner of the house?

G blinked in astonishment. Whom were they after? Could von Grentz's wards possibly have misread where the fence had been breached? Or—might there be a second set of intruders? "What's going on?" G demanded.

"How the hell should I know?" said Wolfe irritably. "Maybe we're being suckered. Maybe they decided to teach a door-to-door salesman a lesson. Or maybe von Grentz just decided now was a nice time to play with the doggies."

She left the cover of the hydrangeas, sprinting toward the rear of the house. G and Chad followed, pounding across well-groomed sod. They joined Wolfe flat against the stone wall of the building, out of sight of any door or window. Just to their right, a stairway led downward to a cellar door. "Just a minute," said Wolfe. She concentrated a bit and disappeared. A shadow slid under the cellar door.

"Where she go?" asked Chad nervously.

"To unlock the door from inside, I expect," said G. She,

too, felt a little anxious; they were too exposed, out here against the wall.

Sidney sprinted from the shelter of the rosebush across a bed of iris and under a weeping hemlock. Ahead of her, cubits away yet, she saw Kraki swing from the limb of an elm tree and onto the sill of a second-story window, Nick clambering up the tree behind him. Of the others there was no sign, although somewhere hooted an owl—Frer Mortise?

That gong sounded again and again. Lights were going on in the mansion, and somewhere men shouted and dogs howled.

Then an excited barking began. Around the corner of the house, a half dozen hounds hurtled, paws eating up the sod.

Sidney yowled and leaped for a branch of the hemlock, clawing her way high up the trunk. Below, the hounds leaped and snapped, eyes glowing brilliant red in the darkness.

They were no mere dogs, she saw: pony-sized, eyes aflame, blue flame flickering about their jaws. She'd never seen hellhounds in the flesh before.

One howled in frustration at its inability to climb the tree; it tensed, holding a point, and made a curious coughing sound.

Flames roared from its mouth, up into the branches of the tree. Leaves curled and blackened where flame touched them. Sidney felt the whiskers on one side of her face singe, and yowled again, leaping higher into the tree.

She wondered what to do. She might turn human once again, but her weapons, like her clothes, were back outside the fence. Treed, she thought in self-disgust, how amateurish.

Sidney glowered at the hellhounds below. The fool creatures wouldn't give up; they leaped and snapped at her, but she was far too high for them to get her, and their blasts of fire merely denuded the lower branches of needles. She was safe, for the nonce, but . . .

One hellhound stood on its hind legs and reached up the trunk. It seemed to concentrate; as Sidney watched, its claws began visibly to grow. After a moment, it dug those now sharp claws into the tree, gave a little growl of satisfaction, and hoisted itself upward, hind claws scrabbling until they, too, found purchase. Doggedly, it reached higher again. Its progress was painfully slow; even with enhanced claws, it was not designed to be a climbing creature.

A second beast was climbing now, on the trunk's opposite side. They whined in expectation, blue-burning slaver running down the sides of their snouts, eyes glowing hateful red in the darkness.

Sidney leapt from one branch to another, but realized she had nowhere to go. There were other trees in the garden, but none close enough for her to reach.

Sidney gave a small, worried meow.

Frer Mortise flitted through the night air, hooting morosely. A mouse scurried through a flowerbed, down below; he fought a powerful urge to dive, seize it in his claws, and bite off its head with his sharp beak. He mustn't give in to such instincts, he told himself; he had more important concerns.

Exactly what they might be, however, he couldn't quite say. He was out of his league here and knew it, a simple hedge priest lost in the big city. His night vision was excellent, and his height gave him a better vantage than any of the others. He saw soldiers forming up on the house's front steps. He saw the hellhounds, clustered about a tree. He saw Jasper's green light, motionless before a window, and von Kremnitz and Timaeus strolling through the garden in leisurely fashion, as if out to sniff the night air. And at the rear of the house, he saw what seemed to be an enormous molehill, and a troll and a woman standing flat against the wall.

He could see a great deal, but what it all meant, and exactly what he should do, he could not say.

IV.

Koi swam in the pond. A steady stream of water emerged from the fawn's mouth and dripped into the pool. "Very nice," said Timaeus, strolling past and puffing contentedly.

"Come on," said von Kremnitz. "I hear dogs." Indeed, in the distance there was a howling.

"I've got a spell prepared," said Timaeus. "Never fear."

They rounded a privet—more of a tree than a bush, a huge old plant bursting with the exuberance of spring—and the mansion's main door came into sight. "Hullo!" said Timaeus. A score or more of soldiers stood there; swordsmen, mainly, though one or two held guisards, apparently a favorite weapon of von Grentz's followers. A man with a severe haircut, barefoot but wearing a breastplate, ordered them into some semblance of formation. And a petite woman in a red robe stood nearby, yawning into her hand.

"Well," said Timaeus, "can't have this." He released his prepared spell.

A fireball tumbled toward the soldiers. The red-robed woman looked up in alarm and started to shout something, but before she could complete her spell, flames exploded.

Thick smoke drifted across the garden, providing some cover for von Kremnitz and Timaeus. They sprinted away, toward the corner of the house. The woman in red was obviously a mage, and equally obviously it made no sense to remain where she had last seen them.

Their caution was rewarded; behind them, a bolt of flames ripped a nasty hole in the privet. "Fire mage," said Timaeus in some surprise, panting as he ran.

"Von Grentz had one at Weintroockle, remember," said von Kremnitz. "Where he ambushed the elves . . . What the devil?"

Beasts were clustered around the weeping hemlock tree ahead of them, peering upward into its branches. The creatures wheeled to face the approachers. They were enormous, as high at the shoulder as von Kremnitz's chest; eyes glowed crimson in the night.

"Hellhounds," said Timaeus. "Delay them." Gesturing with pipe in one hand, he began to chant.

"Delay them?" said von Kremnitz incredulously, surveying the rippling muscles, the enormous fangs, the blue fire playing about their muzzles. One of the monsters peered upward into the hemlock tree, while three others paced toward them. "Personally, I'm more inclined toward headlong flight."

Rather irritably, Timaeus broke off his spell. "Hellhounds are fire-aligned," he said. "I have some power over them—at least I will, if you delay them long enough for me to complete my spell." He took up his chant again.

"Yes, very well," von Kremnitz said resignedly, drawing his épée. One of the monsters suddenly ran three paces and launched itself into a leap, at least a dozen stone of viciousness hurtling across space. Von Kremnitz ducked underneath the hound and stabbed upward with his épée, ripping a line of blood down its belly. The beast landed awkwardly, howled, spun on four legs, and charged again. Von Kremnitz turned to face it, realizing immediately that this might be a mistake; from behind, he heard the patter of paws as the other two hounds charged. He was surrounded.

He whirled again to face the two charging monsters, hoping the injured one would be sufficiently delayed by its wounds that he might deal with the other two first. Not, to be sure, that he thought he could defeat two of the beasts at once; but it seemed his best strategy.

To his surprise, the two charging beasts separated and began to circle him, rather than pressing home their charge. He danced about, trying to keep an eye on all three of the monsters simultaneously; soon they halted, and glanced at one another.

Von Kremnitz realized that he was now encircled by the three, the monsters spaced at equal distances about the circle, separated by 120 degrees each. One of them gave a whine.

All three went into a point. Three black noses pointed directly toward von Kremnitz, three blue-fired bodies straining.

He wondered what this portended. It didn't take long to find out: The hounds breathed fire.

Three long tongues of blue flame darted inward. One, von Kremnitz might dodge; two, he might duck; but three— He flung himself away. Behind, three blue flames met and splashed out in a fireball, smaller than Timaeus's, but quite as deadly.

He stumbled, fell to the sod in a somersault, and lost his épée in the lawn. That was disastrous, but at least he had not been incinerated. He sprang to his feet, somehow retaining his dagger, and spun—

By all the gods, he thought. They work better together

than we. The three beasts ran around him clockwise now; it was difficult to keep track of all three at once.

Behind, Timaeus continued his chant; von Kremnitz could almost feel power gathering about the mage.

The wounded beast broke from the circle and lunged toward him; von Kremnitz stabbed toward the head with his dagger and dealt it another, glancing wound—but the effort threw him to one side. Immediately, another hound landed on his back, driving him face down into the lawn.

He had his dagger still, but face down, hundredweights of beast on his back, it was no use to him. Heart in throat, he flailed desperately, trying to throw off the beast, expecting its massive fangs to crush his skull at any instant, or to lift him by the nape of his neck and rip open his jugular—but instead, there were sudden snarls.

He turned his head far enough to see two hounds faced off above him. They seemed, he thought, to be contesting the right to administer the *coup de grâce*. The one on his back evidently thought that capturing him gave it that honor; the other, injured, apparently felt its wounds entitled it to the kill.

Where was the third hound? he wondered. He turned his head to the other side and saw Timaeus, chanting, smoke from his pipe writhing about his head in arcane patterns. The third hound was charging directly toward the wizard—and von Kremnitz despaired. Timaeus's spell was their only forlorn hope. Von Kremnitz stared in horror as the hound leapt toward Timaeus, the monster's fangs dripping blue fire as it opened its mouth to rip out the unarmed wizard's throat—

Timaeus leapt directly toward the charging hellhound and smashed it on the nose with his pipe. "Bad dog!" he cried.

To von Kremnitz's astonishment, the beast cringed, put its head on the ground between its paws, thrust up its rump, and wagged its tail from side to side in the manner of a puppy chastised for fecal incontinence.

Timaeus had completed his spell.

He strode across the lawn toward von Kremnitz, shouting, "No! Bad doggie!" at the two monsters that kept the swordsman pinned.

They backed away from von Kremnitz. One of the hellhounds whined unhappily, tongue lolling between bluefired fangs.

Timaeus reached down to give von Kremnitz a hand up. "Look as if you were having a bit of a bad spell, there," he said. "You all right, old man?"

"Right as rain," said a white-faced von Kremnitz, trembling slightly.

Timaeus turned back to the hellhounds, and said firmly, "Go home! Go home! Go to kennel, d'ye hear me?"

The monsters whined and wagged their tails sluggishly, as if asking for reprieve, but Timaeus was firm, repeating his command and pointing across the lawn. At last they loped away, peering forlornly behind.

Only one hound remained: the one staring upward into the hemlock tree. Von Kremnitz and Timaeus moved toward it, to finish the job; surprised, they saw that it was not the last hound after all. Two more were well up the hemlock, climbing awkwardly higher, snarling at something still higher in the tree.

"Go home," Timaeus said firmly to the one on the ground and, reluctantly, it did. Timaeus turned his face upward, toward the beasts in the tree, and shouted, "Down! Down, boy!" To von Kremnitz's eye, the creatures' gender was not immediately apparent, but he was willing to defer to Timaeus's superior knowledge.

The beasts looked down at them. One tried to back down the tree but lost its grip, falling onto a branch with a crack, and then heavily to the ground. The other, seeing this, actually leapt, from at least a dozen cubits in the air, onto the lawn. The force of its leap rocked the upper branches of the tree, and Sidney fell out with a yowl, managing to land on her feet not far from von Kremnitz.

"I say," said Timaeus cheerfully, "it's raining cats and dogs."

"It's Miss Stollitt," said von Kremnitz in relief. He sheathed his dagger and tucked her under one arm.

Chad, G could see, was getting more nervous by the minute. His employer had disappeared, they were in the midst of burglarizing the mansion of one of Hamsterburg's most powerful men, he was exposed against the wall, that alarm continued to ring, and from somewhere came the continued snarls and howls of the hounds. He had reason to be nervous, G supposed.

"It'll just be a minute," she said soothingly.

And then, from off across the mansion's grounds, there came an explosion: a flash of red light, a deep bass boom. It gave even G a start, but Chad leapt high in the air and came down running, directly away from the mansion. G recognized the cause of the disturbance almost immediately: Someone had cast a fireball—not a particularly unexpected eventuality, as Wolfe had reported that von Grentz employed a fire mage by the name of Rottwald. The fireball disturbed G less than the departure of Chad; they needed his muscle to get the damned statue out. Before he had taken three strides, G snatched a lead-weighted rod from her belt and spun it toward Chad's legs. The rod had its intended effect; Chad stumbled and fell.

"Come here, you idiot," said G. "We've an amulet against fireballs. If you're as yellow as this—"

Somewhat shamefacedly, Chad got to his feet and returned to the wall. "Chad not yellow," he protested. "Chad green. With brown splotches. See?"

G sighed. Actually, she couldn't see, not by moonlight.

The cellar door swung open at last. Wolfe stood within it. "In here," she whispered.

"What took you so long?" G whispered, following Wolfe into pitch darkness.

"Sorry," Wolfe whispered, off to the left. "This way." Even after a few seconds to let her eyes adjust, G could see nothing. She headed "this way"—and walked into something, hard enough to bruise her forehead. There was a movement in the air as whatever she had struck toppled over, then a tremendous crash, the tinkle of glass, and a sudden strong smell of wine. Red wine, thought G; a full-bodied one, possibly an Alcalan.

"G, you oaf," said Wolfe, in a whisper that came as close to a shout as a whisper is capable of coming. "What the hell—"

"It's pitch dark in here," protested G. "I can't see a thing."

"I see hokay," said Chad conversationally from behind her.

"Shhh!" hissed Wolfe.

"Of course he can see okay," whispered G. "He's a troll. And you're a shadow mage. But I've got no magic; it's black as the Dark Lord's heart in here."

"Here," whispered Wolfe, managing somehow to imbue the whisper with a wealth of irritation. After a moment, a wan point of light appeared in the air before her.

By its meager illumination, G saw that they were, as she had surmised, in a wine cellar. Wolfe wove through the wine racks toward the cellar's nether end, Chad following. G paused briefly to look at the label on a broken bottle; it was indeed an Alcalan, a Rive Palatine, from one of the better châteaux. She made a mental note to snag a bottle on the way out, if it was practical.

Gerlad, Graf von Grentz, marched down the steps of his house with martial dignity. He was naked—so he slept—but unashamed. He exercised an hour a day, he had the body of a man half his age, and he found nothing particularly erotic in mere nudity. He regarded the nudity taboo, like most of the moral strictures of his society, with contempt.

Black char marks marred the marble stairs. Wounded were sprawled across them, a cleric moving from form to form. There was no semblance of discipline. Von Grentz scowled.

"Magistra Rottwald," he said. "What is the meaning of this?"

The fire mage was stooped over the body of a badly burned guisardiere, casting a fire protection spell; it couldn't help the man avoid injury now, but it would at least render his burns less painful until a cleric could attend him. She straightened up and turned toward her employer. "I beg your pardon, your grace," she said. "It appears that among our assailants is another fire mage. I was unable to—"

"Never mind that. Where is Serjeant Kunz?"

"Dead," said Rottwald, pushing back her xanthine hair.

"Where are the invaders?"

Howls, yips, and snarls came from around the side of the house. "Over there, I presume," said the mage.

Von Grentz bit back a cutting remark. They were under attack, and these fools hadn't the sense to find out by whom. "Every able-bodied man, to the foot of the stairs," he bawled. Several soldiers hesitated. "Yes, you, dammit," he said, stabbing a finger at one. He reached down and took a sword from one of the bodies. "You too, Rottwald."

He took the steps two at a time and briefly surveyed the motley dozen who had responded. They looked a little dazed, as well they might; their company just suffered fifty percent casualties, half the group lying on the stairs above, dead or wounded. But he hadn't spent hours drilling the swine for nothing. "You, you idiot; drop that pole-arm. Draw your sword. Now listen to me, you lot. Line abreast,

at a run. Keep an eye on the man to your right, keep up
with him. Drop to the ground the moment you see someone casting a spell. Hold." He turned to Rottwald.
"Magistra, prepare and hold a defensive spell; it is likely
to be a small party. We probably outnumber them on the
ground; your best use is to protect us so we may drive our
attack home."

He turned back to the soldiers. "You will follow my orders with alacrity, or you will taste the lash. Now! Follow
me!"

And he sprinted, barefoot and bare elsewhere as well,
across the lawn, confident that they would indeed follow.

They had been well drilled; they did.

Somewhere out there, there had been an explosion. And
more yaps and howls, and the gods knew what else. From
closer at hand came moans, pants, and gasps of pleasure.

Kraki wondered what to do. It was foolish to wander
about the mansion, blinded as he was; how could he possibly hope to find the statue? Even if he did, he couldn't
see it, and might not even realize it was there. Still, it was
equally pointless to stand here, dithering. What did Nickie
think he was doing, anyway? Yah, kill the men and ravish
the women, all very good barbarian practice, and Kraki
had no particular objection, but still, the battle was still in
progress. You were supposed to slay all your foes first,
then ravish the women.

Kraki counted on his fingers, to make sure he had that
right. One, kill the men. Two, drive their cattle before you.
Three, listen to the lamentation of their women. Pillage by
the numbers, it was called, and it was drilled into every
barbarian from childhood. Kraki wasn't clear on how ravishment and lamentations went together, never actually
having been part of a conquering horde, but the rules
pretty clearly indicated that you dealt with the men and the
cattle before the women, in complete accordance with the

relative positions of men, cattle, and women in barbarian society. They had not, as yet, accomplished step one or two, and Nick was obviously breaking the rules by going straight to step three.

Hounds bayed outside the window. "Egad!" shouted a voice: the woman's husband, Kraki thought. "Down, boy!"

"Good heavens," said another voice—the young man? "I knew Cousin Gerlad was keen on dogs, but hellhounds seem a little—I do believe they're coming at us, Rutherford."

"Come on, you young idiot!" Rutherford shouted, his voice sounding almost parallel to the room now. "Up the tree, you—"

Leaves rustled desperately; a hound bayed victory from beneath the elm. "I say," said Egbert petulantly, "those were my best hose, you brute!"

"Of all the damnable luck," said the old man. "To lose my wand at a time like this."

Kraki was unaccustomed to indecision; he found it most uncomfortable. Yet he could not make up his mind. It was lunacy to stay here, that much was obvious; but should he charge into the mansion, leave by the window, or stay here to protect Nick?

Retreat was the obvious choice; but that was not acceptable. Retreat was for cowards. *Men* stood and died.

"Millicent?" said Rutherford from the window, in a rather suspicious tone. "I say, Millicent, what are you doing in there?" The sounds of lovemaking were evidently audible to him, now that he had climbed the tree.

"Oh, crikey," said Egbert, sounding shaken. "They're ravishing her in truth, the blackguards! You must do something, Rutherford."

"I?" said Rutherford. "I? A wizened old man such as I? No, my boy, you're the young hero here. Up to you, I should think."

There was silence for a moment. Then Egbert said, "Millicent? Millicent, dearest? Are you all right?"

"Go away," said Millicent shortly.

"We're busy right now," said Nick.

"What?" shouted Rutherford, voice quivering in rage. "I say, Millicent, this is quite out of the— Is that smoke, Egbert?"

Kraki sniffed at the air; there *did* seem to be smoke. Something was burning. He couldn't see any flames, though. Well, of *course* he couldn't see any flames; he was blind. Rutherford had carried a lamp into the room, as well as a wand, hadn't he? Could it have set something on fire?

"Ouch!" said Nick suddenly. "What . . . ?"

"Room on fire, Nickie," said Kraki. "Maybe ve leave, yah?"

"Hell of a time," complained Nick.

"Fire?" said Millicent in alarm. "Eeek!" There was the sound of rustling sheets, then the patter of feet, an annoyed "Ouch!", and the creak of a door.

"Wait!" Nick said—but the door slammed shut. Millicent had fled the room.

From the tree, Egbert and Rutherford argued about who should go to Millicent's rescue. Neither seemed particularly eager to brave licking flames and heavily muscled barbarians.

"Let's get out of here," Nick said.

"Tree or door?" asked Kraki.

"Tree," said Nick. "We've—"

"That is retreat," said Kraki with finality. "Retreat is covardice." He could hear Nick getting out of bed and moving toward the window.

"Don't be stupid, Kraki," Nick said.

"Vhat wrong vith being stupid?" Kraki protested. "You civilized fellas too smart by half, you ask me."

Nick snorted. "Listen, Kraki. Hear that?"

From outside came howls.

"Yah," said Kraki. "So?"

"Hellhounds," said Nick.

"Yah," said Kraki, "sure."

"You're telling me it's cowardice to leap into the midst of ferocious, man-eating hellhounds, fell beasts of power able, so legend says, to spit flames at their foes? Sounds pretty damn heroic to me, actually."

"Oh!" said Kraki, in relief. "Yah. Good. Thank you, Nickie."

He ran for the windowsill and balanced briefly atop it . . .

Then leaped blindly out into space, bellowing the name of his most illustrious ancestor.

A stairway led upward from the wine cellar, but Wolfe skirted it, heading instead for the back of the chamber. There another door stood, secured only by a bar on the inside. Wolfe laid aside the bar, doused her magical light, opened the door, and peered through it.

Beyond the door, a corridor led left and right; down to the left was a lamplit room. Not much of the room was visible from this vantage. Wolfe closed the door again and whispered to G, "Down the corridor. I'll be back in a minute."

G nodded in the darkness, trusting that Wolfe would see the gesture. Presently, she felt that Wolfe was gone—an absence of breathing, a sense of emptiness before her; with the door closed and the light gone, she could again see nothing.

An eternity passed. From outside the mansion came the sounds of furious barking, animal yowls, a shout or two. G began to itch; waiting in readiness was almost more tiring than action.

At last Wolfe was back. "There are only five," she said. "The rest must have gone upstairs to investigate. But they're alert and itchy."

G sighed. "Let's go," she said.

Wolfe guided her hand to the latch. G withdrew it, took her crossbow from her back, cranked it, and laid a quarrel in its groove. She tucked another quarrel under her left arm, holding the bow in her left hand. She reached out for the latch with her right hand, took hold of it, and said, "On the count of three. One, two, three."

She flung open the door and hurled herself down the corridor, grabbing the loose quarrel with her right hand. Behind her, Wolfe and Chad ran.

A helmeted man stood at the end of the corridor, half silhouetted in the light of the room. He heard running footsteps and turned toward G. "Hey," he began to say.

G brought up her crossbow. Running, one-handed, she squeezed the lever, snapping off a shot.

"Who—*gluuch*," said the man. The quarrel hit him square in the throat. He began to fall, hands going to the shaft.

G cranked the bow. By the time she reached the corridor entrance, she had laid the second quarrel in its groove.

Wolfe had sketched the room for G, back in the Albertine Lodge, the headquarters of the Ministry. She knew what to expect; in the northeast corner was a door, leading to stairs upward. Across the room was another open corridor, leading to the vault. One soldier stood at each, she saw. The other two sat at a table, but Wolfe had been right; they were alert. They wore chain mail, and each had a weapon within arm's reach.

Above the table was a bell. One of the seated soldiers, a woman who had unwisely removed her helmet, began to rise from her chair, reaching for the clapper.

G shot her. The quarrel struck just above the bridge of the nose. The woman tumbled over backward, knocking down a chair; G suspected the missile had failed to penetrate the nasal opening and that the woman was still alive, but she was down, at any rate, which would do for now. G dropped her bow.

Her left hand had by now drawn a throwing star. She hurled it, neither looking nor aiming, toward the soldier who guarded the opposite corridor. He was charging her while drawing his sword, which he had not yet brought into position; the star missed him, clanging against the stone wall, but he ducked, which threw him off stride and gave her a little more time.

Her right hand had drawn a throwing dagger by the blade. She held it by her right ear and took more than a second to brace herself and take careful aim. The second soldier at the table, a boy of scarcely sixteen, was reaching for the bell. G was impressed that so raw a lad could respond appropriately, so quickly, in a moment of mortal danger; he had potential. She therefore hurled her dagger into his gut—a painful wound that, with any luck, would put him out of action but which, if he got to a healer in time, would neither kill nor permanently cripple him.

The soldier from the corridor opposite had now reached G and was swinging his sword. She was out of position and could not respond quickly enough to block the blow; she had feared this might happen, but had felt that preventing an alarm was worth the risk. She ducked and reached up, to take the blow flat onto the ulna of her left arm—no major arteries there; it might break the bone but could not inflict life-threatening injury—while drawing a kukri with her right hand.

Wolfe dived around G and deflected the man's blow with her épée. His saber passed over G's head, but hit Wolfe's lighter blade hard enough to snap it. Before he could regain control of his weapon, G had driven her kukri under his ribs and—the utility of a curved blade—upward through the rib cage and into his heart. She let go the kukri, letting it fall with her foe.

Crossing her hands over her abdomen, G grasped the hilts of both her swords—the one at her right in her left hand, the one at her left in her right—and drew them both with a flourish, turning toward the final soldier, the one by the door to the stair—

In time to watch the door slam behind him. Coward, she

thought, instantly launching herself into a sprint toward the door.

"No, G!" shouted Wolfe.

Reluctantly, G halted and turned. "He'll give the alarm," she said.

"I'm not having you chasing him around the mansion," said Wolfe. "We'll stick together; we'll just have to work fast."

"Ook," said Chad a little sadly, surveying the gore. Was he saddened by so many deaths, G wondered, or because he'd arrived too late to join in the fun?

Wolfe hustled out of the room and down the corridor to the vault, Chad following. G checked the four bodies; the two older men were dead, the woman breathing but out. The boy was motionless, feigning unconsciousness, but by his tenseness obviously in pain and obviously alive.

G had a craftsman's sense of parsimony. She had no objection to killing in pursuit of her objectives, but had no desire to kill unnecessarily. She gave him a nicely calculated thump to the back of the skull, relieving him of the need to maintain his charade.

Jasper was still pulling at his rings when he heard the boom of Timaeus's fireball. Instantly he realized that the others must be in trouble. The shouts, the baying hounds he had taken for the consequence of the alarm he had triggered, but the flash and boom of a fireball must mean the others had indeed followed.

It was a disaster, he realized; a disaster caused by his own impulsiveness. He felt hot with shame; he was supposed to be an old hand at this sort of thing, and here . . .

Well. He gave up prying at his rings and flew toward the fireball's boom.

Timaeus and von Kremnitz, the latter carrying Sidney, walked across the lawn. From ahead, hounds still bayed;

apparently, another group of the animals continued to harass someone else. Yes thought Timaeus; there they were, by that elm. He hadn't thought to maintain his spell, alas, and so began working on it once again. But just as he began, an owl swooped down and flitted around his head.

"Hoo! Hoo!" quoth the owl.

"Oh, dash it," grumbled Timaeus. "Scat, you—oh, Frer Mortise; I didn't recognize you at first. Good, that just leaves Kraki, Nick, and Jasp—"

"Hoo! Hoo!" said the owl urgently.

"And a hoo hoo to you, too," said Timaeus. "I don't suppose you've seen—"

Frer Mortise came to a landing on a branch of a nearby tree, resumed human form, and said, "The Graf von Grentz has rallied his soldiers, and is heading toward you. We—"

And there they came, at a run, the naked von Grentz in the lead. The red-robed magician lagged a little behind.

Timaeus instantly switched to a different spell, spitting the syllables of magic as fast as he was able. It was risky, spell-casting so fast; a stumble of the tongue and the spell could have unintended, possibly lethal effects. But they had little time before the soldiers closed.

Von Grentz halted below the elm where the hellhounds clustered. The red-robed woman joined him, with a gesture ordering the hellhounds to line up defensively, protecting them both. Von Grentz bawled orders; soldiers ran to encircle Timaeus and the others.

Von Grentz happened to glance upward into the branches of the elm. "Rutherford," he said in surprise. "What the devil are you doing up there?"

Rutherford? Timaeus wondered, even as he worked the spell. "Who was . . . ? It hardly mattered; they were well and truly snared. There were too many soldiers, and they were too spread out; he could not get more than three with a single spell. And that other mage must have something up her sleeve. It all looked rather grim.

Frer Mortise had, discretion being the better part of valor, turned back into an owl. Sidney leaped from von Kremnitz's hands into an overhanging branch. Von Kremnitz, who had retrieved his sword after the fight with the hounds, drew it once more.

A ball of fire appeared in Timaeus's hands. He hurled it not at any of the soldiers, but directly toward von Grentz. Kill the leader and the followers would be more amenable; a reasonable theory, at any event.

A ball of flames tumbled through space, toward the elm. Von Grentz faced it expressionlessly. The soldiers threw themselves flat.

. The ball of flames—

Fizzled.

Timaeus cursed; a counterspell. He should have anticipated that. Instead . . .

The soldiers picked themselves up and closed. Timaeus and the others found themselves at the center of a ring of blades.

"You will surrender," said von Grentz, "or die."

"Surrender?" said von Kremnitz, smiling slightly. "I'm not familiar with the word, I'm afraid. You'll have to define your terms."

Von Grentz sighed. "If you give me your word that you will provide a full accounting of your actions and motives," he said, "I give you my word that I shall set you free."

"How much is your word worth?" von Kremnitz asked skeptically.

Von Grentz stiffened. He was not accustomed to having his honor questioned so directly. "Kill—" he began.

At that instant, someone above him screamed, "Gostorn Pie-Eater!"

Von Grentz looked upward.

Jasper came in sight of von Kremnitz and Timaeus. They were ringed by soldiers; a naked man and a red-robed woman, perhaps a mage, stood under an elm near the Drachehaus, beneath a window from which smoke poured. The man gave off an air of command.

As he feared. The idiots had got themselves captured. What should he do?

Blindly, Kraki plunged through space, shouting his war cry. Well before he should have hit the ground, his left sandal hit something, sending Kraki sprawling . . .

It was von Grentz. The sandal hit the nobleman full in the face, flipping him backward; his head hit a root of the elm with a crack.

Kraki hit the earth awkwardly. In an instant he was on his feet, flailing blindly about with his sword and bellowing, "Take that, foul vight!" Magistra Rottwald dodged out of range of the sword.

The blade bit into the elm. "Aha!" shouted Kraki, turning to face the tree. He began to chop at it, bellowing imprecations. Chunks of wood flew hither and yon.

Nick pulled himself more cautiously into the branches of the elm. Something twisted under his boot.

"I say," said Rutherford, "watch where you put your feet, lout."

"Sorry," Nick muttered. He tilted his head from side to side; his vision was returning, although he couldn't make out much just yet.

The soldiers stared at the body of their leader and the barbarian chipping at the tree. Von Kremnitz took advantage of their momentary confusion to slip under one man's blade and sink an épée into his stomach.

A naked woman dropped out of the elm and onto a third soldier's shoulders. As he crumpled, Sidney clouted him in the temple with her fist and grabbed his sword.

An owl raked at another soldier's eyes.

Timaeus began to chant a spell, well aware that one of these sword-wielders might gut him before he could finish.

But the remaining soldiers were backing away, uncertain and confused. "The graf," one said, "he's down—"

"Feel the wrath of Kronar's son!" shouted Kraki to the elm, chopping away.

Rottwald snapped an order to her hounds. They turned and hurtled toward Timaeus and the others, snarling defiance.

This time, however, Timaeus had thought ahead. His spell would be too long delayed to do much to the soldiers surrounding him; either the others could deal with them, or they all would die. If the latter, no spell would help; if the former, the hellhounds would be the last remaining threat.

He shouted the last Words of his spell. "Bad dog!" he bellowed. "Down! Down! Sit!"

The charge of the hounds broke up in confusion. They halted, looking back and forth between Rottwald and Timaeus, whining. Rottwald was already chanting another spell, and while obviously unhappy with this turn of events, did not care to abandon it to impress her will on the hounds.

"Sit!" Timaeus shouted again, making a sitting motion with his hand. Reluctantly, the hounds complied.

Jasper saw Kraki plunge from the window and onto von Grentz; and instantly he realized what he must do. Quietly, he began the Words for a spell of his own.

The soldiers would be taken aback, a little afraid to see their leader fall; he could work on that fear.

With satisfaction, he saw von Kremnitz kill one, Sidney put another out of action. That would increase their tension. It was a trivial matter to turn tension into . . . terror.

The soldiers backed away, faced with an unexpected attack from those they had thought to be prisoners.

Jasper completed his spell.

They backed away—then turned and fled.

V.

G gaped at the vault's protection.

The end of the corridor was filled by an enormous steel contraption. It had bars, wheels, levers, and gears, interlocking in a fashion that only a dwarven artificer might understand without prolonged study. The steel was highly polished, every element of thick, machined metal, the whole so evidently sturdy that it looked as if it could outlast the city. And the complexity of the mechanism was such that G doubted the cleverest of locksmiths, the most experienced of thieves could undo it.

Moreover, the walls of the corridor bore a number of suspicious-looking depressions and vents. Wolfe stood before the mechanism, turning a wheel; G expected the vents to begin to spew poison gas, or bolts of flame, at any moment. It made G nervous; a living foe she might kill, but this thing was beyond her skills.

Wolfe gave the wheel a precise quarter turn, reached up and played a minuet on an array of levers, and turned three dials—one clockwise, two widdershins. G heard no sounds of tumblers clicking, no indication—save continued existence—that Wolfe had gotten the motions right.

Wolfe fiddled with more rods, cams, and dials; after seconds that seemed like eons, she turned the great wheel again, reversing her original rotation. And the door swung open. G breathed relief.

"How did you do that?" she asked.

Wolfe gave her a glance. "I watched von Grentz do it, of course," she said. G's appreciation of her talents rose several notches.

Wolfe was the first to enter the vault. She jumped as if startled, and said, "Who . . . ," cutting the sentence short almost as soon as she began to utter it. G peered from behind her.

A light had gone on as the door opened; a globe at the back of the room glowed brightly green, emitting faint screams as it did. G didn't know what spell powered it and, judging by the screams, didn't want to know. The statue was there, lying on a table at the vault center; there were shelves and, oddly, filing cabinets; but there were none of the heaped jewels and golden coins G had expected to see.

"The old man again," Wolfe muttered, just audibly enough for G to hear her.

"What old man?" asked G.

"I thought—never mind," said Wolfe. "Trick of the light, I suppose. Chad, come here."

The troll stepped into the vault and began to examine the statue. Dealing with it was his problem; G took the opportunity to take a closer look at the vault. A modest assortment of gold ingots did sit on one shelf, doing something to satisfy her desire to see golden treasure, but filing cabinets occupied the bulk of the room. Could von Grentz possibly value information on his enemies more greatly than money? "This is a great lord's treasure?" G said incredulously.

Wolfe gave her a brief look. "Money in vaults doesn't pay interest," she said.

Of course, G thought. They'd invest the money. Probably those filing cabinets held a good many stock certificates and other—hmm. Other negotiable instruments. She pulled open a drawer.

"No time for that," Wolfe snapped. "Chad, can you carry it?"

The troll was already moving about the statue, tying it in a network of rope. G was surprised at the suppleness of his fingers as he tied the knots; trolls might lurch clumsily, but they did not seem to be clumsy in every respect. "Yah," said Chad. "Hard work, though. Help me get it onto floor." He took hold of Stantius's ankles and, grunting, rotated the statue so that it lay across the table's short dimension. Then, while G and Wolfe heaved up on the shoulders, he tilted the feet down until Stantius was standing atop the vault floor. Taking two heavy ropes, one over each shoulder, he backed up to the statue, crouched down, and pulled the ropes until they were taut. He passed the ropes through a series of loops, knotting them several times, back around the statue, and through his harness. At last he was done. He strained upward and forward, grunting with effort, until at last he stood erect, bearing Stantius on his back. "Let's go," Chad said, his voice revealing more than a little strain.

They did. They left the vault door open. No one had yet returned to the guardroom; G fretted at that, for the escaped guard should have raised the alarm by now. Perhaps the household was still preoccupied with whatever had been going on out on the lawn; she hoped so, for otherwise they were almost certainly walking into a trap. They made their way back to the wine cellar at a run and maneuvered through the racks. Chad moved awkwardly with Stantius atop his back; he knocked another wine rack down, almost onto G, who cursed, but had the presence of mind to snatch a magnum of something as it fell past her. A Sang du Démon, she saw, stuffing it into one of her cloak's voluminous pockets. As she climbed the cellar steps onto the lawn, it banged uncomfortably against her thighs.

Wolfe peered out into the night. The hellhounds had gone quiet, but there were the sounds of weapons clashing, men yelling, and what sounded peculiarly like someone chopping down a tree from their left. "Come on," said Wolfe, and loped out toward the hydrangeas, a saber stolen from one of the dead soldiers in her hand.

G cursed; she would have preferred to reconnoiter first, but there was, after all, something to be said for headlong speed. Chad pounded behind her, his breath coming in gasps.

The gnome was still there, or its remnants; and there was the tunnel lip, down which Wolfe had already disappeared. G dived into the tunnel, scrabbling through dirt on her hands and knees. "Wait," said Chad behind her.

She paused, unable to turn in the cramped confines of the tunnel. "What is it?"

"I can't do this," said Chad. "Statue too big. I get stuck."

G cursed, and shouted for Wolfe. There was no response. She continued down the tunnel, to find Wolfe already outside the fence, bending over her magic pouch, which, as expected, no one had yet stolen. The earth mage was still there, too, talking in his usual slow way. "Uhhhhhhhhnnnnnnng," he said.

"The tunnel's too small for Chad," G said, "with the statue on his back."

Wolfe blinked. "It's always something," she said, and dived back into the tunnel.

G sighed; she had no desire to follow, but supposed she must.

"Clllllle," said the earth mage.

G bent down to enter the tunnel. Uncle? What the hell was he saying "uncle" for?

Rottwald, chanting her spell, ran full tilt toward Timaeus and von Kremnitz. Timaeus was momentarily confused, but quickly realized what she was up to. "Down," he yelled, slapping von Kremnitz on the shoulder.

Kraki, shouting his usual "Yah hahs!" and "Die, foul vights!" continued to chop at the elm.

Von Kremnitz responded to Timaeus's order with alacrity; he didn't know much about magic, but a fire mage, sprinting toward one and chanting a spell, obviously meant trouble.

Timaeus grabbed the fringe of his cloak with both hands and hurled himself atop von Kremnitz, spreading the garment as he did. He prayed that he and his cloak, between them, would shelter his companion; the cloak, like all his clothes, was fire-resistant. That was a necessity for a fire mage; elsewise, an ill-timed spell would leave one starkers, and while the lower classes might not balk at that, a gentleman must adhere to certain proprieties.

Mere steps from them, the woman exploded into flame. Above her, a branch of the elm took fire. Sidney threw herself from the tree, yowling at her singed fur.

A silent moment passed. The breeze began to dissipate the choking smoke. Flames crackled from the Drachehaus window. Kraki had been startled by the bang, but quickly resumed the attack against the elm. "Yah-hah!" he bellowed, sword chunking into heartwood. "Take that, foul giant!"

"Get the hell off of me," said von Kremnitz from underneath Timaeus.

Timaeus got gingerly to his feet; he was uninjured. But then, he'd been at the center of a fireball's blast often enough that it no longer fazed him. "I resent your tone," he said. "I may well have saved your life."

"Next time you save my life, be so kind as to lose a few pounds first," said von Kremnitz. "Whatever happened?"

"She teleported out," Timaeus said, "leaving a fireball behind her. A sensible thing to do, with her allies gone."

With a cry of triumph, Kraki dealt the elm a final blow. While Rutherford, Nick, and Egbert shouted in dismay, the mighty shade tree toppled away from the Drachehaus and crashed into a bed of peonies. Von Grentz lay, unconscious and snoring, by the stump of the fallen elm.

"Ha!" shouted Kraki, brandishing his broadsword triumphantly. "So fare all who face the sword of Kraki! Is that you, Timaeus?"

"Yes, Kraki," said Timaeus. "Ah, there you are, Nick, my boy. Now there's just Jasper." Nick extracted himself from the branches of the fallen tree and joined the others. The center of his vision was still filled with bright afterimages, but he could at least see things at the periphery.

"How do you mean?" asked Jasper, the green light whizzing down to join them.

Sidney gave a hiss and leapt at the green light, which dodged away. "I say, Sidney," said Jasper. "What is the—well, yes, perhaps I was a bit rash to—I am sorry, you're quite—Please! I do not expect such language from a lady ... Yes, all right, you're not a lady, you're a cat, but I must say—"

"Shut up, Sidney," said Nick, to the apparently silent cat. "We'd better get out of here while we have the chance."

"Ho," said Kraki, wandering in their direction. "This vill be a day of vhich the bards vill sing, eh? The day that Kraki Kronarsson slew the giant of Drachehaus! Single-handed, blinded that I be—"

"Ah," said Timaeus, "that explains it."

"In single combat, I slew the monster. I chopped him limb from limb—"

"You've got that right," said Nick.

"And cleaved him from pate to pelvis," declared Kraki with satisfaction. "Behold!" And he gestured toward the fallen elm with his sword, nearly decapitating Nick in the process.

"More like from twig to taproot," said Timaeus. He took Kraki's arm. "Come on, Kraki, O mighty slayer of elms. Aim your heroic feet this way." He began to lead the barbarian away from the Drachehaus and toward the street.

"Vhat?" protested Kraki, as Timaeus and Nick dragged him away. "Vhat you mean, slayer of elms?"

"What do you make of all this?" asked Egbert, as he gave Rutherford a hand down from the branches of the fallen tree.

"Thought Gerlad was a solid sort," said Rutherford, "but, by Dion, he can't even keep order in his own household. How he expects a man to get a little shuteye with fireballs exploding and battles raging in the front garden, I'm damned if I—I say. Here he is in the very flesh."

Rutherford had nearly stumbled over the unconscious body of Gerlad, Graf von Grentz, lying naked by the ragged stump that was all Kraki had left of the elm.

"Cousin Gerlad," said Egbert, kneeling and shaking the graf. "I say, old bean, do wake up."

Von Grentz's eyes opened.

"Sleeping out tonight?" said Rutherford. "Nice weather for it."

Von Grentz sat bolt upright. "Where are—What—" Dazedly, he took in the flames licking from the window of his mansion, the elm afire. His eyes had difficulty focusing; indeed, he was seeing double, slightly concussed from the blow to his head. "Rottwald," he croaked, got raggedly to his feet, and staggered off toward the front of the house.

"Nary so much as a 'How are you, cousin,' " complained Egbert.

"Well, his house *is* on fire," observed Rutherford.

Egbert looked up at the window. "Quite right," he said. It occurred to him that Millicent was presumably still in the house. She was in the house, and the house was burning. She was in the house, the house was burning; therefore, she was in dire peril. She was in the house, the house was burning, she was in dire peril—dire peril from which a gallant young man might rescue her. Just the thing, thought Egbert; a gallant young man going to the rescue of his lady love, cradling her in his arms, striding heroically from the blaze. "Um—ta for now, Rutherford, old man," he said, and set off for the nearest ingress, a bottom-floor window.

Somewhat parallel thoughts had been running through Rutherford's head. "Stop, you rakehell," he shouted, hastening after the younger man.

"All right, Chad," said Wolfe, "back out." She turned to G. "You were right; he doesn't fit."

G had just about changed her mind again; maybe she would kill Wolfe after all. "You think I make these things up for the hell of it?" she snarled. "Of course I was right."

"What do we do?" asked Chad.

"Dig out the hole," said G.

"Right," said Wolfe. "With what shovel?"

"Hands, I guess," said G.

Wolfe snorted. "Take us forever," she said. "Chad, take off the statue."

Chad obliged, more than happy to shed the burden. Wolfe examined the statue, and Chad's ropes, with interest. "Will that cable pull the statue?" she asked.

"It's heavy enough," said Chad. "Double it up to be sure."

Wolfe nodded. "Good," she said. "Unknot some, a long

enough length to run through the tunnel, with, oh, twenty cubits to spare. Is there enough rope?"

Chad blinked, slow mind puzzling over the request. "Yah," he said.

"We going to pull it through?" asked G.

"Something like that," said Wolfe. As soon as the rope was ready, she grabbed it and crawled back down the tunnel.

G sighed. "I wish she'd tell us what the hell she's going to do," she said.

"Soldiers!" said Chad in a sudden panic. He pointed at something behind her back and crouched down, looking as if unsure whether to flee in panic or to dig a hole to hide in. "Bad men kill Chad! Save Chad, G!"

G whirled, hands going to her weapons. Ambling toward them was an old woman, holding an oil lamp over her head with one hand, the other hand bearing a hoe. She was clad in heavy canvas trousers and clogs, and mumbling something toothlessly.

". . . three yearsh before the bloody privet will—Who the devil are ye?" she demanded.

"Kill her, G," whined Chad, groveling in the dirt with fear. "Kill her!"

"You're a disgrace to your species," said G. She turned to the old woman and said, in a soothing tone, "We're just leaving."

"Well, leave, then, by damn," said the old woman. "Not a raise in pay in eighteen yearsh, and the bashtard fightsh a bloody war amid me damned peoniesh! Bigodsh, and here'sh a molehill the shize o' Mount Cernitash. Finish yer damned business and get out, shay I." She turned and wandered back toward the shed.

"She'll bring soldiers!" whined Chad.

"Oh, shut up," said G. "She's just the gardener. Harmless enough."

"G!" came a low voice from the cast-iron fence.

"What is it, Wolfe?" asked G.

"Shove the statue up to the mouth of the tunnel, and get the hell out of there," said Wolfe.

"Coming, darling," said G. "Give me a hand, Chad."

When they crawled out of the tunnel, they found the hansom cab and a rather confused driver standing in the street.

". . . d'ye mean, ye'll go back now?" the driver was saying. "Ye just got here, ma'am."

"Nevertheless," Wolfe insisted, "we wish to return to the Albertine Lodge."

"Whhhhhhhaaaaaaat'sssssss," said the earth mage.

"Not like that," said the driver. "Ye're all covered with muck. I shan't have ye smearing it about in me cab."

"We'll recompense you for that," said Wolfe soothingly. "Here, Chad, give me a hand."

"Goooooooiiiiiiinnnnnnng," said the earth mage.

"What you want Chad do?" asked the troll.

"Tie these ropes to the axle of the carriage," Wolfe ordered, which Chad began to do.

"Now what's this?" demanded the driver. "If ye damage the vehicle—"

Wolfe sighed. "Look here," she said. "Just shut up and do as we say, and I'll pay you ten pounds *argentum*."

The driver sat bolt upright. "It's not illegal, is it? madam?" he quavered. "Me license—"

"The Ministry will answer for any irregularities," Wolfe said soothingly.

"Ten pounds?" demanded G. "Isn't that—"

"I'm under budget," Wolfe said, practically snarling. "Get in." G did.

"Oooooooonnnnnnnn?" said the earth mage.

"Chad done," announced the troll.

"Good," said Wolfe, climbing into the cab. "You get in, too."

Chad began to do so, then hesitated. "What about him?" he asked, gesturing toward the wizard, who was only now, rather confusedly, registering the hansom cab's reappearance.

"Throw him in," said Wolfe, which Chad proceeded to do, bodily picking up the wizard and tossing him into the hansom.

"Now," said Wolfe, sticking her head out a window to talk to the driver. "On the count of three, gallop like the wind."

"Yes, ma'am," said the driver respectfully, touching the brim of his top hat.

Wolfe counted to three. The hansom set into motion, jolting its riders. The horses had just attained a gallop when there was another jolt—the ropes going taut, yanking on the axle.

The cab skittered from side to side, wheels running up against the curb and striking sparks, as its momentum drew the statue through the tunnel. Finally, the statue was free, bouncing off the cobblestones behind them with a noise like Fithold, the god of the forge, whanging on his celestial anvil.

G, who had stuck out her head to watch the statue bounding along behind, pulled back into the cab. "Won't it be damaged?" she asked.

"It's made of athenor," Wolfe said. "Isn't much in the world that can damage it."

G mulled that over. "People on our route aren't going to get much sleep tonight," she said. "Discreet it isn't."

"Stantz didn't tell me to be discreet," said Wolfe illtemperedly. "He just told me to get the statue. Well, there it damned well is."

Timaeus stood by the ragged hole he'd cut in the fence, and took Kraki's hand. "Step up, now, there's a good fellow," he said to the barbarian. Kraki picked up one foot and moved it cautiously forward, the toe of his sandal touching an iron bar; he raised the sandal higher, found the hole, and stepped awkwardly through.

"Are ve outside?" he asked.

"Yes," said Timaeus, offering a hand to Nick. Sidney had already darted through the bars, had resumed human form, and was now donning her clothes, which, miraculously, had not been stolen in her absence. Von Kremnitz was next in line.

"Brother," said Timaeus to Mortise, as the cleric also took on human shape, "can you do something about Kraki's blindness?"

"Yes, perhaps," said Mortise, "but I believe the condition is temporary. Anyhow, I don't recommend hanging about; perhaps we should retire to the pension."

"The Maiorkest is closer," said von Kremnitz.

"What good would going there do?" asked Timaeus. "We've no hard evidence to offer the Lord Mayor."

"Quite so," agreed Jasper. "We'll have to try again, this time with a little planning. Actually, it's astounding we're all in one piece; on the whole, we've been quite lucky."

"If you call it luck," snarled Sidney, "you half-wit."

"Now, Sidney," said Jasper.

"Save the recriminations for later, babe," said Nick. "The padre's right; let's get out of here."

"Babe?" said Sidney incredulously. "If anyone's behavior is infantile, Pratchitt, it's—"

"Oh, please," said Timaeus tiredly. "I've had quite enough for one evening, and the pension is a good mile from here. This way, I think."

Jasper flitted on ahead, embarrassedly avoiding further conversation. Timaeus and the others followed, more sedately.

Clang! A noise resounded from all around, a noise like sheet metal falling on rock from an enormous height. *Clang!* There it was again.

They turned toward the sound. A hansom cab careened around the corner, horses at gallop, metal-clad wheels rumbling over cobblestones. *Clang!*

It tore past, horses alather, the coachman whipping them on. From inside, an alert-looking middle-aged woman, hair close-cropped in the manner of a soldier, peered out. The carriage passed.

Behind the passenger cabin was a platform where trunks and luggage were often tied. There an old man precariously sat, clutching the brass luggage rack for dear life. As he passed, he gave them a toothless grin, and risked taking one hand from the rack long enough to send them a cheerful wave.

A statue trailed the carriage, strung behind on sturdy cable. It flew through the air, fell toward the cobblestones with a—

Clang!

—and bounded into flight once more.

The carriage, and its curious appendage, passed.

Timaeus gaped after it. "I say," he said. "Wasn't that our—"

Sidney was already charging down the street, waving her sword and shouting, "Stop thief!"

"I like that," said Nick. "Pot calling the kettle—"

"I'll trail them, shall I?" said Jasper gaily, as if glad of an opportunity to redeem himself. The green light zipped in pursuit.

Stauer had found them a cold roast squab, some ham, pickled vegetables and mustard, and an undistinguished *vin ordinaire*; they lounged about the sitting room of their suite in the Pension Scholari, in poses indicating varying degrees of exhaustion. Kraki sprawled across a chaise longue, mouth open and snoring; Nick sat at a writing table, scribbling feverishly at something by the light of a candle, yawning from time to time and sipping his wine.

Sidney sat on the edge of her chair, gnawing on a leg of squab. Transformation took quite a lot out of her; she was generally ravenous afterward, and this time was no exception. "What I say," she told Timaeus, "is that you're a damned optimist if you think we'll ever see Jasper again."

"Oh, come, my dear," said Timaeus, lying well back in the soft pillows of the couch, a pickled onion in one hand and a glass of wine in the other. "He is *Magister Mentis*, after all, and more or less invisible to boot. If anyone is well suited to tailing the people who absconded with our statue, it is he."

Sidney snorted. "He's well suited to acting the fool," she said. "If he hadn't flown over that fence—"

"Then the statue would have been stolen from von Grentz, and we'd be none the wiser," von Kremnitz pointed out. The leftenant sat on a pillow on the floor, his scabbard poking rather awkwardly into the rug, a plate balanced atop his crossed legs.

"Perhaps," said Sidney. "However—"

"Who do you think has it?" asked Frer Mortise. He squinted even in the dim light of the candles, his pupils enormously wide.

"Another of Hamsterburg's uncountably numerous factions, I expect," said Timaeus. "Don't suppose you recognized them, Leftenant?"

"No, I'm afraid not," said von Kremnitz. "If Sir Jasper doesn't turn anything up, I'll go to the Maiorkest tomorrow morning; perhaps the Lord Mayor will have heard something."

Sidney cleared her throat. "I think I recognized one of them," she said.

Timaelus raised and eyebrow. "Mmm?"

"The old man who waved at us," Sidney said. "Didn't he look familiar to you?"

Timaeus blinked. "Well, they were moving rather fast," he said apologetically. "I'm afraid I didn't—"

"I think it was Vic," said Sidney.

Timaeus sat up sharply. "Vic?" he said. "Are you sure?"

"No, I'm not sure," said Sidney with irritation. "But—"

"Good heavens, what does this mean?" said Timaeus. "Suppose it is Vic. Does he *want* those people to have it? Is he testing us? Why did he disappear? What the devil is afoot?"

Sidney shrugged. Timaeus looked at Mortise, then at von Kremnitz, but realized that neither of them had met Vincianus, and wouldn't have recognized him under the best of circumstances. However—"

"Nick," he said, turning toward Pratchitt, who was sitting back in his chair and reading a piece of paper with a maniacal grin on his face. "Did you—what have you got there?"

Nick stood up and turned toward his companions. "Just this," he said. He adopted a declamatory pose, and read:

the saga of kraki elm-slayer

"sing now of kraki, he aptly named.
sing of the deed that gave him his fame.

"with brave companions, he raided the dragon,
house of a kingling in far southern lands.
took he his blade, heavy as mountains,
raised it on high with his mighty hands.

"blinded was he by untimely magic
could not espy the mien of his foes.
was he thereby deterred from attacking,
streaked with yellow as the saying goes?

"nay, never kraki! leapt from the building,
shouting the name of his famous forebear,
gostorn gaptoothed, famous for eating,
eater of apricot, apple, and pear.

"swung he his weapon—o, mighty swinging!
felt blade strike hard in the flesh of his foe.
yanked forth the weapon, whacked again fiercely,
shouted his triumph like this: 'ho ho ho!'

"never did man behold such a giant
as kraki did strive with that glorious night
dozens of cubits rose his opponent
many its limbs striking out in the fight.

"'ye shall be cloven,' swore our brave kraki,
'i shall bisect ye from tuchus to *tête*.'
swung he a last time—o mighty swinging!
so mighty a stroke there never was yet.

"down crashed the enemy, limbs flailing blindly,
crashed into flowers that lay all about.
round kraki gathered his brave companions
awed and in reverence, led kraki out.

"'ho,' boasted kraki, 'i have slain giants!
those who are foemen better take care.'
'yes, kraki, certainly,' said his companions,
'henceforth we know ye as kraki elm-slayer.

"'slew ye the elm, battled it mightily,
clove it in twain from taproot to twig.
heroic the deed, as we deem it, certainly,
never did we see a tree that's so big.'

"so let all hail kraki, kraki elm-slayer,
mighty tree-battler, scourge of the wood.
in all of our history never has there been
such a great hero, one half as good.

"so hear me, children: if ye would be like him,
eat up your vegetables as all children should."

In the course of this recitation, Kraki had woken up, and
now sat on the sofa, head between his knees. As Nick fin-

ished, he looked up and said, "Good thing poetry so bad, Nickie, or I have to kill you." He lay back down and turned over as if to go to sleep.

"Poetry so bad!" Nick protested. "What do you mean, poetry so bad? You wouldn't know good poetry if—"

"Scansion hokay," grunted Kraki. "No alliteration."

Nick blinked. "No alliteration?" he said. "So what?"

Kraki looked up. "Vhat you mean, so vhat? Vhat are you, some kind of modernist? Of course poetry must alliterate, so bard can memorize lines easier, resound in the souls of the listeners."

"But it rhymes!" protested Nick.

"Rhymes, shmymes," said Kraki, shrugging into the cushion. "Rhyming for sissies. Nobody in northland listen to newfangled rhyming stuff. Thank the gods, or I be chucklingstock of northland."

"Laughingstock," said Nick automatically.

"I'd suggest you stop arguing, Nick," said Timaeus, standing up and stretching. "If you persuade him of the virtues of modern poetical forms, he'll feel compelled to murder you."

"Yeah, okay," said Nick. "What did you think—" But Timaeus had already closed the door of his bedroom behind him.

Nick turned to the others, but they, likewise, were going to their rest.

He went to the window and peered out it a moment, but there was nought to be seen but the glint of moonlight on cobbles, and chimney pots sticking up from distant roofs. The streets were silent, without birdsong, or insect noise, or the hubbub of humanity to bring them life. Nick sighed and tossed off the lees of his wine, and he, too, turned toward his room and sleep.

VI.

Nick Pratchitt was awakened by distant bangs, the shouts of men, running feet in the street. Groggily he sat up, went to the window of his room, and peered outside. The aperture gave out on an alley; he could see only a slice of street at its end, and nothing untoward there. So he left for the sitting room, and threw back the curtains shielding the French doors.

Somewhere, off across the city, a tendril of black smoke rose skyward; a major fire of some kind. Not far off, in a major avenue—Nick was still insufficiently familiar with Hamsterburg, and did not know its name—a barricade rose. It was hastily made, of furniture, bits of wood, sandbags—of whatever materials, apparently, the builders could find. About and atop it swarmed men and women in leather aprons, some shouting orders to others below.

Elsewhere, people had gathered to listen to orators, while other folk ran through the streets, some with piles of possessions on their backs or in hand-drawn carts.

A bang from behind Nick's shoulder startled him; he very nearly leapt from the balcony. "So it's happened," said Timaeus, puffing on his first bowlful of the morning. The wizard was barefoot, wearing a crimson robe.

"Dammit, Timaeus," said Nick. "Give a guy some warning when you light your pipe, will you?"

"Vhat's happened?" said Kraki groggily. He had been sleeping on the chaise longue in the sitting room, but voices, and Timaeus's explosion, had woken him.

"Look thither," said Timaeus, gesturing toward the barricade with his pipe.

Kraki peered outward. "They build a vall," he said. "The city is invaded?"

"No," said Nick. "There's an uprising. Something's happened; we knew the city was on edge already . . ."

Von Kremnitz, naked to the waist, peered over Kraki's shoulder, cursing steadily. He moved swiftly to the bell-pull and gave it a yank. "Stauer will know something," he said. "Ye gods, it's the ninth hour; we have overslept."

"Has anyone seen Jasper?" asked Sidney, entering from her bedroom.

"Not as such," said Timaeus, "but there's something green on his bed." He shared a room with the mentalist.

Sidney headed toward their bedroom, with the obvious intention of waking Jasper. While she was gone, there was a knock at the door. Nick opened it.

Stauer stood in the hall, looking more than slightly worried. "Good morning, *messieurs et madame*," he said. "Please accept my profoundest apologies, but we will not have fresh eggs today; the city is in disorder, and our usual deliveries—"

"Never mind that," said von Kremnitz peremptorily. "What is the news?"

"Oh, my lord," said Stauer sadly, "they say that the Lord Mayor is dead."

"What!" shouted von Kremnitz. "How did it happen?"

"Not a mark was found on him, so the rumors say; he lay in his chamber, contorted in terror. A spell, perhaps, or some rare poison—but the streets are in chaos. Half the city says the Spider slew him; the Accommodationists are rising, and others assembling to oppose. They say there are armies outside the city, that—"

"Who builds that barricade, over to the east?" asked Timaeus.

"Sir?" said Stauer, blinking rapidly. "Ah—may I come in?"

Nick moved out of the door to permit Stauer entry. Stauer went to the French doors, put his pince-nez to the bridge of his nose, and peered out. "Ah, in the Tetrine Way," he said. "Masons, by their garb."

"And their faction?" asked Timaeus.

"Their guild supported Siebert strongly," said von Kremnitz. "Most of the guilds did; one of his few sources of support."

"Without power on the Council," said Stauer dismissively.

"Or in the *Gentes*," agreed von Kremnitz.

"What are they up to?" Nick asked.

Stauer shrugged. "I suppose you'd have to ask them," he said. "Resisting the Accommodationists, I would assume."

"Fine," said Nick. "Dandy. So the statue is gods know where, in a city in the throes of revolution. Tell you what, let's all go join a religious order; the Josemites, perhaps. We can spend the rest of our lives hoeing vegetables and flailing ourselves with leather thongs."

"There, there, lad," said Jasper, whizzing into the room. "Fear not. Even in these dark hours—"

"Just tell them," said Sidney dangerously, following him from the bedroom.

"Yes, yes, of course, my dear," said Jasper. "You will cast your minds back to the events of last night, please. As you recall, I departed your company in hot pursuit of the statue-nabbers. I followed them, aloft—"

"Excuse me, Jasper," said Timaeus.

"Yes, what is it?" said Jasper, irritated at the interruption.

"Miss Stollitt has expressed strong feelings, on prior occasions, on the subject of discretion," said Timaeus, rather stiffly. He nodded meaningfully in the direction of Stauer, who looked suspiciously back through his pince-nez.

"Ah—no fresh eggs," said von Kremnitz, after an awkward pause, "but can hotcakes be prepared?"

"Yes," allowed Stauer. "Precisely what I was going to suggest. If you will forgive the intrusion—ah—may I ask whether your plans are likely to offer harm, or attract untoward attention, to my establishment?"

"No, sir," said Timaeus. "I do not believe so."

Stauer sighed, apparently rather frustrated to be excluded from their confidence. "It is my strongest belief," he said in a low voice, "that a host should respect his guests' privacy. I shall therefore depart, upon this assurance." He made for the door, turning at the lintel, and said, "I'll send a girl up with your *petit déjeuner* momentarily. Coffee?"

"Tea," said Timaeus.

Stauer shivered delicately; Hamsterians considered tea rather effete, though it was the preferred morning quaff of Urf Durfal. "If you wish," he said.

And he closed the door quietly after him.

"I like your man Stauer," Jasper told von Kremnitz.

"It is a good establishment," said von Kremnitz. "Now, then; what did you learn?"

"I pursued the hansom through the winding streets of the city," said Jasper, "flying at a sufficient height above the vehicle that the occupants did not suspect my presence. Seeing no reason to waste the time spent *en route*, I essayed a number of spells in an effort to read the thoughts of the occupants of the cab."

"Yes, yes," said Timaeus. "Get· to the point, please."

"Testy this morning, what, d'Asperge?" said Jasper. "I shall tell the tale in my own fashion, and at my own pace, if you please."

"I don't please," muttered Timaeus.

"Nonetheless," said Jasper. "Alas, my spells proved fruitless; I was able to discover that the driver was a Luigi Amato, of Seventy-six Slobinstrasse, a member of the Hauliers' Guild—a mere hireling. The cab was occupied by three others: a troll and two women. One of the women wore an amulet against scrying; I was unable to read her at all, and knew she was there only from the perceptions of the others. The other woman had been complexly trained—and, I believe, programmed under hypnosis—so that I was unable to read anything other than the most cursory, fleeting thoughts. She thinks of herself as G. The troll's surface thoughts were in the creature's barbarous native tongue, with which, alas, I am not familiar; I was able to determine that he spent the bulk of the trip in a reverie, thinking of his plans for the rest of the night, which seemed to involve a substantial quantity of ale and a lady troll. Not much help there.

"I did, however, manage to overhear part of the women's conversation, which was unguarded. G's companion was named Wolfe—"

"Renée Wolfe?" asked von Kremnitz sharply.

"I didn't get the first name," said Jasper apologetically. "They went directly to a large building of rather unusual architecture—stucco and exposed beams, the sort of thing one expects in country châteaux. The building itself was warded, and I thought it best not to enter, but scouted about until I found a late-night pedestrian, who thought of it as the Albertine Lodge—"

"Stantz," said von Kremnitz.

"Eh?" said Jasper.

"The Albertine Lodge is the headquarters of the Ministry of Internal Serenity; the minister is Guismundo Stantz."

"The Spider," said Timaeus.

"Yes," said von Kremnitz. "The man who may well have assassinated my master. Renée Wolfe is his woman."

"His paramour?" said Timaeus, in some surprise; it was difficult to think of the dreaded Spider as a man with lusts like any other.

Von Kremnitz snorted. "No, no; his employee."

They mulled over that for a moment.

"You think he killed Siebert?" asked Timaeus.

Von Kremnitz sighed. "I don't know what to think," he said. "The common opinion holds that Stantz tried to assassinate the Lord Mayor before, killing Julio von Krautz by mistake; Siebert himself believed otherwise, that Gerlad von Grentz killed von Krautz, and then tried to pin the blame on Minister Stantz."

He paced for a while between the chaise longue and couch. The others watched him.

"If Stantz were in truth allied with my lord," he muttered, "then Stantz would want to free the statue from von Grentz; but if Stantz were an enemy, he would want the statue anyway, to bolster the position of whomever he supports—ach, I cannot decipher it."

"Does it matter?" asked Timaeus gently. "Siebert is dead; does it matter whether Stantz betrayed him? Either way, he has the statue."

"It matters to me!" shouted von Kremnitz in rage. "If he betrayed my lord, he shall die."

"Well spoken, lad," said Jasper, voice thick with emotion.

Timaeus snorted. "You, raw youth, provincial swordsman; you shall kill the Spider? The Spider, whose web spans all the human lands, whose agents are everywhere?

Whose dungeons are legend, who has outlasted ten lord
mayors?"

"Aye," said von Kremnitz, his aquiline nose in noble
pose, "I shall."

"And we shall aid you," said Jasper warmly.

"Oh shut up, you unbearable idiot!" shouted Timaeus.
"Bad enough you go gallivanting off into von Grentz's
backyard, triggering every alarm in creation; now you
want to—"

"To aid a brave young man in his quest against vil-
lainy," said Jasper severely. "A young man, need I say,
who has offered us every assistance; a young man of un-
stained escutcheon; a young man who aided us when we
were in peril."

Timaeus was turning dangerously red.

"Thank you, Sir Jasper," said von Kremnitz, warmly.
"If, in truth, Stantz is the villain of the piece—"

"Jasper, dear," said Sidney dangerously, "you really
can't commit us, you know. We're on a quest; we can't
rescue every treed cat and help every old lady across the
street."

"Bosh!" said Jasper. "This is no such trivial affair. And
as we are heroes, so we must act heroically."

"Yah!" said Kraki. "Topple empires, slay foemen by the
score, slaughter vast monsters and foul beasts!"

"Um, yes, thank you, Kraki," said Jasper. "If we refuse
to aid those in need, shall not the gods turn deaf ears to
our pleas, when we ourselves need aid?"

"Economy of resources," said Nick economically.

"*Magna est veritas, et praevalebit,*" countered Jasper.
"If Stantz slew Siebert, he is no more than a murderer; and
the truth will out."

"*Omnia vincit amor,*" said Timaeus in disgust. "*Magna
est veritas* . . . Whoever taught you the Imperial tongue did
us no favor. And argument does not proceed by aphorism."

"Again, sir," said Jasper severely, "I am astonished at your lack of feeling—"

"Wait, wait, wait," said Nick. "Look. Let's not argue about this, okay? Stantz has the statue, we know that; we've got to get it back. Maybe he killed Siebert; maybe not. Maybe, in the process of getting the statue, we'll find out—and we can worry about what to do about it then."

"Right," said Sidney. "The important thing is to figure out how to get into the Albertine Lodge."

"Oh, I can get you in, all right," said von Kremnitz. "It's getting out that's the problem."

" 'Allo?" said a voice from the door. "I 'ave your 'otcakes, *messieurs et madame*."

Von Kremnitz led the way, as he knew Hamsterburg best; his hand was at his pommel, for while it would not do to walk the streets with naked blade, still the uneasiness of the city had infected them all. Jasper flew behind and above, height giving him a view of the path ahead. Kraki strode at the rear, to deter attack from that direction, while Nick and Sidney flanked Timaeus and Frer Mortise, protecting their spell-casters.

Folk scurried about, most hugging the sides of the street. Shopkeepers stood in the doors or windows of their shops, not yet closing up, for some were doing a brisk business, in food and the kinds of goods one might need to survive for several days of chaos. Still, they looked worried, and most carried weapons prominently, to indicate their willingness to defend their property. Some had gone so far as to hire some of the neighborhood bully-boys, both to provide muscle against looters and to occupy the people most likely to loot. Sidney saw that with cynicism; a few pence from a shopkeeper would not deter such as they, not if windows started breaking.

Down the center of the street marched a group of men and women, surrounding a man in costly dress: a noble-

man and his clients—a common sight on the streets of the
city, but uncommon to see them all armed. The folk gave
them a wide berth; von Kremnitz led his companions to
the side of the street to do likewise.

After a time, they passed into a rougher neighborhood;
ahead, a barricade loomed. Von Kremnitz called a halt,
asked Jasper to fly upward to reconnoiter, then decided
that detouring was more trouble than it was worth. He
walked on ahead, toward the barricade—for all of them to
go was to risk having the defenders decide this was an
attack—and called upward, to the doughty workingmen
and kerchiefed women who perched there, "We seek passage."

"An' who d'ye be?" demanded a mustachioed man, naked to the waist and tattooed with a spur on one
shoulder—a former cuirassier, for the spur was the symbol
of the Heavy Brigade.

Von Kremnitz considered; to declare his regimental allegiance might give offense—no love lost between the cavalry and the Mayoral Foot—yet it would be dishonorable
to offer a lie. "Pablo von Kremnitz," he said, "of Meersteinmetz; and my companions, foreigners."

"And what d'ye desire?"

"Merely passage," von Kremnitz replied.

The man looked worried; no doubt he saw Jasper flitting
above, and could see that the group he faced had magic.
"The borough of Einhoch is a poor one," he said. "We
seek only to defend our homes; we do not wish to fight ye,
but have no desire to see armed men traipsing about our
streets."

"I give you my word," said von Kremnitz. "We shall offer no harm to any in Einhoch, nor tarry, but travel expe-
ditiously through."

"Your word?" said the tattooed man skeptically. "That
an' tuppence'll buy ye pastry."

Von Kremnitz instantly drew his blade. The heads of

two women appeared over the barricade; they bore cross-bows, with quarrels against the string. "You doubt my word?" the leftenant said angrily. "You have not the manners of a swineherd, you refuse! Come down here and face me, or you are no gentleman!"

The tattooed man snorted laughter. "Aye, true enough," he said. "No gentleman I. And ye must be a true cavalier indeed, to offer me harm beyond the support of your companions, me with numbers and fortification; no one but an honest gentleman would be so daft. Very well, then, give me your word, and ye may pass."

Von Kremnitz waved the others forward; they came, and clambered over the barricade—timbers from ruined buildings, with plaster still adhering; bricks and cobblestones, rickety furniture and broken barrels—under the mistrustful eyes of labor-stooped slum-dwellers and mighty-thewed washerwomen. The tattooed man, who seemed in command by virtue of his military past, dispatched a walleyed youth to guide them—and, no doubt, to report if they should break their undertaking. And then they strode through the sad streets of Einhoch, raw sewage in the street centers and dilapidated buildings slumping into each other, roofs at uneven angles, heaps of trash in every alley, until they came to its nether end and a second barricade. The youth conferred briefly with a commander there, and they were escorted over this obstacle, too.

They found themselves at the foot of a bridge over a narrow canal; and beyond it, once more in a commercial area, the shops somewhat grander here, and many already shuttered.

They strode up the street, doing their best to avoid the occasional armed parties, until—

Off, off in the distance, they heard a sound: A rhythm, repeated. Bom—bombombom. Dum—dumdadum. One syllable; then three. Over. And over. And over.

It was a crowd; not so much a crowd as a mob, the

voices of a thousand, ten thousand, raised in unison. A mile away, they could hear the beat, though the words were impossible to distinguish.

They quailed momentarily, and glanced at each other with unease and awe, but yonder lay the Albertine Lodge, and therein Stantius; and there they must go. Onward they went.

The volume rose as they progressed. Onward, at the end of the avenue, they could see a crowd of people, and around it a mist of others, wandering into the crowd and out of it, the tightly packed mass of the mob thinning out at its fringes. The mob swayed this way and that, swirling in chaotic motion like a fog, the brightly colored clothes of one person showing briefly against the drabber garb of the rest, moving across the crowd and then merging somewhere into its depths; random motion, like that of leaves in a gale, the purposefulness of individual action merged into insensate chaos. Vowels and aspirated consonants are more easily perceived than other sounds; a few blocks away, they began to discern the sounds: "Shtahn—ur-ur-ur. Shtahn—ur-ur-ur. Shtahn—ur-ur-ur."

They were in the fringes of the mob now, almost instinctively moving together, preserving their unity as a party amid the vast collectivity beginning to form about them. That collectivity was not universal; away from the mob came some folk, those spooked by how individual consciousness merged into vast, unreasoning union, or leaving to tend to other matters. And toward the mob came others, drawn by that roar, drawn by the rumors that washed across the city, drawn by the promise of violence or the thrill of participation, drawn by who knows what instinct or what compulsion: drawn toward one of the moments when individual futility becomes, for better or for worse, a moment of collective destiny.

They were amid the crowd now. Even here, with weeping men and bellowing women all about, with banners waving and fists shaking, with people pressing leaflets into their hands, it was difficult to make out exactly what they shouted. One beat; then three. One; three.

"Stantz! Murderer! Stantz! Murderer! Stantz! Murderer!"

They screamed it toward the Albertine Lodge, across the square.

Albertus Square: where the Tetrine Way merges with the Avenue of Regret, *en route* to the Eastern Gate. At its center was the Fountain of Albertus, where a statue of the pudgy former mayor flung coins of water—a clever mechanism, that—into the pool, to figures of the poor and hungry, standing in poses indicating thankfulness. Albertus had been legendary for his generosity, but the mob paid him, and the kinder and simpler Hamsterburg he represented, no heed. A thousand, ten thousand, perhaps many more—a measurable percentage of the population of the *urbs*—they swirled about the fountain, carpeting the cobblestones, packed dangerously close. There were flags and banners, hastily made; there were orators, screaming imprecations to folk who could not possibly hear them against the roar of the mob; there were red faces, tears, angry men.

Across the square, the Lodge: built by Albertus himself, in a peculiar vision of urban rusticity. Its timbers were rough-hewn, whole pine trees; its walls, stucco; its steeply pitched roof, shingle. It had the aspect of a mountain lodge, but it was enormous, occupying a block entire, roomy enough for a mayor's mansion, as it had been, roomy enough to house the whole Ministry of Internal Serenity, with its voluminous files and its innumerable clerks, its vast apparat of spies.

The Albertine Lodge had never been defended in battle; it had not been designed for such, and its innumerable windows made it essentially indefensible. The predecessors of Stantz had no fears on that score, for they had seen

the Ministry merely as a way for the Lord Mayor to keep
tabs on his obstreperous nobility, no more than that; and
Stantz had never seen fit to move quarters to a more de-
fensible site, for he would have taken this, a mob at his
very gate, for a clear indication of failure in his self-
appointed mission. Yet, around it a thin line of defenders
attempted exactly this task: the Serenissima.

For Internal Serenity maintained the Republic's commu-
nications—scrying crystals, stables for the horse-borne express, the semaphore telegraph: It delivered the Lord
Mayor's diplomatic missives, the vital orders of his bureaucrats. And these required defenders: the Serenissima,
the Most Serene.

There were not many, here; a few score, perhaps a century. It was a credit to their *esprit de corps* that they continued to face this mob, shield to shield, pikes held aslant,
a few dozen men pressing out against this vast morass of
humanity.

If the mob chose to move, they would be trampled un-
derfoot in seconds.

So, too, would many of the mob; but mobs do not pause
to make such calculations.

"Stantz! Murderer! Stantz! Murderer!" rose the cry.

Men and women wept for their martyred lord; for the
first mayor in centuries who had tried to curb the excesses
of the *gens*, to restore the privileges of the *populus*. If
Hamish Siebert had never been more than reviled among
the nobility, among the proletariat he was well beloved.

Led by von Kremnitz, a veritable dynamo, reinforced
with the strength of Kraki and the power of Jasper's magical suggestion to give way, they forced their way through
the crowd, and to the lip of the fountain. There they
paused for breath, and to survey the situation.

"Stantz! Murderer!" roared the crowd.

"Looks like you're not the only guy that had that idea,"
shouted Nick to von Kremnitz.

"Their very conviction makes me doubt it," shouted the leftenant back, wiping his brow.

"I've got a bad feeling about this," said Sidney.

Timaeus and Frer Mortise both looked as if they could hardly bear their surroundings: Timaeus, perhaps, from aristocratic fear of the mob; Mortise, a rustic, from unease at the sheer numbers about him. "Is one supposed to get a good feeling?" shouted Timaeus over the crowd.

"We get the statue," shouted Sidney in explanation. "Then the mob storms the Lodge. We are killed in the ensuing chaos."

They contemplated that. Perhaps attempting to regain their statue, in a city in the throes of revolution, from the headquarters of the most hated defenders of the *ancien régime*, perhaps this was not the smartest move in the world.

"This way," shouted von Kremnitz, pushing off from the fountain.

It was hard going, through that morass of humanity, the tightly packed flesh. Without Kraki's strength and Jasper's power of suggestion, they might never have made the mob's edge. At last, however, they neared the wall of shields, the defenders of the Lodge.

The eyes of the soldiers were frightened: determined, but scared. Their shields overlapped, they leaned into their shields, shoulder first, pressing back against the mob that sought to overwhelm them. In this they were at least partially aided by the people at the mob's fringe, people who, however much their emotions had been captivated by the unity of the mob, the passions of the hour, knew that they, unlike those farther back, were in close proximity to killing weapons. If this tentative peace, this uneasy equilibrium of forces, broke down, if the mob surged forward or one of the soldiers lost his head and struck out with a spear or sword, those at the fore would suffer. They would be the ones to die. And so they drew back, as much as they were able, against the force of the folk behind them.

Von Kremnitz pushed the man ahead of him to the side, and came face to face with a soldier. Her eyes widened as she took him in, saw the weapons at his belt, the look of determination on his face; she panicked, brought down her pike . . .

Von Kremnitz's heart went to his throat; she might well kill him, his own mobility hampered by the crowd, his light blade of dubious utility against a wall of shields. But more than that, this one gesture might precipitate chaos: If a soldier were to kill a protestor, that would inflame the passions of the mob, might lead to full-fledged riot. He had no desire to kill her—she, like he, a servant of the city—but more, he had no desire to see the Lodge looted, burned, chaos spreading across fair Hamsterburg. He—

A gloved hand fell on the soldier's shoulder. "Steady, Giselle," barked a serjeant's voice. "Remember your orders."

Shamefaced, she raised her pike once more, brought it back to its accustomed slant, resting on the top of her square shield. And the serjeant pulled her out of the line, motioning another soldier forward to take her place before any of the mob could press through the momentary gap.

"Serjeant!" shouted von Kremnitz, before the man could walk away. "Serjeant! I must speak with you!"

The man turned, looked warily at von Kremnitz. His eyes widened as he took in the man and his diverse companions—and narrowed as he saw the pin at von Kremnitz's cloak, the pin that bore the hamster statant regardant of Hamsterburg.

"I bear the Lord Mayor's safe passage," shouted von Kremnitz. "I demand entry!"

"He's dead," shouted the serjeant. "Or haven't you heard?"

"Nonetheless!" von Kremnitz insisted. "I have vital information!"

The serjeant looked uncertain, but turned to face the Lodge. He whistled, then held four fingers in the air and gave a wave. In moments, four soldiers appeared, apparently summoned from the Serenissima's scant reserve. They formed a semicircle, slightly back from the line, around the serjeant; the serjeant pushed between two members of the shield wall and motioned von Kremnitz through.

"Stantz! Murderer!" roared the crowd. One man, unkempt, unbathed, beard to his chest, threw himself toward the momentary opening, but a soldier merely bashed his head with the side of a shield. Timaeus started forward, then realized that the serjeant had permitted entry only to von Kremnitz.

The leftenant stood beyond the wall, surrounded by soldiers, arguing with the serjeant. He displayed his document, with its impressive seal: the *laissez-passe* that Siebert had given him. He pointed toward the others, but the serjeant merely shook his head.

The serjeant pointed to von Kremnitz, as if to say, "You"—and held up one finger, as if to say, "You alone."

Timaeus could hear not a word of what passed between them.

Over the line, a point of green light flitted. Unnoticed, it circled over the serjeant's head.

Von Kremnitz reddened, enraged; he grabbed the serjeant's breastplate with both hands, screaming into the man's face.

The serjeant's face went slack, as if personality had gone out of it; he nodded, a mechanical nod. He spoke briefly to von Kremnitz, who let go, looking rather confused.

The serjeant spoke again, to the soldiers around them; the four looked a little bewildered, but when the serjeant repeated his order, they shrugged, turned away, returned to their position near the Lodge.

The serjeant pushed his way through the shield line and beckoned Timaeus and the others forward.

Behind them came a cry—"Traitors! Spies for the Spider!"—and the mob pressed forward against the line. Quickly the party darted through the narrow opening in the shield wall, the shields coming together behind them with a clash. Soldiers grunted as the mob smashed into them.

Von Kremnitz, the serjeant, Timaeus, and the others trotted away, toward the Lodge's vast oaken doors. Timaeus gave a worried glance behind; the shield line bowed inward, the pressure of the mob forcing the defenders back—inward, inward . . . In moments, he feared, it would give way . . .

More soldiers came from the Lodge at a run, hurling themselves into the line, pressing back against the mob, a few thin reinforcements; but that seemed to be enough, for the nonce. The line stabilized; the mob withdrew.

The serjeant seemed curiously oblivious to these events for a man with ostensible responsibility for this section of the line. About his head, Jasper continued to fly.

"What did you tell him?" Timaeus asked von Kremnitz, puffing to keep up.

"I don't know," said von Kremnitz. "He wasn't going to let you through—then suddenly changed his mind. I don't think it was anything I said."

"Ah," said Timaeus, casting a glance up at Jasper.

VII.

The Lodge's interior: A-frame beams overhead, darkened with age; frightened bureaucrats hustling to and fro on apparently urgent business. The room was cold, lit by flickering torches that an educated eye could see were magical—no smoke rising from the flames to choke the air, the brands themselves unconsumed by the fire they bore. At the back of the large chamber was a desk, manned by several clerks; from the chamber four corridors led off down rows of offices.

The serjeant led them to the desk. One of the clerks conversed with a bureaucrat, while another accepted a package from a harried messenger; a third was unoccupied. "What is it, serjeant?" he asked.

"These people have the Lord Mayor's *laissez-passe*," the serjeant said, in a mechanical drone. "They seek an audience with Magistra Wolfe."

The clerk's eyebrows gave a leap. "I shall try to locate her," he said, and turned to a bank of speaking tubes.

They waited, impatiently and rather nervously, while the clerk hollered first into one tube, then another, putting his ear to each tube to hear its reply. At last, he turned back to them, and said, "Have you an appointment?"

"No," said von Kremnitz, "but the matter is urgent."

The clerk sighed. "May I see this *laissez-passe*?"

Von Kremnitz laid a parchment document on the desk; it was hastily scribbled in poor penmanship, but bore the Mayor's seal, in red wax, at its bottom.

"It appears legitimate," shouted the clerk into the tube. He listed for the reply, then turned to von Kremnitz. "What is the matter about?" he asked.

Von Kremnitz looked at the others. Timaeus shrugged. Sidney said, "Tell him."

"The statue of Stantius," said von Kremnitz.

The clerk looked mystified, but repeated this to the tube. As he listened to the response, his face went blank. "Yes, ma'am," he said, turned back to the desk, and rang a bell.

In a moment, a young man in a gray tunic appeared. "Jorge," the clerk ordered. "Take these people to Room Six, in the Griffon section."

"Yes, sir," said the boy. "This way, gentles."

They followed him toward one of the corridors. Behind them, the serjeant turned on his heel and marched back toward the main front door. Jasper flew with him briefly, then swerved and met up with the others.

They hustled down the corridor, Jorge setting a swift pace. The walls rose to intercept wooden beams at odd angles, as if the corridor were a late addition, the area through which they passed originally a large chamber, later subdivided. Torches lined the walls at lengthy intervals, providing dim illumination—enough to make one's way, but not much more. Even here, the roar of the crowd could be faintly heard, that one beat and three. Men and women scurried past, some carrying files or papers.

"Dammit," Sidney said in a low voice, "we're doing it again!"

"What do you mean?" asked von Kremnitz.

"You got us in," she said, "as you promised. But we've got no plan, no—"

"Ahem," said Timaeus. "Our guide can hardly fail to overhear us. And a busy corridor is not the best place—"

"Never fear for Jorge," said Jasper. "I have him in a light trance; he'll not remember anything he shouldn't. And if we're discreet, I think the people we pass won't take alarm."

"Good," said Timaeus. "Sidney's right. What are we to do?"

"Find statue," said Kraki. "Take it. Kill anyvone who gets in vay. Leave."

"It has the virtue of simplicity," said Timaeus. "However, I'm not entirely clear on how the first step is to be accomplished."

They came to a large open archway of decorative stone, the capstone carved in the shape of a griffon; through it was a large chamber, with rows of tables, seats, and a lectern at one end. Along the left side of the room were several doors, one numbered "6" in brass. Jorge led the way toward it.

"Wolfe will know where it is," said Nick.

"We hope," said Sidney.

"Can we bushwhack her? Take her hostage?" said Nick.

"Sounds risky," said Timaeus.

"Life is risky," said Kraki.

"She's a mage," Jasper pointed out. They skirted a table. "*Umbrae*, isn't it, leftenant?"

"Yes," said von Kremnitz.

They came to Room Six's door; Jorge lifted a hand to turn the knob—

"Wait!" said Sidney. "We still don't have—"

"Magistra Wolfe isn't in there," Jasper said. "She's to meet us here."

"How do you know?"

"Jorge knows," said Jasper.

"All right," said Sidney. "Let him open it, then."

Room Six had the aspect of a sitting room; there were couches, armchairs, tables. At one end stood a chalkboard, and on the table were piled papers, inkwells, quills, blotters, and knives for trimming nibs. Clearly, it was often used for conferences of one kind or another. Peculiarly, it had no windows, but was lit instead by a globe of glowing white light at the ceiling's center.

"Thank you, Jorge," said Jasper. "You may go now."

"As you wish," said the young man. He closed the door behind him.

"Taking Magistra Wolfe hostage may be risky," Jasper said, "yet here, in the Spider's very web, we are at considerable risk regardless. We do have an advantage; no doubt the Ministry is distracted by the chaos outside. And the building may be stormed at any moment; if it is, we may be able to escape with relative ease, assuming we do not find ourselves a target of the mob's fury."

"Wouldn't it be easier to explain ourselves to Wolfe?" said Timaeus. "Surely—"

"Stantz obviously wants the statue," Sidney said, "or Wolfe wouldn't have stolen it. You think maybe he'll give it back if we just ask pretty please?"

"Guismundo Stantz is not to be trusted," said von Kremnitz.

"Yes, all right," said Timaeus. "Wolfe comes in, we grab her, force her to tell us where the statue is—Sir Jasper, can't you just read the information from her mind?"

"I very much doubt it," said Jasper. "She wore an amulet against scrying in the carriage, remember?"

"Bah," said Kraki. "I grab her. Vith sword at throat, she

talk hokay! Or, *gish!*" He made a motion indicative of de-
capitation.

"Yes, thank you, Kraki, very graphic," said Timaeus.
"More likely, you grab her, put your sword to her throat,
she turns into a shadow—"

"Need spell to do that," said Kraki. "She start spell, and
gish!"

"Shadow mages are taught to subvocalize," said
Timaeus. "Otherwise, they couldn't use magic, in shadow
form; shadows don't have voices. You'd never know she
was working on a spell."

"Bah," said Kraki. "Then I kill her right avay. *Gish!*"

"It is fairly difficult to obtain information from a
corpse," said Timaeus testily.

"Unless you're a necromancer," Nick pointed out.

"True enough," said Timaeus. "I don't suppose you
have unexpected talents along such lines, eh, Pratchitt?"

"No," said Nick.

"Then do shut up," said Timaeus. "We've got perhaps
as much as thirty seconds before Wolfe arrives, and no
time for idiotic—"

"Ahem," interrupted Jasper. "I could detect subvocal-
ization, I believe, even if Magistra Wolfe were to wear an
amulet."

"Eh?" said Timaeus. "Hmm. So Kraki takes her hostage, we tell her we'll kill her if she starts a spell. By
Dion, this might actually work."

"Might have," said a woman's voice—a voice that
seemed to come from the brass ventilation grille at the
room's rear. "All right, Jocko; shut them down."

Instantly the room went dark.

There was a crash as Kraki threw himself against the
door—to no avail. "Door locked," he reported.

Sidney cursed. "Of *course* they'd monitor the room,"
she said. "Of *course*—"

There was a hissing noise.

There was a sudden sense of vertigo, as if the world itself had lurched, as of swift motion toward a far destina-
tion . . .

Unconsciousness.

Now this, thought Sidney with peculiar satisfaction, was
a *proper* dungeon.

She was manacled at wrist and ankle, spread-eagled
against the rough stone wall. It was quite uncomfortable;
the heavy metal manacles bore her full weight, pressing
into her flesh.

There was darkness, broken only by a furnace's red
glow. Before the furnace stood a man: a torturer, in the traditional garb—naked to the waist, black pantaloons, domino mask. He moved slowly, placing irons in the fire,
shuffling them about. He withdrew one, and examined its
tip; it was curved, an S-shape, glowing white-hot in the
darkness of the dungeon.

There was quiet, broken only by the slow drip of water,
the roar of the coals, the sounds of rats scuttering across
the stone—Sidney could see their eyes, out there, reflect-
ing the furnace's fire. She wondered at the noiselessness of
the place; could the roar of the crowd possibly have
ended? Or were they simply so far below the sunlit world
that even the howling of the mob could not be heard?

The air was dank, chill. Perhaps there was the slightest
tang of blood, of burnt human flesh.

The torturer moved aside; and, the light of the furnace
no longer blocked by his form, Sidney made out more of
the chamber. There was a table covered with implements,
gleaming instruments of unmistakable purpose. There were
several other tables, of peculiar design—manacles at the
corners, blood runnels down the sides. Beneath the table-
tops were gears and wheels and latches. Sidney surmised
they permitted the torturer to alter the position of his sub-

ject, to allow an optimal approach—devices not entirely different in function from a barber's chair.

Sidney looked to either side; her companions were likewise chained to the wall. She, apparently, had been the first to regain consciousness, but Timaeus was now beginning to stir.

About his upper arm, Sidney saw, twined a peculiar black bracelet; it looked like a snake, of cast iron, with runes inscribed on its surface. And then, with an intake of breath, she realized it was alive; it moved, constricted, tightened against Timaeus's arm.

Timaeus groaned and opened his eyes. He looked about.

"Timaeus," Sidney whispered. "Can you burn through the manacles?"

Timaeus looked at her, then at the snake-thing. He gave an unpleasant start, as of someone discovering a roach in his tea. He swallowed, and said, "No." Sidney realized he meant that the snake-thing prevented him.

"What is it?" she asked.

Timaeus hesitated. "A sort of demon," he whispered. "It lives by draining mana, magic power. As long as it's on me—" He shrugged, as well as he was able to, spread-eagled against the wall.

Kraki, chained at Sidney's left, opened his eyes. He looked briefly around, then began to pull at the manacles with all his might, trying to free himself through sheer brute effort. Sidney watched for a while; he did not seem to be making progress.

From beyond Timaeus came a clank; Sidney craned to see the source of the sound. Another man was chained there, someone she'd never seen before: a pudgy little man in his forties or fifties, clean-shaven and balding but with long locks at the back of his head. His garb was that of a wealthy man, his hose somewhat soiled; on every one of his ten fingers there was a ring, while his arm bore another of those menacing snakes.

"Good day, sir," Timaeus said to the man. "We find ourselves in similar circumstances; I hight Timaeus d'Asperge, of Urf Durfal. May I inquire—"

The man blinked in surprise, then looked down at himself. "Ah," he said. "It is I, Timaeus; surely you recognize the voice?"

Sidney did; it was Jasper, whom she had never before seen in the flesh. Apparently, the snake-thing did more than prevent spell-casting; it drained the power of Jasper's magic rings as well.

The masked man now stood before them, attracted by the sound of their voices. "Good day, Master Torturer," said Sidney. "Did you do the decorating yourself?"

"You like it?" said the torturer in a pleased voice. "Oh, my dear, you can't imagine what I've gone through to get a proper dungeon look. I mean, heavens, the Lodge was built with timber and plaster; they even went so far as to stucco down here, can you imagine? I had them rip all that rubbish out. And I had to do something with the drainage; quite dry, when I came—all very fine for a basement, but it just won't do for a good, professional dungeon operation. I had pipes specially installed."

"I appreciate it, I really do," Sidney said. "I've been in dungeons in my time, and I've always thought there was something missing. This has just the right sort of menacing sensibility."

"Oh, it's very kind of you to say so, very kind," said the torturer.

"I was imprisoned briefly in Biddleburg," said Sidney, "you know of it? No? Little barony up in the Dzorzia. They actually had a sofa in my cell. Can you imagine?"

The torturer snorted in laughter. "A sofa?" he said. "Whatever can they have been thinking of? Bed of nails, yes, I can see that; lice-infested straw, yes, fine; rotten vegetable marrows with maggots would do quite well, but a sofa? I suppose you just have to chalk it up to provincial ignorance."

"Have you seen the dungeons in Urf Durfal?" Sidney asked.

"Mm?" said the torturer. "No, don't get out of Hamsterburg a great deal, I'm afraid. Just an old homebody, that's me."

"The old Grand Duke filled them up with horse dung," said Sidney sadly. "He was very big on mushrooms, was Mortimer, wanted the space to grow specimens."

"That's criminal!" said the torturer. "Why, the old Durfalian dungeons were legendary! A shame, a crying shame. Ought to preserve such things for posterity. There's a new duke, I hear, though."

"Yes," said Sidney.

"Not a fungus fancier, I hope?"

"I don't believe so," said Sidney.

"Probably want to open the dungeons up again, then," said the torturer thoughtfully. "I suppose they can be restored. Probably take years to get the smell out, though."

"Well, an overwhelming smell of animal dung might go very well, I should think."

The torturer perked up. "Well, yes, it might," he said. "You'd have to work around it, but it could be an effective element."

"Well, at any rate," said Sidney, "I shall be proud to be tortured in first-class surroundings like this."

"I—I really appreciate that," said the torturer, practically choked with emotion. "We don't get many who understand, you know. Probably be just as happy being tortured in a music room, or a salon."

"Would you know when we're to begin?" asked Timaeus hesitantly.

"Oh," said the torturer, "fairly soon, I should think. As soon as Wolfe arrives." He shook his head sadly. "You're

the third lot today, you know; busy, busy, busy. City in unrest, traitors everywhere, a torturer's work is never done."

"It must be very hard for you," said Sidney sympathet-
ically.

"Haste makes waste, I tell them; try to get something
quick, and you'll just kill the subject," said the torturer.
"Violates my contract, it does, so many in so short a time,
but just try to get the Guild interested in a grievance like
that. Excess overtime, too many victims—they couldn't
care less. Now, client stipulating technique, *that's* what
pisses them off. Bunch of sadistic twits, that's what they
are."

"Terrible," said Sidney.

"Look here," said the torturer. "They get you down
here, they're not going to be satisfied without a little pain.
Clients too prone to lie if there isn't any pressure, that's
what they claim. You see? Me, I think folk'll say anything
under torture—especially when I torture them. I'm a professional; seven years apprentice, six as journeyman, eight
as master now. Haven't had a subject yet who hasn't
spilled his guts—figuratively speaking. Well, no, not always figuratively."

"How very nice for you," said von Kremnitz, somewhat
hostilely.

"You think I like it?" the torturer said. "Disgusting line
of work, that's what it is. Appalling. *I* wanted to be a flo-
rist, but my dad wouldn't hear of it. His dad had been a
torturer, and his dad before him, and so on and on and on.
Every first-born Fenstermann is destined to stick burning
bamboo shoots under people's fingernails, apparently." He
scowled. "Well, water under the bridge, and it's a living, I
suppose."

"Um, yes," said Timaeus. "All very fascinating, but see
here, it's really quite unnecessary. If you'll unlock these
blasted manacles—"

"Now look," said Fenstermann hotly. "What kind of a

torturer would I be if I let subjects free without management's okay? Utterly out of the question. A matter of professional pride."

"Yes, I quite see that," said Timaeus, "but might I—"

"No, you might not," said the torturer. "Don't even think about it. Wolfe will be here shortly, and then it'll be onto the table. Now listen up, you lot. You seem like very nice people, for felonious enemies of the state. I said they won't be satisfied without a little torture, and they won't. But please, do cooperate; let's make it a *little* torture, yes? A second-degree burn or two, maybe a small incision; some bandages, and a couple of stitches, you'll be right as rain. But if you balk, I shan't be responsible. Out in a wheelbarrow if you get out at all. I do hope you'll—"

"Making friends with the meat again, Fenstermann?" came a voice.

"Wolfe," said the torturer resignedly, turning. Beyond him stood a woman, clad in loose black blouse and gray pantaloons, a jagged scar across her face and nose, close-cropped graying hair in a helmet above her forehead. The lines about her mouth gave an impression of permanent impatience. Almost, Sidney admired her: The woman projected a strong air of competence, of power, of energy. "You must talk to them upstairs," the torturer continued. "I just can't do an adequate job with this many subjects. I realize there's a revolution on, but—"

"Shut up, Fenstermann," Wolfe said. She walked down the line, examining each of them in turn. When she came to the leftenant, she said, "You von Kremnitz?"

"I am," he said.

"Where did you get this?" She wafted the safe passage under his nose.

"It was given to me," von Kremnitz said stiffly, "by His Serenity, Hamish the First, of the House Siebert, Lord Mayor of the Most Serene Republic of Hamsterburg. It requires you to lend me every assistance; wherefore, I demand—"

"I don't give a good goddamn," said Wolfe. "You clowns were plotting to hold me hostage."

"*Gish!*" said Kraki menacingly, shaking his manacles.

"That too," Wolfe said. "I want to know what you know about the statue, why you want it, and who you are."

"Trade you," said Nick.

Wolfe blinked. "What do you mean?"

"A question for a question," said Nick.

"You're not in any position to bargain," said Wolfe. She turned to Fenstermann. "We'll start with him."

"Oops," said Nick.

"I'd rather torture her," said Fenstermann, pointing to Sidney.

"Why?" said Wolfe.

"She's got a real feel for things," said Fenstermann. "She'll appreciate the technique."

Wolfe snorted. "Fenstermann, sometimes I don't understand you. If you like her—"

"No, it's all right, really," said Sidney. "I'll go first."

Wolfe glared at Sidney. "What are you, some kind of masochist?"

"N-no," said Sidney. But she could always turn into a cat and quite possibly escape, while Nick had no such option. "Anything to be helpful."

Wolfe eyed Sidney warily, and said, "If you want to be tortured, you've got a reason. The man."

Fenstermann shrugged and went to unlock Nick, then carried him over to one of the tables.

"Stiff upper lip, Pratchitt," said Jasper. "Never surrender. You can do it, lad."

"Please," said the torturer in a long-suffering tone. "I *am* a professional, you know. Of course you'll talk. And if you'll take my advice, you'll do it quickly."

"Talk?" said Nick nervously. "You want me to talk? Of

course I'll talk. I love to talk. My mother always said she couldn't get me to *stop* talking, as a matter of fact. And I never could keep a secret, ask any of my friends. Chatterbox Pratchitt, that's me, talk the livelong day. Ask me a question, any question—"

"How about the iron maiden?" said Wolfe.

Fenstermann pursed his lips judiciously. "A little advanced for the start, don't you think? Red-hot pokers against the skin, I'd say."

"Urg," said Nick.

"Well, you're the professional," said Wolfe dubiously, "but I've always thought the iron maiden was very effective."

"True, true," said Fenstermann. "Still, I've got these irons in the fire, might as well use them for something." He picked one out of the blaze. "Here we go," he said, approaching Nick. "Lie still, now; this won't hurt a bit."

"It won't?" said Nick.

"Well, actually, it will, rather," said Fenstermann apologetically.

He brought the tip of the iron, glowing with intense white heat, down through the air, down toward—

"Halt!" shouted a voice. "Put that down!"

Into the furnace's dim illumination strode a man; an old man, but a vigorous one; a man in the robes of office, a man with the jowly appearance of a basset hound . . .

"My lord!" said von Kremnitz, in wonder. "You live!"

"Release them instantly," said Hamish Siebert.

"My lord," said Wolfe in alarm, "you are needed above! The—"

"Quite right," said Siebert. "We haven't much time. Therefore, release them at once."

"But they—they're felons!" Wolfe said. "They planned to hold me hostage, to—"

"Did they really?" said Siebert in interest. "Must have

their reasons, I suppose. Nonetheless, young von Kremnitz is one of my most trusted men, and his companions and I have an understanding. I vouch for their good behavior. And I shall stay right here until you free them."

"You can't do that!" said Wolfe. "If you don't appear before the mob, they'll storm the Lodge!"

"I imagine so," said the Lord Mayor. "Therefore, you'd better release these good people with alacrity, so I may return upstairs as quickly as possible, *n'est-ce pas?*"

"You'll get us all killed," said Wolfe in a disgruntled tone, but motioned to Fenstermann to release the prisoners. He failed to move sufficiently quickly for her taste; she grabbed some of his keys and set to work as well.

"What about—that," said Timaeus, pointing to the black thing on his arm.

Wolfe, looking at it, shuddered slightly and turned to Fenstermann. The torturer went to get a pair of tongs; he used them to pluck away the slug-like thing and toss it into the fire. He repeated the task with Jasper.

"Now follow me," said Siebert. "You, too, Magistra." He began to stride across the floor, setting a surprisingly rapid pace for an elderly man.

"You shouldn't have come down here," Wolfe scolded, easily keeping up. The others, somewhat taken by surprise, lagged behind. "You're running a terrible risk."

"Magistra Wolfe," said Siebert in a censorious tone, "the good leftenant bore my safe passage; it was my sworn duty to aid him—and yours, as well, I might add. If anyone endangers our lives, it is—"

"I say," said Jasper, flitting up to join them, "am I to understand that the Lord Mayor is needed elsewhere as quickly as possible?"

"Yes!" said Wolfe intemperately. "You needn't come if you don't—"

"I have a ring of magical flight," said Jasper. "Why don't I lend it to you, your serenity?"

"Ah! That would be useful, if you would," said Siebert, coming to a halt.

"If I can get the damned thing off—good. Bit of luck, that. Here you are."

"You have my thanks," said Siebert. "Magistra, if you mistreat these people further, I shall have your eyes put out. Hard to be a shadow mage if you can't perceive shadows, what?"

"Go, dammit!" said Wolfe. "Move!"

"Ta," said Siebert. He lifted from the dark rocks of the dungeon and flitted away through the air.

"Now what?" asked Sidney, eyeing Wolfe uneasily and wishing for her weapons. She checked; yes, even the knife in her boot was gone.

"Oh, come along," said Wolfe. "Up these stairs."

The stairs seemed to twine upward forever. At intervals, magic torches flickered. Wolfe led the way.

"I thought you had killed him," von Kremnitz said wonderingly.

"Me?" said Wolfe. "Oh, you mean the Ministry. Actually, I might well have been asked to kill him, if Stantz had wanted him dead."

"How is it that he is alive?" von Kremnitz asked.

"Faked his death, of course," said Wolfe.

"Why?" said Timaeus, breathing hard; his legs were beginning to feel the strain of so many stairs.

"Isn't it obvious?" said Wolfe nastily. "The Accommodationists have been planting rumors for weeks, claiming Stantz had tried to kill the mayor before, and would do it again. And they made Siebert's assassination the signal for their troops to move."

"Didn't you just—do what they wanted to happen?" said Sidney. "Aren't they moving to take over the city now?"

"Yup," said Wolfe. "But in a few moments, the Lord

Mayor will miraculously appear before the people of
Hamsterburg. And then he will lead them toward the
Maiorkest, to rally the folk against tyranny."

"I see," said Jasper. "The Accommodationists had
planned for the mob to storm the Albertine Lodge, but instead, the mob becomes a weapon in Siebert's hands."

"Exactly," said Wolfe. "And—the assassination was not
to occur for several days. Their troops are out of position,
and they won't coordinate properly."

"Excellent!" said von Kremnitz. "I had misjudged you
and the minister, Magistra. And when the Lord Mayor appears with the Scepter and statue of Stantius, the people
will know he is divinely appointed to lead the nation. Patriotic rapture will sweep the *urbs*, men and women will
rally to the sign of the hamster; the Accommodationist
host will melt away like snow in the spring!"

"Ah," said Wolfe. "Hmm."

"It really isn't your statue, Leftenant," Timaeus pointed
out. "I suppose we could permit its temporary use to calm
the city, but afterward, we really must continue on our
quest."

"Yes, yes," said von Kremnitz. "Of course." He spoke a
little too hastily for Sidney's peace of mind.

"What I don't understand," said Nick, "is why, if the
Lord Mayor knew Magistra Wolfe would be snatching the
statue, he didn't let us know. We could have worked together."

"Quite, quite," said Wolfe absently. "Here we are." The
stairs spiraled a final time, and a door came into view.

VIII.

Wolfe brought them through the busy corridors of the Albertine Lodge to a large chamber, apparently a ball-room, for the floor was polished wood and the space was unfurnished, save for a few couches and chairs drawn up against the walls. The late-morning sun shone brightly through the French doors of the far wall, which opened out onto a large balcony. The middle set of doors had been flung open, and through them they could see Hamish Siebert, in his mayoral robes of office, standing before the crowd, arms outspread.

Beyond him was the swirling enormity of the mob, packing Albertus Square from one end to the other. They had ceased their chant some time ago, but their roar was no less for that; there were shouts, screams, orations, yells from across the square, an inchoate noise like that of the sea, battering against the Albertine walls. It gave the air a physical quality, as of waves of pressure washing against the ears.

The Lodge's defenders were out there, still, a thin line against enormity. It was a miracle, Sidney thought, that they had not been overwhelmed, a tribute to their esprit and stamina—and an indication, perhaps, that the rabblerousers the Accommodationists should have had in the mob, to spur it into action, were either cowed or missing.

At first it seemed as if the crowd were entirely oblivious to Siebert's presence; it was minutes before any diminution in that roar could be perceived. But some folk noticed the single figure standing on the balcony, and realized someone wanted to address them; and of those close to the Lodge, some were able to recognize Siebert, while others recognized his robes of office. Word began to circulate to those farther back in the square. Slowly, slowly, the noise died down, silence spreading outward as waves spread from a stone dropped in still water.

It took perhaps ten minutes—and all that time, Siebert held his hands in the air. At last there was silence—or near silence, as much silence as ten thousand are capable of accomplishing: the occasional sneeze or cough or low conversation. Ten thousand people stood, looking upward; waiting for Siebert to speak.

He began.

THE ALBERTINE ADDRESS

My name, if you haven't already figured that out, is Hamish Siebert. Death came for me this morning; but he and I got to talking, and got to drinking, and I left him under the table.

As he slid from his chair, I grabbed the handle of his scythe, because I'd always heard that the blade has a name on it, when Death comes for you. Maybe it says "Cholera," or maybe it says "Age," but it always has the name of the one who fells you. I squinted at the blade, and held it to the light, but the name I read was not that of Guismundo Stantz.

So I grabbed Death's bony shoulder, and shook it a bit. "Charley," I said, "wake up, boy." And he did, a little, and asked me what I wanted.

Well, hell; what do you want? I've got a pretty fair idea. You want a chicken in the pot. You want the rent paid. You want the kids to stop whining. And most of the time, you just want the city to leave you damned well alone.

But some of you may have kept a scrappy little rodent, as a kid. And maybe you kept it not just to have a furry little thing to pet; maybe it meant something more. It stood for the neighbors who told you to get along home to your mother when it started to get dark, it stood for the bustle of the market and the ships at the dock, the swordsmen swaggering in velvet, and the blind beggars on the Tetrine Way who tell stories to the kids while Mom darts in to do some shopping. It stood for a city, our city, the city, once, of empire, and still the center of the human world. Most of the time, you want a chicken in the pot, and perhaps a wee dram after, but you also want something for Hamsterburg, something better than what she's got. You do, or you wouldn't be here.

Why *are* you here?

I know, of course; I'd be deaf if I hadn't heard you, the last hour or two. You thought Stantz had me killed. You came to avenge me.

You don't know how profoundly moved I am, how grateful I am for your assistance. In my short time as Lord Mayor, I've mostly met obstruction and resistance; I had just no idea that so much of the city believed in me, believed we could bring about the changes the city needs, cared enough to mourn me, let alone avenge my death.

But I'm not dead yet. And neither is your hamster, however long since you dug a hole for him in your backyard.

Death asked me what I wanted; and so I told him. I told

him I wanted the city clean. I wanted an end to her decline. I wanted her governance out of the hands of the *gens*, who, however well they guided her in her youth, have descended into corruption; I wanted the city to serve her people. I wanted an end to dissension, and a unity of purpose in restoring the city to her former glory; I wanted the hamster perky, and not dead.

"Give me a corkscrew and a case of the red," Death said, "and I'll give you a little time."

A little time; that's all anyone has, a little time. I said yes, of course. And so I, and you, and Hamsterburg, have a little time left.

What are we going to do with it?

When I was a boy, my dad owned some stables up in the borough of Stuffel. When I got to be fifteen, he told me it was time I got to work in the family business. I told him that was fine, of course, figuring he'd give me a nice, cushy position, overseeing the hostlers, or buying the feed. After all, I was the boss's son. My dad took me out to the stables and handed me a shovel and a broom. "Start to work," says he.

I threw a fit, but he wasn't to be budged; he thought I should learn the business from the ground up. And so I did, though it wasn't so much from the ground up as up from the horse's arsehole. For the next three months, I was up to my knees in horseshit, day after day, and believe me, it did nothing for my popularity with the girls. And the job never ended: however much shit you shoveled, the horses were always making more.

I thought I'd never have a job as hard as that one, but that was before they made me mayor. I feel like I'm back in the stables, after all this time. However much shit I shovel, the *gens* are always making more. But, by all the gods, this stable needs to be clean, and if it's within my power, and it can be done in the little time I've got left, I'm going to clean it.

I've got some extra shovels, though. Care to lend a hand?

Good. There's a particularly noisome stench coming from one stall, over here. Over the stall is a plaque, engraved with the horse's name. And, funny thing, it's the same name I read on Death's own scythe.

The name of the horse is Gerlad von Grentz.

If we shovel a bit, I think we'll find some rats, buried in the muck. They've been going about the town, squeaking in people's ears. "Guismundo Stantz tried to have the Lord Mayor killed," they squeaked. "He'll try it again."

Wondered where that rumor came from, didn't you?

Now, why should the rats want to spread it? Because they wanted you here, today. They didn't expect Hamish Siebert to drink Death under the table; they expected him to fall. And they wanted you here, to storm the Lodge, to smash this Ministry. Why?

Because Guismundo Stantz, for all his faults, is a patriot. And he would never allow any of the *gens* to seize absolute power.

Gerlad von Grentz, say.

Oh, there's more to the plot, to be sure; there are a good many rats, down there in the manure. The noble House of von Grentz maintains its own army; it marches on the city. Von Grentz is allied with other *gens* of similar inclination; their troops march too. My death was to be their signal for rebellion.

But my Death has a weakness for strong drink. And I've got ten thousand friends, with shovels.

You can kill a rat with a shovel, if you move fast. You might have to whack it a couple of times. And rats are all we face.

I know, it's true; some of those rats are armed and trained veterans. And you, you're just civilians. Civilians, citizens, as are we all; *Hamsteriana civitatis sumus*. And they're rats. They expect an easy conquest, a city in unrest, thankful for the restoration of order; they don't expect angry men and women armed with spades. Rats are very bold, but are quick to flee the shovel's mortal smash.

Shoulder up your shovels, and ask yourselves this: Are you mice—or are you Hamsters?

Rats may be bigger, but we are the better rodents.

And we know how to shovel shit.

Von Grentz's stall isn't the only one that needs shoveling, but once we clean that one up, the others will be easier, I think. And you've got to start somewhere, when you've got a stable to clean.

A mile from here is the Maiorkest. The Mayoral Foot is there. I'm going to take a stroll, and join them. If you come along, I don't think the rats will bother us. If you come along, I think they'll slink back to their holes. All we need to show, I think, is that this city holds more Hamsters than rats.

Are you coming?

The crowd roared approbation.

Von Kremnitz wept in a veritable paroxysm of patriotic joy.

Kraki snored.

"Very nice speech, I thought," said Jasper. "I rather liked that last turn of phrase; classic example of chiasmus, wouldn't you say?"

"Chiasmus?" said Timaeus. "You old fool, when did you last study rhetoric? That was metonymy, and quite an effective use."

"Metonymy? Are you daft? I know chiasmus when I hear it. The gods only know what they teach you twits at university these days. Why, when I was a lad—"

Jasper was interrupted by Siebert, who appeared in the French doors, tossing a ring in his right hand. Spotting Jasper, he said, "I say, old man; do you mind if I use your ring to fly down to the crowd? I'll toss it up to you on the balcony, if you like."

"Oh, certainly," said Jasper. "Make a grand entrance, what?"

"Politics is at least half spectacle," said Siebert. "Come along then." He turned to walk back onto the balcony.

"Wait!" protested Sidney. "What about the statue?"

Standing in the doorway, Siebert blinked. "What about it?"

"Why did you not use it to bolster your claim, my lord?" asked von Kremnitz. "Surely it would have been an effective element of your address."

"It is hard to exploit something you haven't got," Siebert said acidly. "We'll try to get it from von Grentz once this is over—"

Von Kremnitz whirled to face Wolfe. "You didn't tell him!" he said.

"Um," said Wolfe.

Siebert hesitated, obviously not wanting to keep the mob much longer. "Tell me what?"

"Internal Serenity's got it!" von Kremnitz said. "Wolfe stole it from the Drachehaus, out from under our very noses."

"I see," said Siebert. "Is this so, Magistra Wolfe?"

"Well, yes," said Wolfe. "We thought it dangerous to permit von Grentz to keep the statue—"

"Quite so," said Siebert. "But as my ally, I do expect you to keep me informed of—"

"We didn't know you had an interest," said Wolfe.

Siebert sighed with exasperation. "I *am* Lord Mayor of this benighted cesspool," he said. "I do expect to be informed of events of striking political import. I shall expect Minister Stantz to explain himself. At considerable length."

"I'll tell him," said Wolfe.

"Mind you do," said Siebert. "And you may tell him, also, to surrender the statue immediately to these people."

Wolfe recoiled. "You're joking," she said.

"By no means," said Siebert. "They are its legitimate owners."

"Legitimate—but consider the political—" sputtered Wolfe.

"Enough," said Siebert with finality. "We can discuss it later, if Stantz insists. In the meantime, I must be off."

"Yes, my lord," said Wolfe forlornly. "Farewell."

"Ta," said Siebert jauntily, and departed. Jasper followed him onto the balcony, to retrieve his ring.

Out in the square, the folk were gradually filtering away. The sheer number of people meant it would no doubt take long minutes before the square was finally clear.

"Well, Magistra?" said Timaeus, pipe at a defiant angle. "Our statue, if you please."

Wolfe dithered for a moment, then shook her head. "Stantz has to make that decision," she said. "I couldn't just hand it over to you, even if I knew where it's stored."

"Fine," said Sidney. "Take us to Stantz."

"*Tout de suite,*" said Jasper.

"I can't," said Wolfe. "He's in the War Room! There's a rebellion on, or hadn't you noticed? He's up to his neck in planning—"

"Goodo," said Timaeus. "Then take us to the War Room."

"Not likely," said Wolfe. "You're not cleared. Besides, you're aliens! I can't think of a more drastic security breach than—"

"My dear lady," said Jasper, "the Lord Mayor did say to give us the statue 'immediately,' did he not? I don't believe the word is susceptible to much interpretation."

Wolfe smiled at that. "You haven't done much business with government, have you?" she said. "There's 'immediately' as in 'this instant.' There's 'immediately' as in 'as soon as practical.' There's 'immediately' as in 'follow normal procedures but put this at the top of the list.' There's 'immediately' as in 'I want to be able to blame you for the delay, but please take as long as possible.' And then there's—"

"Oh, shut up," said Sidney. "Take us to Stantz. Do it now!"

Wolfe peered at Sidney. "Shut up yourself, dear," she said sweetly. "I'm not scared by gutter toughs like you."

"I kill her?" asked Kraki with interest.

"No, no, no," said Frer Mortise.

Kraki scowled. "Civilization," he swore. "In northland, you have dispute, you kill. Simple. Here you talk, talk, talk, nothing gets done."

"If we kill her," Timaeus said patiently, "she won't be able to tell us where the statue is."

"Yah, hokay," said Kraki, "but it be more fun."

Wolfe went to a bellpull that ran against one wall and gave it a yank. "I'll have you shown to the Green Room," she said.

"Oh, no you don't," said Sidney. "You're not gassing us again."

Wolfe scowled at her. "I'm not going to gas you," she said. "The Lord Mayor would have my head. But I can't take you to the War Room, so you'll just have to wait. In the Green Room."

"No," said Sidney. "Take us with you."

"Impossible," said Wolfe. "A messenger will be here shortly to take you there. Goodbye." She started toward the heavy doors at the ballroom's far end.

Sidney trotted along, waving urgently at the others to follow. "You can't get rid of us that easily," she said determinedly. "We're sticking with you until you get us the statue."

"Oh, come on," said Wolfe. "Can't you wait—"

"For how long?" demanded Sidney. "*I've* dealt with government. We could be in your Green Room for weeks. I'm not letting you out of sight."

"Sorry," said Wolfe. "I forbid it. You may not come."

"How do you propose to stop us?" demanded Sidney. "By force? Do you think the Lord Mayor will appreciate that? Bring us the statue, or we're coming along."

"I can't allow that," said Wolfe.

"Try and stop us," said Sidney.

Wolfe contemplated that. "All right," she said. And turned into a shadow. She began to slide toward the door.

Sidney whirled to face the French doors; the morning sun shone brightly out there, rays slanting into the long hall. She looked down at her own shadow; it was etched clearly against the parquet floor.

Sidney sprinted after Wolfe's shadow, reaching for a dagger that—wasn't there. That's right, she realized; their weapons had still not been restored. She then raised her fists, holding them up against the light until they cast clear shadows against the floor. She threw a fist forward. . . . The first itself struck nothing, moving through empty space. Its shadow, however, smashed into—Wolfe's.

Wolfe's shadow recoiled.

Sidney struck out with her other hand. It felt strange, to box against nothing. For good measure, she kicked the air, her foot's shadow kicking Wolfe's.

There was a sense of magic transition; and then a corporeal Wolfe stood in the hall once more, a prominent bruise around one eye. She swiftly drew her blade and put its point to Sidney's neck. "Stop that," she practically snarled.

"I kill her now?" said Kraki.

"No, no, no," said Frer Mortise, Timaeus, and Jasper, practically in unison.

Kraki pouted.

Sidney spread her hands. "I've stopped," she said. "See?"

Wolfe breathed heavily for a long moment, then finally sheathed her weapon. "Oh, all right," she said finally. "Look, I really can't take you to the War Room. Why don't I take you to Stantz's office?"

Sidney considered that. "All right," she said at last.

IX.

"Hallo, hallo, hallo," said the fat man.

He was, thought Timaeus, rather astoundingly corpulent. He had known Guismundo Stantz was supposed to be fat, but the sheer bulk of the man was impressive. The chair behind his desk was large, but even so, Stantz filled it to overflowing, folds of flesh squeezed between and over the arms. It was amazing, Timaeus thought, that the man could still walk.

"I thought you were in the War Room," said Wolfe.

"Pooh," said Stantz, waving a hand the size of a dinner plate. "The staff can handle things. Good as over."

Kraki wandered into the room and looked about in the dimness. He spotted the cheese, cut off a wedge the size of his head, and started gnawing. The others moved in more slowly, blinking at the oddly appointed space: the strange contraption lighting the papers on Stantz's desk, the innumerable speaking tubes, the newscrystal.

Wolfe snorted. "You've got more confidence in Siebert than I do."

"Perhaps so, perhaps so," said Stantz genially. "And who are these people, whom you have so gaily escorted into my *sanctum sanctorum*? No little breach of security, I might add."

"Friends of Siebert, apparently," said Wolfe.

"May we be seated?" asked Timaeus. Kraki, still munching on his cheese, was now examining the flask of syrup of greep that stood on the sideboard, along with glasses and a pitcher of water.

"Of course, of course, please," said Stantz. "And might I inquire as to your business?" Kraki picked up the syrup of greep and unstoppered it.

"The Lord Mayor says they're to be given the statue of Stantius," said Wolfe.

"Difficult, that—I say, that's prime-quality greep syrup there, my man. Put it down, please, you don't quaff it like ale."

"Why is it difficult?" ask Timaeus.

"Don't have it any—I say, look, put that down. I'll make you a greep spritzer, if you like."

"*What?*" shouted Timaeus.

"Greep vhat?" asked Kraki.

"A greep spritzer," said Stantz. "A blend of soda water and syrup of greep. You won't find a better or more healthful quaff. Well I know, for I came to maturity in Hamster-Dzorzia, where elven magic lingers, where the finest greeps in all the world are grown. It seems so long ago . . ."

"That statue!" said Timaeus. "What about—"

"Wait!" said Sidney.

But they were too late: Stantz was on a roll.

SYRUP OF GREEP

It seems so long ago, so long ago that I roamed the hills of Hamster-Dzorzia. The world was young then, always green, soft spring winds wafting eastward with the hint of rain, young flowers nodding in the meadows, the greeps putting forth their first green fruit. Oh, I suppose it wasn't always so; were there not winters? And scorching days? And hours of labor totting up figures in dusty rooms? But that isn't what sticks in the memory, from that distant time. No, it is the skirl of pipes, the coolness of the gloaming, the scent of the greeps' new blossoms.

For that land had once been elven, long time past; and here and there, about it, traces of elven magic lingered still. There was power, hither and yon, slowly dying with the elves' absence, but enough of it present to support the greep.

I see you do not comprehend. It is simple enough; the greep is a magic plant. It draws sustenance not only from rain and earth and sun, but from the magic energy that permeates certain soils. It will not grow in mundane ground.

And its fruit; ah, its fruit. If you have not tasted the fresh greep, new-plucked from the vine, you have no inkling of nirvana. This side of the grave, there is no closer taste of paradise. It is tart, but not too tart; sweet, but not too sweet; words betray me. It is trivial to describe a sight, not much harder to describe a noise, but taste—the language does not suffice.

The greep perishes quickly; it is a delicate fruit, and cannot withstand much handling. It must be preserved, if it is to become a commodity: They pickle it, can it, turn it into jelly. They make greep vinegar, greep schnapps—and, of course, greep syrup. Well I know, for my father was an *haut bourgeois*, a trader in products of greep. He shipped the fresh fruit, by fast pony, sometimes by pegasus or dragonelle, to Hamsterburg, where gourmets dined on its exquisite flesh. There was great demand for greeps among true connoisseurs, for different soils breed clear differences in taste: Greep grown by a magic spring tastes of the cool freshness of the waters, while that grown where a basilisk nests has a pungent, earthy scent. My father was always on the lookout for magical places where the greep could be grown, for practically each new site meant a slightly different taste, a new variety for his demanding clientele.

Because of this, I saw him little, for he was constantly on his rounds, and only briefly in the little market village we called home. His absence, indeed, gave me my freedom. I was sixteen that spring, old enough that, my father gone, no one in the household could impose his will on me. I was too old to be biddable any longer; too young, yet, to be encumbered with a share of the family's financial burdens. And so, oft of a soft spring morning, I would sneak away from my chamber, before the hour at which I was required to meet my tutor, and roam the hills at will.

More often than not, I would meet with Rudy. He was a year or two older than I, of equally respectable family; and I had worshiped him from boyhood. He had a quality of sober joy I found ceaselessly fascinating, a keen intelligence he applied to our amusement, and a reckless daring that kept me in awe. In the best of circumstances, I think he would have wound up dead, or imprisoned, for he was the sort of boy who steals the clappers from the bells of the town clock, makes off with women's clothes while they bathe, and casually pockets merchandise while the shopkeeper looks elsewhere; not, I think, the sort to make a success of himself in the sober world.

We climbed the hills, swam in the streams, taunted bulls, played jokes on the local yokels, and otherwise amused ourselves. His skin was fair, his arms speckled with a light golden down, his face chiseled in such exquisite lines that, more than once, despite our friendship, I was overwhelmed by shyness in his presence, a diffidence his

sudden grin would instantly shatter. Together, we roamed
the spring-soft hills, and took pleasure in each other as we
found it.

One of our favorite places was an oak grove, down in
the fold between two hills, where a little stream ran. The
stream, I think, marked the boundary between two peasants' properties, which may, perhaps, be why the grove
had not been felled to make room for crops; that, or perhaps they, superstitious as peasants often are, felt some
sense of the power there.

The oaks were tall, centuries in age, undoubtedly dating
from the era of elven dominion. The ground was carpeted
with soft leaf mold, dotted with harder acorns. The trees
abounded with squirrels, chipmunks, and various birds
who survived on the mast the oaks produced; it was a veritable little forest, one of the last great stands of trees in all
the cultivated land. Even in the hottest days of summer,
the high branches of the trees cast a cool, green shade
within the grove, a shade we found inviting. Often, in the
afternoon, we would go there, drink at the stream, make a
rude lunch of bread and cheese, and lie together in the
green dimness of the grove.

Oh, there was magic there, sure enough; the everyday
magic of the play of leaf-dappled light on earth, of the
purling of the stream, of squirrels chattering from the
branch. But I had not realized that there was more, not until the evening I went to see Rudy there, later than we usually met.

I snuck away after dinner, out into the gloaming. The
sky was that strange indigo that painters cannot seem to
capture, the luminous fading of the light, a time almost
magical in itself. I knew the grove as a place of green dimness, but in this already dim light, it now seemed dark,
mysterious. As I entered it, I heard the sound of voices:
Rudy's, and—a girl's.

Surprised that he would bring a wench to our private

place, I crept softly toward the stream, hiding behind the trees. And there was Rudy with—with a creature. Oh, female, to be sure; but hardly human. Her skin was pastel viridian, her hair bedecked with long, fine, willow-like leaves, her eyes of an elven cast. She moved with a catlike litheness and she, and Rudy, were obviously entranced.

Astonished, I could hardly move, but watched, crouching behind the bole of an oak, while they murmured to each other, Rudy mustering the full force of his enormous charm. It hardly seemed necessary, for she intended much as he, and by the time full darkness fell, they were in each other's arms. It was black, by then, in the oak grove, no moon that night, and the trees obscuring even the meager light of the stars; I saw little of them, hearing only their soft breathing.

I stumbled away, half in pain, half in rage. Rudy had defiled our place, had defiled what we had together, and had done it, moreover, with a creature not of our kind. Why did I react with such intensity? It is hard to say, now, so long after. Certainly, Rudy had had wenches before; he was a careless, charming lad, of respectable family, and had induced many of the local girls to spend a hour or two with him, in a hayloft, or amid the soft greenery of the meadow. And that had never bothered me, for I had known that they meant nothing to Rudy, nothing more than an afternoon's pleasure, nothing by comparison to what we shared. But this, I sensed, even from that moment, this was different.

And it was. With me, he grew distant; the intimacy we once had shared was gone. Never did he tell me of his lover, but I could see it in his eyes, his attention far away; he would gather wildflowers for no apparent purpose, and take them to the grove. He would bring nuts and berries for the squirrels, lie there, his back to an oak tree, for hours at a time, staring upward into the leaves and sighing. Never would he speak to me of his new passion, but it was clear, not only in his actions, but in his lack of action, his unwillingness to roam with me, to play the games that were our wont. Perhaps I should have confronted him with what I knew, but that seemed fruitless. What could he say? What could he have done? It was true, I knew; he had been captivated by that creature, enraptured in her spell, and what we had once shared was gone forever.

I began to hate him, as only one whose love is betrayed can hate; hate him nearly as much as I loathed that inhuman, green thing with which he lay. And I began to plot my revenge.

The grove was magical; I knew that now. A dryad lived there, Rudy's love. That information had value.

Great value. For the greep grows in magical soil, and even in Hamster-Dzorzia, there were few enough patches of that, few places where the fruit could be grown. Fell those trees, and the grove would be a perfect place for a stand of vines—rich bottomland, well watered by the stream, the soil imbued with magic. Moreover, none of the greep orchards from which my father bought were planted in a dryad's former grove; greeps planted there would possess a novel taste, would provide my father with a new variety to titillate the jaded palates of the *urbs*.

And as it happened, he was home.

I told him what I knew. Oh, not of Rudy, nor what had passed between him and the dryad; but of the dryad's presence, of the grove's power. My father slapped me on the back and, I think, for the first time in my life, was proud of me. Canny merchant that he was, he began at once to ponder how best to acquire the property, how to obtain it from the peasants who tilled the adjoining fields without raising their suspicions as to its value.

I slept soundly that night, savoring my victory. If I could not have Rudy, I could serve him as he had served me, betray him as I had been betrayed. The next day I met him, on the hill overlooking the town, and told him what I'd done.

All color drained from his face. "No," he said, "you can't have done." When I insisted I had, and provided corroborating detail, he struck me, a sudden vicious blow. I had not expected it, and it flung me to the ground. I think I lost consciousness for a while, and when I awoke found a reddening bruise about one eye.

That very afternoon, I went out to the grove in the company of my father, with two woodsmen and a sorcerer, the former to fell the grove, the latter to protect us if the dryad proved to have unexpected powers. They set to work on the outer trees, while I went with my father inward, to show him the stream, the largest oak wherein, I thought, the dryad made her home—

Oh, what dolor greeted us there. Where there had been green coolness was warm blood, almost black in the darkness of the grove; gray steel, deep in Rudy's belly, pale flesh lifeless on the moss beneath the tree. The blood ran everywhere; it was hard to believe one man could hold so much gore. I cried out, ran to him, cradled his head; but it was too late. Life had departed his form hours before.

My father scowled, cursed under his breath, hauled me away from Rudy, saw the tears coursing down my cheeks, and slapped me, hard. I think he understood it all, in that moment, understood that Rudy and I had been more than friends, understood what Rudy had done with the creature of the wood. He was disgusted; he despised me, as I think he always had, an unforgiving man. But worse, from his perspective, was this:

The grove was ruined. Rudy's blood would taint the soil, would taint the greeps, if we grew them there. They would taste of metal, of blood, of death; they would win no praises at the tables of the city.

He called the woodsmen to a halt, and hauled me roughly away from Rudy's form. He swore to kill me if I let the townsfolk know of my—unnatural desires, he called them; odd how natural they seemed, by comparison with Rudy's, Rudy's love for something beyond nature. And he told me he would send me to university, banish me from my home. I hardly cared.

Rudy had known what his blood would do; how could he have not? Though there were wheatfields, apiaries, and vineyards in Hamster-Dzorzia, the lifeblood of its commerce depended on the greep, and we had known its ways from infancy. He had slain himself, not out of despair, but out of love; not in mourning for the loss of his dryad, but to protect her from the ax. He had cheated me of my vengeance, cheated me thricefold: First, of his love; second, of the despair I had wished him to feel; third, of the dryad's death. And most of all, he made me realize that I, too, had never been more than a passing fancy, for him, little more than one of his girls; would he ever have sacrificed his life for mine, as he did for the spirit of the oak?

From high in the oak's stately branches, I caught a hint of a laughing face, a sardonic glint of the eye; the dryad was there, mocking me. Had she planned this from the start? Had she known that, in this region, it was merely a time before she fell to the ax? Had she *plotted* all this, as a means of mere survival—betrayed Rudy as fully as I?

In rage and frustration, I darted from the grove, took an ax forcibly from the woodsman's hands, and ran back, to fell that mighty tree. At the least, I would slay that thing, that green-skinned thing, that mockery of humanity.

But my father knocked me to the ground; he forbade it. "We thrive on the gleanings of departing magic," he told me later. "Wouldst destroy what little remains, not for gain, but from sheer spite?"

A nice sentiment, but it did not prevent him from selling the grove, at a handsome profit, before the news of Rudy's death became known. So he came out of it without loss; would that I had done as well.

For years afterward, I tortured myself with what I had done; but now, so many years later, it seems to me that we were like actors in a drama, virtually fated to do what we did. And if my motives were vile, still it was not I who slew Rudy, nor did I do more than advance the date at which the grove might have been felled. We did as we felt we must, Rudy, the dryad, and I, and I can blame myself hardly any more than they. The world is full of tragedy; much of it we cannot hope to prevent, but only to ameliorate.

"And so," said Stantz, "when I sip of the greep, I remember the bittersweet days of youth; and in this, the hour of triumph, it is meet to remember that life is not always thus. Can I fix one for you?"

"Urg," said Nick.

"No, thanks," said Sidney.

"None for me, thank you," said Jasper.

"Does it have a kick?" asked Kraki.

"No," said Stantz, "it is not an alcoholic beverage."

"Then vhat good is it?" complained Kraki.

"I'll try one, if I may," said Frer Mortise, raising one hand hesitantly.

The others stared at him, while Stantz poured syrup and water into a glass and chanted a brief incantation.

"The statue," said Timaeus brokenly. "The statue. Yes? Can we talk about the statue yet?"

"Certainly," said Stantz. "What about it?"

"Where the devil is it?" Timaeus said.

"How should I know?" said Stantz.

"You *had* it, didn't you?" said Sidney.

"Yes, certainly," said Stantz. "Why are you interested, if I may ask?"

"The mayor says they're the statue's legal owners," said Wolfe.

Stantz snarfed a noseful of spritzer and had to be patted

on the back for quite some time afterward. "How so?" he asked at last. "If legend be true, Stantius himself is the legal owner, or perhaps the Dark Lord."

"Right of salvage," said Timaeus. "We found it in the dungeon below Urf Durfal."

Stantz looked off into space thoughtfully. "Yes, there was—hmm. Just a second." He reached down and pulled open a desk drawer. It was filled with files, Sidney saw; that was reasonable enough, but the lever fixed to the side of the drawer was unusual. Stantz yanked downward on the lever, the motion of someone working a pump; with a whirr, the files spun into motion, a blur of paper inside the drawer. It was as if, Sidney thought, the drawer opened onto a wheel stuffed with files, as if working the lever spun the wheel, displaying a few feet of files to the drawer at a time, as if the small file drawer somehow contained whole cabinets of paper, accessible through the yank of a lever; impossible, Sidney scoffed to herself.

Or perhaps not, she considered. She'd heard of purses containing an infinity of coin, wineskins capable of dispensing wine eternally. If magic could create such things, why couldn't it store an entire department's paperwork in a single file drawer? And wouldn't it be like the Hamsterians to put the romantic mystery of magic to such mundane function?

At last, Stantz gave a grunt of satisfaction and pulled out a single file folder. He placed it on his desk, opened it, and pulled over his light, on its pulleys and gears, to shine on the folder's contents. He read for a moment, then put his finger to a line of text. ". . . a party of adventurers in the employ of one Timaeus d'Asperge, *Magister Igniti*, a gentleman of Athelstan," he read.

"I am he," said Timaeus.

Stantz looked up. "I suppose you can prove that?"

Timaeus looked faintly disgruntled. "My passport is

back at the pension," he said. "I had not expected an in-
quisition. It can be fetched, if—"

"Never mind," said Stantz, waving his enormous hand
and flipping through the file. "I shall take you at your
word. Now wasn't there—yes, here it is. Ah. Vincianus
Polymage? How extraordinary. Is he still alive?"

"Technically," said Timaeus. "The body survives, albeit
the mind has seen better days."

"Taking it to Arst-Kara-Morn?" said Stantz, still scanning the file. "My good man, how absurd!"

"How did you know that?" Sidney demanded.

Stantz looked up, smiling faintly. "We do have our
sources, my dear," he said. "Sir Ethelred of Athelstan may
think he has the finest espionage establishment in the human lands, but he is in error."

"You have a spy in the Athelstani Foreign Ministry?"
said Jasper.

Stantz blinked. "Do you expect me to comment?" he
asked. "Take it to Arst-Kara-Morn? Suppose the Dark
Lord captures it? Idiotic idea."

"See here," said Timaeus, somewhat angrily, "it's no
concern of yours. It belongs to us; the Lord Mayor has
specifically ordered you to surrender it to us; we demand
it. If you don't have it, the least you can do is tell us who's
got it, why, and how we can get it back."

"The Lord Mayor specifically ordered?" said Stantz. "Is
that so, Ren?"

Wolfe cleared her throat. "Yup," she said.

Stantz frowned. "Well, well, well," he said. "Damn." He
wheeled his chair over to one of the speaking tubes, and
uncapped it. *"Kant!"* he shouted down it. *"Are you
there?"*

He put his ear to the tube and listened briefly, then put
his mouth to it again. *"Kant! The statue! Did they pick it
up?"*

"Did who pick it up?" Sidney demanded, but Stantz shushed her as he put his ear to the tube again.

"Damn," he said to himself as he listened. *"At what time?"* he shouted, then frowned at the response. *"Thank you, Kant!"*

He moved to another tube, uncapped it, and shouted, *"Bleichroder! Immediate message to the Alcalan frontier! Are you there, dammit, Bleichroder? Yes, good. Halt all elven travelers. Search possessions for a life-size statue of a human male, cast of athenor. Yes, athenor, dammit, Bleichroder. At once! By crystal, of course. Good. Thank you."*

He wheeled back to his desk. "We'll try to recover it, of course," he said, "but I suspect it's unlikely—"

Everyone started babbling at once. For long minutes, there was pandemonium. At last, Sidney shouted, *"Shut up!"*

And miraculously, there was silence.

"To whom did you give it?" Sidney demanded.

"The elves," said Stantz.

"Why?" asked Sidney.

Stantz shrugged. "They asked for it," he said.

Sidney snorted. "If an orc had wandered in off the street and asked for it, would you have said, 'Sure, here it is, my compliments to the Dark Lord'?"

"No, of course not," said Stantz in irritation. "But why *not* give it to the elves?"

"Why *should* you give it to the elves?" Sidney demanded.

Stantz spread his hands. "It's a hot potato," he said. "Look what chaos it's wrought in Hamsterburg; if I kept it, seventy-three discrete political factions would start plotting to get it away from me. Getting rid of it seemed like an excellent idea."

"But what do the elves *want* with it?" asked Timaeus plaintively.

No one had an answer for that.

After a long silence, Frer Mortise cleared his throat. "Well," he said, "I've always wanted to visit the elven domains."

"*I* haven't," said Jasper nastily.

"Twinkle-toed little snots," snarled Nick.

It was hard, thought the lich as it drove its horse to the limit of endurance, to know which was the more otiose: the normal, everyday tedium of humdrum existence, or the occasional bursts of desperate activity continued survival required.

It didn't know why it bothered. Continued survival hardly seemed worth the bother. The true death would be almost welcome.

Although, it reflected, the terrified horse's hooves pounding recklessly across some poor peasant's field, smashing sprouting wheat to the earth, the difficulty with Dark Lords was that they wouldn't let you stay dead. Its own existence was testimony to that. It was compelled to action not so much by the need to survive as by the need to avoid spending the next millennium at the bottom of a dungheap, say, or functioning as a birdfeeder. It had spent three centuries as a birdfeeder once, its skull affixed to a post and filled with seed, and it still had a strong urge to smash songbirds into bloody pulp whenever it heard them.

Arst-Kara-Morn was a lot bigger on the stick than the carrot.

Some peasant came running out of a shack, waving a sickle and cursing. He ran to intercept the lich's horse, whose hooves were pounding the peasant's crop to mud. The lich pulled back its cowl.

Its skull grinned emptily in the daylight. The peasant's eyes went wide in fear; he stumbled away from the horse in terror.

It should never, thought the lich, have allowed von

Grentz to keep the statue. How quickly the fool had lost it! And now the elves had it.

It had a chance, albeit a slight one, a chance of getting it away from them.

And presenting it on a platter to the Dark Lord. That would save its bacon.

Not that it had any bacon to speak of. Or anything in the way of meat, actually. Meat rots. Bones last a little longer.

Too long by half, it mused glumly.

The horse stumbled, slowed, collapsed to the ground. The lich jumped lithely from its back, then went to examine the beast.

It was dying, heart burst from its exertion.

Casually, the lich drained the last of its life energy, then went to look for another creature to run into exhaustion.

THE, UM, INTERMEZZO